PRAISE FOR **TEGEN JUSTICE**

**Maxy Awards Winner ~ Best SciFi - Fantasy
London Book Festival ~ Honorable Mention ~ Fiction**

"Action anyone? It never ends in Goss's sci-fi crime thriller, every page
is worth reading." —*Maxy Awards*

"This book has non-stop, on the edge of your seat action, and will
keep readers obsessively reading from the very first page until the very
last." —*Chris Fischer, Readers' Favorite Reviewer*

"This book is a page turner. Drug running. Organized crime. Murder.
Mayhem, love and lust." —*Wanda, WaAr*

"This is a sci-fi-gang crime busting thriller which is crisply written,well
edited and fast paced." —*Amazon Reviewe*

"spectacular and action packed thriller novel." —-*James Verne*

"The mixture of underworld figures, who are cultured while at the
same time vicious and ruthless, combined with a heroine who is both
extraordinarily powerful but simultaneously vulnerable…this series
definitely has the potential for bestseller status."
—*Ray Simmons, Readers' Favorite Reviewer*

Tegen Justice

Inge-Lise Goss

Published by Olivebranch Press

IN LOVING MEMORY OF MY FATHER,

ORVILL HESS THOMSEN

.

CONTENTS

ACKNOWLEDGMENTS

My gratitude goes out to author C. Michelle McCarty who read, re-read, and generously gave numerous suggestions and edits to help improve my story. I am especially grateful to my husband, Peter, for reading very rough drafts and always giving me encouraging words to continue writing. I wish to extend a thank you to Ernest Walwyn, Nancy Buford, Jo Anne Plog and Debbie Prince, members of the Rainbow Writers Group, for their professional critiques of my work. I also want to thank my outstanding editors—Christine A. Walsh, Marsha Coons, and Nancy Buford. Last, but not least, I want to give a special thanks to the readers of *The Tegen Cave*, without you this book would not have made it out of my computer.

PROLOGUE

Strolling up the grass-covered incline on Memorial Day weekend, I smelled the fresh bouquet of flowers in my hands through an opaque black veil that hid my face—a critical precaution. Over a year had passed since I visited my parents' gravesite and I felt guilty about staying away so long. San Diego had become a dangerous place for me, but I missed my parents and wanted to pay my respects before embarking on my perilous new project.

I reached the crest of the hill, looked toward their gravestone and fear surged up my spine when I saw Conner heading in my direction. My former lover who believed I was dead. I turned around quickly and approached a fresh flower-adorned mound encircled by people. Disappearing into the crowd, my eyes darted around for any familiar unwelcome faces. I stopped at the closest deserted gravesite and stood solemnly at the foot as if a loved one had been buried there. I spotted Conner walking toward the narrow road that ran through the cemetery.

Two broad-shouldered, muscular men in dark suits were standing by the hood of a black limo. They were watching Conner descend the small hill. My heart pounded erratically. A lump formed in my throat. No matter how hard I tried to forget him, a day seldom went by that I didn't long to be with him. And here he was, less than a hundred yards from me, but I couldn't budge. I remained frozen, only able to see him from a distance, and my heart ached, knowing he'd never come looking for me. *But what was he doing here today?*

With my head bent toward the stranger's grave, I spied the limo driver open the door for Conner and held my breath when he turned and looked up the hill. For a brief moment, I thought his eyes focused on me. Then he climbed into the vehicle, the door closed behind him, and he was gone from sight.

After the limo drove away, I felt safe enough to continue toward my parents' gravesite. As I got closer, the sweet fragrance of lilacs, my favorite flowers, filled the air. Then I saw the source. Next to my parents' headstone sat a rose-colored one with bouquets of lilacs and red roses spread over the grave. My eyes filled with tears as I read the inscription carved into the stone: "Sara Jones" under it my birth date followed by the day Conner believed I died. Below that it read: "Beloved Daughter of Martin and Samantha Jones and Sweetheart of Conner Crussett."

About ten months ago when I thought he might kill me, I had told him I wanted to be buried by my parents. Realizing Conner had given me my last wish, I choked back tears even though a stranger now occupied the spot.

As I laid flowers on my parents' graves, tears flowed. My adoptive parents, Martin and Samantha Jones, had loved and cared for me the first twenty-one years of my life until a tragic accident claimed both their lives. I didn't have a clue I wasn't their biological child until right before my twenty-fifth birthday. Then, I met my biological father, a Tegen, and had to decide if I wanted to join his group or die. I chose to transform into a Tegen, a species which never ages, is capable of repairing itself, and has poisonous venom lingering in its organs, ready to flow out to kill in an instant. Though living forever requires deadly maintenance and sacrifices, that wasn't the reason I ended my relationship with Conner. I had to leave him when I discovered he was a member of an organized crime family. Since his older brother had met with an untimely death, Conner now ran the family business. In order to keep some fraction of my humanity in my new existence, I planned to slowly destroy that business before it destroyed me. Tegens had only one deadly enemy: fire. The last time I tangled with the Crussetts, I almost perished in a roaring blaze. Staring at my parents' graves, I wondered if I'd be lying close to them next Memorial Day.

1

PROJECT BEGINS

Part of my mission entailed thirty days of covert spying on Mitt Thurman, which currently found me sitting in my rented metallic green Chevy concealed by a truck. My eyes were fixed on the side mirror, watching the tall, 32-year-old Mitt talking to a bald, burly man. They stood in front of a vacant one story building with boarded-up windows that belonged to Mitt's father, Orson Thurman, a valuable Crussett customer. After I arrived in Baton Rouge, I checked out all of Thurman's properties, except his personal residence, hoping to locate the place he stored illegal drugs. When I realized the building behind Mitt didn't have an alarm system or anyone stationed at that site, it was scratched off my list.

I learned about the Thurman family's drug trafficking business through documents I had seen and copied in Houston, Texas while living in Conner Crussett's house. The Crussetts were a cautious, powerful organized crime family and never dealt with new customers without a comprehensive investigation, which included searching for secrets that could be used to the Crussetts' advantage if they ever needed leverage. Periodically, the Crussetts had old customers re-investigated in case new dirt could be scrounged up. That was when a crucial secret Mitt kept hidden from his father had been found. A secret printed in bold letters on a copied page I left in my home in North Dakota, a house where I lived with my biological father, Lance Alston. My goal was to ruin the Thurmans' illegal business by getting close to Mitt and destroying it through him. In turn, it would have a negative impact on the Crussetts' business.

Seeing Mitt and the burly man enter the boarded-up building, I climbed out of the Chevy, went to the side of the building, and noticed a wood slat dangling from a ledge, revealing a partially exposed, broken window about ten feet above the ground. Out of view from the street traffic, I took off my sandals. Since spider DNA was encoded in my genetic makeup, I projected clusters of hairs on my hands and feet that worked like climbing claws, and crept up the building.

With half my face hidden behind the wooden slat, I peered through the broken window and found I was less than fifteen feet from a muscular, heavyset man slugging a guy tied to a chair while a short, husky man stood by his side. Mitt and the burly man looked on with stern expressions on their faces.

The victim moaned and groaned as blood trickled from his nose and lip.

"Ready to talk?" Mitt said, moving closer to the bound man.

"They...were there," the victim stammered. "Honest."

Mitt leaned toward the man. "How did you get them?"

"Just showed up."

"Come on, Frank, spill," the burly man said.

"Don't know," the victim mumbled.

"Fingers," Mitt said.

The muscular man took a pair of clippers off of a bench, and, with the aid of the short guy, secured the squirming man's little finger between the blades.

"No, no," the restrained man pleaded.

Biting my bottom lip, I felt a queasy sensation run through my body and blood draining from my cheeks as I gazed at the gruesome scene unfolding in front of me.

When Mitt nodded toward muscular man, I turned away, not wanting to witness the continuing torture. A bloodcurdling scream rang out. The urge to rescue the man grew inside me, but I couldn't help him without exposing my poisonous Tegen ability.

"Anything to say now?" Mitt asked.

"Please...no more...please...don't...kill me...I'll do...whatever... you want."

"I want answers."

"Told...everything."

Another scream echoed through the building, followed by the sound of shuffling feet.

"He's passed out, boss," a deep voice said.

I looked through the broken window and saw the battered man slumped in the chair with blood-soaked hands.

Mitt held a pistol, screwed a silencer on the end of the barrel, and pulled the trigger. The top of the victim's head exploded, splattering blood, bone, and gray matter on the floor.

I cringed, swallowed hard through the lump in my throat. What had the slain man done to warrant that punishment? Under all the blood covering him were remnants of a suit. I had seen Mitt watching his gang of thugs handle others who crossed him—beating them, breaking bones—, but this was the first time I had witnessed his involvement in a killing, and the first time a victim wore a suit. Was the murdered man important to my project?

Mitt opened his suit coat and holstered his weapon. "Dump the body in the usual place." He headed toward the door with the burly man.

I hurried down the structure, slipped on my shoes, and moved closer to the front of the building to be within earshot of the two men exiting.

"You think there was any truth to his story?" the burly man asked, stepping onto the sidewalk.

"Pictures? No. It's been over two years. They would have surfaced before now. We wouldn't be here if they existed."

Could he be talking about the incriminating pictures I saw of him last year at Conner's house?

"Probably just a bargaining chip to stall for time. Every inch of his place was searched."

"No one took pictures, but someone told him about it," Mitt said. "Any ideas?"

"Only Ben comes to mind, and he's already been taken care of. And now Frank Montoya has been silenced."

"That news might not sit well with some people."

"Losing a relative never does."

Montoya? That name didn't sound familiar among Thurman's associates. Who was he related to?

"Check his office. We might be able to recoup some of the money."

"Will do," the burly man said. "See you at Christie's tonight." He climbed into a red Corvette with a swirly, white strip on each side that ran the length of the vehicle.

"Dan, did you take care of that other matter?" Mitt asked.

"Sure did." Dan closed the car door and the Corvette's engine roared as he drove away.

Mitt gazed at the boarded-up building and rubbed his forehead while he walked to his white Maserati.

Waiting for him to drive off, I thought about all the times different Tegens told me I'd eventually feel differently about seeing someone killed, and it would stop bothering me. A year ago, I had been involved with so much bloodshed I figured by now I should be immune, but listening to that man pleading for his life brought back those gory events. Will I ever reach the point when it no longer fazes me, or will it always haunt me? With that question on my mind, I hurried to my car and left the scene of the crime. Thirty minutes later, I pulled into the parking lot behind the Baxter Apartment Building.

Since arriving in Louisiana, besides keeping track of Mitt, I had hired a sweet gray-haired, 80-year-old, fragile-looking woman to pretend to be my grandmother. I gave her the last name, Jablon, to use. A Tegen computer whiz inserted the elderly woman's first name, Agnes, into a background identity for Sally Jablon, the fictitious name I adopted when I stepped off the airplane in Baton Rouge.

I rented a two-bedroom apartment on the fifth floor in the Baxter building across the street from Christie's, a classy steak-and-fish restaurant frequented by Mitt and his buddies, and the place he would be meeting Dan for dinner. Unfortunately, he never mentioned a time and his evening eating schedule fluctuated between eight and ten. Tonight, I planned to be there with hired Granny.

At 7 p.m., I showered and blow-dried my newly cut and dyed, short, strawberry-blonde hair, a color I assumed appealed to Mitt after seeing him with other women. I brushed my hair so the ends curved up and the bangs covered most of my forehead. I fixed my make-up and inserted light-blue contact lenses over my brown eyes. Besides adjusting my appearance to attract Mitt, I needed the disguise. Since I had never traveled with Conner on business trips, I doubted any of his customers would recognize me. Still, there was a chance Conner might have shown someone my picture he carried in his wallet, or a customer could have met with him in Houston at his family's investment company, a place I had previously worked. I would have opted for some plastic surgery, but that wasn't a possibility for any Tegen. Knives can't be used to alter the way we look. When we heal, we return to our former appearance as if we had never gone through any surgical procedure. Tegens can gain or lose weight, add or reduce muscles, but it has to come through a natural process. Nothing induced externally works.

I put on a pair of maroon slacks, a cream-colored, well-tailored blouse that revealed part of my cleavage and a pair of five-inch stilettos. I touched my black Tegen ring, which had bonded with my body, and wondered if I should leave it in my nightstand drawer. Gazing at it, I admired its beauty and felt comforted by having it next to my skin. Conner would immediately recognize it, but I doubted Mitt would even notice it, and if he did, he'd have no reason to mention it to Conner. After mulling it over, I decided to leave the ring where it belonged, on my finger. I headed into the living room to make sure Granny was dressed for the evening.

She sat in the overstuffed, upholstered chair watching television. When she saw me, she said in her weak, scratching voice, "I'm ready," and waved her hand over her navy-blue dress with a row of pink flowers embroidered in the bodice. "You sure do look nice, honey. I still can't figure out why you don't have a whole bunch of fellas buzzing around you. You've got to be the prettiest girl in town."

Granny had been given very little information when I hired her. All she knew was I needed an elderly woman to pretend to be my grandmother. She wasn't to pry into my life. I had interviewed eight senior citizens before I offered the position to the compliant woman who now shared my apartment.

"Thank you, but I don't want a man in my life right now," I said in a southern twang, a twang I had taught myself preparing for my self-imposed mission. I planned to use it as long as I remained in Louisiana. Previously, I had been recorded without my knowledge. If that ever happened again, I didn't want anyone from my past human life to recognize my real voice— Sara Jones' voice.

"We leaving soon?" Agnes asked.

I checked my watch. It read 7:55 p.m. Not knowing exactly when Mitt would show up at Christie's, I replied, "Our reservation is for 8:30, but I'm expecting an important email, so it could be a little later than that."

She nodded, then turned back to her television program.

In the process of tailing Mitt, I surreptitiously attached a tracking device to his car, a device as yet undiscovered. If it was, thanks to the computer whiz, it couldn't be traced to me. I picked up my laptop, sat in a chair close to the window overlooking the restaurant, and flipped it on. Checking the tracking program, I saw Mitt's white Maserati, represented by an orange blip, on the move, and it looked like it could be heading toward Christie's. My eyes swept over the street below, and I saw Dan's red Corvette. I glanced at the computer scene again; it showed the blip still heading this direction.

"Got the email," I said, putting away my laptop. "Ready to go to dinner?"

She turned off the television, held onto her walker, and rose to her feet.

Gripping the handles of her walker, Agnes trudged along at a slow pace. It took us almost ten minutes to make the journey to the other side of the street. Shortly after 8:30 p.m., we arrived at Christie's. As the Maitre d' approached us, I noticed Dan sitting alone at a table in the corner, not far from the door to the restrooms.

"Do you have a reservation?" the Maitre d' asked.

"Yes, under the name of Sally Jablon."

The Maitre d' looked at a list and picked up two menus. "This way, please." He led us down the aisle and stopped at the table right next to the one occupied by the Corvette driver.

Granny was seated with her back toward Dan, and I moved her walker to the wall and sat across from her where I could easily observe his table.

After Agnes and I ordered drinks and an appetizer, I noticed Dan staring toward the main entrance as he sipped his beverage. Sitting the glass down, he glanced at his watch, and then drummed his fingers on the edge of the table.

The waiter had just delivered a Shirley Temple for Granny and a glass of Sauvignon Blanc for me when Mitt finally arrived, dressed in a dark gray Armani suit, but he hadn't come alone. He was accompanied by a petite, dark-haired, olive-skinned woman, not indicative of his usual dates, at least not in appearance. I had seen her before with one of Mitt's buddies at a bar he visited a week earlier. The woman sat on the side of the table closest to us, and Mitt took the chair by the aisle, a good spot for me to discreetly watch him, and hopefully, catch his eye.

"Everything looks and smells so good," Agnes said, between sips of her drink. "I can't decide between a steak and the grilled salmon. What are you going to have?"

Mitt had not once glanced around the restaurant since he sat down, and I had only been able to pick-up a few words of their conversation. Nothing helpful. "Salmon," I said, thinking about how to get his attention.

After we ordered, I excused myself to go to the restroom. As I headed back to the table, I *accidently* dropped my purse by Mitt's feet. Bending down to retrieve it, I bumped into him. "Oh, I'm so sorry."

Tiny lines of annoyance appeared between his hard eyes, which immediately faded when he turned and saw my face. "No problem," he said with a faint smile creasing his lips.

I sensed him staring at me as I returned to my seat. "Well, that was embarrassing," I said to Granny in a tone loud enough for Mitt to hear.

"Honey," Agnes said, sounding motherly. "Ladies sometimes drop their handbag. Men understand. You have nothing to be embarrassed about."

While Granny and I enjoyed our dinner, out of the corner of my eye, I saw Mitt occasionally looking at me as I wondered about the murdered victim. Why had Mitt carried out that punishment instead of ordering one of his men to do the deed? The Crussetts ordered hits, but I doubted if Conner ever pulled the trigger. In fact, I never noticed him packing.

As we finished our dessert, Agnes appeared a little pale and tired. I figured it was because she wasn't used to being out this late, and she normally ate dinner around six. "Do you want to go home or would you like another cup of coffee?"

"I want to go home, if that's all right?"

"Of course." I gestured for the waiter to bring the bill.

After the waiter returned the leather bill folder with my credit card inside, I jotted down the tip, signed the receipt, and deliberately left my credit card in the folder. With Mitt's eyes focused on me, I moved to the other side of Agnes' chair, retrieved her walker, and placed it by her.

As she began to rise, her walker slid away from her and the chair tilted. I grabbed Agnes' arm and the waiter caught the chair before it tipped over.

"Oh, I'm sorry," Agnes said in shaky breaths. "I didn't set the brake."

"Granny, are you okay?"

She slowly bobbed her head.

"Can I have someone help escort you to your car?" the waiter politely asked Agnes.

"No, thank you, young man."

"We just live across the street," I said, guessing Mitt was listening. I held onto Granny's arm and she clasped onto the walker's handles. I picked up my purse, and we headed to the door.

"Miss Jablon," the waiter said, hurrying after us. "You forgot your credit card."

I turned toward him and took the card. "Thank you," I said, hoping Mitt caught my last name.

The following afternoon, what I wanted to accomplish at Christie's came to fruition. I saw Mitt in front of the Baxter building, talking on his cell phone as he stood next to his parked Maserati. He wore a nicely tailored blue-striped suit, and his tawny hair blew slightly in the warm, June breeze. Grabbing my purse, I left my apartment.

"Hello, Miss Jablon," Mitt Thurman said when he saw me on the front stoop.

Stepping down to the sidewalk, I lifted my eyebrows. "You ... you were at the restaurant last night. How do you know my name?" I asked in my southern twang, sounding irritated.

"Miss Jablon, I overheard the waiter say your name, and I wanted to get to know you better," he said. "I apologize if I have upset you by showing up here. Had I been able to acquire your phone number, I would have called first."

Gazing at Mitt, I recalled reading he had attended an Ivy League school. He clearly possessed the demeanor of a man with that background and didn't talk like a person involved in drug trafficking. Then Conner popped into my head. He was also an Ivy League man. "I'm not upset. It's just I was startled when you said my name, that's all."

"I still would like to get to know you. Can I take you to lunch?"

"Oh," I hesitated and twirled my ring around, trying not to appear over eager.

"Do you like Italian food?"

"Well, yes," I said slowly and glanced over my shoulder toward the Baxter building. "But Granny might need me soon."

"Fratelli's Restaurant is only a few blocks away. I'll have you back here in an hour."

"An hour?…Well, I guess I can be gone that long."

Mitt drove five miles to a small, intimate Italian restaurant. There was no way I'd be back to my apartment in an hour, nor did I care. My goal was to get close to Mitt Thurman, not to worry about the time, and Granny was more than capable of taking care of herself.

After spending two hours with him at the restaurant and occasionally pretending to call Granny to make sure she was all right, he invited me to a Saturday afternoon garden party at his parents' house. I accepted, trying not to show too much enthusiasm.

2

VISITOR ARRIVES

As I climbed out of bed on Friday morning, a cell phone chirped. It wasn't the pink one lying on top of my nightstand, so I opened the top drawer and took out the black phone I had brought from North Dakota. Glancing at the caller ID, I saw Brett's name. He had been my Tegen handler and helped me through some rough times while my body went through changes before I completed the transformation. Now, he was the man I shared a bed with often, and he referred to me as his girlfriend. I was confused about my feelings for him, since I couldn't shake Conner from my thoughts.

"Hi," I answered.

"How's your project coming along?" Brett asked.

"Not bad. I'm starting to make some progress." Brett knew nothing about my project. He had tried to pry it out of me, but if I told him, he'd either attempt to sway me from going to Baton Rouge or he'd insist on coming with me. I didn't want to deal with either of those options. Yet, I suspected he probably had guessed it had something to do with Conner's business.

"Sara, Wendy's been moping around for the past couple of weeks and seldom talks," he said, his voice filled with concern for Wendy, his biological daughter.

Wendy had been a Tegen for two years, over a year longer than I. From what I'd seen and heard from other Tegens, she was on an emotional rollercoaster. She fluctuated from being severely depressed to spouts of being pleasant, which could change in a split second to angry outbursts. Trying to snap her out of her depression, Brett suggested she take some classes with me—yoga, karate, kickboxing, and various types of weapons training. She became quite a good marksman and that perked her up. Brett calling me about her could only mean one thing—she had gone downhill since I left.

"She wants to see you and her folks," he said, referring to her adoptive parents. "Can I send her to you?"

I didn't want any Tegen to be with me while I worked through my project, but Brett seemed lost when it came to dealing with his emotional daughter. Wendy didn't resemble him in any way—neither looks nor personality. They weren't close. He had never seen her before she turned twenty-five. Still, he was her father and wanted to help her. "Sure, but I don't have an extra bedroom. She'll have to sleep on the couch," I said, wondering how to keep Wendy entertained and oblivious to my activities and whereabouts.

"I doubt that will be a problem. And if you're busy on your project, a short visit should be enough, and then she can go see her folks. They live in McComb, Mississippi. It's only about a ninety minute drive from Baton Rouge. Can you take her there?"

Last time Wendy rented a car, she attempted a U-turn over a six-inch raised island. That maneuver destroyed the bottom of the vehicle, earned her a costly ticket, and did appreciable damage to her driving record. Since then, she hasn't rented a vehicle.

"Sure. Maybe on Sunday. You know, she's spent at least three months with them since I became a Tegen. Won't it be harder if she continues visiting them that often?" I thought about how Tegens must sever their relationships with their adoptive parents since we never age.

"There are some Tegens who have managed to stay close to their folks—makeup, disguises, and pretending to be grandchildren. Even those who end that relationship, it sometimes takes ten to fifteen years. There's no rush."

"I'm glad to hear that. Until she gets some professional help for her depression, it probably isn't a good time for her to even think about cutting off her parents. Did you get a chance to talk to Dr. Driggs?" Dr. Driggs was a Tegen and a psychiatrist who I hoped could help her.

The Tegens who had spent time with Wendy when she first joined our species told me she used to be outgoing, and then something changed. All of Brett's Tegen friends, including me, suspected her problem might stem from realizing her life had permanently changed. That sometimes hit new Tegens months after the transformation, but most learn to cope with it and move on. At any rate, she needed help and couldn't go to a non-Tegen for therapy.

"Yep," Brett said. "He'll start seeing her next month when he's back in the country. Are you still planning to go to the gathering in Jackson?"

"Yeah, I need the energy." Consuming human blood and flesh had once horrified me. Now I looked forward to participating, something I never imagined possible. "It's a week from tomorrow, right?"

"How about getting there a day early, so we can spend a couple of nights together?"

"I had already planned to do just that. What about Wendy? Does she need to go?"

"No. She went to one last month."

Standing by the baggage carousel at the Baton Rouge airport, I waited for Wendy. She should have arrived three hours earlier, but her connecting flight had been delayed. Finally, I spotted the five-foot-six woman with a cute round face, and long brown hair that she wore in a ponytail. Wendy had a warm smile, but seldom used it.

As she came closer, I noticed the strained, solemn expression on her face, her furrowed eyebrow and her slumping shoulders. "You okay?" I asked in my southern twang as I put my arms around her.

"I need some *venotrolia*," she said, her voice quivering.

Since commercial flights had restrictions on liquid quantities in carry-on luggage, *venotrolia*, human blood tainted with poisonous venom and a nutritional necessity for Tegens, became a problem when flights were significantly delayed. But normally, Tegens only needed to consume *venotrolia* three times a week unless they'd been injured or they were in a stressful situation. Flight delays sometimes brought on anxiety, causing a Tegen's body to ache for the precious red liquid. And, I suspected, Wendy might require it more often because of her mental problems. "Didn't you drink any before you went through the security screening?"

"I got mixed up," she stammered, "and threw the wrong bottle away after Brett dropped me off."

When I learned the plane was going to be late, I stuck a thermos of *venotrolia* in my oversized purse. "Don't worry, I've got some." I led her into the restroom.

After Wendy gulped down the *venotrolia*, we collected her luggage and headed to my rented Chevy. Climbing into the car, she asked, "Why are you talking so funny?"

"That's my southern twang. I don't want anyone in Louisiana to recognize my voice," I said without offering her more of an explanation. Switching back-and-forth between my regular voice and the disguised one, might mess me up. Staying in character was important if I didn't want to get caught.

"Why?"

"Ask Brett about it. He can explain it better than I can." He'd be just as confused about it as Wendy, but let him stammer for an explanation since he sent her here.

"Well, if you don't want to talk about it," she said with an edge to her voice.

"I don't."

While we drove toward the apartment building, I tried numerous times to start up a conversation with Wendy to no avail. Then, I flipped on the radio and an old rock-and-roll song blared through the speakers.

"Do we have to listen to that?" she grumbled.

"No. Why don't you find a station you like?"

"I don't want to listen to any music."

"Okay." I turned off the radio. For forty minutes, we drove in silence. Parking behind the apartment building, I asked, "Did Brett mention you'd have to sleep on the couch during this short visit?"

"Yeah. Why didn't you rent a two-bedroom?"

"I did, but I have an elderly lady living with me. She's pretending to be my grandmother."

Wendy wrinkled her nose. "Why?"

Not wanting to divulge any part of my project to Wendy, I said, "I didn't think it was a good idea to live alone in this city."

Her eyes popped wide open. "You're a Tegen. Dangerous. Just bring out your poisonous needles. You can handle anyone that messes with ya."

"If I needed to defend myself, I'd use the skills learned in the classes we took together. Poisoning someone could raise a lot of questions; questions that would be difficult to answer."

"Only if someone finds the body," she said without showing any emotion.

"Wendy, you know the Tegen rules. Unless we are in imminent danger and trapped with no other options available to us, we don't poison anyone," I said firmly as the trail of victims I had left on a ship swirled through my mind.

"How about to feed?"

"Well, those individuals have been carefully selected. I've never participated in the kill. Have you?"

"No," she said, fidgeting with her fingers before changing the subject. "The old lady living with you… can't you kick her out while I'm here?"

"On Sunday, I'm planning to drive you to your parents." I stifled a deep sigh, already regretting my decision to let her visit. Dealing with a difficult Tegen was never meant to be part of my Baton Rouge agenda. "You'll only be sleeping on the couch a couple of nights."

She threw her arms into the air and her cheeks reddened. "Well, I guess that will be okay."

"Agnes is a sweet, elderly lady. You'll like her," I said, hoping I was right.

Entering the apartment, I smelled tomatoes, garlic, herbs cooking, and saw Granny standing by the stove, stirring the spaghetti sauce with her right hand while she supported herself with her left hand wrapped around the edge of the counter. Her walker stood a foot away. Before I left for the airport, I had told her my cousin would be staying with us for a few days.

"Agnes, that smells wonderful," I said, surprised to see her at the stove. She had not prepared one meal since she moved in, nor had I expected the frail woman to cook.

Agnes turned and smiled. "I thought you might be worn out from waiting at the airport and your cousin might like a home cooked meal."

"Can I help you?"

"I got it under control. Just take care of your cousin."

I introduced the two women and felt relieved, like I made it over the first hurdle, when Wendy patted the old woman's shoulder. "That sure smells good," she said, giving Granny a sweet smile.

While the sauce simmered, I led Wendy into my bedroom and showed her the little fridge tucked in the corner which held a supply of *venotrolia*. On top of the fridge stood a dark wine bottle filled with the stuff. "I like to drink it at room temperature, like a red wine." I picked up the bottle. "Let's have some." I got two wine glasses out of a kitchen cabinet and poured the red liquid.

Wendy sat on the couch and took a big gulp. "Oh, this tastes so good. I still felt thirsty after drinking the bottle you brought to the airport."

Agnes glanced over her shoulder with squinted eyes and her lips clamped together as she looked at Wendy.

After we were all settled at the table to eat, I filled the wine glasses.

"Can I have a little sip?" Agnes asked.

"With the medications you take, aren't you supposed to stay away from alcohol?" I asked, not that *venotrolia* had any alcohol in it, but it certainly wasn't anything Granny should be consuming.

"A half a glass won't hurt."

"If you're absolutely certain." I raised the wine bottle and slightly twirled it. "This one's polished off. I'll get another bottle. I took a bottle of merlot out of a cabinet, uncorked it and poured some in a glass for Agnes.

She carefully took a small sip, allowing the liquid to barely touch her lips. "Oh, it is good."

3

GARDEN PARTY

Saturday morning, I made my daily call to my father, and then sat on the edge of my bed trying to come up with an excuse to give Wendy about why I'd be gone most of the afternoon and maybe part of the evening. I showered and got dressed before a feasible explanation popped into my head.

"I'm thinking about investing in some vacant land outside Baton Rouge. I have an appointment with a realtor today to see some available sites. After that, the realtor and I will be meeting with a developer."

"Can't you wait until I'm gone?" Wendy asked.

"No. It's been scheduled for a while."

Wendy narrowed her eyes as an irritated expression flashed on her face. She plopped down on the couch, stared at the television screen, and refused to say another word.

Around 2 p.m., I put on a rose-colored silk skirt, a blouse a shade lighter, and a pair of light-brown sandals with four-inch heels. I had purchased a new wardrobe when I arrived in Louisiana, one consisting of nicely tailored, but inexpensive clothing—clothing a woman on a limited budget might buy. Wearing something that Sally Jablon wouldn't have been able to afford, might raise suspicion.

Fifteen minutes before Mitt was due to pick me up, I left the apartment as Wendy sat on the couch scowling and Granny crocheted while she watched television. Stepping into the foyer, I bumped into Mitt, waiting for the elevator.

"You're early," I said, glad I caught him on the ground floor. The lies I had given Wendy would've been shattered if Mitt had rung the doorbell.

But looking at him, I thought maybe he could pass for a realtor in his light blue shirt, red-and-blue stripped tie, light-brown slacks, and dark brown sport coat. From head to foot, he wore designer brands. I suspected just his necktie cost more than my entire outfit.

"You were worried about your grandmother when we had lunch. I wanted to see how she was doing before we left."

"My cousin's in town for a few days. She'll watch over Granny while I'm gone."

"Good," Mitt said, escorting me out of the building.

Climbing into his Maserati, I noticed a freakishly tall, sinister-looking guy with a square jaw and deep set black eyes standing close to the curb. Since I was a Tegen, I shouldn't be afraid of any mortal man, but something about him sent a shiver up my spine. As Mitt drove away, I kept my eyes on the tall stranger until he faded out of sight. Though I had never seen the man before, I wondered if he was one of Mitt's employees or someone sent to check up on him. My ex-boyfriend's organized crime family had enemies, and I suspected the Thurmans had just as many if not more since they distributed directly to drug dealers, people that sold to the final consumer.

"Where does your cousin live?" Mitt asked, snapping me out of my reverie.

"In McComb, Mississippi," I replied, giving him the name of city where Wendy's parents lived.

"That's less than a couple of hours away. Did she drive into town?"

"No. She's been away from home visiting friends." Leaning back in my seat and not wanting to dwell on Wendy any longer, I changed the subject, "What a great tune," I said, referring to the song coming through his speakers. "Growing up, I constantly listened to all of Michael Jackson's albums."

"It's too bad he died so young."

We talked about Jackson's music and his death while we continued along the highway.

Two weeks prior, I had scouted out Orson Thurman's house. It was a thirty minute drive from my apartment. Mitt executed a left turn at a corner where he should have gone right.

"I need to make a quick stop on the way," he said, driving along a deserted road with lush green foliage on both sides of the pavement. No houses were in sight.

My stomach churned as an uneasy feeling vibrated through my body. Had I somehow screwed up? Did he know I wasn't a former bank teller who had moved to Baton Rouge to care for her aging grandmother, the woman who had raised Sally Jablon—the person I had portrayed myself to be during our lunch date? Anyone doing a background check on Sally should have run across those details along with an associate degree in business I claimed I earned at an Alabama community college.

Knowing if there was a problem, I wouldn't be the one ending up being the victim, but then all the research I had done on Mitt Thurman and the time I had spent in Baton Rouge would have been wasted. I bit my lower lip and pondered over every move I had made since I met the man sitting next to me.

Mitt turned onto a curvy road that ran between rolling hills dotted with clusters of wild grasses and trees. He glanced at me, patted my leg, and said, "Don't worry, we won't be late. Guests start streaming in around three, but normally the last one doesn't arrive until after four."

I forced a smile, assuming he must have noticed a concerned expression on my face. "Since I've never meet your parents before, I think it's important to be on time to their party."

"They're used to me showing up a little late. They won't blame it on you, and my father is responsible for this little side trip." Mitt turned off the road onto a cement driveway between dense bushes and oak trees. Then, a two story glass-and-steel house with a cobblestone walkway leading to a crimson-red, double-door appeared before us. Off to one side of the structure was a two-car garage with a black Porsche parked in front of it.

"I'll just be a sec," he said, stepping out of the car.

I watched as he made his way to the door. A tall, slender woman with long blonde hair opened it and led Mitt inside. Through the house's glass façade, I saw them go into a room where a long, white leather couch sat against the window. The almost blinding glare of afternoon sunlight reflected on the glass prevented me from seeing any other room furnishings.

Mitt remained in my view, but the woman could no longer be seen from my vantage point. When I spotted her again, she held a large padded envelope and handed it to Mitt. Staring at the two, they appeared to be chatting about the package. I wished I had attached a bug to him. Could I have gotten away with that? Or would someone at Orson's house be checking for unseen devices?

A minute later, Mitt opened the car door, scooted into the driver's seat, and leaned the package against the console between the seats. "Sorry. That took a little longer than I expected." He turned the key and the Maserati roared to life.

"Not a problem," I said, looking his direction, but my eyes had dropped to the envelope. There weren't any markings or names on the exposed side. Driving down the driveway, I noted the number 9369 on the mailbox next to the road. "What a nice house, but it's so far away from the city and there aren't any neighbors close by. Reminds me of Capote's *In Cold Blood*, which still gives me the heebie-jeebies when I see an isolated house. I spent a summer on my Uncle's farm, five miles away from the closest neighbor, and never stopped worrying about home invaders. I hope your friends have an alarm system."

"They're business associates and well prepared to handle anyone who would be foolish enough to try and break in." His lips curled up slightly. "Don't worry about them."

As Mitt turned off the small winding road, I saw the street sign—Fulmer Lane. In case my GPS didn't work properly in this remote location, I studied the markings and signs along the main road so I could find my way back to the glass-and-steel house if something came up that required a look inside.

Mitt stopped at a white wrought iron gate leading to his parents' house. He reached up and pulled a plastic card out of the visor, and waved it in front of a pole at the edge of the driveway. The gate swung open.

I had driven by the place several times, but couldn't see the house from the road. Parked cars lined one side of the driveway. I spotted three men dressed in suits wandering around and suspected each carried a weapon strapped to their chests, hidden under their suit coats, yet easily accessible.

As we continued along the pavement, a large sleek ultramodern house with single story wings flanking a two story central area came into view. The size of the structure surprised me since it appeared to be twice the size of Conner's father's large house, and three times the size of Conner's.

Two valets, ready to park the next vehicle, stood by the curve of the driveway in front of the house. Mitt ignored them as he drove to a four-car garage situated about a hundred feet from the house and parked in front of it, blocking two of the stalls.

Walking toward the front door, I noticed a couple of blowtorches behind the cabinet used by the valets. Goose bumps rose on my arms; every nerve sprang into full alert. Fire was the only thing capable of destroying Tegens. Pointing at them, I asked Mitt, "What are they for?"

"Spiders."

"Spiders? Wouldn't pesticide work better?" Thinking about the harm it could do to my spiders, a queasy sensation pulsated through my stomach.

"Possibly, but not the person carrying them. If someone shot that person, the spiders could escape and they'd be hard to track down."

"You're afraid of spiders?"

"Lethal ones. Yes. They were used to murder several of my colleagues."

"How would you know if someone had one of those spiders?"

"We've been working to solve that problem. Until we do, no one is allowed to enter my father's estate without proper clearance."

I wanted to ask what would happen if someone did, but doubted I'd get a straight answer. Strangers caught trespassing were not dealt with lightly by the Crussetts, and I suspected the Thurmans took the same approach. I glanced at the blowtorches one more time as we stepped through the doorway, wondering if that was their protocol in handling all uninvited guests.

The interior of the house was exquisitely decorated with modern, expensive furnishings and abstract expressionistic paintings adorned the walls. Mitt led me through the house as voices came from off in the distance. Looking around, I tried to figure out the location of his father's den. Through the patio doors lining the back exterior wall, I saw a horde of people outside and assumed we were headed there. Instead, he turned down a hallway and knocked on the first door.

"Before I barge in, I want to make sure he's alone," he said, and I guessed he was referring to his father since he had the package securely tucked under his left arm. He waited a minute. When no response came from the other side of the door, he turned the doorknob. "Wait here. I'll be right back." Mitt stepped into the den, leaving me in the hallway and the door wide open.

From where I stood, I studied the layout of the room. A bank of windows on the far side faced the front of the house. Those windows could offer either an escape route or a point of entry when I found an opportunity to explore Thurman's den without Mitt by my side. I suspected a wealth of incriminating information was hidden in the room. Information that might help me further my goal of ending the Thurmans' drug trafficking enterprise and causing some damage to the Crussetts' organized crime business.

Mitt unsuccessfully tried to open a drawer in the desk. Then he turned to a credenza. The first two file drawers didn't budge as he tugged on the handles. The third one glided open. He pushed the files forward and dropped the padded envelope toward the back of the drawer.

I smiled to myself, thinking I must be doing a good job in my new role since he didn't make any effort to conceal the package from me. On his way to the door, he took off his sport coat and flung it on the couch situated on the opposite side of the room.

"Can I leave my purse in here?" I asked, wanting an excuse to go into the den later. Before I left the apartment, I had carefully packed my handbag in case personal belongs were somehow checked.

"Sure." He took it from me and dropped it next to his sport coat. As he returned to the hallway, his cell phone buzzed. "I meant to put it on vibrate when we got here." He pulled it out of his pant pocket and glanced at the screen. "I better take this. Wait here," he said in an authoritative voice, almost like an order. He hurried back into the den and answered it.

His tone irritated me, but I wasn't here to build a personal relationship with him. What I wanted was information, nothing more. Seeing the door ajar, I perked up my ears.

"Friday," I heard Mitt say. "Different routes...No...three...the furniture truck...."

High heels clicking on the tile floor caught my attention. I moved away from the door and stepped toward the foyer.

A middle-aged woman with short brown hair, smartly dressed in a calf-length flowing white skirt and a soft pink blouse, entered the hallway. "Hello," she said, a faint smile creasing her lips. "I don't believe we've met. I'm Tessa Thurman." She stretched out her hand.

Noticing a suspicious look behind her pale blue eyes, I shook her hand and said, "I'm Sally Jablon. I'm here with Mitt."

Her face scrunched in confusion. "Mitt?" she said, moving her head back and forth. "Where is he?"

"Right here, Mother." He strolled out of the den and gave his mother a brief hug. "Let me introduce—"

Waving her hand, she interrupted him. "Ms. Jablon has already introduced herself, and you're late."

While we headed toward the patio doors, Mitt explained to his mother he had a business matter he'd dealt with which took longer than anticipated. Since he never mentioned his father had sent him on an errand, I wondered if Mrs. Thurman was kept in the dark about her husband's business. And, if so, what did she believe her husband did to afford their lifestyle?

The guests meandered around an Olympic-sized pool while servants made their way through the crowd carrying trays of hors d'oeuvres and champagne. I spotted a lone teenage boy, looking bored, leaning against a planter a distance away from the people milling about. He was the only person at the party wearing jeans, a t-shirt, and sneakers.

After Mitt's mother left us so she could talk to some of the other guests, Mitt held my hand and headed to the teenager. "Sally, Dwayne, my brother. Dwayne, Sally," he said.

"Glad to meet you, Dwayne." I shook his hand. He made a sound I took to be a mumbled greeting. I felt sorry for the kid, assuming he'd follow in his father's footsteps whether he wanted to or not just like the Crussett family.

"Dwayne turned sixteen yesterday."

"Happy belated birthday," I said, and Dwayne gave me a lopsided smile. My eyes moved to Mitt. "Do you have any other siblings?"

"A sister. She's at UCLA. Dwayne, where's Dad?"

Without saying a word, the teenager pointed to a gray-haired, tall man with a prominent square jaw talking to a group of people at the edge of the crowd. Although I had never met him, I recognized the face from a picture.

Mitt motioned to a server. A woman hurried over to him, lowered her tray, and waited as he took two champagne flutes. "Hope you like Dom Perignon," he said, handing me a glass.

"Thanks." I took the champagne without answering his question. Since

Sally wasn't a wine or champagne connoisseur, I avoided commenting on brand names and revealing any knowledge I possessed regarding fine wines.

He guided me in the direction of the gray-haired man, stopping several times along the way and chatting with guests. As soon as he reached the man, he whispered something in his ear, and then he proceeded to introduce me to Orson Thurman, his father and one of Crussetts' valuable customers.

A stocky, short man standing next to Orson, asked, "Any word?"

"Not yet," Mitt said without elaborating.

As I wondered what that was all about, Mitt asked the stocky man, "How did you enjoy New York?"

While the three men talked, my eyes drifted over crowd, but I kept my ears on high alert in case they mentioned anything useful. On the other side of the pool, the petite, olive-skinned woman whom Mitt had taken to Christie's chatted with his mother. Then Mitt's mother's confused expression when I told her I was here with her son popped into my head. Was the olive-skinned woman meant to be his date? Both women turned and looked in our direction. The olive-skinned woman walked away from his mother and headed toward us.

I tapped him on the arm. "I need to powder my nose."

"Just go further down the hallway we were in before, and there's also one right inside that door," he said, nodding toward a side entrance to the house, and then his attention returned to the two other men.

Suspecting the olive-skinned woman might keep Mitt occupied for a while, I walked back into the house. After checking the hallway, I ducked into the den and locked the door behind me. I took a pair of thin latex gloves out of my pant pocket and slipped them on as I went to the credenza. I pulled out the third file drawer, grabbed the package, and carefully pried it open. Inside were several small labeled plastic bags filled with white powder substances and a folded sheet of paper. I lifted out the sheet, spread it open, and saw a handwritten note. It read: "All of our products are of the highest quality. We can offer them to you at a price substantially less than our competitors. Monique."

Conner's competition, I thought. Interesting. Glancing around the room, I saw a fax/copy machine combo sitting on the far side of the credenza. Without hesitation, I stuck the page into it, pushed the copy button, and chewed on my lower lip until the machine stopped. Removing the documents, I heard loud voices in the hallway. I quickly placed the original note into the padded enveloped and pushed it back in the file drawer where Mitt had left it.

The doorknob rattled. I clutched the copy in my hand, ducked behind the couch, and hunkered down as a wave of panic swirled through me. I didn't want to be caught before I had a chance to implement my plan.

Controlling my breathing, I knew no one could see me unless someone bent down and looked under the couch. Still, that comforting thought didn't slow down my rapidly pounding heart or prevent my stomach from tightening into knots. Pressing my lips together, I briefly closed my eyes and tried to rein in my nerves.

After the clicking sound of a key turning in the lock, the door swung open. "Mitt must have locked it," Orson said, as feet shuffled across the hard floor.

The clinging of a key chain drifted through the room, followed by a soft creaking noise, like a drawer sliding open.

Orson continued, "We need to move the stuff as soon as it gets here."

"Where to?" a man with a raspy voice asked.

"The other warehouse. Here."

"Is it still coming in three vehicles?"

"Yeah. Crussett wants it that way."

"Don't blame him after what happened."

Happened? What happened? I doubted he could be referring to the problems I caused the Crussett family eleven months earlier when I sabotaged a shipment of another type of merchandise.

"Only the furniture truck will be traveling on I-10."

"And the other two?"

"Don't have any specifics," Orson said. "Just know they'll be coming on different routes."

"Any idea what time they'll be here?"

"After eight."

"I'll have the men in Livonia before then. We'll move each shipment as soon as it arrives."

"Check the purse," Orson ordered.

Suddenly, Mitt's sport coat and my purse slid off the couch and landed on the floor about two feet from me. A cold chill washed over me, suspecting any second I'd find myself staring at a man's face as he stooped down to retrieve them. Pushing my back tight against the wall, I held my breath and waited.

"I said check the purse, not dump it and Mitt's coat on the floor," Orson snapped.

"Didn't mean to," the raspy-voiced man said.

A suit clad arm reached down in front of the couch and grabbed Mitt's sport coat and my purse. I inhaled deeply and slowly breathed out the air while I listened to the man unzip my purse and rummage through it.

"Belongs to your son's girlfriend….Sally Jablon."

"It was lying on his coat. Tell me something I don't know."

"There's not much here—a driver's license, a credit card, a picture of an elderly lady, a couple of twenties, a bag filled with make-up, a receipt from

Christie's, a comb, a pen. That's it, Boss."

A chair scraped along the tile floor.

"Let's get back to the party," Orson said.

The door opened and slammed shut. I remained in my spot for another few minutes and listened. Besides the faint voices off in the distance and the rapid beating of my heart, I couldn't pick up any other sounds. Confident I was alone again I scurried out from behind the couch, folded the copy of the note, eased it under my blouse, and secured it in place with the bottom band of my bra. I flung the strap of my purse over my shoulder, removed the latex gloves, put them in my pocket, and then leaned my ear against the door. Not hearing any movement in the hall, I inched open the door and edged into the hallway. As I pulled the door shut, a muscular man I had seen earlier stepped into the hallway. His hard eyes darted between me and the den door. Holding up my purse, I said, "I needed to get this."

He didn't budge or speak while I walked around him and into the foyer. Just in case Mitt had missed me, I needed to be able to account for my time and decided to check out the paintings. While I studied the third one in the living room, heavy footfalls pounded on the floor behind me.

"Where have you been?" Mitt asked with a tinge of anger in his voice.

I turned my head toward him. "Admiring the paintings. I love abstract artwork. This is a wonderful collection." I waved my hand around the room toward the paintings.

He silently stared at me. I moved closer to him and flashed a coy smile. "I'm sorry. I just don't do well in crowds. Since you were busy talking to everyone, I thought you might have a better time if I made myself a little scarce. Do you mind me looking at your parents' paintings?"

"No, that's fine. If you don't like crowds, why did you agree to come here?" he asked in a suspicious tone.

I took his arm. "I wanted to go out with you again and meet your parents. But honestly, I had no idea there would be so many people here. I thought somewhere between ten or twenty, not over a hundred."

"Do you want to go?" he asked, squeezing my hand.

"No. I want to meet some more of your friends and my mouth is starting to water from the whiffs of steaks, fish, ribs, or whatever is being grilled."

It was almost 11 p.m. when I entered my apartment and felt a little disappointed I hadn't learned more about the Thurmans' drug trafficking business. As much as I had eavesdropped on conversations during the evening, I didn't hear much I didn't already know from my visit to Orson's den. While Mitt and I sat at the same table as his parents, Orson began talking to Mason Buckley, a guest Mitt had introduced me to earlier, about the man's warehouse. Unfortunately, Mitt's mother immediately cut him off by saying, "No business talk today."

Waiting for the elevator, I mulled over the Friday night drug shipment—three vehicles arriving after eight in Livonia. Once I had tracked Mitt's Maserati there. It was a small town, fifty or sixty miles from Baton Rouge. A furniture truck, one of the delivery vehicles, would be traveling on I-10. Even though I didn't know the exact location where the merchandise would be shipped from, I knew it was somewhere around Houston.

As I stepped into my apartment, Wendy leapt from the couch. "Who was that guy?" she snapped.

"The realtor?"

"Sure," she said in a tone that left no doubt she wasn't buying it. "A realtor that takes clients out in a Maserati? Is he a new boyfriend? Does Brett know about him? Is he why you *had* to come to Baton Rouge? Is Agnes his grandmother?"

"Hey…hey," I said, holding up my hand with my palm facing her in a stop motion. "It's late. I'm not up for an interrogation tonight. We can talk about it tomorrow on the way to your parents' house." My eyes darted to the empty chair Granny normally occupied. "Where's Agnes?"

"In bed. What an old fuddy-duddy. I asked her about the dude that drives the Maserati. She acted like she had no idea who I was talking about. She even claimed you hadn't dated since she's been living with you. As if she thought I'd believe that bullshit."

"Wendy, I'm tired. We'll have plenty of time to talk about this tomorrow."

"Are you cheating on Brett?" she asked through gritted teeth.

"Cheating? Wendy, Brett and I don't have any kind of arrangement where we have agreed not to see other people."

"That's not what he says," she retorted.

"I'm going to bed. Goodnight." Closing the bedroom door behind me, I heard her grumbling on the other side as she paced the floor. Sitting down on the edge of the bed while I took off my shoes, I tried to figure out the reason for Wendy's outburst and wondered if she cared more for Brett than she had led anyone to believe. She would never acknowledge he was her father, and she always acted as if she hated being around him. Most of the time, she refused to even talk to him. Was it all a performance? Or part of her depression? All I really knew was that Wendy needed professional help to deal with her issues.

Lying on the bed, I jotted a few notes about my findings at Thurmans', and questioned the best way to expose Monique, whoever she was. Any drug trafficker I could help put out of a business would be a win for society. And maybe in the process I could better cope with what I required to survive, which still haunted me. I fluffed up my pillow and climbed under the covers. I immediately drifted off and dreamt about being in Conner's arms again.

4

TRIP TO MCCOMB

Since I had painted Granny as a woman who needed almost constant supervision, leaving her alone to fend for herself was not an option. "Agnes, I'm taking Wendy to her parents today. Could you visit your sister while I'm gone?" She had lived with her sister before I hired her, and planned to live there again after I no longer needed her services. Her sister's house was a little over six miles from the apartment.

"Marsha would like that," Agnes said as she sat at the table, reading the newspaper. "What time should I go?"

"We'll be heading out in about an hour. I'll drop you off on the way."

Wendy had showered, dressed, and eaten breakfast without bringing up any of the questions she had spouted last night. From the hostile expression on her face, I knew they were still percolating inside her and assumed she was holding back another eruption until we were alone.

I put my notes about the upcoming Friday delivery, the address of the steel-and-glass house, and the copied note Monique had written into my purse. Then I loaded some of my remaining bottles of *venotrolia* into a styrofoam cooler, took it to the car, and put it in the trunk next to Wendy's suitcase.

Besides hiring Agnes to play the role of my grandmother, I anticipated that her presence in the apartment would be enough to deter unwanted visitors when I wasn't there. I didn't expect her to defend the place if an intruder barged in, nor did I think anyone would harm a frail elderly woman. Yet, I would be informed if someone unexpected dropped by.

Since no one would be left in the apartment, I collected my spiders from a large container in my bottom nightstand drawer, eased them into a smaller, black, ovoid case covered in pin-like holes, and put it in my purse. I stuck my computer into a duffle bag and scanned the room to make sure I wasn't leaving anything behind that I wouldn't want a stranger to see. Satisfied, I escorted Granny to my rented Chevy and got her situated in the front passenger seat. Wendy glared at Agnes for a minute, and then reluctantly climbed into the backseat while I put Agnes's walker behind the driver's seat.

I stopped in front of Agnes's sister's house, pulled out the walker, and held onto it while Agnes gripped the handles. Before she reached the sidewalk, Wendy jumped from the backseat and into Granny's vacated spot.

"Why'd she have to sit up front?" Wendy asked, as I slid behind the steering wheel.

"It's easier for her to get in and out of the car." I pushed the accelerator and sped away from the curb.

Wendy's eyes narrowed into thin slits and her jaw tightened as she glared at me.

Ignoring her scowling, I headed toward the freeway and drove along for about fifteen minutes as I waited for her to pick up where last night's inquisition left off. "Yesterday, you had a lot of questions. Do you want to talk about them?"

"No," she hissed, staring out the windshield.

Though I didn't like her attitude, I was relieved I wouldn't have to endure a question-and-answer session and make up a stream of lies I'd have to remember if she brought up Mitt again. "How long are you planning to stay with your folks?"

"Don't know." She leaned back and closed her eyes.

Obviously, Wendy wasn't in a chatting mood, I stretched out my hand to turn on the radio, but immediately drew it back, remembering she didn't like music. I focused my attention on the highway and kept checking the mirrors to make sure we weren't being followed. Since it would take about ninety minutes to reach our destination, I lifted my water bottle out of its holder, took a sip, and began speculating about the Friday night's drug delivery. Would the Thurmans be informed about the other two vehicles—type and route—carrying the drugs before the scheduled delivery? The drugs were being shipped in three separate vehicles because something happened that made Conner extra cautious. What? Had the police confiscated a shipment of drugs, had they been stolen, or was it something else? Biting my bottom lip, I wondered how to weasel it out of Mitt without setting off his internal alarm.

"Turn off at the next exit," Wendy said, snapping me out of my deliberation.

Seeing the sign to McComb, I was surprised how quickly the time had passed.

Wendy directed me to her parents' house, a two story white frame structure with a porch stretching the width of the main floor. The lawn and the flower bed looked perfect; not a blade of grass out of place. Wendy jumped out the passenger door and opened the trunk before I turned off the engine.

"Do you want my help?" I asked as she swung her bright pink duffle bag over her shoulder and lifted out her suitcase.

Without answering me, she hurried up the walkway and entered the house. I contemplated whether I should visit for a few minutes or just drive off. While I stood by the car thinking about it, her adoptive mother, a pleasant-looking, stocky woman with gray-streaked brown hair, stepped out the front door and headed toward me.

"Hello, hello. You must be Sara Alston," the woman said with a warm smile. Alston was the last name I began using when I moved into my biological father's, Lance Alston, home in North Dakota.

"Sara Jablon," I said in case she ever tried to contact Wendy at my place in Baton Rouge, I didn't want any potential flags raised. "Alston was never my legal last name." I also wanted to tell her my first name was Sally, but couldn't think of a logical explanation.

Still smiling, she said, "Hello, Sara Jablon, I'm Beth Adams, Wendy's mother. Thank you for bringing her here." She put her arm around my shoulders and began leading me up the walkway. "Come on in the house. I've made some lasagna for lunch, Wendy's favorite. I'm sorry her father won't be here to join us, but he can't get away from work. You know how construction goes—you have to work ten hour days, if not more, until the job's done.

Walking through the front door, the wonderful smells of baked lasagna enticed me. The inside of the house had a nice homey feeling with family pictures lining the mantle and comfortably worn furnishings. I followed Mrs. Adams into the kitchen where the table had already been set for our arrival. On the counter top, I noticed a tray stacked with chocolate chip cookies.

"Take a seat," she said as she checked the timer on the oven. "Ten more minutes." She went to the fridge and pulled out a pitcher. "Lemonade?"

I bobbed my head.

"We drink this with almost every meal. Wendy loves it." Mrs. Adams filled the glasses on the table. "Have you lived in Louisiana long?"

"Not long." I said, giving a vague answer. Wondering what Wendy had told her mother about me and not wanting to contradict any of it, I needed to stir the conversation away from me. "Your lawn and flower bed look immaculate. You or your husband must spend hours working on them."

"Every Saturday." Her eyes dropped to my hands resting on the table. "Your ring. Wendy has one just like it. You girls must have gone shopping together."

I nodded, pleased Wendy's mother believed that.

She glanced out the kitchen doorway. "I thought Wendy would be down here by now. Let me get her." The stocky woman hurried up the stairs.

A minute later, Wendy yelled in an angry tone, "Mom, I'm not ready to come down yet."

When Mrs. Adams returned to the kitchen, her cheeks were flushed and her lips quivered. "Sorry about that. Wendy will be down in fifteen or twenty minutes." She turned off the oven and slightly opened the oven door.

Perhaps Wendy's mother could shed some light on Wendy's mental state—depression, mood swings, or whatever it was. "I've noticed that Wendy seems to get easily upset. Has—"

"Oh, yes," her mother interrupted, sitting down at the table. "She's been that way ever since Hank disappeared."

"Hank? A boyfriend?"

"Wendy and Hank were engaged for over a year." She shrugged her shoulders. "Then something went wrong, and they broke up. Before he went to work in New Orleans, he used to live only two houses away with his folks. Wendy and Hank went to grade school together, middle school, high school, and even went off to college together. They were such a cute couple. I always thought they'd get married someday."

"How long has he been missing?"

"It's been over a year. Let me think," she said, tapping her fingers on the edge of the table. "Maybe nineteen months. His poor folks still keep handing out flyers every weekend. Last Sunday, they were in New Orleans passing them out. I don't think there is much hope, but I suspect I'd be doing the same thing if Wendy were missing."

Poor Wendy. Maybe her mental condition had nothing at all to do with becoming a Tegen. "How's the police investigation going?"

She shook her head. "Right after Hank was reported missing, the police talked to everyone around here. We were questioned a few times. Wendy more since she had a long history with Hank. But, according to Hank's folks, nice people, the police never came across any good leads. His mom told me she thought the police had given up on the case, so she had to work harder. She's not about to give up until he's found."

"That's probably how every parent would feel," I said, hearing footsteps descending the stairs.

"Mom." Wendy beamed as she wrapped her arms around the stocky woman. "You cooked my favorite. And chocolate chip cookies."

"Sit down, dear, and visit with your friend while I dish up." Her mother affectionately squeezed Wendy's arm.

Talk about mood swings. I had never seen Wendy this happy before.

Now I was beginning to understand why she wanted to spend so much time with her parents—she was in her comfort zone and cared for by a doting, loving mother. I suspected her father treated her the same way.

While we ate, I learned that Wendy had a younger brother who was in the military and stationed somewhere overseas. He was expected home in a couple of months for a short visit. As Wendy and her mother chatted about him, I wondered how long she could hid the fact that she wasn't aging from him—five years, ten, or maybe longer.

An hour later, I drove away and felt both relieved and sad. Seeing Mrs. Adams caressing Wendy's arm and touching her cheek, a dreadful grief had washed over me as it brought back cherished memories of my mom. Sitting in the kitchen, I had a hard time keeping my tears at bay. Now a few drizzled down my cheeks as I wished I could feel my mom's arms around me again.

Wanting to snap out of my mournful thoughts, I flipped on the radio, concentrated on the soothing classical music and enjoyed the lush green scenery. My tranquility abruptly ended when Hank, Wendy's former fiancé, flashed into my head. Maybe she had hoped to rekindle the flame with him before he went missing without a trace. What happened to him must prey on her mind all the time. Was he dead? Murdered? Did he have an accident? Did he run off to start a new life? The possibilities were endless. Even though I couldn't be with Conner, at least I knew he was alive. I wanted to destroy his corrupt business, but not the man. I wanted him safe. My eyes became moist, my lips trembled, and my heart ached just thinking about him. Unable to focus on the highway much longer, I took the next exit, stopped on the shoulder of the road and breathed deeply, trying to get my emotions under control. But it was a useless attempt. I cupped my hands over my face and the tears flowed unrestrained.

When I finally composed myself, I pulled out my black cell phone and called Brett. He answered on the second ring. After we greeted each other, I told him I had just dropped off Wendy, and then got right to the point. "Wendy's former fiancé is missing. That could be the cause of her depression."

"Missing? An old boyfriend?" Brett said, sounding bewildered.

"Yeah. Her mom told me about him. His name is Hank Davidson."

"Did he live in McComb?"

I filled him in on everything Wendy's mother had told me about the former boyfriend.

"A boyfriend? Let me check into it," he said with a tinge of doubt in his voice, like he questioned the possibility Wendy would be concerned about a former fiancé, or that she even had one.

"Well, anyway, I thought you might like to know. I want to get back to Baton Rouge. See you on Friday."

31

When Agnes and I were back in the apartment, I checked my cell phone, the pink one I had left in my nightstand. It showed two missed calls and a message from Mitt. The message said to give him a call. I clicked on his number and pushed the send button. The call went to his voice mail. "Hi. This is Sally returning your call. I'll be in the rest of the evening if you want to talk," I said, and disconnected.

5

WAREHOUSE OWNER

After a leisurely breakfast the following morning, Agnes watched television in the living room, and I set up my laptop and portable printer on the kitchen table. I got my notes about the Friday night delivery along with the copy of Monique's note and began researching 9369 Fulmer Lane, the address of the steel-and-glass house. A picture of it appeared and I printed that page. Going to the county treasurer's site, I discovered it was owned by a company called "White Lace and Supplies." A smile crept across my face as I stared at the name thinking how clever—a nice vague reference to what they distribute. Based on the drug samples I saw at the Thurmans', most of their merchandise was different shades of white. I googled "White Lace and Supplies" and couldn't find anything about the company.

Staring at Monique's note, I wanted to know her last name and assumed she was the woman who had given Mitt the package. Should I break into the glass-and-steel house? Mitt had told me they had a good security system, but that didn't worry me. The only thing that did was the possibility of someone seeing my face. "I guess it's time to buy a ski mask," I said to myself.

Next, I searched the name "Mason Buckley," the guy Orson had talked to about a warehouse at the garden party. To my surprise, only three people with that name lived in Baton Rouge. They had different middle initials, J. C. and T. There was always a possibility there were more just not in the system. Checking on those three, I found Mason T. Buckley had a Facebook page and clicked on it. A picture of a twenty-something guy with blond hair appeared. The Buckley at the party was over fifty. As I prepared to close his page, I noticed he had posted his favorite hang out spots. One was "Sammy's Place," a bar frequented by Mitt. Was this guy Mason Buckley's son? He had also posted a picture of his girlfriend and the street where he lived, but no house number. So much for keeping anything in this guy's personal life private. After jotting down some information about him, I moved on to the other two Buckleys. Mason J. Buckley owned a facility called "Mason Storage Units," and he was in his mid-fifties. I suspected he might be the right guy and wrote down the address. In case I was wrong, I continued looking for the third Buckley, Mason C. Buckley. I managed to locate an address for a Mason Buckley, no middle initial. It wasn't on the same street as the Facebook Buckley, and I had no way of knowing if it belonged to the owner of the storage unit.

An idea sprang into my mind and I hurried into the bedroom, slipped on a pair of latex gloves, took an envelope and a manila folder out of the boxes sitting on the shelf in the closet, and went back to the table.

I printed Mr. Crussett and Conner's address on the envelope and slipped it into the folder. I picked up my oversized purse and carefully placed the folder in it along with Monique's note, the picture of the house with the address clearly displayed along the top and the ownership page.

As I cleared the table, the pink cell phone rang, and I glanced at the caller ID. "Hello, Mitt."

"Where were you yesterday?" he demanded to know, as if I had to report my whereabouts to him.

"Away," I said, irritated.

The phone went silent, and since I wasn't through using him to obtain information, I worried I might have been too curt. "Mitt, are you still there?"

"Yes," he said sharply.

"It was my aunt Abby's birthday yesterday so Granny and I went to Alexandria for a short visit." I reluctantly justified my absence, but given his tone it seemed necessary. "Since it's a long drive we were gone must of the day. I called as soon as we got home."

"Would you like to accompany me to the Symphony on Thursday evening?"

"Oh, I'd like that," I replied in an upbeat tone.

"I'll pick you up at seven-thirty." He clicked off.

Annoyed by his rudeness, even though I knew he had personality flaws, I plunked my cell phone onto the table. From what I learned before arriving in Baton Rouge, Mitt seemed to change girlfriends every couple of months. I figured he liked variety and didn't want to be tied to anyone, but now I wondered if it was him or the women who ended those relationships.

"If someone calls on the landline or stops by the apartment," I said to Agnes as I placed the phone on the end table beside her. "Tell them I had to go and pick up some prescriptions, and then call me."

She nodded while she continued looking at the television screen and crocheting.

After I climbed into my rental car, I drove ten miles away and started looking for a place that had a copy machine, a place where I might go unnoticed. It took me twenty minutes before I spotted a public library, parked behind the building, and walked through the entrance.

Within ten minutes, my copies of Monique's note and the documents applicable to the steel-and-glass house were lying in a tray. Making sure my right hand was out of view from everyone nearby, I yanked on a latex glove, grabbed my copies, and pushed them into the folder tucked in my purse. I slipped off the glove, and dropped them in next to the folder along with the originals.

With my task completed, I returned to the apartment and ate lunch with Agnes. Then I grabbed my laptop and headed out to find "Mason's Storage Units."

It took me about an hour to reach the storage units, which looked similar to other repositories—rows of metal buildings and roll-down doors. Parking close to its gated entrance, I walked along a chain-link fence surrounding the exterior perimeter and scrutinized every aisle. Two pickup trucks unloaded into different garage doors, hauling nothing unusual—just miscellaneous household items.

I scanned the surrounding area and saw a large lumber store, a strip mall and a residential neighborhood. Nothing about this facility struck me as a likely spot to store large quantities of drugs. Too exposed. People could come and go from their storage unit at all hours, but I wasn't ready to completely discount it or eliminate Mason J. Buckley since he might own other properties.

I got the laptop out of my trunk, climbed into the driver's seat, and looked for the location of Mitt's Maserati. Seeing the orange blip moving along a city street, I sighed with relief—my tracking device was still attached. At the same time, I wondered why he wasn't at work in the downtown building owned by his father. He had a suite of offices there with "Thurman Property Management" printed on the main door.

During the weeks when I had kept a close eye on him, with the exception of lunch and the time I tailed him to the boarded-up building, he seldom left his office before five. At the bottom of the computer screen it showed: 3:48 p.m. The blip appeared to be heading out of town, the opposite direction from where I was parked. If he reached his destination soon, it would take me over an hour to get there. Still, I wanted to know where he was going. I placed my computer on the passenger seat and drove toward the blip.

An hour and a half later, I found myself approaching Fulmer Lane, the street where Mitt had picked up a package two days earlier. Since Mitt had no idea what type of car I had, I turned onto the road and proceeded toward the steel-and-glass house. Driving slowly by it, I looked down the driveway and only saw slivers of the second floor through the tall trees.

I stopped on the edge of the pavement a few hundred feet from the driveway and checked the blip again. It hadn't budged for the past thirty minutes. Wondering if Orson Thurman had decided to give Monique his business, I slid out of the Chevy, locked the doors, and moved along the shoulder of the road toward the driveway. If Mitt left the steel-and-glass house, he'd be going the opposite direction toward the main road. Yet, I kept my ears perked for the roar of a sports car engine, and I was prepared to leap behind an overgrown brush or tree.

Fifty feet from the driveway, I ducked into the heavy foliage, crept between the trees, and worked my way to Monique's garage. A dog barked in the distance. I stood completely still and waited for the sound of the animal running through the vegetation. The barking stopped, and then the only noises I heard were the pounding of my heart, and air being drawn in and out of my lungs. I continued trudging toward the house. Through the tree branches, I spotted Mitt's Maserati. Like the last time I was here, a black Porsche was parked in front of the garage. I stealthily moved to the side of the building and peeked around the corner. I saw the couch inside, but I couldn't see any people. Because of the glass façade, I hesitated going closer to the house and doubted I'd be able to hear Mitt's departing words from my location.

My pink cell phone rang, startling me. I yanked it out of my pocket and turned it off. Wanting to make sure no one inside the house had heard the ringing, I peered around the corner, saw the front door remained closed, and exhaled a long deep breath. I quickly moved to the back of the garage and checked the cell phone. The missed call was from Agnes. She had never called me before.

Feeling concerned, I returned her call. "Hi, Agnes. Is something wrong?" I whispered after she answered.

"A man just delivered a package," she said, following my instructions to call if anyone came to the door.

"Package? Does it have a return address?"

"No, but it was postmarked in McComb, Mississippi."

"Thanks for letting me know." Guessing it came from Wendy and wondering what she had sent, I turned off my cell phone and slipped it in my pocket. I snuck along the side the garage, crouched down, and crawled over to the Porsche. I inched my way to the front bumper, glimpsed at the house, and suspected I was still too far away to hear anything that might be said on the front stoop.

While I thought about my next move, the red door flew open. I dropped to my stomach as my eyes focused on the house. Mitt and the blonde-haired woman, who I assumed was Monique, stepped outside. Though I couldn't make out anything they were saying, the upbeat sound of their voices and body language suggested they were on good terms. Maybe a deal had been made. I watched them shake hands and became convinced I was on the right track. Mitt turned and headed toward the Maserati.

Since Mitt could easily spot me from the driver's side, I slithered toward the back of the Porsche and hid from his view.

After he pulled out of the driveway, I remained low to the ground and inched back into the heavy foliage, scrambled to my feet and treaded my way to the road.

Driving away from Fulmer Lane, I wondered how Conner would react if he learned he might be losing a valuable client. Most likely given his family's connections, it wouldn't affect his business very long. He'd probably have no trouble finding another buyer. Yet, I knew he had dirt on the Thurman family, things they wouldn't want revealed, especially Mitt's secret. Even if they wanted to give someone else their business, I doubted the Thurmans would be able to sever their working relationship with the Crussetts. Maybe that wasn't their intention, and they planned to purchase from two sources. Expand their business.

As soon as I entered the apartment, I opened the package from McComb and lifted out a note and a gold bracelet with a kitten-shaped charm hanging from it. The note read: "Dear Sara, Thank you for letting me stay with you for a couple of days and for driving me to my parents' house. I'm sorry I wasn't a nicer guest. Love, Wendy."

I admired the delicate bracelet while I thought about the sender. Poor Wendy, her irritation over Agnes living with me, her tone when she questioned me about Mitt, her scowling and moping around, and then, she does something sweet and sends me a thoughtful present.

"Oh, what a lovely bracelet," Agnes said.

"It's from Wendy."

"Wendy?" she said with raised eyebrows in a tone of disbelief.

The following day, I drove to the address that, according to the internet, belonged to one of the Mason Buckleys. Entering a rundown neighborhood with graffiti splattered on the buildings, I couldn't imagine the polished and expensively attired Buckley I met at Thurmans' party would reside anywhere around here. As my eyes swept over the conglomeration of commercial buildings, storage yards, apartment complexes and houses, it occurred to me that the address might not be his residence, but a business location, perhaps an old structure used as a warehouse.

Meandering through the neighborhood, I reached my destination and went slowly by a single story white house with a sagging front porch and paint peeling around the windows. The front door stood wide open along with a few windows, not a place anyone would house drugs or a place a guest of the Thurmans would reside. I shook my head in disappointment and headed back to my apartment while I contemplated my next step in locating the warehouse owner.

Shortly before 8 p.m., I went to Sammy's Place and parked across the street. Keeping track of Mitt's car on my computer, I saw the blip moving and knew he wasn't close by. I had an urge to go inside and look for the twenty-something Buckley, whose picture I had memorized from his Facebook page, but without my computer I wouldn't know if Mitt's Maserati pulled up outside. Reluctantly, I stayed put and focused on the entrance, hoping Buckley would either enter or leave the establishment.

Two hours later, I became restless and suspected I was wasting my time. Only a few people had left Sammy's Place and just three people had entered during the past half hour. The blip on my computer screen showed the Maserati was parked near Christie's, the restaurant across from my apartment, and it hadn't moved for over an hour.

I decided to check out the inside of the establishment and climbed out of the driver's seat. Jaywalking across the street, I almost came face-to-face with Buckley as he walked out the door. I quickly turned and sauntered down the sidewalk until I could duck behind a truck and watch to see what type of car Buckley drove. He sprinted to the other side of the road and opened the door of a yellow Mustang parked right behind my rented Chevy. As he climbed in, I ran across the street, dodging a car along the way, and squatted down between two parked vehicles.

When the Mustang moved away from the curb, I jumped into the Chevy and discreetly tailed the young Mason Buckley. He went to a high rise apartment complex that had a security guard who greeted everyone entering the building. Since the apartment building wasn't on the street he had posted to his Facebook page, I assumed he didn't live there. After waiting past midnight for him to emerge, I suspected I had made a wrong assumption. I retrieved a small black plastic bag from under the front passenger seat, unzipped it, and took out a tracking device along with a page of instructions prepared by my computer whiz. Following the instructions, I entered the information into my computer. Cautiously, I attached the device above one of the Mustang's back wheels while I kept an eye on the high rise. Wishing I had done that task earlier, I started my car and eased into traffic.

For the next day and a half, I tailed the Mustang's blue blip on my computer screen. I had expected him to go to a work location and stay put for a while, but he roamed all over the city, making numerous stops at apartment buildings and stores. Was he peddling drugs at each stop? A few times I almost followed him inside, but I had to remind myself my goal in tracking young Buckley wasn't to catch him selling drugs. Since he hung out at a bar Mitt frequented, I suspected they knew each other and the Mason Buckley who owned a warehouse was young Buckley's father. If I stayed on his tail, hopefully he'd lead me to his father. And, if I was right about young Buckley being in the drug business, he might go to the warehouse to restock his inventory.

When Buckley parked in front of Sammy's Place, I went around the block and stopped across the street in a spot I knew well. Wanting to get a glimpse of his buddies inside, I turned off my computer and waited for a break in traffic. A white Maserati zoomed past me. Irritated with myself that I hadn't recently checked the screen for Mitt's car, I flipped back on my computer. The orange blip was only a few blocks away from me, heading the same direction as the Maserati I had just seen. Mitt's car. An icy chill crept up my spine. Did someone follow me while I tailed Buckley? Was Mitt suspicious about me? Had he spotted me?

6

SYMPHONY DATE

Dressed in a crepe, light pink dress that flowed three inches below my knees and wearing four-inch stilettos, I was ready for my date with Mitt. I pulled a container of *venotrolia* from the small fridge in my bedroom and took a huge gulp. If Mitt was on to me, I needed enhanced physical power to avoid a possible deathtrap planned in lieu of a musical treat.

Earlier I set the stage of Agnes' inability to stay alone by incorporating a neighbor to unknowingly assist in my deception. When I came into the living room and saw fifty-something Esther chatting with Granny, relief washed over me. To abate Mitt's suspicion my scenario would reinforce my role as Granny's caregiver.

The doorbell buzzed and I opened the door encountering a pleasant expression on Mitt's face as he stood in the hallway. "Come in." I introduced him to Granny and Esther, and they chatted while I went into the bedroom to get my purse.

As we headed to the elevator, he said, "Your grandmother seems in good spirits."

"She's having a good day." I planted the seed indicating she also had bad days.

At the symphony he introduced me to a few people. Sizing them up, I doubted they were involved in illegal businesses, but I had learned appearances can be deceiving. *Mozart's Symphony No. 40* was the evening's concert and the orchestra played it to perfection. I kept looking for signs that Mitt had grown suspicious about me, but I never saw any. He was the perfect gentleman.

After the concert, he took me to a rooftop with a magnificent cityscape view. Recalling how Mitt snapped at me on the phone when he couldn't reach me on Sunday and not wanting a repeat performance, I invented an excuse for my upcoming absence. "I'm taking Granny to see my aunt tomorrow in Shreveport."

"Shreveport? That's a four-hour drive."

"Yeah, I know. It's a distance, but Aunt Margie isn't doing well and Granny wants to see her. We'll be staying a couple of nights. I probably won't be back until late Sunday." Then, trying to find out if a theft had caused Conner to be extra cautious about shipments, I added, "And I sure hope I don't have any problems like I did last time I went out of town."

His brow furrowed. "Problems? What problems?"

"Someone stole a bag I had in my backseat and a car dented my bumper. Who knows, it might have been the same person," I said, slightly shaking my head and pressing my lips together.

"Did you report it to the cops?"

"No. I have a thousand dollar deductible on my insurance. So I figured calling the police wouldn't make any difference. It only contained a few purchased drug store items. Nothing expensive."

"Where did this happen?"

I went on with my made-up story, "Outside a café on the way back from Alexandria. Have you ever had anything stolen from your car?"

"No. But it happens all the time. You're lucky they didn't snag anything of high value. I have an associate who had a large bundle stolen."

"Expensive?"

"Yeah."

"Did he call the police?"

Mitt drank his cocktail as his eyes fixed on the table. After a noticeable pause, he looked at me and said. "He called them."

"Any luck in getting his stuff back?"

"Nope. Doubt it'll ever show up."

"I read somewhere that if the police didn't recover the stolen items in a week or two, they're probably gone forever," I said, attempting to pry more details out of Mitt. If it had anything to do with drugs, no cops would've been called.

A hint of a smile crossed his lips and his eyebrows slightly bounced. "Two weeks? Well, then he's got a few days before it's gone forever."

Lifting up my wine glass, I mulled over the amused expression on Mitt's face. Was he talking about a drug shipment and did he play a role in its disappearance? Sipping my Sauvignon Blanc, I wanted to ask more questions about his friend's theft, but I knew I'd be treading on thin ice. Before I blew my cover, I still needed to learn so much more about Thurmans' illegal activity, especially the location of the warehouse, in order to carry out my goal.

****

As soon as we finished breakfast, Agnes asked, "What time will we be leaving?"

"A couple of hours."

The day before, Agnes had made arrangements to stay with her sister again while I went away for a few days.

In my bedroom, I took my suitcase out of the closet, opened a concealed compartment hidden on one side of it, and pulled out the folder containing copies of Monique's note to Orson Thurman, an image of the steel-and-glass house, and the ownership page. I slipped on a pair of latex gloves and wrote FYI in bold letters on the copy of the note. I folded the documents, eased them into an envelope I had addressed earlier to Mr. Conner Crussett, sealed, stamped, and returned the envelope to the folder. Then I shoved it and my latex gloves into my oversized handbag.

I moved all the *venotrolia* into the suitcase along with my laptop and clothing for two days. Next, I transferred my precious spiders from their cage to my black, ovoid container and fed them some kernels of a granulated potion, specifically designed to keep Tegen spiders healthy. I slipped the container in my handbag, dragged the suitcase into the living room, and found Agnes ready to go.

After dropping off Agnes, I started looking for a partially hidden payphone and spotted one on side of an old building tucked between two larger structures and slightly concealed by two parked cars. Above the building's entrance hung a dilapidated sign that read, "Manny's Tattoo Parlor."

I parked a block away from the building, took a bag out of the trunk, and returned to the driver's seat. I opened the bag, yanked out a baseball cap, and slipped it over my hair. I pulled out a voice-altering device, put it in my purse, and then hid my eyes behind oversized sunglasses. I stepped out of the Chevy, grabbed my purse, and locked the car. My eyes darted back and forth as I headed to the tattoo parlor.

Seeing the parked cars next to the building hadn't moved, I sighed with relief and walked around them. With my back to the street, I slipped on my latex gloves, lifted the receiver, and attached the voice-altering device. I called the Louisiana State Police and rattled off everything I knew about the drug shipments scheduled to arrive in Livonia after 8 p.m. When the officer started asking questions, I interrupted him and said, "This is an anonymous call. The information I have given you is accurate. Now it's up to you to deal with it." I hung up, removed the device, and dropped it along with the latex gloves into my purse.

Back in the Chevy, I leaned my head against the headrest and briefly closed my eyes, wishing I could've given the officer the location of the warehouse where the drugs would be taken after the delivery. Maybe someday I would place that call.

Then I searched for a mailbox and found one in front of a strip mall. I slipped on the latex gloves again, took the envelope out of the folder in my purse, and hurried to it. Seeing the next pickup time was on Saturday, I dropped in the envelope, knowing it couldn't arrive at Conner's house until after the drug shipment. If the police managed to seize part of it and if Conner had experienced a prior theft of a shipment to Thurman, he'd probably suspect it was an inside job. The letter could add fuel to his brewing suspicion. He might think Monique was involved. *Eliminate the competition.* "Let's see how this plays out," I mumbled, hoping for some serious damage to the drug business.

7

THE GATHERING

Around 6 p.m. as I rolled my suitcase through the Hilton Hotel lobby in Jackson, Mississippi, a blue-eyed, tall, well built, gorgeous guy strolled up to me. I ran my fingers through his short-clipped beard.

Brett wrapped his arms around me. "Boy, have I missed you," he whispered while taking my suitcase. "We're all checked in." He squeezed my hand and led me to the elevator.

As we ascended, I gazed at his face and felt my heart and mind warring against one another, a war I was having a difficult time winning. My mind told me Brett was the man for me. He was charming, good company, and a great lover. Yet my heart wanted Conner. I found it an obsession that sometimes left me feeling numb and almost grief-stricken. Conner had even tortured me when he knew I played a role in his brother's death. He believed I was dead. He buried me. Although, after witnessing his profound mourning over a gravesite he believed was mine, I knew his love for me had not died. Conner was as corrupt as his family. *Why do I cling to the memories of being in his arms? Loving him? Why can't I break that connection?*

"You okay?" Brett asked as we stepped out of the elevator.

"Yes. I was just thinking about my project."

"Any problems?"

"No. A couple of glitches, but nothing I can't handle."

When we reached the room, he enveloped me in his arms and passionately kissed my lips as he unbuttoned my blouse. It didn't take us long to strip, pull down the blankets, and climb into bed. He kissed my neck and his fingers trailed up my leg while his warm breath and muscular chest pressed against my body. My pulse quickened, my breathing came in wild gasps and thoughts of Conner vanished as our flesh intertwined.

In the warm afterglow, I laid my head on his shoulder and he tightened his arms around me. "I don't want to share you with anyone." He brushed my hair away from my face. "Let's eat dinner in here. How does room service sound?"

"Good," I said, enjoying the feel of his body next to mine.

Brett raised his head, gently kissed my lips and my neck, and then passion consumed us once more as our bodies molded together. He made me forget Conner for the rest of the evening, but when I dozed off, Conner crept into my dreams again.

In the morning, I rose when a hint of dawn filled the room. I slipped on a robe, went out onto the balcony and admired the sunlight seeping over the distant ridge, illuminating the peaks of the tall buildings. Breathing in the fresh air, I watched the spectacular sunrise. Everything seemed so peaceful until the noise of the city began to come to life on the streets below, interrupting my reverie.

Brett ordered room service again and we ate on the balcony as the traffic sounds throughout the city increased.

Wendy flashed into my mind. "Did you check into Wendy's former fiancé?"

"Yeah," he said between bites. "According to her handler she didn't have a boyfriend or anyone even close to one in her life while he was keeping track of her. But there was a guy in her past she had been engaged to. They broke up two years before she became a Tegen, and the guy became engaged to another woman."

I thought about the way Wendy's mother had talked about her daughter and Hank. She had mentioned they broke up, but not a word about him being engaged to someone else. "Hank Davidson?" I asked, wondering if it could be a different guy.

"Since it didn't seem important at the time, the handler doesn't remember the name of the guy, but he did recall that Wendy went to school with him and they lived close to each other."

Filling our coffee cups, I said, "It's got to be the same person."

"Agreed. Did Wendy's adoptive mother say anything about Hank's fiancé?"

"No. Absolutely nothing. She talked as if Wendy and Hank might have gotten back together had he not gone missing."

"I had an investigator check out Hank Davidson. Before he disappeared, he lived in New Orleans with his fiancé, a woman named Marilee Kent. She moved out of the city shortly after he vanished. The investigator is working on tracking her down."

"Hank went missing in New Orleans?"

"The police aren't sure. He had been visiting his folks in McComb. No one saw him after he left their house. His car was found in New Orleans, but not close to his apartment."

"Fingerprints?"

"Only Hank's and his girlfriend's."

"What do you think?" I asked, wondering if he thought Hank's fiancé had played a role in his disappearance or worse—if he suspected Wendy was involved.

He shook his head. "The police cleared everyone they interviewed. Let's see what the investigator turns up." Brett rose to his feet, came to my side of the table, and took my hand. "Enough talk about Wendy. Time for us."

Gazing at his face, I saw excitement in his eyes as he led me back to the bed. My skin tingled with anticipation when he held me close, smothered my lips with his, and untied my robe. It dropped to the floor while he scooped me up into his arms, kissed my neck and gently laid me down on the mattress.

Darkness had fallen over the city when Brett and I headed north out of Jackson to the location of the gathering.

Brett executed a right turn into a heavily wooded area that snuffed out even small beams of moonlight. Ten minutes later, he turned onto a well-maintained gravel road protected by a metal gate with a thick, combination padlock. Brett got out, dialed the padlock until it sprung open, and then swung the gate to one side.

"When and how did you get the combination?" I asked as he scooted into the driver's seat.

"All our gathering spots with gates use the same combination, eliminating a need to memorize so many number sequences."

"I've never come across a lock before."

"You've only been to two places—Billings and Bismarck. They're well hidden, but they still have a fence around the outside perimeter. You just never saw locks because you've entered at the back of private residences. Most sites have padlocks."

I completely understood the need to keep out trespassers. Gatherings entailed ceremonies in which Tegens consume a human body poisoned by our spiders thus should never be witnessed by non-Tegens. Spider venom has permeated the organs, flesh, and blood of each victim, providing Tegens nutritional food mandatory for their survival.

Brett drove beyond the gate, got out of the car again, closed and padlocked the entryway. He continued moving along the gravel road. Within minutes, we heard laughter and chatting off in the distance.

"That sounds more like a party than a gathering," I said. People talked and laughed at gatherings, but it was always a little subdued. The ones I attended lacked the gaiety of tonight's sounds drifting through the air.

"I should have warned you. This won't be like any gatherings you've attended. Kendall, our host, likes to party with the intended victim."

"What?" I said in disbelief. Victims selected for the gatherings had committed heinous crimes, but I couldn't understand anyone wanting to share a good time with someone they planned to kill.

"Kendall is an enforcer," Brett announced, sending a chill up my spine. Enforcers were the Tegen police force, and they carried out the ultimate punishment—the death penalty to any Tegen who broke the prime role: no killing humans for revenge or sport. "He's one guy I wouldn't want knocking on my door."

A two story, gray, wood-framed Victorian house with a wraparound porch appeared in front of us. Light illuminated around the edges of the dark window coverings on the main floor and a candle glowed from an upstairs octagon window. A long row of cars lined one side of the gravel road. Brett stopped behind the last one.

A lump grew in my throat. "Is the victim a Tegen?"

"No," he said, squeezing my leg. "No. That punishment isn't administered at a gathering. We can't consume each other, and we don't die from being bitten by one of our spiders."

"Sorry, I wasn't thinking. The enforcer thing got me a little rattled. Why would Kendall want to be friendly to someone he's going to kill?"

Brett held my hands. "Sara, sometimes we have to get close to people we might have to kill. Handlers. Remember...I had to watch over you before I knew you had the right DNA." He raised my hand and kissed it. "You have no idea how relieved I felt knowing you could become a Tegen. But had it gone the other way, it would've been better for you to die than to suffer the fate of Tegen offspring who can't become Tegens."

I knew those children died an agonizing death with uncontrollable stiff hairs protruding all over their bodies unless someone put them out of their misery. "When handlers get close to someone, they don't know how things will turn out, but the intended victim in that house," I said, pointing at the Victorian, "is going to die. There's no possibility of another outcome."

"Kendall claims it's a training exercise. It helps him keep his abilities toned up to stay mentally detached if he has to punish a Tegen....someone he might know."

"Can't he excuse himself if he knows the Tegen?"

"Nope. There are only six enforcers and that's what they signed on to do."

"Can they quit?"

"Yes, but they can never be reinstated. All enforcers have a team available to help them track down a hiding Tegen who has broken a rule, and they all volunteer to get our food, so Kendall isn't the only one who enjoys the hunt."

Hunting people. I would never volunteer for such a task. Walking with

Brett toward the house, I glanced at all the parked cars and listened to loud voices, laughter, and music. "It looks and sounds like a big crowd. Will one body be enough to feed all of us?"

"Doubt it. Kendall never runs out of food or *venotrolia* at a gathering so they'll be another body or two."

"Partying?" I asked, wanting to know if more than one victim was having a good time inside the house.

"Only one."

We went through the foyer and stepped into a large exquisitely decorated room. The painting hanging on the wall closest to me depicted the Tegen Cave. Four musicians along with a male singer were situated on a raised platform next to the dance floor performing popular music from the sixties and seventies. A long table covered with food stood against the far wall. Several women wearing aprons over black skirts and white blouses carried trays of champagne glasses or hors d'oeuvres and served the guests.

"This looks more like a nightclub than someone's living room."

"You're right. Kendall hosts gatherings often, so he must like it this way."

My eyes swept over the crowd. No faces looked familiar.

Brett was greeted and hugged by several people. After he introduced me to them, he said quietly to me, "It takes a while to get to know everyone, and there are some you'll probably never meet. It's good we can identify another Tegen by the pheromone in our arms if we touch each other."

"Yeah, it's nice to know who's in our club," I said, taking a deep breath.

"Otherwise, we might accidentally divulge a Tegen secret to a non-Tegen."

"Are the musicians and servers Tegens?"

"Yes," he said, hesitantly, and then he gave me a mischievous smile. "Unless one is our dinner."

"Brett." I nudged his arm. "That isn't funny."

A spasm of panic suddenly surged through my body, and I swallowed hard when I saw the guy I had seen once outside my apartment, the freakishly tall, sinister-looking man with deep set black eyes. To make matters worse, he was walking toward us.

"Hello, Brett," he said in a cold, gruff voice that matched his physique. "I haven't seen you for a while."

"Kendall." Brett shook the man's huge hand. "Let me introduce you to Sara Alston. Sara, our host, Kendall Vickrey."

"Miss Alston, I've heard so much about you," he said as his course, rough hand encased mine.

"What have you heard?" I asked, feeling uneasy that he knew something about me, and wondering why he had been outside my apartment.

"How lovely you are. Rumors don't do you justice."

"Well, thank you," I said, surprised this man with cold, penetrating eyes had a charming streak in him.

"Kendall." A tall, slender, young woman wrapped her arm around his. "Let's dance."

While Kendall introduced us to Mandy, I briefly looked at her hands. No Tegen ring. Gazing at her round face covered with a thick layer of make-up, I suspected she was his prey.

"Don't you just love his black eyes?" Mandy said, admiring Kendall's face. "So mysterious. Doesn't he look more like a spy, you know, a man with secrets instead of a farmer?"

Now, I knew she was the victim. "Farmers can have secrets, too."

"Suppose so. But he doesn't even know how to use a gun." She stroked his arm. "Come on, babe, the dance floor is calling."

When the happy couple strolled away, I pondered if I should tell Brett about seeing Kendall by my apartment. I decided it probably wasn't a big deal, after all, I only saw him once, and he could've been there for reasons irrelevant to me. "Kendall's been dating her?"

"Apparently," Brett said, taking champagne glasses from the tray held by a server.

"She looks so young." I took a sip of champagne. "Is she old enough to drink?"

"No. Not legally. She's nineteen."

"How do you know?"

"Heard about her and her boyfriend last week."

"Boyfriend? Kendall?"

"No. A guy named Bernie."

"Boy. I thought she had the hots for Kendall. Where's Bernie?"

"Probably out back, waiting for us," Brett said, referring to a body on the stone altar. He took my hand. "May I have this dance, Miss Alston?"

Brett guided me onto the dance floor and held me in his arms while we danced to a slow melody. I closed my eyes, rested my head on his shoulder and focused on the words coming out of the singer's mouth, wiping Mandy and her boyfriend from my thoughts. Then *Sugar, Sugar* started. Brett twirled me around the dance floor. He pulled me into his chest when the band began playing *Angel.* I noticed Kendall and Mandy dancing not far from us. If I didn't know better, I'd think they were a couple who really cared for each other. Looks certainly can be deceiving.

When we finished dancing to *Girls Just Wanna Have Fun,* I said, "I need a break."

As we walked to the edge of the room, Brett grabbed two more champagne glasses and handed me one. He introduced me to a crowd huddled around a punch bowl. Some of the guys told jokes, and I laughed with everyone else. It didn't take long before I had met most of the Tegens at the party. I doubted I'd remember their names, but I'd probably run into them again at another gathering.

The music stopped and the female singer grabbed the microphone. "Okay, ladies, step up." She motioned for us to come to the platform.

"What's this?" I asked Brett.

Before he could answer, Mandy grabbed my arm. "Come on, Sara." She led me toward the women on the dance floor.

"Sing along," the female entertainer announced. The music started. *I Am Woman* blared through the speakers. Voices erupted from the women on stage and those surrounding me. I joined in. While they continued singing, the women started dancing. Mandy took my hands and we danced, sang, and then giggled as we tripped over a couple next to us.

Strolling back to Brett, I thought, what a great party. Even though Kendall was an enforcer, he knew how to have a good time. Glancing at Mandy, I felt a tinge of sadness and wondered what crime she could've committed that warranted a death sentence.

Brett ushered me back to the dance floor, held me in his arms and we danced to *Take My Breath Away*. He whispered, "How true. I can't get enough of you, Sara Alston."

As the band played *Mandy*, I sensed Mandy wouldn't be partying much longer. Feeling an uneasy sensation surging through my body, I swallowed hard. My eyes darted around the dance floor, searching for her. I spotted her close to the platform with her arms wrapped around Kendall's neck and her hips swaying to the beat.

"Whatever happens," Brett said softly, "don't react."

I assumed he was talking about Mandy's demise. I wanted to look away from her, but I couldn't. Brett turned and I adjusted myself so I was staring at her back and Kendall's face. His eyes appeared to be darkening. I wondered if that was possible with black eyes or if it was my imagination working overtime.

The song ended. In one swift move, I watched him raise his hand and scrape it along Mandy's bare arm.

"Ow," Mandy yelled, pushing away from him. "Kendall, you scratched me."

The room became silent.

Mandy lowered her head toward her arm. "Kendall, look! I'm bleeding!"

"I know," he said with a stern expression, not showing any signs of emotion. He dropped a spider on her chest.

Mandy screamed, "What are you doing?"

Kendall nodded toward the band. *Welcome to My Nightmare* started.

"Kendall, what's wrong with you?" Mandy shouted, hitting his chest. "Talk to me!"

Ignoring her, the Tegens around us began dancing. Brett gripped my hands and swung me to the beat of the music. A thump rang out and I saw Mandy lying on the floor. Out of the corner of my eyes, I kept watching Kendall. Though his face looked impenetrable, devoid of any emotion, I sensed he was enjoying Mandy's suffering.

Within a few minutes, four male Tegens were by Kendall's side lifting Mandy's listless body and marching her away with a horde of Tegens following.

"What was her crime?" I asked Brett.

"Let's talk outside," he said, leading me through the foyer. We sat down on the porch swing. "She's Mandy Katz."

The name rang a bell. "Mandy and Bernie....Mandy Katz and Bernie Dason? The teenagers who killed sixteen people?"

"Yes. That's them. Tortured their victims."

"They were all over the news. Some of their victims were so badly disfigured dental records and DNA had to be used to identify them. Mandy and Bernie's pictures are plastered everywhere. I should have recognized her. The police, FBI, everyone's looking for them. How were they found?"

"They hid in the wrong place. A cabin not ten miles from here. On property owned by Kendall."

"You're kidding?"

"No. He stumbled across them when he was looking for a spot to bury remains."

"Remains?"

"Yes. There are always remains. We don't eat bones. Can't have that stuff laying around for someone to find."

"Mandy and Bernie weren't the intended victims?"

"No. There were already two other people selected for tonight. They'll be used at the next gathering."

"Why do you think those two teenagers did it?"

"They started out robbing houses to finance their drug addiction. It escalated from there. Who knows, maybe they were high and hallucinating. After Kendall ran across them, he asked them if they wanted to stay at his house."

"He put them up?"

"Both Bernie and Mandy were high as kites, completely drugged out. Kendall managed to separate them. Only Mandy stayed at his house. She thinks Bernie ran off."

"What happened to Bernie?"

"He was imprisoned by another Tegen until the drugs were out of his system. It wouldn't hurt a Tegen to consume blood laced with drugs, but it's better if we can eliminate the extra buzz accompanying it."

"You don't want happy Tegens?"

"Not a problem if everyone slept over, but we don't want any car accidents. Too difficult to explain how someone walked away unscathed from a mangled cars while others weren't that lucky." He pulled me into his arms and passionately kissed me. "Why don't you come back to Denver with me?"

"I want to finish my project."

"Well, then, let's hurry and finish our celebratory feast so I can get you back to the hotel," he said and lightly kissed my lips.

I walked with Brett on an unlit path, grateful my transformation into a Tegen endowed me with night vision as I gingerly dodged boulders and low bushes that abutted the trail.

Off in the distance I heard voices, which got louder as we moved along. The sound of laughter and feet pounding against the dirt trail came from behind us. A group of five Tegens rushed past us. "They must be hungry," Brett said. "But don't worry there will be plenty to eat."

When we reached the other Tegens milling about, my eyes scanned the large open space surrounded by overgrown shrubs and trees. I saw a huge granite slab with a bare-chested man's body lying on top of it. Small dots were scurrying over his face, arms, and chest. I knew the dots were our spiders injecting poisonous venom into his torso.

Wondering where Mandy had been placed, I heard commotion near a tree at the edge of the clearing and saw several people moseying in that direction. I worked my way through the crowd toward the tree. Then I stopped in my tracks when I saw the limp body of Mandy lying on a table. Next to her another table stood with her boyfriend, Bernie, on top of it. Gazing at the two victims, I knew they were 19, but they looked younger, more like 17. I cringed seeing the blank stare in their eyes, their pale skin, and drawn lips. Some of our spiders were being dispersed on the teenagers. I wanted to look away, but felt frozen as the horrific sight in front of me swirled through my mind. Two young people were about to be slaughtered, such an awful ending to their lives.

My stomach churned, my lips curled in disgust, and I forced myself to turn on my heels and walk away. I needed to feed, but I didn't need to see their bodies carved into edible pieces. Without saying anything to Brett, I went and sat on the bench at the far end of the clearing, a place hidden behind the crowd. I lowered my head, rubbed my forehead, and closed my eyes, trying to erase the image of the young couple from my mind.

"What's wrong?" Brett touched my shoulder.

I raised my head and looked at him. "Mandy and her boyfriend," I said, my voice trembling. "I know they committed monstrous acts, but they're in their teens. I've never been to a gathering before with such young victims."

Brett sat down next to me and put his arm around my shoulder. "I know. We all know. But had the authorities caught up to them before

Kendall did, they would have been killed or spent the rest of their life in prison. What type of life is that for anyone? Actually, we're doing them and the authorities a service—no trial, no prison costs and no lawyer fees. You don't need to feed on them. Kendall's going to start by serving the man over there." Brett pointed toward the granite slab. "That guy murdered his wife and three children."

8

MONIQUE'S HOUSE

After a morning of passion ended in sated bliss, Brett kept his head on the pillow while slipping his arm under my neck. "I love you," he said, gently trailing his index finger across my lips.

I looked into his glowing blue eyes and saw he was hopefully anticipating I'd declare my love for him too, but the words wouldn't come. I gave him a warm smile and caressed his cheek as I wondered what was wrong with me. Why couldn't I spit out the words? Part of me truly did love Brett. It was the other part that worried me. The part I feared would always love Conner. The man I also loathed for the lives his family's business had destroyed, and now he ran that business. Conflicting emotions bombarded me. Somehow I needed to find a way to appease my internal struggle.

"Hey," Brett said, snapping me out of my contemplation. "Don't look so worried." He kissed my cheek. "It takes time."

Sensing he knew exactly what I had been thinking about, I snuggled closer to him. Though I couldn't control my heart, Conner belonged in my past and that was where I planned to keep him. I inhaled Brett's musky, powerful, sexy scent as I hoped he'd wait for me to overcome my irrational feelings that still lingered for Conner.

Shortly after lunch Brett left for the airport, and I left for Baton Rouge anxious to know if the police had intercepted part of the drug shipment. If an article didn't appear in the newspaper about the seized drugs, I'd have to find a creative way to find out. Various possibilities bounced around in my head.

Pulling over to the curb in front of Agnes's sister's house, I found her sitting on the porch waiting for me. While I climbed out of the car, she stuck her head in the doorway and said goodbye to her sister.

When we were settled back in the apartment, I turned on my laptop, went online, and brought up the *Baton Rouge Advocate* to search for drug busts. One article appeared. I read the first paragraph. Nope, nothing to do with the shipment I had informed the police about. I went to the *Baton Rouge Post* and ran into the same disappointing results. I scanned through other Louisiana newspaper sites. Nothing. I gave up and clicked on the surveillance program that tracked Mitt's car.

I shook my head when no orange blip appeared on the screen. The tracking device must have been located and destroyed. Wondering when and how it was detected, I clicked on the tracking program for Mason's Mustang, the blue blip. A wide smile crossed my face and my eyes lit up when I saw it meandering along city streets. I almost yelled, "Yippee. He hasn't discovered it."

Cooking dinner, I occasionally glanced at the computer screen and saw the blip still moving around town. While the vegetables were steaming and the pork chops baking, the blue blip stopped. I zoomed in on the location and saw the Mustang was parked by Mitt's condo complex.

Shortly after I arrived in Baton Rouge, I had thoroughly searched Mitt's penthouse condo and didn't find a shred of anything that would link him to the drug business. Not a wall safe, list of phone numbers, or a stash of cash. Absolutely nothing. Even though his condo complex had security guards, visitors needed to be cleared at the front desk, and in the elevator, a special code needed to be punched in for it to stop on Mitt's floor, I suspected despite all that he still didn't view the building being secure enough to leave anything incriminating in his condo.

I wondered if Mason was just hanging out with Mitt or if it meant something more—maybe a meeting. Curious, I plucked the pink cell phone out of my pocket and called Mitt. It went to voice mail, and I left a message, "Hi, Mitt, this is Sally. I just wanted you to know I'm back in town with Granny. Talk to you later." I disconnected and slipped the phone back in my pocket as I thought about why Mason was there. Was it a good sign that something unexpected had happened in their drug business?

After the dinner dishes had been put away and no word from Mitt, I checked the computer screen again. The blue blip hadn't budged. If part of the drug shipment had been confiscated and Conner couldn't or wouldn't send another one, the Thurmans might be looking for product elsewhere. I quickly changed into a black jogging suit, grabbed my computer, and told Agnes I needed to run some errands.

Thinking Monique could fill orders if there was a problem, I drove toward the steel-and-glass house to get answers. Darkness had fallen like a shroud when I stopped by the side of the road a few hundred feet from the driveway. After I got my backpack from the truck, I pulled out a ski mask, a sheath with a double-bladed knife inside, and a holstered pistol. I raised my pant leg, secured the sheath to my calf, strapped the holster over my waist under the top of my jogging suit, and yanked the ski mask over my head as I climbed out of the car.

I flung the backpack over my shoulder and stealthily worked my way through the overgrown foliage that shielded the steel-and-glass house from the road. As I crept closer the canopy of trees squelched the moonlight and no light came from the direction of the house. I came out of the thick vegetation near the rear of the garage and peered around it. The house was completely dark, not even a porch light was on. The front door caught my attention. It stood ajar. Had something caused the occupants to flee in a hurry? Then my eyes darted to the Porsche parked by the garage doors. Would they have left it behind?

Cautiously, I inched around the house. Using my ability to see in the dark, I looked through the windows and didn't see anyone inside or any signs of movement. Gripping the handle of my pistol, I raised it out of the holster and held it firmly in my hand as I pushed the front door open, ducked inside, and eased the door shut. Perking up my ears, I remained motionless and listened. No sounds drifted through the house.

I slipped on a pair of latex gloves and stepped into the living room. My mouth fell open when I saw the scene in front of me. Two cushioned chairs had been overturned. Broken pieces of porcelain, clay pots, and lamps were strewn over the tile floor. Pictures with broken frames lay smashed next to knocked-over end tables. Obvious signs of a struggle. While I holstered my weapon, my eyes swept around the space, searching for clues. In the corner, a clock lay face down on the floor. I went and turned it over. Cracked glass covered the dial fixed at 7:22. Wondering if that was a.m. or p.m. and what day the struggle had taken place, I glanced at my watch. It said 9:36 p.m. Not wanting to be in the house any longer than necessary, I search for the den and found it behind the first door I opened off the living room. I quickly rummaged through the white-and-stainless steel desk and didn't run across anything about the drug business.

I went to a white four-drawer lateral file cabinet that stood against the wall. It was locked. I took picks out of my backpack and managed to open it. The top drawer contained small plastic bags filled with a variety of substances, probably samples. The second drawer held alphabetized labeled manila folders. I thumbed through them looking for "Thurman" and found two—"Thurman, Mitt" and "Thurman, Orson." Mitt's folder only held a CD in a hard plastic container. Wondering about the contents, I slipped it in my backpack. In Orson's folder was a handwritten note documenting a phone call. Studying it, I noted it was dated the day before, the caller Mitt Thurman, and he wanted to discuss placing an order. At the bottom it said,

"He'll be here at 7 p.m." Was he responsible for the struggle in the living room? In case it was him, I stuck that folder and the empty one labeled "Thurman, Mitt" back in the file drawer. I began sifting through the other folders, and it appeared they contained information about customers and suppliers. I stowed as many of them as I could in my backpack.

Opening the third drawer, I heard the roar of car engines outside and lights streamed in through the house's glass façade. I crouched down and closed the drawer. Making sure I stayed in the shadows, I crept toward the back of the house. When I reached the kitchen, hidden from the light now illuminating the house, my eyes roamed over the back yard. I spotted a bush swaying though there was no breeze in the air. A muscular man, dressed in black slacks and a long-sleeved black t-shirt emerged from the foliage and headed toward the back door. At the same time, the front door opened and the interior of the house lit up.

I ducked down on the other side of the kitchen island where I was out of sight of the back door. Since gunshots would draw anyone who might be waiting outside into the house, I decided against pulling out my pistol and opted for my knife. I raised my pant leg and slowly eased it out of the sheath. Thinking I might need more than a sharp blade, I freed my hands from the gloves so my poisonous needles would be accessible, but that weapon would be a last resort. I had to guard the secret of the Tegens' existence. Poison spider venom had killed some of Conner's men and a couple of his relatives less than a year ago. Using it now could draw unwanted attention.

A rough, harsh voice rang out, "Get all the files. You two, clean up this mess."

The back door handle rattled, but the door didn't open. I assumed it was locked. Since the living room was being straightened up, whoever called the shots didn't want anyone to know a struggle had occurred less than thirty feet from me. The sounds of feet crunching on broken glass, something scraping along the tile floor, and objects hitting metal echoed through the house.

"Find another broom," the man with the harsh voice said.

"Hey, boss," a raspy-voiced man said. "Should we also take this stuff?"

Heavy footsteps pounded on the tile floor moving in my direction, sending a rush of adrenaline coursing through my body. As chattering continued in the living room, a fist slammed into the granite counter above me. Holding my breath, I slithered around the corner of the island and saw dark leather shoes under black slacks within arm's reach of me. My stomach tightened into a knot and a foreboding pressure built up in my chest. I didn't want to be caught before I inflicted as much destruction as possible to Thurman's illegal drug business.

Peeking around the corner of the island, I watched the man open a pantry door next to the cabinets and saw he wore rubber gloves. From a shelf inside, he grabbed a box of large plastic bags and closed the door. He went to a door by the fridge, opened it, and pulled out a broom and dustpan. Looking at his shoes retreating back into the living room, I guessed the cleaning crew had neglected to bring enough supplies with them.

I remained on high alert and sat on the floor, my back flattened against the island cabinet while I contemplated escape routes. A phone rang. I jumped, lightly hitting my head on the protruding counter top above me. Lowering myself back to the tile floor, I doubted with the phone ringing and the ruckus going on in the living room that anyone could have heard a small bump in the kitchen. Still, I listened intently for footsteps heading my direction. Satisfied no one had picked up the sound, I inhaled deeply.

After the phone rang over four times, the answering machine clicked on and a familiar voice came through the landline. "Monique. It's Mitt. Give me a call as soon as you can."

"Boss?" a man asked.

"Take the answering machine," the harsh-voiced man said. "Andy, start searching the rooms upstairs for documents, anything that's been written on. It's all coming with us."

So Mitt wasn't behind whatever went on here? I mulled over the possibilities. Someone else who was at his dad's barbeque? A disgruntled customer? An unpaid supplier? Knowing it wouldn't be long before someone started searching the kitchen cabinets and drawers, I moved into a squatting position and worked my way to the back door, staying out of the line of sight from anyone in the living room. I gazed out the windows, looking for any signs of movement in the backyard. Nothing. Quietly, I unlocked the door. Glancing over my shoulder, I held onto the doorknob, turned it silently, and pulled the door open a few inches. As I slinked out, I eased the door shut behind me.

A short, muscular man stepped into kitchen. "Did any of you hear that?" he asked as I dropped to the ground and crawled backwards away from the door.

Entering the kitchen, a heavyset man with a harsh voice said, "Hear what?"

"A door shutting."

As I ducked behind a bush at the corner of the house, the back door flew open and the harsh-voiced man walked outside. Peering through some branches, I saw his head turning back and forth, scanning the yard. "Andy said the back door was locked." He moved back into the house, and yelled, "Hey, did any of you guys go out the back door?"

From my location, I couldn't hear a response.

The heavyset man walked out the door again. "Well, someone did," he said as his eyes drifted around the area. He stuck his head into the house. "Jim and Leon put silencers on your pistols and check around outside. If there's an intruder, shoot him."

Instead of heading toward the road, I moved further into the backyard behind high wild grasses, trees, and bushes. I took off my shoes and socks, tied them to a strap on my backpack, and projected clusters of hairs on my hands and feet that worked like climbing claws. I scurried up a large Cherrybark Oak tree and stretched out on a branch about fifteen feet above the ground, a place where I had a good view of the house and the surrounding area.

Two men, with their weapons at the ready, came out of the house, and began combing through the foliage. As one moved closer to my tree, I squinted and my mouth popped open when I recognized the man. I didn't know his name, but I knew he worked for the Crussett family or, at least, he used to. He was among the security guards who protected the Crussetts inside their compound after Conner's brother, Cameron, had been killed. I ran my hand over the ski mask that hid my face. If the man caught a glimpse of my face, I suspected he would also recognize me.

Could the Crussetts be behind the struggle that occurred in the house? When I dropped the letter to Conner in the mailbox on Friday, I checked the pick up times. The next one scheduled was Saturday, so the earliest he could receive it was tomorrow, Monday. Did he already know about Monique trying to steal his customer? Or was killing off the competition commonplace? If a Crussett drug shipment had been stolen earlier, was Monique the thief? So many questions buzzed around in my head that I doubted the answers to most of them would ever be within my grasp.

As I heard twigs snapping and the rustling of leaves below me, my eyes roamed over the house. A man was upstairs in a bedroom, and it looked like he was meticulously going through the drawers, making sure all the items were put back in the same place he found them. I continued watching the men inside that I could see from my concealed vantage point and patiently waited for them to finish their tasks.

Two hours later the lights inside the house flicked off. Hearing car engines humming in the distance, I scooted off my branch and climbed down the tree. I slipped my socks and shoes back on, and inched toward the side of house. After seeing taillights moving out of the driveway, I walked at a normal pace to the front of the house, stopped and gazed at the front door, surmising the couple who had lived here would never be going through that door again. Wondering if they had been tortured before they met their fate, I turned away from the steel-and-glass structure and walked up the driveway.

9

A NEW DISCOVERY

The following morning, I sat at my computer disgusted by photos on the CD I had snatched from Monique's. The images were identical to the ones I discovered at Conner's house months earlier when I rummaged through his credenza. Pictures Mitt had been keeping from his father showed a puffy face, bruised, and bleeding woman, chained to a wall while Mitt stood inches from her—Orson's lover of ten years, and who he still searched for, offering enormous rewards for information leading to her whereabouts. The body of Orson's mistress being buried in the last picture as Mitt watched with a pleased smirk on his face. Why torture her? If she had betrayed his father and he wanted names, Mitt should've provided Orson with the evidence against her and allowed him to handle it. Then I thought maybe Mitt feared his father wouldn't be able to torture his mistress enough to get the answers he wanted. Conner had a tough time interrogating me after he learned about my involvement in his brother's death.

I emailed the gruesome pictures to my account at a secure private Tegen website while I pondered about the photographer. Who was he? He could have been handsomely paid by Orson if he had turned the disk over to him. Why didn't he do that? How did Conner acquire those pictures? Who gave a set to Monique? Tapping my fingertips on the edge of the table, I suspected the answers to these questions would also remain out of my grasp. And for that matter, I didn't need those answers to finish pursuing my plan. I deleted the 'sent email' file from my computer, ejected the CD, and put it back into the plastic container.

Holding it firmly in my hand, I went into my bedroom, closed the door, and opened the bottom nightstand drawer that held my precious spiders. I unlatched their tightly woven cage and lowered the plastic container to the bottom of it, making sure the spiders weren't underneath. Raising my hand, I saw the silky cobwebs covering my fingers. Before I brushed the delicate fibers from my hand, I inhaled deeply the luscious sweet scent and held it in my lungs until I gasped for air. With my other hand I snapped the cage shut, knowing the spiders' habitat was the safest place for the disk. Anyone who attempted to take it would be found on the floor, staring at the ceiling with motionless eyes.

Wearing a pair of latex gloves, I took the manila folders out of my backpack and skimmed through them. I opened a folder for a supplier and saw invoices from a Central American company that ships into the country, the same way Crussetts acquired some of their merchandise. Only symbols appeared next to the prices, no names. Another folder, with the word 'lab' in the heading, held receipts for supplies, summaries of finished products, and a list of employees along with their hourly rates. Based on those documents, I suspected Monique had a stake in the lab—possibly the principal or a partner.

A folder labeled "Buckley, Mason" peaked my curiously when I found only one handwritten note: "Ford van, pay Buckley for storage-$5000/month. Paint and dispose in August." Along the bottom of the page, illegible scribbling revealed the word "street," which I figured previously displayed an address for the storage facility. Who would pay that kind of money to store a vehicle? If Monique hadn't intended to keep it, why not just get rid of it? Several possibilities sprang into my mind. Maybe the van—or more importantly the cargo—might be behind the struggle that occurred at Monique's house. Buckley—father or son?

Excluding the Buckley folder, I separated the others into three piles—supplier, lab, and clients, and then placed contents of the lab folder in a large envelope. Using the internet, I printed a label for the state police department, affixed to envelope, and put it into my oversized purse. Not about to risk having folders in my apartment, I stuffed them into two envelopes and addressed them to my home address in North Dakota, and stowed them alongside the Buckley folder in my backpack.

Next, I used my computer to locate young Buckley's Mustang, and found it stationary across town, thus made a mental note of the address. I removed the gloves, slipped on my backpack, and carried my purse and laptop to the Chevy.

I stopped at the post office, mailed the envelopes addressed to myself, and purchased stamps. Sitting in my car, I tugged on a new pair of latex gloves and put postage on the other envelope before dropping it into a curbside mailbox.

Merging into the traffic, I hoped my parcel to the police would yield an investigation and prosecution of the lab company. I wanted it permanently out of business.

Approaching the place Buckley's Mustang had been earlier, I pulled over to check my computer and learned it remained in the same spot. Seeing his Mustang in front of a two story, red brick house in an upscale neighborhood, I parked a few doors away to keep watch on the house while searching county records for the owner. Raina Montoya Buckley. Was she related to Frank Montoya, the guy murdered in the boarded-up building? And how was she related to Mason? Mother? Sister? While I pondered those questions, Mason stepped out of the house, climbed into his Mustang and sped away. As I flipped a u-ey to follow him, the two story house garage door opened and a silver Mercedes backed out. Since the tracking device was still securely attached to the Mustang, I decided to tail the Mercedes and catch up with young Buckley later.

The silver luxury car passed and I recognized its driver, a middle-aged woman who had attended Thurmans' party. She was the wife of warehouse owner, Mason Buckley, and I surmised the mother of young Buckley.

She stopped at a dry cleaners a few blocks away, and was leaving when a petite, slender woman came charging out after her, yelling, "Raina, you forgot your credit card."

Raina said something to the woman, took her card, hung the dry cleaning, and climbed into the driver's seat. She drove to a supermarket, but I didn't want to waste time waiting for her to do her grocery shopping. I checked my laptop for the Mustang's location—only a couple of miles away—and decided to switch gears and pursue young Buckley. Then Raina reappeared, carrying a small prescription sack, and changing my game plan. I tagged after her to monitor any other stops she made before heading home.

At the intersection, Raina went the opposite direction from her house. I stayed a few cars behind her despite doubting she would be looking for anyone on her tail. She drove onto the interstate and headed away from the city while I remained a comfortable distance from her.

The Mercedes soon took an exit ramp, and turned into heavy traffic where I managed to blend in with other cars. Within a few miles, other vehicles thinned out and my Chevy wound up directly behind her. I slowed to a snail's pace and a Jeep passed, but did not pass Raina, allowing me to keep a respectable distance. Warehouses and industrial buildings with cars in their lots, shot up around me as several semis moved on the pavement. The Mercedes stopped in front of a metal structure almost hidden among the trees and overgrown bushes. Driving by, I caught a glimpse of Raina taking the dry cleaning bag out of her vehicle.

A block away, out of Raina's line of sight, I u-turned, stopped on the shoulder of the road, and pulled binoculars out of the glove compartment. From my vantage point, I could only see a sliver of the building and a blue truck parked next to her Mercedes. I stepped out of the Chevy, opened the trunk, grabbed my backpack, and headed for a closer view. Crossing the street, my pink cell phone vibrated in my pant pocket. I ducked between two bushes and yanked it out, glancing at the caller ID. "Hello, Mitt." I feigned excitement over him calling me.

"Sally, dinner tomorrow night?" His voice all business-like, he got right to the point.

"Oh, that sounds good."

"I'll pick you up at seven-thirty," he said and clicked off without allowing me to agree to the time. I looked at the phone and said sarcastically, "Sure. That works for me." The more I got to know Mitt, the more I understood why he didn't have long term relationships with women. Only women with half a brain would put up with his arrogance, but I had to tolerate him to gain crucial information.

Putting my phone away, I kept my knees bent as I crept through the trees and worked my way toward the metal building. A six-foot chain link fence with three rows of wires strung above it appeared before me. It stood about twelve feet from the structure, and there were no trees or foliage on the other side of it, nothing to obstruct my view. The building was at least two hundred feet deep. No windows or doors were on the side of the building I faced. I stepped back into the trees and stealthily edged toward the back corner of the structure. As I got closer, voices drifted from the building. Staying concealed in the foliage, I peeked around the building and saw a window ajar.

"...won't," a woman with a sweet, motherly voice said. "Do you want me to?"

"Absolutely not!" a husky male voice barked. "You stay away from her place."

I heard a knock on a door.

"Yes," the man with the husky voice snapped.

"Mr. Buckley," a man said, "how late do you want me to work this evening?"

"Ten, but don't leave until Jeff gets here."

A door snapped shut.

"Mason," the sweet-voiced woman said. "Monique's had electrical outages before. Maybe her cell phone went dead and she can't recharge it. It's probably nothing more than that."

"No. Something's going on. There's a problem."

"Just because you can't reach her doesn't mean she's involved. She's family."

"Yeah," he said in an irritated tone. "Not blood. She's married to your

63

cousin, a cousin who hasn't lived with her since last year."

"Maybe she's with Frank."

"Wishful thinking. She never took his last name. What kind of a marriage was that anyway?"

Could Monique be married to the late Frank Montoya? If so, Raina might have been right. Monique might be with Frank, lying next to him under the ground someplace.

"Oh, Mason, a lot of women these days don't take a husband's last name. It's not a big deal."

"Raina, she's not..."

Suddenly, I couldn't hear the voices. I carefully moved closer, hoping to pick-up their conversation again. Just above a whisper, I heard Buckley say, "...blame me."

"Come on, Mason," Raina said in a gentle tone. "Monique isn't the law. You only introduced her to Orson. That's all you did."

"How about..." his voice trailed off again, and I couldn't get any closer without shimmying over what might be an electrified fence.

From behind me came the sounds of bushes rustling, twigs snapping, and feet crunching on dry leaves. I dashed to the nearest tall tree, ejected clusters of hair on my hands and clambered up it.

I stretched out on a thick branch and watched a guy with a baseball cap perched on his head wander through the foliage. He stopped next to the fence in the same spot I had just vacated and glanced around. Then he moved along the fence line, checking the ground abutting it. Occasionally, he touched the fence so I knew electricity wasn't running through it.

While I waited for the guy in baseball cap to vanish from my sight, I noticed a wooden fence surrounding a small, brown log building a hundred feet behind the metal structure. Since I couldn't see a gate in the wooden fence, it piqued my curiosity.

Five minutes later, I climbed out of the tree and treaded carefully toward the metal building while I remained on full alert for any signs of the guy in the baseball cap. Reaching the back edge of the chain link fence, I turned and looked for any indication of movement coming from the metal building and surrounding area. Satisfied no one had heard me, I climbed over the wood fence and listened for potential sounds coming from the log structure. Leaves swayed with a soft breeze floating through the trees, but I couldn't pick up any voices or people moving about inside.

My eyes drifted over the enclosed area, searching for surveillance cameras. Not spotting any, I quietly and cautiously looped around the interior parameter of the fence, looking for a concealed gate or anything that could open to allow access to the log building. Nothing. Next, I checked the exterior of the fifteen-by-fifteen foot log structure and saw a double door the size of a garage door situated on the side of the structure closest to the metal building and only two feet away from the wooden fence, making it a tight fit to bring anything through the doors. At the same time, since there wasn't any access to that area, usage of the double doors seemed a moot point. I continued wandering around the building and discovered a padlocked door on one side. As I began to pick the lock, a loud clang rang out from the direction of the metal building. Did the log structure belong to Buckley?

Thinking I might have triggered an alarm, I rushed to the wooden fence closest to the metal building, dropped to the ground and pressed my back tightly against it. This was a place I wouldn't be spotted if someone looked over the six-foot fence and, also, a place where I could easily escape from the enclosed area if someone climbed into it from another direction. Feeling my heart rapidly pounding and my mouth becoming dry, I forced myself to take slow shallow breaths. While I anxiously waited for the sound of running feet or any sign someone was heading toward the log building, my hand came to rest on the cement that secured one of the wooden poles in place. Gazing at it, I wondered why it wasn't covered with dirt like the steel poles I stood next to earlier. Upon closer examination, the wooden fence running along this side of the log structure appeared to be almost new.

I hunkered down a few minutes without hearing any movement before venturing out to check the rest of wooden fence again, this time to determine if it was all new. Every pole contained exposed cement and the dark fence color came from paint cans, not aging. Strange? The log building lacked easy access, thus seemed illogical for storing drugs. On the other hand, it might be a good place to hide them.

I headed to the structure and looked around for an electrical box. Nothing outside. I needed to check inside and pulled my picks out of my backpack to jimmy the lock. I managed to open it, and then slipped on a pair of latex gloves, wiped off the padlock and laid it on the ground. Inching the door slightly open, I listened for a beeping or humming sounds from inside before pushing open wide enough for me to squeeze inside. Closing it behind me, I noticed several oil lamps on a workbench next to the door as darkness doused all the light except for a ray underneath the double doors. Using my night vision, I looked around the one-room structure for small blinking lights or any signs indicating I had tripped an alarm. No lights or surveillance cameras.

In the center of the room, a white Ford van with green-and-yellow colorful advertising on the sides: "Johnson's Plumbing Supplies" occupied most of the interior space. Phone numbers included a Houston, Texas area code I recognized. The van Buckley was storing for Monique, which needed to be painted to unload. If this was the same van used by Crussetts to transport drugs, was it the cause of Conner's increased shipment security?

Had Monique swiped the drugs? But more important—who told her about the shipment? Buckley?

Looking for answers, I opened the passenger door and saw dark stains splattered on the driver's side of the van—seat, dashboard, gear shift, door and ceiling. Upon closer inspection, I had no doubt the spots were dried blood. The windshield and the driver's side window appeared clean. I stuck a gloved finger in a hole in the back of the driver's seat, touched something hard, grabbed a screwdriver from the workbench and pried out a squashed bullet. After putting it in my pocket and considering the slope of hole along with only a few splattered stains on the passenger seat, I figured the shooter had occupied that seat. I checked the glove box and under the seat. Not a trace of anything. I jumped out of the van, opened its back doors and climbed in. I searched through every nook and cranny including the spare tire compartment. Nothing.

I moved to the driver's side and discovered the window along with the windshield hadn't been cleaned; they were missing. I ran my hand under the driver's seat. Nothing. As I slid into the seat, my feet crunched on shards of glass on the floor. Assuming it came from the driver's window, I continued my search and pulled down the visor. Nothing.

Feeling disappointed, I leaned back in the seat, glanced around, and spotted a shiny object wedged between the driver's seat and the gear shift. I stuck my hand down and made a useless attempt to retrieve it from the small space. With the aid of a screwdriver, I dislodged the object—a cell phone. I doubted it had any juice, but I still pushed the on button. The screen remained black. I stowed it in a pocket on my backpack.

Then I looked underneath the van, checked around the wheel wells, and opened the hood. I located the VIN number and jotted it down. Satisfied I couldn't find anything else in the vehicle, I fished the pink cell phone out of my pocket and took pictures of the van.

For the next two hours, I searched the log cabin's shelves and workbench. With grease and grime covering my gloves and having gone through every container in the place, I stepped out of the building, put back the padlock and snapped it shut. After I tugged off the filthy gloves and pushed them into a plastic bag in my backpack, I headed to the fence, brought out clusters of hair on my hands, and scurried over it.

Moving stealthily through the trees and bushes, it took me over ten minutes to reach the Chevy. When I drove by the metal building, the Mercedes was gone.

10

PLANTED CLUE

A few miles from Buckley's building, I turned onto a side street, parked behind a group of trees to shield my car from the main road, and took out the cell phone I found in the van. In case it had a built-in GPS, I didn't dare charge it inside or anywhere near my apartment. Connecting a portable charger to the vehicle's cigarette lighter, I plugged in the cell phone, and the screen immediately lit up. I waited while it charged a few minutes, and although the battery was low, it had enough juice for me to give it a try. I clicked on its menu and located recent calls. The last call sent went to a Houston number seventeen days earlier at 10:32 p.m. There were over three dozen missed calls between 11 p.m. that day and 9:46 p.m. last night. I recognized the name attached to the eleven o'clock caller—Sam Phillips, an employee of the Crussett family. I roamed through the calls listed and saw they all had the Houston area code. Searching the menu, I located the number belonging to the cell phone, scribbled it down, and then skimmed through the contact list. Many names belonged to Crussett employees. I clicked on messages—there were 18 unheard voice messages and 67 text messages.

I opened the text messages. The oldest one had been sent by Sam at 11:12 p.m. seventeen days ago. It read, "Tyler, are you someplace where you can't answer your phone? Text me." Following that one were several other similar messages. A day later came a message from a woman, "Babe, why haven't you returned my calls. What's up?" After that a different woman had sent him a text. "Oh Baby, got the bubbly chillin', dressed the way you like me, get your butt over here."

Going through the other text messages, I read a large number from women. Each day that passed, the tone in most of them became angrier. Guessing Tyler was probably dead and suspecting at least one Crussett employee was monitoring for the GPS signal from the phone in my hand, I straightened my back, realizing by now spies had been given enough time to hone in on an approximate location.

As I drove back toward the log building, I thought, *Warring and fighting within the illegal drug business leaves less work for me to do. Let them kill each other off.*

The sun had set and darkness was falling over the landscape when I stopped a block away from the metal building. I grabbed my long-sleeved black t-shirt, tugged it on, and unhooked the cell phone. After sticking it in a front pocket on my backpack, I headed into the trees and stealthily moved through the vegetation until I almost reached my destination, the wood fence surrounding the log building. As a precaution, I pulled the ski mask out of my backpack, slipped it over my head and put the cell phone in my t-shirt pocket. Since I could move faster without carrying my backpack, I hid it up in the nearest tree. I stepped to the edge of the heavy foliage and scanned the area, searching for anyone moving about. Not spotting a soul, I quickly scampered over the fence, checked to make sure the cell phone was turned on and concealed it in tall grass abutting the log building.

With my task accomplished, I hurried over the fence and walked at a brisk pace toward the nearest tree.

"Hey," a male voice rang out, "Stop right there!"

I swung around toward the direction of the voice and saw an average-sized man in his late twenties moving along the exterior of the fence with his pistol drawn and aimed at me. My pulse spiked and blood surged through my veins as I felt annoyed with myself for not being more cautious. How could this man have gotten so close without me even sensing his presence?

"Raise your hands," he said, staring at me.

Ignoring his order, I charged into the dense foliage covered by a canopy of tree branches and only lit by filtered moonlight. A gunshot rang out. A bullet buzzed by my ear and ripped through a bush next to me and hit a tree trunk, spreading splinters of wood. I leapt behind another tree and dived under an overgrown brush.

"Get out here," he shouted. "You can't escape from the woods."

While I controlled my breathing and heart rate, I heard his footsteps shuffling in the thick wild grasses, heading toward me. Peering through a small opening between the branches, I saw a beam of light skimming through the foliage and his athletic shoes. He stopped a few feet from me. Slightly raising my head, I spotted a flashlight in one of his hands and a pistol in the other.

He suddenly dropped the flashlight and its light beam hit my eyes. Squinting, I carefully adjusted my position. The last thing I wanted to do was to draw attention to myself. Could I find a way to prevent it?

"Jeff, Greg here," the man said.

Stretching my neck to see him, I caught a glimpse of a cell phone next to his ear.

"We have an intruder…Phil's in the warehouse…wood area outside the fence…she didn't get in the warehouse…a woman…face mask…no…could be…yeah, I spread it…I'll know if she attempts to get out of here…it's been electrified…ten minutes."

I watched as he put the phone in his pocket, bent over and picked up the flashlight. Suspecting I only had ten minutes before reinforcements arrived, I slowly lifted up my pant leg, gripped the handle of my knife, and lifted it out of the sheath attached to my calf. In one quick motion, I jumped out of my hiding spot and, with the blade of my knife, scraped the man's forearm down to the pistol holding hand. His weapon went off as it tumbled to the ground. The bullet grazed my arm right below the elbow, but now wasn't the time to dwell on it. His blood streamed from the laceration I inflicted as he went to retrieve his gun with his other hand. I kicked him hard in the chest, sending him flying backwards into the bushes.

I had seen enough bloodshed last time I tangled with thugs and didn't want to add another kill to my growing list. Still, I couldn't have the wounded man trailing after me and when he tried to get to his feet, I plunged my knife into his leg.

Buckling over in pain, he moaned and groaned as he landed on the hard ground. "You… won't… get away," he mumbled as he briefly looked up, and I saw the rage flashing from his green eyes.

Knowing I was running out of time, I charged to the tree that held my backpack, quickly retrieved it and sprinted toward the street, dodging trees and bushes along the way. Recalling the phone call I had overheard, I came to a halt when I spotted the road ahead of me. The man had mentioned he had spread something, something that would let him know if I left this wooded area. What could it be? Instead of going closer to the road, I stayed hidden in the trees and moved parallel to the road in the opposite direction from the warehouse. I had gone about four-hundred feet when headlights lit up the pavement and cars came to screeching stops somewhere behind me.

As I picked up my pace, a short burst of gunfire crackled in the direction of the warehouse. What? Who's shooting at whom? Wondering if there was another uninvited guest cruising around the warehouse, I sprinted until I reached an eight-foot fence with warning signs posted on it saying, "Beware of Dogs," and "No Trespassing."

It would be a simple to poison the dogs and any scratches or bites I received in the process would quickly heal, but I didn't want to tangle with them and I wanted to get back to the apartment as soon as possible. I left the security of the woods and darted to the street, stumbling over some meshing material on the way as I heard commotion, a few gunshots, and loud banging off in the distance.

When I reached the Chevy, I scooted in, looked at my blood soaked sleeve, and touched the wound without feeling any pain. It wouldn't be long before it was completely healed. I started the engine, slammed on the accelerator and moved farther away from the warehouse. Winding through mostly deserted country roads, it took me over ninety minutes to reach the intersection leading to the highway, a drive that would have taken me less than thirty minutes had I gone by the warehouse.

In the apartment building parking lot, I removed my long-sleeved blood-stained t-shirt, pulled another one out of my backpack and slipped it on. I dropped the ruined t-shirt into the garbage bin and went into the Baxter Building.

As I stepped into the apartment, Agnes said, "You look bushed."

"I feel bushed." I inhaled the wonderful aromas of cooked seasoned meat and gravy.

"Hope you're hungry. I made meatloaf. Let me dish it up for you." She took the handle of her walker and began to rise.

"No. I can do it. Enjoy the rest of your TV show."

"The super came by to make sure the kitchen faucet wasn't leaking," Agnes said. "Never said why he needed to check it. He sure is a grumpy fellow. Now, I know why you make sure the chain lock is in place before you go to bed. We certainly don't want him coming around when we're sleeping."

I smiled without showing it as I thought the super was the last person I worried about sneaking in this apartment. There were others who were much more dangerous. If anyone recognized me lurking around or perhaps my Chevy parked down the street from the warehouse, one or maybe more of those dangerous people might come knocking on our door or bust in uninvited.

11

A MISSING TEGEN

Thinking someone would have reported the gunfire around Buckley's warehouse the night before, I searched the internet for Baton Rouge and surrounding area news articles and found nothing. Since I still didn't know if the police had stopped the furniture truck carrying illegal drugs Friday night, I also looked for articles about drug busts. I ran across a couple of small ones, but not the one I wanted to read about. Wondering if there was a way I could find out about the gunfire or a drug seizure from Mitt during dinner without raising any suspicion, I tapped my fingertips together as different ideas swam through my head and suddenly, a plan sprang into my mind.

Then I checked the tracking program on my computer and saw the blue blip, the Mustang, moving along a major highway. Reminiscing about the shooting at the warehouse, I decided to spend the day tailing young Buckley. But first, I needed to rent another car just in case someone recalled seeing a metallic green Chevy down the street from the warehouse. A strong possibility since it was the only car parked nearby.

I opened my top nightstand drawer to put back my black phone, and as I went to turn it off, I noticed a message from Brett, received shortly after I had talked to my father earlier. The message said, "Give me a call."

"Hey," he answered on the second ring. "How are things going?"

"Fine," I said, wondering if he called just to chat.

"You're probably busy, so I'll get right to the point. Have you seen Wendy?"

"Wendy? No. Not since I dropped her off at her folks. Isn't she there?"

"No, she isn't." He sounded irritated.

"She doesn't have a car. Did you ask her parents where she went?"

"Last time I talked to her mom, she seemed extra nice and friendly like Wendy had told her we were friends. But when I talked to her today, she was curt and slammed down the receiver."

"Then how do you know Wendy isn't there?"

"I did get that much out of her mom, but nothing else."

Trying to figure out Mrs. Adams' attitude, I asked, "Did you have a fight with Wendy over the phone or anything like that?"

"No. This morning was the first time I called her since you took her there."

"Strange. Did she try calling you, and you never returned her call?"

"Nope."

"Maybe she just wants to be alone for a while. I'm sure she'll show up. She still could be at her parents' house. She could've told her mom to tell you, or anyone who called, she wasn't there. Her mom dotes on her, she'd do whatever Wendy wanted. And it's not like you need to worry about her being in an accident." All injured Tegens quickly heal.

"This can't wait. She needs to be found," he said in an agitated tone.

"Brett, what aren't you telling me?"

"The investigator looking into Hank's disappearance tried to talk to her yesterday morning. She hung up on him."

"Did he insinuate she was involved?"

"I doubt it. He told me he just wanted to clear up a few loose ends, but things have gotten worse since then."

"What do you mean?"

"Another investigator was following the trail of Hank's girlfriend, Marilee Kent. The woman died in a car crash six months ago."

"What does that have to do with Wendy?"

"The accident occurred right after Marilee had been visiting Hank's folks. A one car rollover, two miles from McComb, at a time when Wendy was staying with her parents."

Knowing that Tegens weren't allowed to use their venom or their spiders to inflict revenge, I said, "You're not saying…"

Brett interrupted me, "That's a possibility."

"How will you know?"

"No autopsy was done. Everyone assumed the accident was the cause of death. We're working on trying to get permission from Marilee's parents to have her exhumed. That's the only way we'll know if she was poisoned by Tegen venom."

I wanted to ask some questions, but I couldn't spit them out, fearing I already knew the answers. I closed my eyes and the image of Wendy, the loving daughter, and her mother sitting at the kitchen table popped into my head.

"Sara?"

"Yeah, I'm still here. Are Marilee's parents reluctant?"

"Yep, but hopefully they can be swayed. Call if you see Wendy."

"I will, Brett."

"Tomorrow I have to go out in the field for a couple of weeks, a place that doesn't have cell phone coverage. The boss is bringing a satellite phone for emergencies. Call the office and tell whoever answers that it's an emergency. Someone will pick up regardless of the hour. They'll get in contact with me. Do you have the number?"

"Yes."

"Sara, if you need me for any reason don't hesitate to call that number."

"I won't." Turning off the cell phone, I hoped Marilee's death was an accident and nothing new would be revealed if an autopsy was granted. Then I thought about Wendy's emotional ups-and-downs. Could she kill an innocent woman out of revenge? Revenge—for what? Stealing her boyfriend? And, if so, did she also murder Hank? Or, did she think Marilee played a role in his disappearance?

12

BUCKLEY'S MEETING

It only took minutes to swap my rented metallic green Chevy for a light blue Dodge Dart, after I lied about hearing a worrisome humming noise under the hood.

I transferred my belongings to the Dodge, and then checked the Mustang's location. The blue blip showed up a few miles from Raina Buckley's house, so I cut into traffic, and headed toward young Buckley's car, occasionally glancing at my computer to make sure his route did not change.

Twenty minutes later, I turned onto Buckley's street. As I approached the house, I saw a dark gray Ford truck parked on the road in front of it and a blue Silverado and a black Volvo in the driveway. The Mustang was across the street. Guessing a meeting might be in progress, I drove past the house and stopped a distance away between several vehicles so my car wouldn't stand out. Since it was broad daylight, my disguise options were limited. I unzipped my duffle bag, pulled out a Yankees' cap, a long-sleeved t-shirt, and a pair of oversized sunglasses and slipped them on. I put the duffle bag in the trunk, grabbed my backpack, and locked the Dodge.

Walking at a normal pace, I remained on the sidewalk until the two story brick house was in sight. My eyes drifted over the parked cars, looking for waiting passengers. All the vehicles were empty. I scanned the neighborhood for people moving about. A few houses away, a woman was taking groceries out of her car. No one else was outside. I strolled away from the Buckley house as I waited for the woman to finish her task. Then I swung around and went back toward the house. Reaching it and making sure I couldn't be spotted through a window, I treaded cautiously to the bushes that lined the side of the structure. I ducked behind them and knelt on the ground in a place where I couldn't be seen from the street.

I took a mini directional mike out of my backpack, inserted the earplugs, pointed the gadget toward the closest window, and turned it on.

Loud static came through the listening device. Squinting and wrinkling my nose, I adjusted the volume. "...not a thing," a deep, raspy male voice said.

"Let's go over this one more time," a husky voice said, a voice I recognized as belonging to Mason Buckley, the man who owned the warehouse. "Her clothes were there."

"Right. Her closet was full along with her drawers, but women like to shop. That might've been just a fraction of what she owns."

"Mason, I just can't believe...," Raina said.

Buckley interrupted, "Raina, get the boys some more coffee."

"But Mason...," Raina said.

"Coffee," he snapped.

"Dad, we've known Monique for a long time," a man with a baritone voice said. His voice sounded younger then Buckley's and I assumed the guy was his son, Mason, the person I had been tailing.

"Mase, not you, too," Buckley said. "The woman Greg described fits Monique. She won't return my calls. She's taken all her files. Every drug she normally stores in her house has been cleared out. Her car's gone."

"How about her clothes?" Mason asked. "And Greg never saw the woman's face. Why would she try to rip you off? She's married to Uncle Frank."

"Estranged from Frank, probably soon to be an ex. And I've never seen Monique wearing the same outfit twice," Buckley said. "Half of her wardrobe could be missing and her closet would still look full. Yes, the woman creeping around the warehouse had on a ski mask, but she was the same size as Monique. She knew Thurman's drugs were stored there and Crussett's delivery van was in the shed outback. For Christ's sake, I'm storing it for her," his voice rose angrily with each word. "Had Greg not spotted her climbing that wood fence, who knows how things would have gone last night?"

I figured I was right about the Crussett crew following the GPS signal on the phone I found in the hidden van, and it led them to Buckley's warehouse. They were probably responsible for the gunfire.

"Oh, let me get some more sugar," Raina said.

I heard clanging of spoons against glass, and chatter about pastries Mrs. Buckley had set out. Besides the sounds of people eating and drinking, the room became silent. While I waited for them to start talking again, I racked my brain trying to figure out if I was right and Conner's guys ended up at the warehouse, then how did Buckley's men handle the situation without a blood bath, or were there casualties I didn't know about.

"Jeff, where did you take the cell phone?" a male with a tenor voice said. He sounded like he was about the same age as young Buckley.

A chuckle echoed through the listening device. "Monique's."

"But you were at the warehouse last night," Mason said.

"Huh?" Jeff, the man with the raspy voice, replied, sounding confused.

"Mase got here late," Buckley clarified.

"That's right," Jeff said. "Greg called and described the intruder when he was looking for her. I suspected Monique right off the bat. After she stabbed Greg, I didn't have any problem using her to get rid of Crussett's men. I told them Monique had been here and left a few minutes ago. Those guys wandered through the warehouse and around the outside while I had the barrel of a pistol aimed at my head. When they couldn't pick up Tyler's cell phone GPS again, they must've bought the Monique story since they put away their weapons and left without hassling us anymore."

As I wondered how he found the cell phone, he continued, "Who else would know about Tyler's cell phone? She must have snatched it while I unloaded the drugs. I searched that van from top to bottom looking for it. Never did trust that woman. Couldn't figure out why she didn't get rid of that van that night. Her lame excuse that the guy at the junk yard wouldn't crush it for her didn't make sense to me. You pay anyone enough, and they'll do whatever you want. She'd stab anyone in the back for a buck."

"I had a gut feeling she was up to something when she wanted that van stored and not destroyed until later," the tenor-voiced man said.

"If it hadn't broken down a block from the warehouse, I never would've agreed to it," Buckley said.

"Monique probably planned that too," Jeff said. "I could smell she was up to something fishy or she wouldn't have gone to that shed. I hustled over that fence and looked around. The padlock hadn't been jimmied. Not finding Tyler's cell phone still kept bugging me. On a hunch, I called his number. It rang three feet away from me. I'm telling you that woman was trying to set us up."

"Any idea why?" Buckley asked.

"Not a clue," Jeff said.

"Had that stupid cell phone been found by Crussett's men we'd be out of business," Buckley said.

"What a bitch!" Jeff said.

"Dad, think about what Mitt told you about Orson," the tenor-voiced man said. "Maybe he's involved."

"Never. Mitt's a liar. He's after his father's business. Reese, don't believe a damn thing he says," Buckley explained in anger. The room fell silent except for a slurping sound and shuffling of feet.

Interesting. Mitt and his father have had some kind of a rift. Orson's tortured lover flashed into my mind, but I doubted Mitt would have divulged that to anyone.

"Gotta get back to the warehouse," Jeff said, snapping me out of my contemplation.

"You're sure none of Crussett's men recognized you?" Buckley asked.

"Positive," Jeff replied. "I had never seen any of them before and not one asked my name."

"Stay armed and keep the back door rigged," Buckley said.

"Will do. I'd kind of like to watch her walk over that threshold. Seeing her hair flaring out and pain on her face would make my day."

Pulling out the pink cell phone, I listened to heavy footsteps and a door creaking open while Raina announced lunch would be served soon. After separating some of the branches, I snapped a few pictures of a tall man with light brown hair as he walked away from the house. He stopped and turned to say something to someone on the porch. I couldn't see who he was talking to, but I saw Jeff's heavy eyebrows and prominent chin as I kept shooting pictures of him. He turned and strode to the dark gray truck parked in front of the house. He climbed in and then the loud, diesel engine roared to life. I watched the vehicle pull away from the curb.

Business talk turned to chitchat between clanking of glasses and utensils, so I glanced at my watch and figured their 2:15 p.m. late lunch wouldn't likely offer me further information. I flipped off the mini directional mike, pulled out the earplugs, tucked them into my backpack, and peered around the bushes. The coast was clear as I crept away from the house and walked at a brisk pace on the sidewalk back to the Dodge.

Settling behind the steering wheel, I mulled over everything I had heard. Why had Conner's guys peacefully left the warehouse? Whatever had gone on at Monique's house, I thought they were responsible for it. I assumed she was dead and her body disposed of someplace where it would never be found. Was I wrong? Her Porsche was parked outside last time I was there. Did she come back to get it or had it been driven away by one of Conner's employees? A fight had clearly happened in her living room. From what I overhead Buckley say the day before, she wasn't living with her husband, but maybe she was living with someone else. If she's still alive, why did Conner's men clean up her place? She would have noticed broken lamps, cracked picture frames, and files missing. But if she was dead, why did they walk away last night? Was it to catch a bigger fish? Questions continued buzzing around in my head as I started the car.

Driving toward the apartment, I got the urge to stir up a little trouble, especially since my Tyler cell phone plan had failed. Crime families should never feel safe. I stayed on heavily traveled streets until I ran across a Wal-mart. In the parking lot, I downloaded the photos on my cell phone to the computer and transferred them to a memory stick. After removing my long sleeved t-shirt and Yankee cap, I went to the Photo Department and had the pictures printed. Before I left the store, I purchased a box of envelopes, two disk mailers, and a package of white paper.

Then I backtracked to a library I had passed earlier. In order to use a typewriter that sat in a small room off the foyer, I had to get a library card. Reluctantly, but doubting anyone could trace a note to this location, I filled out the form, showed the clerk my driver's license, and then received my library card.

Sitting in front of the typewriter, I slipped on a pair of gloves and typed the note. It read: "Mr. Crussett, if you know this man, he now works for Mason Buckley at a warehouse located at" then I proceeded to type the address. "You might also be interested in a missing van. The man in the photo knows where it is." Next, I addressed an envelope to Conner Crussett, stuffed the pictures and note in it, and put a generous amount of stamps on it. Heading toward the Dodge, I dropped the envelope in the mailbox near the library entrance and speculated about possible repercussions. Could it put the Buckleys out of business, or maybe worse?

13

HIDDEN AGREEMENTS

Around 7:30 p.m. the doorbell rang. When I opened the door and saw Mitt standing there, the images on the disk of a woman being tortured drifted through my mind. A torture scene the man in front of me had instigated. "Come in," I said with a forced smile.

While I picked up my purse, Mitt greeted Granny and Esther, the neighbor who sits with Agnes when I go out with Mitt.

Leaving the apartment building, I noticed Mitt seemed uptight; his face looked drawn, his shoulders were rigid and he hardly spoke. When we were settled in his Maserati, I asked, "How's work going?"

"Not good," he replied, pulling away from the curb. "Client problems."

"Oh, I'm sorry," I said, stroking his arm. "I'm a good listener. Anything you want to talk about it?"

"No," he said firmly.

To no avail, I kept trying to start a conversation with him. His mind was definitely elsewhere, and I wondered why he hadn't cancelled our date so he could deal with problems, which probably had to do with Monique and Buckley or perhaps the drug shipment. On the other hand, I couldn't think of any way he could resolve the problems—the damage had already been done. Or had it?

We drove in silence for several minutes. When he turned onto a road that wound through a heavily wooded area, I became concerned and a cold chill ran up my spine. Was I the cause of his aloof behavior? Had someone spotted me or my car in the wrong place?

Mitt pulled onto a paved lane behind a sign that read: *Alfonso's*. He stopped in the packed parking lot next to a wooden chalet and escorted me inside. We were seated in a secluded corner, and I thought Mitt had finally decided to get a little romantic. On our other dates, he had given me a quick kiss when he said goodnight, but that was it. I glanced at the menu while Mitt ordered a bottle of wine.

"Everything here is delicious," he said. "Their filet mignon is superb. The best I've ever tasted."

After the server poured the wine and we had ordered, Mitt pulled his cell phone out of the inside pocket of his sport coat and glanced at it. Since I hadn't heard it ring, I assumed he had it on vibrate. "I need to take this," he said and headed toward the restrooms.

I drank a glass of wine and patiently waited for him to return. Our salads had been delivered ten minutes before he sat down across from me again. "Sorry about that," he said. "Business."

"More trouble with a client?"

"Yes." He stroked my hand. "But we don't need to worry about that tonight."

While we ate, we chatted about the symphony. Then he invited me to an opera on Saturday night. After I accepted, I asked, "Did you do anything fun last weekend when I was out of town?"

"That's when my client problems began." Mitt paused as the server filled our wine glasses. "Had you been in town we would've eaten here Friday night." He cocked an eyebrow and gave me a hint of a smile. "So it was your fault I had to handle problems instead."

Feeling my heart rapidly beating and my stomach churning, I smiled at him as I thought he had no idea how true that statement was. "Your clients call you at night?" I asked, prying for more information.

"All hours. I seldom get a day off."

"Oh, that's terrible. Can't you route those calls to an answering service, and then call them back the next day?"

"The competition is fierce. I'd lose too much business if I didn't take care of their needs as soon as they arise." He ate the last morsel on his plate and laid down his fork.

"You need to get a partner to help out with your workload." I picked up my wine glass.

"I'm working on that." With an irritated expression on his face, he yanked out his cell phone and looked at the screen. "What now?" His eyes moved to me. "Be right back." He walked back toward the restrooms again.

As I slowly sipped wine, I wondered if the urgent phone calls had anything to do with Monique since she was the focus of the conversation I heard at Buckleys'. Had the Crussetts been linked to her disappearance?

Mitt tapped my shoulder, snapping me out of my reverie. "Ready to go?"

"Yes." I sensed he was in a hurry as I grabbed my purse to leave and looked back at my untouched crème brulee on the table.

Sliding into the Maserati, I noticed a grim expression on his face. "Is everything okay?"

"Why?"

"You seem upset."

"Too many business problems," he said, pulling out of the parking lot. "I want to show you my condo—great views of the city."

"That sounds good," I said, recalling the time I broke into his condo and couldn't find anything tying him to the drug business. Gazing out the windshield, I wondered if that had changed. As a precaution before I left my apartment, I had stuffed some strong sleeping powder into an empty lipstick tube and dropped it in my purse in case Mitt decided to get extra friendly.

Thirty minutes later, Mitt unlocked the door to his condo, and we stepped in. His place was decorated like an upscale New York apartment with modern furniture and a large open floor plan. On one side of the room were double doors that led to the master bedroom. Mitt's den was behind the closed single door on the opposite wall. I headed straight to the floor-to-ceiling windows and admired the cityscape, something I couldn't do the last time I was here. I saw the traffic below, the tall lit buildings, the mixture of rooftops and trees bathed in the light of the full moon. Soft music drifted through the room.

Feeling Mitt's arm going around my waist, I said, "You're right, this is a magnificent view. It's too bad you can't work from here instead of your office."

"Sometimes I do. Would you care for a glass of wine?"

"Yes. Please."

"Sauvignon Blanc. Right?"

I nodded, surprised he remembered what I had ordered the night I went with him to the symphony. My eyes continued roaming over the city as he went to the kitchen area and I listened to him uncorking a wine bottle and pouring. Glancing over my shoulder, I watched him put the bottle in the fridge, and knew it would take him a little time to get refills.

He handled me a glass and we went to the couch. "I've turned off my cell phone so we won't be disturbed."

"You need time to relax," I said in a flirtatious tone as I peered into his blue eyes.

Giving me a sensual smile, he said, "That's exactly what I'm planning to do later." He wrapped his arms around me and pressed his lips against mine. His kiss was wet and sloppy, not what I had expected. He trailed his mouth down my neck and caressed my thighs, but instead of moving slowly, he seemed to be rushing it, like he was on a time schedule.

"Oh, Mitt, you're going to get me hot and bothered before I finish this glass of wine," I lied.

"That's the idea."

"Let me catch my breath." I drained my wine. "Would you mind getting me more?" I held up the empty glass.

"Of course." He took my glass and walked away. I quickly reached in my purse, pulled out my lipstick tube filled with sleeping power and adjusted myself in the seat so he couldn't see me pouring it into his glass. Hearing him close the fridge door, I dropped the tube back into my purse.

In a decidedly unladylike manner, I stuck my finger in his glass and twirled it around. I had just pulled out the finger and wiped it on my skirt when Mitt appeared and handed me the filled wine glass. "To us," I said, raising the stem in the air. I waited for him to pick up his glass, and then we clicked our glasses together and drank.

Setting his glass back down on the coffee table, Mitt squinted and stared at it for a few seconds. "Does that wine taste okay to you?"

"I think it's delicious. You don't like Sauvignon Blanc?"

"No. That's not it. This seems to have a little bitter aftertaste."

I took another sip and moved the liquid around in my mouth. "I can't taste any bitterness at all. Maybe it was from something you ate at the restaurant. Take another sip and see if you still taste it."

Mitt sipped a little more, and I smiled to myself seeing his glass was almost empty.

"No. I still taste it."

I didn't want him to dwell on it any longer, so I moved closer to him. "Now where were we before you filled my glass?" I began loosening his tie.

Without saying a word, he unbuttoned my blouse as I continued removing his tie. He rose from the couch and took my hand. "Let's finish this in the bedroom."

I obediently allowed him to lead me through the double doors. Next to his king-sized bed we continued undressing each other as I hoped the sleeping powder would hurry up and kick in. When we both stood naked, he backed away and scanned my body from head to foot, which I found disgusting, but I forced myself not to show it. Being intimate with him was not part of my plan. My mind churned, searching for a way to stall him until the sleeping powder took hold.

His eyes flashed hot with desire. "You're gorgeous. Every inch." Mitt yanked down the covers, scooped me up in his arms and laid me on the bed. He eased down by me and began kissing me again as his fingers trailed over my chest. His head dropped, striking my forehead.

"Ow," I said as his body went limp. "Mitt?" I nudged him, wanting to make sure he was completely out. After waiting for a response, I slid out of his king-sized bed and put my clothing back on except for my bra. I left it lying partially hidden under the foot of the bed. I opened his nightstand drawer and saw packages of condoms. I opened two, took out the condoms, and left the empty packages on his nightstand. Knowing he'd be out until morning, I headed to the den, stopping on the way to grab a pair of latex gloves out of my purse.

Slipping them on, I sank down in his desk chair and recalled seeing women's names in his appointment book, but I couldn't remember any of them. At that time I had assumed the women listed were dates. Now, I wasn't sure. The book sat next to his telephone. I thumbed through it and stopped on numerous entries three weeks earlier with the name Monique penciled in. Going forward, her name appeared often. She was also listed Friday and Saturday night, the nights I had gone to Jackson, Mississippi for the gathering. Next to the Sunday night entry her name had a question mark by it. Was she a business associate or was he dating her? When he stopped by her place on the way to his dad's house, nothing struck me like he even knew her. He seemed stiff on her doorstep. Strange. Could Mitt have been the one who had told Monique about the prior drug shipment?

I continued looking through his appointment book for names that were repeated often. I noticed Mason's, Don's, someone else named Reese. Was Reese one of the guys who attended the meeting at Buckley's house? Aside from those names and Monique's, the rest only appeared a few times, including the name I was using, Sally.

Wondering if he had a picture of Monique, I opened the bottom drawer where I had seen a stack of women's photos when I searched his apartment before. To my horror, on top was a picture of me. I held up the nine-by-twelve picture of my face. I saw the trim of a rose-colored silk blouse and knew the picture had been taken the day I attended his parents' party. The photo looked like it had been taken by a professional. I hadn't seen anyone running around with a camera hanging around their neck. Feeling a sticker on the other side, I flipped it over and saw a white label with Sally Jablon printed on it. I took the stack of pictures out of the drawer, turned them over, and shuffled through them for the name Monique. I found one that said: Monique Torren. I spun it around and gazed at a very attractive woman with long blonde hair. The day I sat in Mitt's car at her place, I hadn't been able to make out her features. Staring at her photo, I noticed her light blue eyes were lacking any trace of a sparkle. I shuddered as I concentrated on her face. There was something foreboding about her, or had I been swayed by what I heard earlier at Buckley's house. I shook my head, turned over all the photos and carefully placed them back in the drawer, making sure my picture remained on top.

I began searching through Mitt's other desk drawers. In the one above the knee opening, I found a manila folder that contained documents applicable to a real estate transaction. Since Mitt ran a property management company, at least part-time, I would expect to see documents like this in his den. Still, I pulled out the folder and laid the contents on the desk. The top document was a purchase agreement for a large parcel of land that included six structures, among them a warehouse. At the bottom of each page was a place for the buyer's initials—MT. On the sixth page, Monique Torren appeared on the buyer line. Though she wasn't responsible for what happened at Buckley's warehouse the night before, she did have a hidden agenda for wanting him to store an incriminating van. She now owned a warehouse and had a reason to want to put Buckleys out of business. A warehouse situated on a large parcel of land, ideal to conceal a large cache of drugs. Buckley was her competition. Besides getting Thurman's drug business, I suspected she also wanted his drug storage business. I went through the document again and didn't see Mitt's name listed as the buyer's or seller's agent.

Leaning back in Mitt's desk chair, I figured he was going to get something out of the deal; otherwise there would be no reason for him to have this document. His father and Buckley seemed like old pals at the party. Could he somehow have acquired a copy of the agreement and planned to tell his father about it? I doubted that was the situation since he had met with Monique often, and he would've handed it over to his father as soon as he got it. Whatever business dealing Mitt had going with her I suspected Orson Thurman wouldn't approve, leaving Mitt with two secrets to hide from his father. Checking the dates on the document, the purchase should have been finalized the prior week.

My eyes darted around the room looking for a copy machine. There wasn't one. I got out the pink cell phone and snapped a picture of each purchase agreement page. If I hoped to connect Mitt to that transaction, I needed something with his name on it, and I couldn't imagine he'd enter into a deal with Monique on a handshake, especially since there was real estate involved, a legal transaction. I thumbed through the rest of the documents lying on the desk. None of them had his name on it. After I put the folder back in the drawer, I searched through the other drawers. Nothing. Then I began going through the credenza. Within an hour, I had rummaged through everything in the den. Not one document linked him to Monique's business.

I moved to the kitchen and went through the cabinets and drawers. I hated returning to the bedroom with Mitt conked out on the bed, but it had to be done. I scrounged around in all of his drawers, even pulled them completely out, looked underneath, and found nothing interesting, just like last time I searched them.

It was almost three in the morning when I decided to call it quits. I grabbed my purse and headed toward the door. There, I stopped and gazed around the large open room. My eyes became fixed on a heat vent. Would Mitt hide something in one of them, like I'd seen in the movies? I headed back to the den, looked at the vent, and saw a little bit of paint had been chipped off next to a screw. I remembered seeing a small screwdriver in his top desk drawer and went to get it. Then I went in the other room and brought back one of the dining table chairs. I placed it below the vent and stood on it. It took me a few minutes to remove the cover. After setting it on the floor, I peered into the vent and saw a black plastic bag. I stuck in my hand and had to yank hard to free it from the vent. Inside I found a partnership agreement. Mitt was listed as Monique's silent partner. I laid it on the desk and shot pictures of the pages. Then I put the document back in the plastic bag and discovered a long rip at the bottom, probably caused when I tugged the bag out of its hiding spot. There was no way I could conceal the tear. I got the tape dispenser sitting on his desk and taped the bottom of bag together. If Mitt looked at it, he'd know someone had found it. Yet, I doubted he'd suspect me.

As I secured the last screw, I heard a moan echo through the condo and feared Mitt was waking up. I finished tightening the screw and quickly climbed off the chair. Trying not to make a sound, I tiptoed over to the desk and put the screwdriver back in the drawer. I picked up the chair and crept toward his dining table. When I sat it down, a loud thud came from his bedroom. I grabbed my purse and hurried to the door leading out of his condo as footsteps pounded on the bedroom carpet.

Easing the door open, I glanced over my shoulder and saw part of Mitt's leg in the bedroom doorway. I ducked into the hall, closed the door, and heard him yell, "Who's there?"

I pushed the elevator button and bite my lower lip until the doors opened. Reaching the lobby, I thought about having the security guard call a taxi, but immediately decided against it. I didn't want to draw attention to myself and needed to get quickly away from Mitt's condo. I walked at a brisk pace along the dimly lit street through the damp air until I ran across a 24-hour pharmacy. I stood inside the door and called for a taxi.

14

THE ENCOUNTER

"Sally," I heard Agnes say.

"Huh," I mumbled, forcing my eyelids open. I felt disoriented, and then the fog began to lift as Agnes, peering into my room, came into focus.

"Dear, are you okay?" she asked, her voice full of concern.

"Yes. Why?"

"It's almost noon and you haven't stirred. Not even each time the phone rang. You've been as quiet as a mouse. I peeked in early just to make sure you were here."

"I got in late," I said, remembering glancing at the clock before I closed my eyes. It said 5:58 a.m. "Who called?"

"A fellow named Mitt Thurman. He said he tried to reach you on your cell phone."

"I turned it off when I went to bed. Did anyone else call?"

"Yes, but when I picked up the phone, the person hung up. Probably a wrong number."

"You've been cooped up here for a few days. Let me take you to lunch."

"Oh, I'd like that."

I quickly showered and dressed, fed my spiders, and made my daily call to my father. Then, I dialed Mitt's number.

He answered on the second ring. "Sally, how are you feeling?"

"Fine," I said, baffled by his question.

"Good. When I called earlier, your grandmother told me you were under the weather and needed a little more sleep."

Pleased that Agnes had covered for me, I said, "Well, I did need more sleep. You wore me out last night. Thank you for such a great time."

"When I woke up this morning, I had hoped you'd be lying next to me."

"I had to get home to Granny." I wondered if he had other nights he couldn't remember what went on since he was going with the flow.

"How did you get home?"

"It was after one and you had just fallen asleep and you looked so peaceful I didn't want to wake you, so I called a taxi."

"You left something behind," he said with a mischievous tone.

"I know. I couldn't find it," I said, referring to my bra, the garment I had planted by the edge of his bed.

"It will be here waiting for you. How about tonight?"

Since I had already searched every inch of his condo, there wasn't a reason for me to go there again. "I hate asking the neighbor to sit with Granny again so soon, especially since I was home so late."

"How about if I get someone to sit with her?"

Based on his persistence, I assumed he was anxious to see me again because he couldn't remember our intimate encounter the night before, an encounter that never happened. "She doesn't do well with strangers. Let me talk to Esther and see how she feels about it."

"There's an Italian restaurant not far from you that I've heard has great food. You up for Italian food again?"

I still needed to appear to be his girlfriend and agreed to go out with him providing I was home by midnight and Esther was okay with it. As soon as I disconnected, I pondered how I could avoid a bedroom scene with Mitt and came up with a plan. Sometime during the evening, maybe just as we reached Mitt's condo, I'd pretend to get a call from Esther saying Granny wasn't feeling well.

After Granny and I had lunch at a Mexican restaurant a few blocks from the apartment, I took her home. Then I went to Wal-mart and waited for the pictures I shot the night before to be developed. Some of the words on the agreements came out blurry on the photos, but enough was legible so anyone looking at them would know what the documents were. The signatures were clear, although Mitt had bad handwriting. A person would either have to be familiar with his signature or study it to make out the letters.

Wondering who I should send them to—Orson Thurman, the older Mason Buckley or the Crussetts, I couldn't decide where the most damage would be inflicted. I settled on keeping them for a day in case Mitt revealed something during dinner that might help me make the decision.

It was just past eight when I climbed into Mitt's Maserati. He seemed exceptionally happy to see me, though I saw worry behind his blue eyes and a tightness in his jaw. Guessing it stemmed from his missing partner,

Monique, I wondered if he had learned anything new.

The air in the quaint restaurant was redolent of garlic, oregano, seasoned sauces, and sizzling meats. We were seated at a small round table covered with a red-and-white checkered tablecloth. Wildflowers in an ornate vase stood in the center.

"That Sauvignon Blanc didn't agree with me last night," Mitt said. "How about a bottle of Pinot Noir?"

"That sounds good."

While we sipped on wine and waited for our meals to be served, I asked, "Still having client problems?"

"They'll never end." His voice revealed an undertone of anger.

"Anything you want to talk about? Remember, I'm a good listener."

"No." Plucking his cell phone out of his breast pocket, he said, "Dammit." He gazed at it. "Not important." Mitt laid his phone on the table without answering it.

I gazed at it, feeling irritated I hadn't gone through his phone the night before.

As we ate, we chatted about different types of food and places he had traveled. He mentioned some South Pacific islands, and without thinking, I blurted out my favorite ones, the Yasawa islands. "When were you there?" he asked in a suspicious tone.

According to my phony background, Sally Jablon didn't have a passport. She never needed one since she had only traveled to a few states. "Well, actually, I've never been out of the United States, but I had a friend in school that went a lot of places. She showed me pictures and I fell in love with those islands. They've been in my dreams so often, I feel like I've been there."

Mitt leaned across the table and squeezed my hand. "Maybe I'll take you someday."

"That would be wonderful." I gave him a warm smile and picked up my wine glass.

"Can your grandmother…," he began, and then abruptly stopped as his eyes rested on my wine glass while I took a sip.

Sitting the glass down, I asked, "Is something wrong?"

Mitt grabbed my right hand. "When did you get that?" he snapped, referring to my black Tegen ring.

Surprised by his angry tone and the fact he noticed my ring, a ring he had seen often, but had never paid any attention to it. "I've had it for a long time," I replied, giving him a vague answer.

"I've never seen it on your hand before."

"Mitt, I wear this ring all the time. What's going on? Does someone else you know have a ring like this?"

"No." His eyes narrowed as he released my hand. "I need to make a call." He stood, snatched his cell phone and walked toward the restrooms.

Thinking about his changed demeanor, I mulled over the past couple of days and then a possibility hit me. I wasn't wearing gloves when I stabbed the man in the wooded area next to the warehouse. Had he mentioned my ring to someone? The day before no one had talked about it at Buckley's house. Maybe they had discussed it before I began listening, or the victim recalled it after he had been stitched up and rested. But since he was in pain that night, I couldn't imagine he would have remembered every detail of my ring. He probably would've just said it was black.

When Mitt returned to the table, he said, "Let's go." His tone sounded more like an order, than a request. I stood and he held my hand as we walked to his car. "I thought we'd stop for a drink before we go to the condo."

From the way he acted after noticing my ring, I had doubted we'd be going to his condo. Now, he seemed pleasant and attentive, but I sensed he was up to no good. Whatever he had planned for me, I was well equipped to handle it. My only problem was that I didn't want our relationship to end this soon. Mitt was my ticket to getting to know his crime family and their friends who also skirted the law. Without him I'd have to scout out someone else who could introduce me to the right people.

It was almost 10 p.m. when he cut to the curb and parked in front of Sammy's Place. Looking at the structure, I wondered why he had chosen to bring me to his hangout place where he drank beer with his buddies and not to a nice lounge, like the one he had taken me to before.

He escorted me inside the noisy establishment and over to a table where three men sat: Mason, the guy I had tailed often, Dan, the burly man with Mitt at the boarded-up building when Frank Montoya was tortured and killed, and another man. Mitt greeted them and pulled up two chairs. Three pitchers of beer and a few empty clean glasses stood in the center of the table. Mason filled two glasses and placed them in front of us while we sat down with our backs facing the door. I would have rather sat on the other side of the table so I would know if anyone I needed to be concerned about entered.

Without giving any last names, Mitt introduced me to Mase, Reese, and Don. I made a mental note that Mitt referred to Mason as Mase. That was the same nickname Buckley called him. That must be how friends and family differentiated between the two Masons. Gazing at Reese, he appeared slightly younger than Mason. They both had blond hair, square faces, blue eyes and muscular arms.

"He's the ugly one in the family," Mason joked, poking Reese in the ribs.

"But you're the sloppy one," Reese retorted. "That's why Mom kicked you out."

They continued chiding each other for a few minutes, and then the conversation switched to sports. While they all chatted about it, I laid my right hand in my lap and used my left hand to hold the beer glass. Because of Mitt strange reaction to my ring, I didn't want any of the other guys to notice it.

About a half an hour later, Mitt turned toward the door. "When's Greg coming?"

"He should be here soon," Mason replied.

From what I heard at Buckley's house the guy I had stabbed two nights before had that name, and I assumed he was the Greg Mitt was expecting. Feeling a pang of uneasiness, my body tensed. I forced myself to take a sip of beer, hoping it would calm my nerves. I knew Greg wouldn't be able to recognize me, but he might remember my ring. Having my ring examined by him was probably the only reason Mitt had brought me here. Maybe I was just feeling jittery because of the way Mitt acted about it. His reaction might not have had anything to do with what Greg mentioned about his assailant, but if that wasn't the case, why did Mitt seem anxious to see him? I had the urge to take off my ring and slip it into my purse, but hiding it would only make matters worse. Then instead of going to his condo later, I'd be taken somewhere away from the city. I doubted he'd attempt to have me killed before he tried to extract information—why I was prowling around the warehouse and who I worked for. I would probably have plenty of opportunity to defend myself, and I'd rather do it in a remote location with only a few observers than anywhere with potentially a lot of spectators.

Based on the wound I had inflicted to Greg's leg, he'd be walking with the aid of crutches. I kept my ears alert to the sound of crutches thumping on the floor as my eyes moved to the restroom sign. Since I didn't want to leave a trail of poisoned victims, I speculated about retreating to the restroom and finding a way to escape from here. They'd track me down, but it might give me enough time to obtain my manmade weapons to fend them off.

As I took another drink of beer, loud footsteps pounded on the hardwood floor behind me, but not the thud of crutches. It sounded like several guys were heading our direction. I noticed anxious expressions on Mason's and Reese's faces, the two men who sat across from me, as their eyes focused on something behind me.

"What?" Mitt said.

Mason nodded toward the door. Mitt gazed over his shoulder and Don looked passed me, leaving me the only one at the table not staring at the people moving toward us. Out of the corner of my eye, I saw the men, dressed in suits, less than a foot away from the table as I sat down my glass. Keeping my head bent, I guessed there was a problem and contemplated excusing myself to go to the restroom.

"We need to talk," a voice I'd never forget blurted out. I assumed he was talking to Mitt, but I wasn't about to look up to be sure. Attempting to hide my face, I raised my hand and fidgeted with my hair while my stomach churned and my heartbeat raced.

"Don, take Miss Jablon home," Mitt ordered.

"I'm going that way. I can drop her off," Mason offered, and I wondered how he knew where I lived.

With Mitt's chair right next to mine, I didn't have enough space to swing out of my seat in that direction. There was no way I could avoid moving right past the three men standing close to the table. I picked up my purse, and keeping my chin down, I slid out of my seat, bumping into the man who wanted to talk to Mitt.

As I edged by him, he touched my arm. A familiar touch I knew well. "Miss Jablon?" he asked, sounding puzzled.

"Yes." I emphasized my southern twang, and kept my head down to avoid eye contact.

He raised my chin, and I found myself looking at Conner's face, a face I had dreamt about often. "Miss Jablon?" he asked again while his eyes studied me. My body tingled as I felt his warm breath against my cheeks, smelled his cologne, and saw a glow in his light brown eyes.

"Yes, sir."

"Would you like Miss Jablon to stay?" Mitt asked, his tone dripping with sarcasm.

"No," Conner replied while his eyes remained fixed on me.

"Sally, are you ready to go?" Mason asked.

"Yes." I stepped away from Conner and sensed him watching me as I headed to the exit with Mason.

Greg, sporting crutches, entered when we were only a few feet away from the door.

"Not now," Mason said to him, as I studied the man I had injured.

"But Mitt wanted to see me," Greg said while he checked me out. I didn't see the slightest hint he recognized me.

"Something's come up," Mason said.

Greg looked behind us, fear gripped his features, and he swallowed hard. "Problems?"

"I suspect so," Mason said, but he didn't seem fazed by it.

"If Mitt asks, tell him I tried to see him," Greg said, turning around. The three of us left the establishment together, and Greg headed to a Toyota close to the entrance.

Climbing into Mason's Mustang, I saw one of the men who had accompanied Conner into Sammy's Place, getting into a black Cadillac Escalade parked across the street. I suspected he planned to follow us. "That was strange," I said. "I've never been sent home from a date before."

Mason started the car and pulled into the traffic. "If you're going to continue dating Mitt, you'd better get used to it."

"Why?"

"Sometimes business associates want to meet on the spur of the moment."

"I feel a little rattled over that. Are you up to having another drink?"

He glanced at me, squinting. "At your place?"

"No." I recalled he had announced to the world on Facebook that he had a girlfriend. "That's not what I meant. I live with my grandmother. I thought we could stop someplace on the way back." Looking at the side mirror, I saw the Cadillac a couple of cars behind us. I didn't want Conner to know where I lived, and doubted he'd ask Mitt for my address.

"Sure. There's a small bar not far from your apartment. We'll stop there."

Mason hadn't exaggerated when he said the place was small. It was a rustic-looking narrow bar with five booths lining one wall. On the opposite wall a long counter stood with a bartender filling beer glasses behind it and a row of barstools in front of it.

Two booths were unoccupied. We took the one furthest away from the door. "Want another beer or something else?" Mason asked.

"Wine. Sauvignon Blanc, if they have it."

"I'll see what they've got." He went to the counter. A few minutes later, he returned carrying a glass of wine and a bottle of beer. "They didn't have anything on tap I like," he said, sliding back into the booth.

I took a sip. "It's good. And thanks."

He smiled. "Not a problem. I wasn't ready to go home either. Talk about ruining an evening. Three nights in a row."

"Three nights?" I knew about two of them and wondered about the third one. "Do those guys show up each night expecting a meeting?"

"No. No. A couple of nights ago, someone tried to break into a warehouse my dad owns, so I had to run over there to make sure nothing was missing, and last night we were busy hunting down the person."

"Did you help the police catch the guy?"

"Nah. We're not sure it was a guy."

Popping my eyes wide open, I asked, "A woman?" sounding shocked.

"Oh, let's not talk about my bad days. So, Sally Jablon, what do you do?"

"My job?"

He nodded. Then I proceeded to tell him the same story of my life I had given to Mitt ending with, "So I came back to Baton Rouge to take care of Granny."

"Who's watching her tonight?"

"A neighbor. Driving here you mentioned those guys that came to see

Mitt were business associates. I just can't figure out why they couldn't talk to him during the day, regular business hours. Showing up like that makes no sense to me."

"The one guy I know." He grinned and cocked his brow. "The guy you obviously enchanted. Never seen him act that way before, but I haven't seen him around a gorgeous woman before either."

"Oh, stop it. I didn't enchant anyone, and I'm not gorgeous."

"You certainly are. That's how Mitt describes you—a gorgeous, blue-eyed, strawberry blonde. When he walked into Sammy's with you by his side, I knew who you were before he introduced us."

Blood rushed to my cheeks. "Mase, you're embarrassing me."

"Sometimes Mitt doesn't treat girlfriends all that nice, so why don't you dump him and start going out with me?"

"Mase, I'm dating Mitt. Girlfriends? How many does he have?"

"Only one at a time," he said as his cell phone beeped. "Sorry, I should have put it on vibrate." He pulled it out of his pocket and glanced at it. "I need to take this." He moved away from me to the last barstool, sat on it and faced the wall.

I perked up my ears and strained to listen. I caught the name of the person on the other end of the line—Don, and enough snippets of the conversation to know they were talking about the meeting taking place at Sammy's.

He tucked his phone in his pocket and returned. "Business," he said, sounding irritated as he scooted into the booth. "Now what were we talking about." He gave me a big smile. "I know. You. What's it going to take for you to dump Mitt?"

Not wanting to be the cause of a riff between the two men, I glanced at my watch without answering his question. "I better get home. I promised the neighbor I'd be back by midnight and it's quarter to."

As we drove to my apartment, I noticed the black Cadillac tailing us. I had hoped Conner would have summoned the driver to return to Sammy's to pick him up by now.

Mason parked in front of the Baxter Building and I asked, "How did you know where I lived?"

"Mitt mentioned how he had met you at Christie's, and you lived in an apartment right across the street. This is the only building that fits that description." Mason walked me to the elevator. "Don't forget my offer when you decide you've had enough of Mitt." He pulled a business card out of his shirt breast pocket and handed it to me. "Just call my number."

"I'll remember." I stepped into the elevator. As the doors closed behind me, I looked at the card. Only his name and phone number were on the card. Staring at it, I thought if I had to pick between Mitt and Mason to be my boyfriend, I'd definitely take Mason. It wouldn't even be a contest.

Entering the apartment, I saw Agnes's door was closed, the television was off, and Esther hadn't waited for me to come home, which was all right since Agnes didn't need anyone taking care of her. Having Esther here was strictly show for Mitt's benefit, nothing more.

15

UNPLANNED KILLING

I awoke to the sound of someone pounding on the door. Feeling groggy, I glanced at the clock: 1:05 a.m. Had Mitt brought Greg here to inspect my ring? The knocking continued as an uneasy sensation vibrated through my body. I grabbed my robe and slipped it on while hurrying to the door. Keeping the chain in place, I opened it and saw Mitt leaning against the door jam. No one was with him. "What are you doing here?"

"We need to chat," he said loudly, almost shouting, as he glared at me.

Seeing his hostile, furious expression, I doubted he'd leave if I refused. "Okay, let me remove the chain." After I had taken care of it and turned on the light, I pulled the door wide open, and Mitt strode in. "Take a seat, but try to talk quietly so you don't wake up Granny."

He plopped into Granny's chair, and I sat on the couch opposite him. "What are you up to?" he growled.

"What?"

Mitt's nostrils flared and his eyes flashed with anger. He stood, moved toward me, and grabbed my arm as he sank down on the couch. "Don't play dumb with me," he hissed.

"Mitt, I don't know what you're talking about, but Granny's sound asleep and if you don't keep your voice down you're going to wake her."

"Granny? Is she even your grandmother?" he asked as his grip tightened around my arm.

"Mitt, what has gotten into you?"

"First, I noticed your black ring."

I looked at it. "What is it with you and this ring?"

"The woman who stabbed Greg wore a black ring."

95

I rolled my eyes. "Mitt, don't you realize there's more than one black ring in this world? And who is Greg?"

"Greg works at a warehouse. Two nights ago a woman wearing a ski mask was spotted creeping around. He caught her. She stabbed him and escaped. He described a ring she wore, and Sally, your ring matches that description. If Crussett would have just shown up a little later at Sammy's, I would've known for sure. But then seeing the way that man looked at you, I knew you two weren't strangers. Do you work for him?"

"No," I said, shaking my head. "You know I take care of Granny. I don't have another job. And I had never seen that man before."

"Stop lying. That punk thinks I had something to do with a shipment he lost, and I also had something to do with the cops confiscating another shipment on Friday night. I didn't have a damn thing to do with the cops. He threatened me. Gave me forty-eight hours. Who the hell does he think he is? You had to be the one who told him about the van."

"Punk? What punk?"

"Crussett. Who else?"

"Shipments? Van? Someone named Crussett? Mitt, you've lost me. You don't talk business with me. How would I know what you're up to?"

"He has a spy here, and it's not one of my men."

"So that makes it me? Why? Because I slept with you? Is everyone who sleeps with you a spy?"

"You went with me to Monique's house. You even asked about her security system. Now she's missing. Did you have anything to do with that?"

"Who's Monique?"

"You know damn well who she is."

Trying to calm him down, I stroked his cheek. "I haven't got the foggiest idea where you're coming from, but I'm not a spy, and I don't know anyone named Monique. I thought we had something special going."

"So did I until I saw that ring," he said, his eyes boring into mine. "Cameron would know exactly how to handle a bitch like you."

"Who's Cameron?" I asked, though I knew it was Conner's brother, a man I had killed before he could carry out his plan to terminate my life, Sara Jones' life.

He shook his head. "Come on, Sally, Conner wouldn't even be running the family business had his girlfriend not knocked off Cameron, the punk's brother."

Since Mitt had not referred to Conner by that first name earlier, I asked, "Conner is Mr. Crussett?"

"So you're going to keep playing dumb." He whipped out a pistol from inside his coat and screwed on a silencer.

"What are you doing?" I said, opening my eyes wider and lifting my eyebrows. "Put that thing away."

His eyes darkened with rage and his face hardened. "Get up," he said, brandishing his weapon. "You're going with me."

"No, I'm not." I feigned a trembling voice like I feared for my life as I stared at the silencer. Did he intend to shoot me right here if I didn't comply?

"Yes, you are," he snapped, raising his voice and dragging me off the couch.

"But Granny needs me."

Suddenly, Granny's door flew open. Wendy charged out and leapt on Mitt. Swinging his pistol, he jerked around and slammed his weapon against Wendy's head while I yelled, "Stop that. Wendy, get off of him."

Holding onto her head where Mitt had struck her, she stumbled backwards and crashed into a wood chair, breaking off one of the spiral back supports. Then I saw the deep scrape on Mitt's cheek, and knew Wendy had scratched him with her poisonous needles. He cupped his hand over the wound as he aimed the barrel of his gun at her. "Who the hell are you?"

"She's my cousin," I answered for her. Though, there no longer was any point in answering any of his questions. The relationship I had worked to establish with Mitt was gone. Before Wendy poisoned him, I thought there was a slim chance I might be able to find a way to salvage it, not anymore.

Mitt swayed and staggered as the poison streamed through his veins. I suspected it wouldn't be long before his body went limp. "Wha--," he murmured, stumbling over the coffee table and discharging his weapon.

The bullet penetrated Wendy's stomach. She moaned and buckled over in pain.

A loud thud rang out.

I turned toward the noise, and saw Mitt sprawled on the floor motionless. I rushed into the bathroom, grabbed a handful of towels, and pressed them against Wendy's abdomen.

"It hurts," she said, the pain etched on her features. "The bullet didn't go through. You need to get it out."

I squinted. "What? I don't know how to do that."

She inhaled deeply, and blew out air. "The pain's starting to go away, but I think we still need to take out the bullet. Do you know if it will just pop out as my stomach heals?"

I shook my head. "Don't know. Should I call my father?"

"No...no. We'll take it out." She ran her hand over the wound. "It's already starting to close. We better hurry. Get a knife."

I charged to the kitchen, opened the utensil drawer, and stared at an assortment of knives. "A butcher knife?"

"No. Something smaller. A steak knife." She stretched out on the floor.

As I bent down next to her, someone knocked on the door. Guessing the person had come to investigate the noise, I went to the door and cracked it open. "Yes?"

"I heard shouting and a commotion coming from your apartment. Is everything okay?" an elderly man asked.

"Yes. My cousin startled me and I knocked over a lamp. I hadn't expected her until tomorrow. I'm sorry it woke you."

"I don't sleep much at night, probably because I nap all day. Glad you're okay."

"Thanks for your concern." As he walked away, I closed the door and secured the chain.

"You need to hurry. The wound is almost closed," Wendy said, moving her finger over it. After I knelt next to her, she pointed. "Cut here."

"Wendy, I don't know about this."

"I'd do it, but I can't see it. Just cut, and I'll try to pull out the bullet."

As I wiped away the blood trickling from the hole in her stomach, I noticed another bloody spot at her side, close to her waist. Thinking she had been scraped by the chair's broken wood spiral, I ran my finger over it, but what I touched was metal. "Wendy, turn," I said, carefully pushing her until her side was exposed to me. "The bullet. It's coming out."

"Really?"

"Yeah, I can see it."

She eased her fingers over it. "I can feel it. Why don't you take the knife and see if you can flip it out."

"No. Let's give it a few minutes."

She bobbed her head.

"How do you feel?"

"Better." She stroked her stomach. "It's not bleeding anymore."

While we waited, I went to Mitt and saw his wide open, glassy-looking eyes, fixed on the ceiling. "Wendy, why did you do that?" I asked in a sharp tone.

"I heard him through the door. He had a gun. I had to do something."

"And look, you got yourself shot. Wendy, I can take care of myself. I doubted he was going to shoot me in the apartment and even if he had, I would be healing. Just like you're healing. Tegens heal." Anger boiled up inside me. "You had no right coming in here and poisoning him. What are the rules? We only use our poison for two reasons. To feed, and those victims have been selected; and to protect ourselves if we, or any potential Tegen, are in danger and there is no other option. We have to keep our existence a secret. We can't let anyone know we're different. Don't you get it?"

"I'm sorry," she said as her eyes filled with tears. "I just wanted to help."

Realizing no matter what I said there was no way I could undo the damage she had caused, I gently patted her shoulder and saw the bullet protruding from her side. "I think I can pull it out the rest of the way." I put the corner of the towel over the bullet and gave a tug. "Got it." I held it up.

Wendy took it from me. "I've never been shot before. I'm going to keep this as a souvenir."

"How's your head?" I gazed at the bump.

She touched it. "It's going down. It'll be fine, but I think it might take an hour or so for the hole in my abdomen and side to completely heal," she said, rubbing them.

Looking at her blonde hair, I raised a few strands, "When did you do this?" I asked since she was a brunette when I dropped her off at her folks.

"Yesterday, do you like it?"

Studying her face, the blonde hair seemed to fit. The color brought out her blue eyes and rosy cheeks. "Yes, it suits you." My eyes moved to Mitt's body lying on the floor. "We'll need to get rid of him. Do you think you can help me?" I hoped her injuries wouldn't make it an impossible task to move him out of the building.

"Let me see." Pressing her palm against her stomach, Wendy stood up and paced the room while I soaked up the blood on the carpet with a towel. "Yeah, I can help."

Granny flashed into my mind. "Where's Agnes?"

"I got here right after you went out on your date," she said, emphasizing the word "date." "The old fuddy-duddy took a taxi to a relative. I guess she doesn't like me."

"What about Esther, the woman watching her?"

"What a busybody. That woman wanted to know everything about me. She rattled off more questions than you can believe. Felt like I was being interrogated."

Recalling what Brett had told me about the Wendy investigation, I asked, "You didn't hurt Agnes or Esther, did you?"

"No, I didn't touch the phony granny or her busybody friend. She wanted to go to her sister's house. Busybody left with fuddy-duddy to wait for the taxi. Good riddance."

I doubted she was telling the whole story, but I needed to get Mitt's body moved before I dug into it any more. I also felt Agnes was safer at her sister's than being in the same apartment as Wendy.

Since both Wendy and I had night vision, I flipped off the light, peeked out the edge of the drapes and scanned the neighborhood. At two in the morning, only one person walked along the sidewalk and traffic was almost nonexistent. Mitt's Maserati was parked out front, a straight shot from the apartment entrance. I figured Wendy and I could get him into the passenger seat of his car. Then I'd drive it to some remote location and Wendy could follow me in the rented Dodge.

A wave of panic surged through my body when I noticed a black Cadillac Escalade on the other side of the street. The dark tinted car windows made it impossible for me to see if anyone was inside, but I assumed someone was in it, a Crussett employee assigned to watch me. The minute I saw Conner at Sammy's, I knew he'd want to find out more about Sally Jablon. I just hoped some doubt still existed in his mind that Sally Jablon and Sara Jones weren't the same person.

To avoid revealing anything about Conner to Wendy, I said, "Mitt's car's right out front, but one of his employees is sitting in a car across the street, probably waiting for him. We're going to have to take him out the back." Eyeing her bloody clothes, I added, "If your wound hasn't completely closed, cover it with bandages. Leave your bloody clothes in the bathtub and put on sweats or something like that, but it has to be dark, preferably black."

After I changed into a black sweat suit, I returned to the living room with a bottle of *venotrolia*, and sat it on the coffee table. I searched Mitt's pockets and found his car keys. I picked up his pistol and put on the safety. I still thought he never intended to use it, probably just a scare tactic. Since my face was covered when I went to the warehouse, no one there could identify me. Yet he acted like there wasn't a shred of doubt I was the woman who stabbed Greg. My ring caused him to get suspicious, but had Conner not stared at me, I might have been able to patch it up. And the chances Greg could clearly remember every detail of my ring when he was moaning in pain were pretty slim.

As Wendy stepped into the living, I handed her the *venotrolia*. "Drink this."

"Thanks. I need it." She took a big swig.

Dropping Mitt's keys and gun into my backpack, I noticed his cell phone lying under the coffee table. I scooped it up, pushed the off button, removed the battery, and put the phone inside my spiders' cage. They'd take care of anyone who tried to retrieve it. I stuck a wet clean towel into a plastic bag, wedged that into my backpack, and pulled out two pairs of latex gloves. "Put these on." I handed a pair to Wendy.

"But I won't be able to use my needles if someone catches us with a dead guy." She sat the empty *venotrolia* bottle on the table.

That's the idea. Leaving the apartment with a lethal weapon ready to strike was not anything I wanted to do. "Wendy, fingerprints. And Mitt isn't dead yet. He's in something like a comatose state right now. Since we're not going to preserve him for later consumption, he'll be dead in a few hours. If someone should see us, we can tell them we're helping a friend who's had too much to drink."

"Why don't we preserve him and take him to the next gathering?"

"Wendy, where would you propose we keep the body?"

Her eyes darted around the room. "Oh, I didn't think about that." Then she grudgingly yanked on the gloves.

After putting on my backpack, I bent down next to Mitt's head, slid my arm under his back and instructed Wendy to do the same on the other side of his body. I placed his arm around my shoulders and Wendy followed my movements. Then we each held onto one of his hands, draped his arm over our shoulders and attempted to get him up into a standing position. It took awhile, but finally we managed. The lower part of his legs and his feet dragged along the carpet as we trudged to the door.

"You doing okay?" I asked.

She nodded. "Yeah. I feel a strange sensation in my stomach, but no pain.

I opened the door and peered out into the hallway. Seeing it was empty, we stepped into the hall with the heavy weight on our shoulders. Wendy closed the door behind us. We moved slowly toward the elevator. Huffing and puffing, I pushed the button.

As we got in, Wendy asked, "Can we put him down for a few minutes?"

"Let's lean him in the corner." We got him situated, and then removed his arms from our shoulders. Wendy inhaled and exhaled deeply, and stroked her stomach as we descended.

Voices came through the elevator shaft below us.

"Someone's waiting for the elevator," I said as we passed the third floor. I pushed the button for the second floor. "We need to get out."

"Really?" Wendy moaned.

"Yes." The doors slid apart. I took off my backpack and dropped it in the door track to keep the door from closing while we adjusted Mitt's arms back on our shoulders. Glancing down the hallway, I picked up my backpack as we pulled Mitt out of the elevator. I nodded toward the exit sign at the end of the hall. "That way."

"We're going to take him down the stairs?"

"Do we have a choice?"

She moved her head back-and-forth, looking for an alternative. "Guess not."

Mitt's weight along with the backpack in my hand increased with every step we took. It seemed like a half an hour had passed before we made it to the exit, but in reality less than five minutes. I pushed open the door and leaned my back against it, preventing it from automatically slamming shut before we maneuvered him into the stairwell. As soon as we cleared the door and stood on the landing, I said, "Let's put him down for a minute."

We released him and he sank to the cement floor.

I secured my backpack.

Wendy sat down on a step. "How much does that guy weigh?"

"Probably around two hundred pounds, but felt like over three hundred. We need to change how we're moving him. I'll take his upper body and you take his legs."

After we both had a chance to catch our breath, we got situated and began to raise Mitt off the landing. It took all my strength to lift him up a few inches from the floor. Seeing Wendy's arms securely wrapped around his legs, I said, "Let me know if this gets too hard for you."

"I will."

We managed six steps before the stairwell turned. Getting him around the corner proved to be too much for us. As Wendy grabbed hold of the railing, Mitt's legs slid out of her arms, and with the added weight, I couldn't hang onto him. His body banged against the steps as it tumbled down.

"Oh, my God, we've killed him." Wendy said as her hands covered her mouth and she stared at the crumbled body lying in a heap at the bottom of the stairs.

I shook my head and briefly closed my eyes. "Wendy, you already killed him upstairs."

She lowered her hands. "Oh, that's right. What do we do with him now?"

"We still need to get rid of the body. Nothing's changed." I hurried down the stairs to check if there was some life left in his body. His pulse was extremely slow, but he had one. I felt relieved since I didn't want him to take his last breath until we had him settled in another location. "He's not dead yet. Wait here."

I went outside, unlocked the Dodge, and moved my duffle bag from the trunk to the backseat. Then I spotted a dolly near the dumpster and pushed it around to make sure it worked properly. Satisfied, I placed it next to my car.

Entering the building, I saw Wendy bending over Mitt with her mouth pressed against his. "What are you doing?"

She turned toward me with blood on her lips. "Blood's seeping from his mouth. I love fresh *venotrolia*. Want some?"

"No. Did you put one of our spiders on him?"

She nodded. "Don't worry, it's back where it belongs."

Gazing at the delicious red liquid covering Mitt's mouth, I licked my lips and forced myself to suppress my desire to indulge. "We don't have time for a picnic right now. Let's get him upright again. My car's not far away."

After struggling with Mitt's limp body, we finally managed to get his arms around our shoulders again, and dragged him toward my car. I had just opened the trunk when I heard footsteps shuffling on the pavement somewhere in the parking lot. Before turning around, I slammed down my trunk lid.

"Why'd you do that?" Wendy asked, holding Mitt against the side of the car with his head and shoulders slumped on the roof.

"Shhh. Someone's close by," I whispered, opening the Dodge's back door. "We're putting him in here."

"Well, hello again," a male voice said.

I looked over my shoulder and saw the elderly man who had knocked on my door earlier. Trying to appear like nothing was wrong and hoping he didn't notice the thin, transparent gloves covering our hands, I said, "You do stay up late. Been out for a stroll?"

"The streets are so quiet this time of night. Best time for a walk." His eyes darted to Wendy and Mitt. "A drunk boyfriend, so that was all the noise. Need help getting him into the car.

"No, we can manage." I pulled Mitt's arm further down over my shoulders. Wendy and I yanked and jerked Mitt until we got him on the backseat. Then I closed the door while the elderly man remained by our side.

Nodding toward the dolly standing by the Dodge, the man asked. "Are you taking the dolly?"

"I'm borrowing it so we can get my cousin's hope chest out of storage."

"Why don't you wait until morning? I know Bruce would give you a hand. He lives on the same floor we do."

"We can handle it."

"If you change your mind, I'm in apartment 512."

"Thanks, we appreciate your concern." I watched the elderly man walk away and step into the building as I lifted up the dolly to place it in the trunk. Its handle protruded beyond the trunk latch. I pulled it out and stuck it in the backseat on top of Mitt.

"Does everyone who lives in your apartment building like to talk?" Wendy asked, climbing into the car.

"No. Most of them keep to themselves." I drove out of the parking lot, wondering if the black Escalade would follow us. I kept checking the mirrors for any sign of the vehicle. After not spotting it for several miles, I deviated from my planned route and went up and down side streets while my eyes drifted between the car's mirrors. The black car was nowhere in sight. I inhaled deeply and softly blew out the air.

"What about Mitt's Maserati?" Wendy asked.

"We'll deal with that when we get back."

"Where are we going?"

"A deserted house. It'll take us a while to get there."

Wendy leaned her head against the window and closed her eyes as I tried to figure out how to dispose of Mitt's car so no one would suspect I was involved with his death. On top of dealing with the Mitt problem, I needed to let Brett know Wendy was at my place. I shuddered as I thought about making that call, fearing the worst.

Almost an hour later, I stopped about a hundred feet from Monique's driveway. "Wendy." I nudged her arm.

"Huh?" she mumbled, adjusting herself in the seat.

"I need to check on something. Stay in the car." After she nodded, I scooted out of the vehicle and crept down the driveway, staying close to the foliage. Not one light illuminated the inside or outside of the steel-and-glass house. To make sure there wasn't a soul around, I rang the doorbell six times. The chimes sounded through the door, but no movement. I went back to the car, started the engine, and drove the Dodge down the driveway.

Wendy stared out the windshield. "This house is deserted?"

"No one's living here."

"You sure?"

"Yes." I fished three bungee cords out of my duffle bag, pulled the dolly off the backseat and rolled it over to the other side of the car. "We're going to strap him to this," I explained as I placed it flat against the pavement. Per my instructions, Wendy climbed on the backseat and pushed out Mitt's legs. Working together and using the bungee cords, we secured his chest and legs to the dolly. His head and shoulders slumped as we rolled him to the backyard. Then we removed all the cords, and Mitt's body fell to the ground.

"I have to get a few things." I took the dolly and bungee cords back to the car, stuck them on the backseat, and grabbed my backpack.

Returning to the backyard, I said, "We need to get him sitting on his legs." I lowered my knees to the ground and sat my bottom on my feet. "Like this."

"Why?"

"I'll explain later."

We toiled on trying to position him for fifteen minutes, but his body was too limp to make it work.

I exhaled a deep breath and said, "Let's give up." Gazing at Mitt, I came up with another way to position his body. "He needs to be lying on his stomach with his head furthest away from the house."

We proceeded to wiggle him around until we had him situated. Then I plucked his pistol out of the backpack.

Wendy stared at the weapon. "What are you going to do with that?"

"Execute him."

"But he's already dead or close to it."

"If he's found with a hole in his head, everyone will think that was the cause of death. No one will look further." I touched his pulse. It was weak, but still beating. "He's alive." I released the pistol's safety and laid it down.

I gripped his shoulder, and following my lead, Wendy wrapped her hand around his other shoulder. We struggled to raise his upper body, but his forehead flopped forward and hit the ground. "This isn't going to work," I said, releasing his shoulder.

Glancing around for something to slide under his chest, I spotted a flat boulder about the size of two basketballs at the corner of the house and pointed at it. "Let's use that."

Given the weight of the boulder, we had to push it. When it was next to Mitt, I grabbed his shoulders and used all my strength to raise the top part of his body off the ground while Wendy forced the boulder under him. After we had rested for a few minutes, Wendy crouched down beside him and held his head up. I picked up the weapon and pressed the barrel against the back of his skull. "Blood will probably spray everywhere, so look away." A second later, I pulled the trigger.

Sure enough, blood splattered, but not one drop landed on me. Wendy wasn't as fortunate. It was all over the side of her black sweatshirt, cheek, hair and gloved hands. The blood also left a large arc on the ground.

"Yuk." Wendy rubbed her cheek, and then licked her gloved fingers. "Good. It's streaming from his forehead. Can I drink a little?"

"Nope. Someone might get curious if there isn't a lot of blood. We have to move the boulder back."

Careful not to get any blood on my clothing, I raised Mitt's shoulders again. Wendy worked the boulder out from under him as Mitt's blood pooled around his head. When we placed the boulder back where it belonged, I took the damp towel out of the plastic bag in my backpack and wiped off all traces of blood. A soft breeze blew toward me and I caught a whiff of his tainted blood. I stood by his body, inhaled the luscious smell and noticed Wendy sticking her gloved hands in the blood and sucking them. It was too much. I had to have a taste. "We can only drink a little."

Wendy's face lit up as she edged closer to him and gulped up some of the inviting red liquid. I joined her for a minute, then blotted my mouth on the towel. "That's enough." She ignored me. "Wendy, stop! We can't drain him dry. There has to be blood at the scene."

"Okay," she said, sounding disappointed. She looked at the blood on her gloves and licked it off.

"Do you want to use the towel?"

"No. I'll take off my sweatshirt and use the inside of it to clean up."

I cleaned the surface of the pistol. "I want to brush away our footprints, so why don't you head to the car?" After she had gone around the corner of the house, I used the towel to sweep around Mitt's body, then laid the pistol next to his head. I continued brushing the towel over the ground until I could no longer see any more footprints. Walking out of the backyard, I dragged the towel behind me, dusting away the indentations I made with each step.

As I opened the car door, she asked, "Can I take off these gloves now?"

"Yes. We're through here."

Driving away from Monique's house, I glanced at Wendy to check how she was doing getting herself cleaned up. She held out strands of her hair and rubbed them with her sweatshirt. "How's it going?"

"Not good. If you don't want me to walk into your apartment building looking like I've killed someone, find a gas station with a public bathroom."

Minutes later, I stopped next to a gas pump. "The restrooms are on the side." I filled the car's gas tank and then listened to the radio while waiting.

Wendy strolled toward the car with her damp hair draping over her shoulders, leaving wet splotches on her tank top.

"Put your sweatshirt in here," I said, handing her a plastic bag.

She pushed it into the bag and asked, "Now what?"

"We deal with Mitt's car."

16

MITT'S MASERATI

It was after 5 a.m. when Wendy and I stepped back into my apartment. I looked out the window and saw the Cadillac hadn't budged. "Change your clothes. You're going to have to drive the Maserati."

Her eyes popped wide open and a smile crossed her lips. "I get to drive it?"

I nodded. "It's a stick shift. You do know how to drive one, right?"

"Yeah. That's what I drove in college."

After she took a quick shower and dressed, I said, "Here's the plan: See that black Cadillac across the street?" She bobbed her head, and then I continued, "I'm going to jog around the block. As soon as that car leaves, you drive to the gas station where you cleaned up."

"I can't remember where it is."

"Then turn right at the first corner." I pointed toward the intersection. "And drive until you see Betty's Diner. You can't miss it. It has a big sign by the road. Pull into the parking lot and wait for me." I handed her Mitt's keys.

"Got it."

I jogged a couple of blocks and stopped to tie my shoe. Glancing over my shoulder, I saw the Cadillac pulling into a parking spot on the other side of the street and spotted a man dressed in a dark suit duck into a doorway behind me. I figured the Cadillac must've had two occupants and one was enjoying the morning fresh air with me. I sprinted for a half a mile and sensed the man in the suit had no difficulty keeping up with me. Leaning against a tree, I looked around and saw the Cadillac close by. I turned and moved at a slower pace back to the apartment, giving Wendy more time to get away.

As I approached the building's entrance, I took a deep breath. The Maserati was gone. Step one accomplished. I walked straight through the lobby and out the back door, then scanned the parking lot for the man in the suit. He was nowhere in sight. Assuming he had returned to the Cadillac, I climbed into the Dodge and dressed in my usual disguise before driving out. Checking the rearview mirror, I didn't spot the Cadillac behind me, but, as a precaution, I zigzagged up and down side streets while making my way to the diner.

The parking lot was busier than anticipated. The Maserati was parked between two vehicles. I pulled into the first empty slot and got out of the car. Walking toward the Maserati, I cringed when I saw the damage.

The car door flew open. "It wasn't my fault," Wendy said, stepping out of Mitt's car. "That guy shouldn't have had those long poles sticking out of his truck. They were almost dragging on the road. It was his fault."

Staring at the badly dented fender and the dislodged headlight, I suspected she had been traveling at a pretty good speed when she rammed into the pole. I squatted next to the front wheel and ran my hand around the tire, making sure the car frame wasn't touching it. "Did the guy stop?"

"No." She handed me a deposit slip. "I wrote the license plate number on this."

"Does the Maserati still drive okay?"

"The engine didn't get hurt."

"We're switching cars. Follow me in the Dodge."

"I can't drive the Maserati?"

"Wendy, you don't have a driver's license. A policeman could pull you over and ask about the damage."

"Why?"

"Checking for a possible hit and run."

Grimacing, she said, "Have it your way."

I moved my backpack from the Dodge to the Maserati, and drove away from the diner with Wendy right behind me. It was broad daylight when I pulled over to the side of the pavement on Monique's street. The Dodge stopped behind the Maserati. I got out of the car and headed to Wendy. "I'm going to park Mitt's car in front of the steel-and-glass house we visited earlier. Stay here."

"What if someone has come home?"

"Then I'll have to deal with that someone," I said, doubting the possibility and suspecting it was too early for visitors.

I drove the Maserati down the driveway and parked it. Pulling the keys out of the ignition, I decided to take them with me. I climbed out of the car and heard a soft humming sound coming from the garage, a sound that wasn't present during our earlier visit. Fearing it was some kind of alarm, I quickly wiped off the stirring wheel and door handle, snatched my backpack and sprinted up the driveway.

Wendy sat in the passenger seat when I reached the car. I jumped in, started the engine, flipped a u-ey, and sped away from Monique's house.

"What's the hurry?" she asked.

"I heard a noise, thought it might be an alarm."

"We didn't hear anything like that last night."

"I know. It came from the garage. Maybe someone else has been snooping around there."

"Hey, is that the black Cadillac that was parked across the street from the apartment?" she asked, pointing at a car moving on the other side of the road, heading in the direction of Monique's.

Was it possible? Could a tracking device be on my car? "I don't know."

"Hey, look. There goes another one." Her head swaying back-and-forth as another Cadillac zoomed past us.

One might have been a coincidence, but two, not likely. When we reached a more populated area, I turned down a side street and cut to the curb. "We're going to check for tracking devices."

"Tracking device? Since the guy was waiting for Mitt, wouldn't that be on the Maserati?"

"Well, I still want to check," I said, getting out of the driver's seat.

"Do you know what a tracking device looks like?"

"They come in different sizes. Just look for anything that doesn't belong on the car."

As I meticulously searched around the third wheel, Wendy stood by the front pumper and said, "Got something here. Do I yank it off the car?"

I hurried to her, pulled off the gadget, and looked at the small gray tracking device, similar to the one I had placed on Mason's Mustang and the one previously on the Maserati.

"That's it?" Wendy asked. "It's so small. Can they hear me talking?"

"No. This isn't a listening device. It only keeps track of the location of the car." My eyes roamed over the neighborhood as I wondered how long the device had been on my car. Could the Dodge have been tailed to Monique's when we took Mitt there and shot him? Seeing a red truck a few houses away with exhaust streaming out its tailpipe, I ran to it and stuck the device under its back bumper.

When I returned to the Dodge, Wendy asked, "How long do you think it'll take someone to find out the tracking device is on the wrong car?"

"It depends on how closely it's being tailed and where the truck goes. It might be soon or it could take a day or so."

Heading back to the apartment, I thought about Mitt's body. How many days will it take for someone to discover it? If the men in the black Cadillacs were Conner's employees and he was responsible for Monique's disappearance, would they wander around her property to figure out why I had been there?

17

THE CONFESSION

After sleeping for less than three hours, I fed my spiders, reached into their cage and removed the disk containing the pictures of Mitt with the tortured woman, Orson's mistress. Guessing Orson might not be too anxious to find Mitt's killer if he knew he was responsible for his mistress's death, I set up my laptop and searched for Orson Thurman's office address. Unable to find it, I typed his name and home address and printed a label. After slipping on a pair of gloves, I cleaned off the disk cover, inserted it into a padded envelope, and stuck the label on it, hoping Thurman's wife didn't open mail addressed to her husband.

To make Mitt look even worse, I considered including pictures of the documents found in his condo, but a better scheme flashed into my head.

I sealed the padded envelope, put stamps on it, dropped it in my purse, and then peeked in on Wendy. She was sleeping soundly. I left her a note saying I'd be back soon.

The Cadillac driver tapped ashes off of a lit cigarette through the open front window and frequently stopped along the side of the street while I walked at a leisurely pace to the nearest mailbox.

When I returned to the apartment, Wendy sat at the table, sipping coffee. Her face looked pale and her eyes were pinched with worry. "Are you okay?" I asked, wondering if she was upset about the way we handled Mitt or if it was something else.

She put down her coffee mug and cupped her hands over her face. "Oh, Sara, I've done something terrible," she said, her voice quivering. Tears trickled down her cheeks.

I placed a box of tissues on the table in front of her. "We've taken care of Mitt." I pulled up a chair and sat beside her. "No one will know you poisoned him."

"That's not it." She sobbed, wiping her eyes as the tears flowed.

I put my arm around her shoulder. "Come on, it can't be that bad," I said, though I wasn't sure if that was true.

She sniffled, "Have you talked to Brett today?"

Earlier I had thought about calling him, but decided to stall telling him Wendy was here. Yet, I knew I couldn't put it off much longer. "No."

She grabbed my hand. "Please. Please. Don't tell him I'm here."

"Why?"

"I've done something really terrible. Unforgivable. I've broken a Tegen rule."

What I had feared Wendy might have done, I had been hoping she hadn't. Now hope had vanished. "What did you do?" I asked, needing more confirmation she was guilty.

Her hands shook and her lips trembled. "Hank, my old boyfriend, I poisoned him." She gripped my arms. "I didn't mean to. It just happened."

"The guy you were once engaged to?"

"Yes," she mumbled. "Who told you about him?"

"Your mom. When I dropped you off and you were upstairs."

"She shouldn't have mentioned him." She sat up straight, clenching her teeth, as an irritated expression crossed her face erasing the sad one that had been there a second earlier.

I worried about her dramatic mood swing. "Wendy, your mother wouldn't have said anything if I hadn't pried. I was concerned about you and asked her if she know of something that might be bothering you. She told me Hank, the guy you had been engaged to, was missing."

"Did you tell Brett?" she snapped.

"No," I lied, figuring she'd run off if I told the truth, and I didn't want her spreading poison because she was mad.

"Some new investigator is checking into Hank's disappearance. I've been through an investigation before. No one even suspected me. Hank's been gone for over nineteen months. Why would the investigator want to talk to me now if someone hadn't sicced him on me?"

"According to your mom, Hank's parents haven't given up on finding him. Maybe they hired an investigator."

"You think so?"

"Possibly. Parents want to find their missing children." I wanted to ask her about Hank's fiancé, but I couldn't think of a way to bring it up without disclosing too much since her mom never mentioned the woman.

"Mmmm," she muttered. "Then why did Brett call my cell phone and the landline at my parents' house wanting to talk to me? He's only called me once before when I've been staying there."

"Well, he's trying to set up some sessions for you with Dr. Driggs. Maybe that's why he called."

"How do you know he wants me to see Dr. Driggs?"

"Wendy, we're all concerned about you. Brett told me."

"So you all think I'm nuts?"

I stroked her arm. "No. We think you might be having trouble dealing with your new existence as a Tegen. That's all."

"You haven't been a Tegen as long as I have. Why aren't you having trouble?"

I shrugged my shoulders. "I guess I approached the change differently."

"Hank wouldn't be dead if I weren't a Tegen and he didn't have that stupid fiancé. It's really her fault."

"Fiancé?" I said, playing dumb.

"Yes. Marilee Kent," she said, sarcastically. "The woman who thought she had snagged him."

"Maybe Marilee hired the investigator?" I said, though I knew she was dead, but I didn't want Wendy to know Tegens were looking into the cause of her death.

Without answering my question, Wendy's eyes filled with water again. "I miss him so much. Sometimes I go to the lake and wish he'd pop up, like he had been swimming. The way we used to in the lake. But now when I dream about him, it turns into a nightmare. His staring eyes haunt my dreams. How can I tell that to Dr. Driggs?" She brushed a tissue over her eyes, and then wrapped her arms around me. "Sara, you've got to help me. They can't find out what I did."

I didn't know how to respond since I was one of the fearful *they*, Tegens. Wendy's secret was one I couldn't keep. "Let me call Brett and find out why he called you."

"No. No. You mustn't," she pleaded, terror radiating from her voice. "If he called about Hank, he'll know I'm here. Please, please, I'll do anything you want, but don't call him."

"Let me try to figure out a solution." I knew there wasn't one. She was guilty. There would be no trial, only punishment.

"Would you?" she said, sounding excited. "I was sure I could count on you to help me." Wendy hugged me.

Feeling guilty for lying to her, I wanted to give her a day or two before I called Brett. "Wendy, I have to run a couple of errands. In case someone drops by the apartment, can you tell them I had to pick up a prescription for Granny? Pretend she's sleeping and you're watching her. Will you do that?"

"Sure. I promise I'll do whatever you want me to." She gave me a big smile, which made me feel even worse.

18

THE ATTRACTION

Before I left the apartment I placed a call to Mitt's cell phone, and as expected it went to voice mail. "Hi, Mitt. Can you give me a call?" I wondered if anyone would ever hear the message.

I didn't make any attempt to lose the black Cadillac tailing me as I headed to Mitt's condo. Recalling Mitt didn't use a code when he exited from the parking structure, I followed a car in and parked in Mitt's reserved spot on the second level.

As I stepped into the lobby, the doorman greeted me. Then I headed to the security guard desk. "I left something in Mr. Thurman's condo. He gave me his keys so I could get it." I held them up.

"Mr. Thurman hasn't called to inform us to let you into his condo," the security guard said.

"Can you give him a call?"

The guard opened a drawer, pulled out a leather bound notebook, and searched for Mitt's name. He placed two calls, one to Mitt's cell phone and one to Mitt's office, and left messages. "I'm sorry, I can't reach him so I can't let you get on the elevator. If you want, you can wait in the lobby until he returns my call," he said, gesturing toward a couch.

Not wanting to wait in the lobby forever, I said, "I'll come back later."

Going back to the parking garage and feeling disappointed the keys hadn't worked to allow me access to his condo, I planned to get in the same way I did once before. I grabbed my backpack out of the Dodge and took the parking elevator to the top level. Near the side closest to the condo complex, I removed my shoes, stuck them in my backpack and pulled out a rope. Holding the end of it, I oozed a sticky web-like substance from my hands onto it. I looked around for spectators. Not seeing any, I flung the rope over the fifteen foot span that separated the building from the parking structure and watched it attach below a window. Gripping the other end, I swung over with the clusters of hair protruding from my hands and feet.

Within a few seconds, I clung to the side of the building, wrapped up my rope, placed it over my shoulder, and scurried up to the rooftop. Reaching my destination, I glanced down to see if I had been observed. From past experience, I knew if someone had seen me, they would either doubt what they saw or assume I had climbed using some kind of equipment.

I slipped my shoes on and stowed the rope in my backpack. I picked the lock on the door leading into the building and hurried down one flight of stairs to the fifteenth floor, Mitt's floor. Yanking on a pair of latex gloves, I moved through the hallway to his condo. Before I attempted to enter, I rang the doorbell and waited a minute. I decided to use a key in the lock instead of picking it and began trying the keys in the lock. The third key worked. Closing the door behind me, I stood quietly and listened. Mitt had a security system, but it hadn't been set the prior time I was here. I didn't hear any peeping sound or any noise indicating it had been activated and assumed he hadn't set it when he left his condo.

Grabbing a chair, I went into the den, took the screwdriver out of Mitt's top desk drawer, and retrieved the plastic bag containing the partnership agreement from the heating vent. As I finished securing the vent cover, the phone rang, startling me. I jerked and the chair tilted. I jumped off of it before it tipped completely over.

"Mitt," a male voice came through the answering machine. "He's at a restaurant with Sally. It'll be taken care of." The phone clicked off.

I walked out of the den and stared at the answering machine. What was that all about? Sally…did Mitt know another Sally? I wondered why the guy had called his landline and not his cell phone; maybe he had and left the same message. At least now I knew Mitt's body hadn't been discovered yet.

I returned the chair and screwdriver to their rightful places. Then I took the folder holding the purchase agreement from his desk drawer, and placed it along with the partnership agreement into my backpack. Next, I went searching for my bra, and found it nicely folded between his jockeys, inside the top dresser drawer—the last place I wanted it to be. Mission almost accomplished.

Walking back into the living room, I debated whether to leave through the balcony door or go out the same way I came in. Hearing commotion in the hallway, I quickly made up my mind and hurried back into the bedroom. As I stepped out onto Mitt's balcony, the creaking sound of a door opening and voices drifted through the condo.

Cautiously, I slid the glass door closed and ducked into a corner where I couldn't be seen from inside the bedroom. I removed my shoes and tucked them into a pocket on my backpack. After ejecting clusters of hair on my hands and feet, I climbed over the railing, scuttled up to the rooftop, and moved to the side of the building facing the parking garage.

Within ten minutes I was settled in the Dodge's driver's seat. To cover my bases, I called the front desk of Mitt's condo unit and asked if Mitt had returned the security guard's call.

"I'm afraid he hasn't," the guard said. "His cleaning crew is working on his condo now. They'll let me know if he left anything there with your name on it. If they find something I'll give you a call."

"Thank you," I said, and then rattled off the pink cell phone number. After I disconnected, I called Mitt's office and left a message with his secretary to have him give me a call.

Opening my apartment door, I smelled the wonderful aroma of lilacs, my favorite flowers. I closed my eyes and inhaled the fragrance. Then it struck me and my eyes popped open—Conner. He's been here. I saw the bouquet of lilacs and red roses on the table. An arrangement he had given me often since he knew how I felt about lilacs. I softly tapped on Wendy's door. "Wendy?"

No answer. I knocked again. I inched the door open and peeked in. She wasn't there. Had Conner taken her out to learn about me? Impossible. She'd never allow that. Then suddenly a worse thought sprang into my mind. Had she poisoned him? Please, not Conner. My eyes became moist and my lips trembled as I looked around the apartment for any sign of a struggle. Everything appeared in order, and I doubted she could remove a body without someone helping her. On top of that, it was broad daylight. Even if she had managed to drag a body out by herself, she would've been seen.

I went to the window and peered out. The Cadillac was parked across the street, the same car that had followed me to Mitt's condo. There were no other Escalades and the other vehicles along the side of the road didn't fit Conner's taste. Had he driven himself, there'd be some kind of fancy sports car parked close by.

I sunk into the couch, feeling both irritated and worried. Wendy should have stayed here and pretended to be watching Granny. She promised. Where did she go? Had something spooked her, so she ran? Then, I heard laughter in the hallway, just outside my apartment. Playing things safe, I eased into my bedroom, closed the door, and intensely listened. The front door opened and voices flowed into my apartment.

"Thanks for lunch," Wendy said.

"My pleasure," Conner replied. "Sorry about the commotion. Next time, we'll have to go to a quieter place. Give your grandmother my best."

"When will..." Wendy's voice trailed off.

I pressed my ear against the door and strained to hear what she was saying. I picked up a word here or there, but nothing that made sense. Then came the soft click of the apartment door shutting. After waiting a minute and only hearing footsteps and the sound of a chair scraping along the floor, I strolled out of the bedroom.

Seeing Wendy sniffing the bouquet, I asked, "Why did you leave the apartment?"

"Oh, I had the most wonderful lunch." She sank down into a chair. "Conner, he's the guy who took me out, came by to give Granny some flowers. He's a friend of that old man in 512. You know the guy who saw us in the parking lot."

"Granny? Flowers?" I asked, puzzled.

"Yeah, Conner just lost his grandmother, so he has a soft spot for elderly women. The old man told him about Agnes. He thought he'd cheer her up with a bouquet of flowers. Isn't that sweet?" Her eyes sparkled and her face glowed.

Conner's grandparents had been dead for years, but there was no way I could tell that to Wendy. Obviously, she had succumbed to his charm and was smitten by him. I couldn't fault her one bit.

"Yes. But you were supposed to stay in the apartment and pretend to be watching Granny," I said, enunciating each word, annoyed she had broken her promise.

She nervously fidgeted with her fingers. "Well. He was so nice. He wanted to talk to Granny to find out if he could help with anything. I just had to tell him the truth."

My body tensed and my stomach tightened into a knot as a lump formed in my throat. "The truth?"

She waved her hand in front of me. "Not that truth."

I flopped into a chair and rubbed my fingertips across my forehead. "Then what truth?"

"That Granny had gone to her sister's place for a few days."

Relieved, I inhaled deeply. "Then he asked you out to lunch?"

"He saw I was all alone, and he doesn't like to eat alone, so I went with him. I worried a little bit about you coming home before I got back, but I figured it wouldn't be a big deal. Was it?" she asked, sounding concerned.

"No, but I was worried about you. You should have left a note."

"Sorry." Suddenly, her face lit up. "Oh, you should see him. He is dreamy. I think he's interested in me. He asked so many questions. He really wanted to get to know me."

"What kind of questions?"

"Where I had lived, traveled, went to school, stuff like that. He asked about my father—Jablon. Since we were cousins, I told him our fathers were brothers. He thinks my last name is Jablon."

"Where did you tell him you lived?"

"McComb. I'm glad I did too because I was able to describe it and tell him about the schools I went to without having to make up stuff. He seemed surprised I had never been in Alabama or Alexandria, Louisiana. He must like those places."

I knew exactly why he had brought them up—they were in Sally Jablon's phony background. Her father was born in Alexandria and grew up there. Sally had lived in Alabama while she attended a community college there. Tucking a loose strand of hair behind my ear, I thought about how I could repair the damage Wendy had done to my cover. There was no point in getting mad at her. She couldn't take back her words, and I doubted Conner would mention it to anyone else.

"Is he going to call you? Or do you already have another date?"

"He's in town on business. He lives in Houston."

At least he didn't lie about that.

She continued, "We might be going out tomorrow night. He's going to call me and confirm. It just depends on how his business is going. Oh, he wants you to come too, probably to find out more about me." She began spinning her bracelet around her wrist, and I sensed she was holding something back.

"Wendy, did anything else happen at lunch?"

"Well." She hesitated. "Nothing."

Noticing a guarded look in her eyes, I wanted to know. "What aren't you telling me?"

"Well, I promised him I wouldn't tell anyone."

Glaring at her and clenching my teeth, I asked, "So you feel you should keep a promise you made to a complete stranger where you didn't have any trouble breaking the promise you made to me?"

"He's not a stranger anymore." Her eyes drifted over my face. "Okay. Okay. There was a little problem at the restaurant, but a guy Conner knows took care of it. I think that guy and another guy work for Conner since they followed his orders and called him sir." She tapped her bottom lip with her index finger. "Tell me, does almost everyone in Baton Rouge tote a pistol?"

"No. Why?"

"Last night Mitt had one, Conner's guys had guns, and so did the woman in the restroom."

Baffled, I asked, "A woman in the restroom brandished a weapon?"

Wendy nodded. "Yeah."

"Do you know why?"

"She thought I was Conner's girlfriend. She kept calling me Sally. Since you don't even know him, she must've been talking about another Sally. I asked Conner about that. He told me he didn't have a girlfriend and he couldn't remember ever dating anyone named Sally."

I recalled the message left on Mitt's answering machine. The 'he' the caller referred to most likely was Conner, and someone thought Wendy was me—probably because they spotted him leaving my apartment building with a blonde. But just because he looked at me at Sammy's, calling me his girlfriend was a little dramatic. "Getting back to the restroom, what did she want you to do?"

"To go with her out the bathroom window. She continued poking me with that stupid gun. If I didn't heal quickly, I'd be bruised all over. You should have seen her—six feet tall, bulging muscles protruding under her blouse, pointed nose, and piercing green eyes. She looked like a muscle building witch. That woman could easily take care of any mortal woman and most guys. Had I not been a Tegen, I would've been in serious trouble."

"What did you do?"

"Now don't get mad. I had to defend myself. Didn't I?"

"You brought out your needles and poisoned her?"

"I had to. There wasn't anything else I could do. Living in this town, I think I'll have to start carrying a pistol in my purse."

"And what did you do with her body?"

She grinned. "Oh, this is the good part. When she jabbed the gun harder into my ribs I screamed and scratched her at the same time. Some guy, later I found out he was with Conner, charged into the restroom. The woman swung her pistol around to shoot him, but he plugged her first. She fell backwards into a stall and landed right on top of the toilet seat. Blood soaked through her blouse." Her eyebrows bounced. "It was so cool!"

I squinted, trying to understand why she was excited about it.

Wendy went on, "Don't you get it? No one will know I poisoned her, just like how you shot Mitt. Had that guy not come in, how could I explain a body in the bathroom? Had I used her gun to shoot her, everyone in the restaurant would have heard the noise. But that's what I would've done if that guy hadn't taken care of it."

I wasn't happy about what had happened, but I was pleased Wendy had a plan to cover her reckless murder. "How did the shooter handle the noise? Were police called?"

"The guy wanted me to tell everyone a car had backfired and startled me. I dropped my makeup bag and a couple of bottles splattered all over the floor. So that's what I told three or four people heading toward the restroom door. Then a server blocked everyone from entering so the mess could be cleaned up."

"People were okay with that explanation?" I asked, knowing I wouldn't be.

She bobbed her head. "Yeah. We were eating lunch late. The restaurant wasn't very busy. And I think the owner knew Conner because I noticed them nodding at each other a few times after the woman tried to kidnap me."

"How did they get the body out of there?"

She shrugged. "No idea."

"Anything else?"

"No, but Conner is in trouble, someone wants to kill him."

"What makes you think that?"

"The woman said my boyfriend was a dead man." She pressed her lips together, and her features lined with concern. "I wish I could protect him."

"You said he had a couple of guys working for him. I suspect they might be bodyguards. They'll protect him. You don't need to worry about him."

"I think I'll give him a call to make sure he's okay," Wendy said, moving toward her bedroom.

19

PHONE CALLS

Wondering how Conner would respond to Wendy's concern for his safety, I went to my nightstand and took Mitt's cell phone out of my spiders' cage. I stared at it, wanting to put the battery back in it and turn it on, but it had GPS. I doubted I could go through his phone before it was tracked to the Baxter building. That would lead them right to my apartment. Planning to check it when I was a distance away, I stowed it and the battery in my backpack. Then I rummaged through my purse and pulled out Mason's business card.

"Hey, Sally," he answered. "I hope you're calling because you decided to dump Mitt."

"No. I'm looking for him. He's not at his condo and he hasn't returned any of my calls. Have you seen or heard from him today?"

"Nope, but I didn't expect to."

"I was supposed to let him know if I could find someone to sit with Granny so we could go out tomorrow night. And," I hesitated.

"And what?"

"Last night he left a couple of folders in my apartment."

"Last night?" Mason asked, sounding confused.

"Before we went out. He didn't want to leave them in his car." Suspecting someone might know that Mitt had been in my apartment after his meeting with Conner, I said, "He came to see me after you dropped me off. Since he had woken me from a sound sleep and I felt groggy, Mitt didn't stay long. He never asked for his folders. I had completely forgotten about them until I saw them this morning on my dresser. The way he had acted about them, I thought they were real important. So if you see him will you remind him they're at my place?"

Ignoring my question, Mason asked, "Did you find someone to watch Granny?"

"Granny's staying with her sister for a few days."

"You can go out tomorrow?"

"Yes."

"How about going out with me if you don't hear from Mitt?"

"Mase, I can't do that. I'm dating Mitt."

"Suppose I see him out with another woman?"

"Well…maybe in that case."

"Let me see if I can track him down."

Before I could turn the folders over to Mason, Mitt's body needed to be discovered. I slipped my backpack strap over my shoulder and went into the living room. Wendy stood by the kitchen counter putting baking ingredients into a large bowl. "What are you making?"

"Cookies. Chocolate chip, my favorite. I hope Conner likes them."

"Is he coming over?"

"Sometime. He didn't answer when I called him, so I left a message. During lunch, he told me he had a busy schedule. He's probably in a meeting or something. In case he can get away and he comes here, I want him to try the cookies—Mom's recipe. She won a prize for them at the county fair."

"I'm sure he'll like them," I said, thinking she had it bad for him. I doubted Conner had led her on that much, but I also doubted Wendy had a relationship with any man after her engagement to Hank ended. "I have to run a few errands. Can I count on you to stay in the apartment this time?"

She nodded. "Unless Conner comes by and wants to go and do something, but I'll make sure to leave you a note."

Behind the apartment building, I searched the exterior of the Dodge for bugs and found two. Since it didn't appear another car would be pulling out of the parking lot soon, I took them with me. I stopped at a drug store and, carrying the bugs, I entered the store and picked up a bottle of hand lotion. While I stood in the check-out line, I dropped one into the handbag of the woman who stood in front of me.

In the drug store parking lot, I attached the other one to a car with its engine running. Even with the bugs gone, it still took me over a half an hour to lose the Escalade tailing me. Then I drove for another five miles, darting in and out of traffic, as I continued to glance at the car mirrors for any sign another vehicle might be in pursuit. Not seeing any suspicious car, I stopped at a chain grocery store anticipating it had a similar configuration as the one closer to the apartment, with a payphone down a hallway several feet past the restrooms.

The phone was occupied, so I waited for the man using it to finish his call. A second after he put down the receiver, I held it in my gloved hand, and with my other hand, I reached into my backpack and pulled out the voice-altering device. I adjusted my body so anyone walking down the hallway toward the restrooms couldn't see my face. I slipped the device over the mouth piece and dialed the police department. It took a while to go through all the choices announced over the answering litany and reach a person on the other end of the line. "There's a body at," I began, and then proceeded to give Monique's address.

Without further ado, I hung up, removed the voice-altering device, and left the store at a brisk pace. Climbing behind the steering wheel, I decided this might be the ideal spot to check Mitt's cell phone. I assumed it wouldn't take the police long to discover the anonymous call they had just received came from this location. If someone matched that up to the last GPS signal on Mitt's phone, they'd find it was from the same place. I guessed they'd suspect the culprit, or an eyewitness, might have made the call and in this case they'd be right.

I turned on Mitt's phone and went to recent calls. The last one was placed by Mitt at 12:30 am, about forty-five minutes before he came to my apartment. I noted he had called Mason Buckley and wondered which one. The phone number didn't match the number I had dialed earlier to reach the younger Buckley, so I assumed it was the father. I scrolled through the calls and stopped on two he made during dinner on the evening he saw my ring. No name appeared next to the numbers, so I jotted them down. The second call occurred within a minute after the first. He probably hadn't reached anyone on the first call. I guessed the second number belonged to Greg, the guy I had stabbed, but I wanted to check it out to be sure.

As I continued scrolling through the calls, I was surprised how often Mitt and his mother called each other. During all the weeks I tailed him, he never once took his mother to lunch and she never went to his office. I hadn't realized they were close. Then I noticed the week before I went to Jackson, Mitt and Monique had exchanged numerous phone calls—two or three times a day. My eyes opened wider when I spotted Conner's number, surprised that Conner would've called Mitt instead of Orson Thurman, his customer. Then it suddenly donned on me it was a call sent, not received.

The wail of a siren blared off in the distance. Was the grocery store their destination to check out the payphone? I doubted they'd do that before they determined whether or not it was a crank call. Had Mitt's body been discovered before I placed the call? As a precaution, I turned off his phone, took out the battery, started the engine and moved to the far corner of the parking lot, a spot where I could quickly leave if the situation arose.

The siren continued getting louder, and then I saw a cruiser with blinking red-and-blue strobe lights slowing down on the street. It executed a left turn into the store's parking lot. Easing into the traffic, I thought about ditching Mitt's cell phone, but decided against it. When the police start investigating Mitt's death, I might be able to use it to draw them to someone who would make an excellent suspect. Right now, I had no idea who I wanted to try to pin it on with so many prospects swimming through my head.

Driving around the corner near my apartment building, I saw two black Cadillac Escalades parked out front. Feeling certain that whoever was inside the vehicles had already spotted my car, I pulled into the parking lot behind the building. Since there were two Cadillacs and I had managed to lose the tail, maybe Conner had decided to pay another visit to Wendy for more information. Torn between my heart's desire to see him and my mind telling me to stay away from him, I locked my backpack in the trunk and wandered around the exterior of the building to the sidewalk. Without glancing at the Escalades, I headed to a coffee shop on the corner and ordered a mocha. I sat at the counter next to the windows and sipped the beverage while I kept track of the Cadillacs, hoping at least one would leave soon.

"Mocha," a voice I often heard in my dreams said, and I wondered how he got in here without me noticing. Was he here when I arrived? I turned my head toward him.

Conner eased down on the stool beside me. "I knew someone who always ordered mocha when we went to coffee shops."

My pulse rate spiked and my heart skipped a beat, then pounded in a chaotic rhythm. Attempting to reign in my emotions, I said, "Mr. Crussett?" as if I were guessing his name.

His eyes shimmered and a faint smile flickered on his lips, perfect lips I could never forget. "I'm so glad you remember. I wasn't sure you would since we had such a brief encounter. And please call me Conner," he said in a formal, polite tone.

I dropped my right hand to my lap, palm up, hiding my ring from his sight. "Conner? Interesting. My cousin's dating a man by that name."

He cocked an eyebrow. "Dating?"

"Well, they just started going out. He took her to lunch today and he's going to take her to dinner the first night he's free from his business obligations."

"What's your cousin's name?" he asked, not showing the slightest hint that he already knew.

"Wendy. Wendy Jablon. Do you know her?"

"What a coincidence. I took a woman by that same name out to lunch today. She lives in the Baxter Building."

I gazed at him, squinted, and tilted my head. "Five-foot-six, blue eyes, shoulder-length blonde hair."

"That fits Wendy."

"I think you took out my cousin."

"I enjoyed her company, but I wouldn't say we were dating. She mentioned she was staying with her cousin, but she never said your name. I suggested that the three of us should go out to dinner one evening."

"Did you now?"

"Yes." He studied my face, making me fidget under his gaze. "She told me about her background. How your fathers were brothers, and they were born in McComb, Mississippi. The same place you both went to school. By the time we were through eating I knew Wendy and her cousin."

"Wendy has some mental problems and has a hard time remembering details of her childhood. Our fathers were born in Alexandria, Louisiana. After her father married, he moved to McComb with his wife. That's where Wendy was born and raised. I never lived there."

"She told her history with such enthusiasm and attention to minute details, I never would have guessed parts weren't accurate."

"Yes, she can be very convincing."

He laid his hand on my forearm, sending a warm, tingling sensation up my arm. "If I can adjust my appointments, would you be free to join us for dinner tomorrow evening?"

Yearning to reach out and caress his face, I forced myself to turn away from him and look out the window. While I watched people crossing the street, I took a few quick breaths and finally managed to say, "I've already got a date."

He squeezed my forearm. "Anyone I know?"

"I believe you do. Mitt Thurman."

He cleared his throat. "Mitt Thurman?"

"Yes."

Conner raised his hand and gently brushed it against my cheek. Feeling my emotions tugging inside me, I turned and met his sensual light brown eyes. I wanted to blurt something out, tell him to remove his hand, but the words wouldn't come.

"If for any reason Mitt can't make your date," he said, tucking a strand of my hair behind my ear, "will you give me a call?"

Since Conner had taken a bouquet of lilacs, Sara's favorite flower, to my apartment, I assumed he knew I was Sara. Was I wrong? Or was he just playing along with my fake identity? "Conner, I've already got a back-up date."

His eyes narrowed. "And who's that with?"

I wanted to tell him it was none of his business, but instead the answer flowed out of my mouth, "Mason Buckley. Do you know him?"

The corner of his mouth slightly rose, that I took to be a smile. "The old man or his son?"

"What do you think?"

"That's one lucky son."

"I can't imagine Mitt will cancel our date, so I doubt I'll be going out with Mason."

"I wouldn't count on that if I were you."

"We'll see. But Wendy's free this evening and I know she's looking forward to going out with you again." The pink cell phone rang. I plucked it out of my purse, glanced at the monitor, and saw the caller was Wendy. Since I'd be seeing her soon, I might have ignored it, but I couldn't take sitting this close to Conner much longer without surrendering to the desire bubbling up inside me that I was struggling to suppress. "I need to take this."

I stepped out of the coffee shop onto the sidewalk with Conner right behind me. I had expected he'd remain inside and allow me to have a private conversation. Answering the phone, I turned so my back faced him. "Is something wrong?"

"Two policemen were here a few minutes ago. When I opened the door, I thought they were here for me. Not that I'm glad they wanted to see you, but I wouldn't have known what to say if it was about the woman at the restaurant."

"Policemen?" I said, thinking out loud. "Did they mention why they wanted to see me?"

"No, but one left his card. He wants you to call him as soon as you get home."

"I'm on my way." I disconnected and began moving toward the crosswalk.

"A problem?" Conner asked.

Since he had been standing only three feet away from me, I was sure he had heard every word I had said. "Maybe," I replied, wondering if I had somehow screwed up and left a piece of evidence behind that could tie me to Mitt's murder.

Conner crossed the street with me. "Don't worry. Sally Jablon, the former bank teller and now caregiver for her grandmother, couldn't possibly be suspected of any crime," he said, emphasizing "crime."

Without a doubt, I knew he had learned about Mitt's untimely death, and I had anticipated he would check Sally Jablon's background, but it surprised me he would mention it. Did he say it to let me know I was on his radar? With a black Cadillac on my tail wherever I went, I'd have to have tunnel vision not to already know that. Sticking to my Sally cover, when we reached the other side of the street I asked in an irritated tone, "How do you know that much about me?"

"Wendy told me."

"Earlier you said Wendy hadn't mentioned my name."

"She hadn't, but she told me those facts about her cousin."

We walked in silence to the apartment building stoop. Was he planning to stay by my side all the way to my apartment? "Are you going up to see Wendy?"

"No." He handed me a card with a phone number on it. "Give me a call if you change your mind about dinner or if you have any problems you can't solve."

Looking at the card, I squinted. The number on it wasn't Conner's. At least, it wasn't the number in Mitt's cell phone, the number Conner had when I lived with him.

"It's not my cell phone number," he said as if he knew exactly what I was thinking. "You can call my cell phone, but sometimes I'm not in a position to answer it. But this number will be answered twenty-four-seven by a live person, not a recording. If you're calling about a problem, you'll get immediate attention. If you're calling about a personal matter—like dinner, the person on the other end of the line will give me the message."

Putting the card in my purse, I smiled at him, and then left him standing on the sidewalk. As I mounted the stairs, I sensed his eyes following me and my heart ached for his touch.

20

MURDER INVESTIGATION

After two rings, a male voice answered, "Detective Karl Gilbert."

"Hello, this is Sally Jablon."

"Miss Jablon," Gilbert said. "We'd like to talk to you about Mitt Thurman."

"Mitt? Is he in trouble?" I asked in a worried tone.

"I'll explain when we see you. Would you rather talk at the station or in your apartment?"

"At the station," I replied, not wanting Wendy to be present during the questioning.

"Can you come in tomorrow morning at ten?"

"Yes," I said and requested the address. As I hung up, I glanced at the clock: 8:10 p.m. I wandered back out into the living room and saw Wendy making a sandwich. "Conner's not taking you out to dinner?"

"He hasn't called and I'm hungry."

The following morning when I arrived at the station, I was escorted into a windowless, light gray room with a large mirror on one wall, which I assumed was a one-way window. A rectangular table and four chairs stood in the center of the room. I was instructed to sit on the side facing the mirror. Detective Gilbert and his partner, Detective Moss, took seats across the table from me.

Gilbert asked, "Miss Jablon, are you okay with us recording this meeting?"

I nodded.

Gilbert flipped a switch on the edge of the table, stated the date, time, and gave the names of everyone present in the room. After those formalities, he adjusted himself in his seat and began, "We wanted to talk to you about a murder."

"A murder? Who?"

"Mitt Thurman."

"Oh, no! Not Mitt" I threw my hands to my mouth and brought tears to my eyes by thinking about my beloved, departed adoptive parents. "I thought something was wrong when I couldn't reach him, but not this." I sniffled and sobbed.

Detective Gilbert handed me a box of tissues. "Miss Jablon, I'm so sorry. We had been told you had only gone out with Mr. Thurman a few times. We didn't realize you'd be so attached to him."

"Our... our relationship... was very special." I stuttered as tears streamed down my face. "And now you tell me he's gone." I reached across the table and touched Detective Gilbert's hand. "Please, please, tell me you've made a mistake."

He patted my hand. "Miss Jablon, Mitt Thurman's body has been identified, both by his parents and the medical lab. There's no mistake."

"But how," I said, dabbing my cheeks. "I saw him Wednesday night. Who killed him? Why?"

"That's what we're trying to find out. Are you up to answering some questions, or would you like to come back later?"

"No. I'll do whatever it takes to put whoever is responsible behind bars. How can I help?" I sat up straight and wiped the last tears from my face.

"You said, you saw Mr. Thurman Wednesday night. Can you remember about what time that was?"

"Late. He came to my apartment around one a.m."

"Early Thursday morning."

I bobbed my head up and down. "He woke me up, and when he realized the time, he didn't stay long, just long enough to ask me out to dinner. We had a date earlier, but it got interrupted when he had a meeting."

"Yes, we know about that. About what time would you say he left your apartment?"

"That I can remember because I glanced at the clock when I climbed back in bed. It was 1:29 a.m."

"We understand you live with your grandmother. Did she hear him come or go?"

"My grandmother is staying with her sister for a few days so she wasn't there."

Gilbert's brow furrowed. "Aren't you her caregiver?"

"I am, but my cousin came for a visit and since I live in a two-bedroom apartment Granny decided she'd stay with her sister while my cousin was in town. Her sister used to be her caregiver before I moved back to Baton Rouge."

"What's your cousin's name?"

"Wendy Jablon."

"Was she awake when Mr. Thurman was at your apartment?"

"She woke up when we were talking and stepped out of the bedroom as he was saying goodnight."

"She can substantiate the time he left?"

"I'm not sure. She went right back to bed, and I don't know if she looked at a clock," I said, giving a vague answer in case Wendy is questioned about it, and she can't recall the time I was planning to tell her. The neighbor, who lives on my floor, saw us with Mitt in the parking lot, and could completely blow my story. I had to deal with him before the police questioned him about that night.

Gilbert flipped through a folder sitting on the table in front of him. "Besides the killer, you two were probably the last people to see him alive."

"Why do you say that?"

"According to the coroner's report, Mr. Thurman died between three and three-twenty a.m. Thursday morning."

"That's over an hour after he left my place. Didn't the security guard at his condo see him?"

"Mr. Thurman didn't go to his condo. His body was discovered a distance from his place, at least a forty-five minute drive."

"When he left he said he was going straight home to bed. I wonder why he didn't do that."

"We suspect the detour wasn't by choice."

"Murdered?" I bit my lower lip. "He wasn't tortured or anything like that, was he?"

"No. If it's any consolation, he died quickly from a gunshot wound."

I briefly closed my eyes. "Thank goodness. I couldn't bear to think of him suffering."

Detective Moss scribbled notes on a yellow notepad. "Miss Jablon, do you know if Mr. Thurman had any enemies?"

I shook my head. "No, but I don't know any of his clients or anyone like that. We went out alone. A couple of times, I heard him arguing with someone on the phone, but I couldn't tell you what it was about."

"Did you catch a name?" Gilbert asked.

"No," I said, shaking my head again.

Detective Gilbert ended the interview and told me he'd call if he had any additional questions. "Would you like me to have an officer drive you home?"

I dabbed a tissue across my eyes. "I'll be okay. Do you know the name of the funeral home?"

"Mr. Thurman's body is still in our morgue, I'll let you know when his body will be moved to a private funeral home."

"Thank you. I appreciate that."

The two detectives escorted me into the lobby. As I left the police station, I noticed Mason's Mustang in the parking lot a few stalls away from the Dodge. Since I hadn't seen it when I arrived, I suspected he would be the next person interviewed by Detective Gilbert.

As I entered the apartment, Wendy jumped off the couch, hurried over to me and stroked my arm. "You look like you've been crying. What did the police say to you?" she asked, her eyes pinched with worry.

"I had to pretend I cared for the man." I sank down on the couch.

"What questions did they ask?" She sat in Granny's chair.

I proceeded to tell her everything Detective Gilbert asked about and my responses. "I didn't get the impression they thought I was involved in Mitt's murder; in fact, quite the contrary. I'm his distressed girlfriend."

"But you told them he was in the apartment." Wendy sounded a little irritated I had given them that information.

"Wendy, his car was parked out front, and who knows who might have seen him in the building? I'm a little worried about the old man in apartment 512. He saw us put Mitt in my car."

She leapt to her feet. "We better take care of him right now," she said, moving toward the door.

"Wendy, sit down. We can't solve the problem that way. Remember, we have to keep the existence of Tegens a secret. We need to maintain a low profile. We can't do anything that might draw unwelcome attention. Spreading poison around certainly isn't what we should be doing. We'll figure another way to handle the neighbor."

She frowned and returned to Granny's chair, giving me the impression she would have enjoyed using her poisonous needles again. Gazing at her, I hoped I hadn't made a mistake by not calling Brett right after she confessed what she had done to Hank. Wendy had pleaded with me not to tell him she was here. All I wanted to do was give her a couple of days before I told anyone about her confession. Earlier when I spoke to Father, I didn't even mention she was here. But now if I told him, she'd probably be whisked away for breaking the prime Tegen rule. Her quick departure from Baton Rouge could appear suspicious to the police. She was my alibi.

Guilt ridden about keeping Wendy's whereabouts a secret from Father and Brett and mulling over how to deal with the man who lives down the hall, I leaned back in the couch and tapped my fingers together. "Didn't Conner tell you he was a friend of the old man in apartment 512?"

Her brow rose. "He did." She stood up and smiled. "I'm going to call him," she said with childlike enthusiasm as she hurried into Granny's bedroom.

Still thinking about the neighbor, I went to the kitchen and got a Coke. I sat next to the window and sipped it. Two black Cadillacs were parked across the street. Was Conner in one of them? Then a movement in the shadows next to Christie's caught my attention. A tall figure stepped away from the building. A shiver sprang up my spine. It was Kendall, the sinister-looking Tegen enforcer who romanced and killed a victim at the gathering I attended with Brett. What was he doing here?

"Hey," Wendy said from behind me. I turned and saw a cell phone in her hand a few inches from her ear. "Conner wants to know if you'll go to dinner with us. Then we can talk there about the neighbor."

"I already have a date for tonight." Even though I hadn't locked in anything with Mason yet, I didn't want to go to dinner with Wendy and Conner. If he gave me more attention than her, she'd probably have an unpleasant mood swing with deadly consequences. "Ask him if he can come here sometime this afternoon to talk."

She pressed her phone against her ear. "Sally has a date tonight. Can you come here this afternoon? …Okay, see you at three." Wendy clicked off. "How much are you going to tell him about that night?"

"Not much. But what, I haven't figured out yet. Just something so he'll ask his friend in apartment 512 not to say he ran into us in the parking lot with Mitt."

"I'll agree with whatever you tell him."

"I need to make a call before he gets here." I headed into my bedroom and closed the door behind me. Sitting down on the edge of the bed, I took the pink cell phone out of my purse and called Mason.

"Sally, I was just about to call you," Mason said in a concerned tone. "I heard you had a rough time at the police station. How're you doin' now?"

"Oh, Mase," I said in a voice heavy with despair. "It's awful. Who would want to kill Mitt? He was such a prince."

"Sally, not everyone would agree with you. Mitt had enemies."

I sighed deeply and swallowed hard, making sure he could hear. "That's right. You said he didn't treat all his girlfriends well. Do you think one of them murdered him?"

"Possibly. I'm on my way to Mitt's condo to meet his mother. Do you want to talk later?"

"You're the only friend of Mitt's I know well enough to talk to about him. I feel so lost. I've never known anyone who's been shot before. I don't know how to handle this. How's his poor mom doing?"

"She's holding up pretty good. I'm going to help her with the funeral arrangements."

"You're so nice. And Mitt's dad, how's he doing?" The line went silent for a minute. "Mase, are you still there?"

"Yeah. Can I pick you up at seven? Or would you rather we talked at your apartment?"

"No. Not here. Not in front of my cousin. She almost fell apart when I told her a friend of mine had been murdered, and she didn't even know him. She's worried that Baton Rouge has become too violent a place for Granny and me to live."

"See your point. And I don't want you leaving Baton Rouge. Are you up to going out to dinner, and then talking at my place?"

"Mase, I don't want to go to a restaurant. Can we do take out and eat at your place?"

"Sure. See you at seven."

Setting the pink cell phone down on the nightstand, I pondered why Mason didn't answer when I asked about Mitt's father. Didn't he like the man, or was there another reason?

21

THE WITNESS

Before I left my bedroom, I stared at my black, beautiful Tegen ring and hated to take it off my finger. Though I already suspected Conner probably had figured out that Sally and Sara were the same person, I didn't want to give him any further assurance. If he noticed my ring, any doubt lingering in his mind would be wiped out. Begrudgingly, I slipped my most valuable possession from my finger, wrapped it in my palm and clung onto the comforting feeling it generated through my body for a few minutes. Then I opened my bottom nightstand drawer and laid my ring inside the cage that held my spiders.

Stepping into the living room, I saw Wendy sitting in a chair by the window and looking out. "Have you noticed there's a black Cadillac Escalade parked in front of Christie's almost all the time even when the restaurant isn't open?" she asked.

"Maybe it's the owner's car," I said, hoping that explanation would satisfy her.

"I doubt it. Sometimes the driver's window is down and I've seen a guy sitting in it. The owner of Christie's would be inside the restaurant, not in his car. Conner took me to the restaurant in a car just like that. He has a driver so he sat next to me on the backseat. It was nice."

"Maybe the person in the Escalade is someone's driver."

She shook her head. "This isn't that fancy of a neighborhood to have chauffeurs. Oh, another Escalade stopped in front of our building. I bet it's Conner... Yep, it's him." She stood and ran her fingers along the side of her hair. "How do I look?"

"Good," I said with a smile. "Don't forget to let me do all the talking."

"I won't."

A minute later, Wendy answered the door and introduced Conner to me. I was relieved that he didn't say we had already met. Wendy motioned for him to sit on the couch, and she eased down right beside him so their bodies were touching. I took Granny's chair.

He looked at Wendy and said, "On the phone you mentioned you had a problem with my friend in apartment 512. How can I help?"

"Well," I began. "A couple of nights ago, a friend, who had way too much to drink, stopped by the apartment, waking us up. He didn't stay long, but in his condition he stumbled around, tipping over a chair and knocking a lamp to the floor. It made quite a racket, and your friend in apartment 512 came to inquire about the noise. I didn't want to tell him a drunk was in the apartment so I lied and told him my cousin," I nodded toward Wendy, "startled me and I tripped, knocking over some things."

Noticing Conner intensely looking at me, my heartbeat fluttered and blood surged into my cheeks. I lowered my eyes to the carpet, forced myself not to show any emotion, and went on, "A friend called my visitor and wanted to meet him outside Sammy's." Realizing Wendy didn't know about that establishment, I added. "It's a bar fifteen minutes from here. Since Mitt, that's my friend, wasn't in a condition to drive—"

"Mitt? Are you talking about Mitt Thurman?"

"Yes."

"How do you know Mitt?" Wendy asked, sounding puzzled as she laid her hand on Conner's arm.

"We're business associates."

Since I didn't want Wendy to dwell on that relationship, I steered the conversation back to the man in 512. "Wendy helped me get Mitt into my car. Your friend saw us doing that."

"You don't want my friend, Eldon, to tell anyone that Mitt was drunk?"

"No. That's not it." Hating having to ask Conner for help, I paused and bit my lower lip, wondering if there was another way to deal with the neighbor.

"Then what is the problem?" he asked, gazing at me. His brown eyes twinkled and his eyebrow slightly bounced, giving his face an amazed expression.

Beyond any doubt, I knew he was completely aware of the problem. Was he curious about how I planned to spell it out?

"We want him to say he never saw us," Wendy blurted out.

His eyes darted to Wendy. "Why?"

Without involving Conner or letting Wendy handle the neighbor her way, I couldn't think of another way to take care of the man in 512. In this situation, Conner became the more palatable solution. "Mitt was murdered after we dropped him off at Sammy's, and I never told the police we drove him there."

"And why is that?"

"I don't want the gunman to know that we dropped Mitt off at Sammy's. I'm sure he knows someone drove Mitt there since he was so intoxicated, but I don't want him to know it was us."

"You're afraid he might come after you?"

I nodded and Wendy followed with a nod. "We never saw him so we can't identify him. And frankly, I don't want to take the chance that we could be in danger if I told the police about dropping off Mitt."

"Did Mitt drive to your apartment?"

"I don't have any idea how he got here. Maybe a taxi?" I replied, not wanting to make up an explanation about the Maserati. "Can you ask Eldon not to say anything about the noise in my apartment and seeing Wendy and me in the parking lot?"

"I'll talk to him, but I can't make any promises."

I suspected Conner probably wouldn't have any problem getting Eldon not to say anything. At the same time, knowing how the Crussetts operated, Eldon and Conner might not even be friends. Did he recruit a neighbor to keep track of me, or was Eldon an employee, a new tenant in the apartment building? I leaned my elbows on the armrests and tented my fingers. "We appreciate that."

Conner's eyes met mine. "Are you sure you can't join us for dinner this evening?"

"Sorry. I have other plans."

"How about tomorrow night?" he said with a boyish smile.

I had managed to keep my longing for him in check during the meeting, but could I sustain it for a whole evening? Even having Wendy there might not be enough to stop me from showing any signs about how much I wanted him.

"Come on, Sally, go to dinner with us?" Wendy urged, and I knew it was because it would ensure she had another date with him tomorrow night.

"Okay," I agreed against my better judgment, thinking Wendy might start wondering if something was wrong if I continued to turn down invitations.

"Tomorrow at eight?" he asked, his eyes studying me closely.

I reluctantly nodded.

"Good," Wendy said, giving me a big smile.

Conner turned toward her. "I'm going to go and talk to Eldon," he said, rising to his feet.

"Do you want me to go with you?" she said, standing up.

"No. I better handle this alone."

Pondering how I could get out of the date I had just made, I remained seated while Wendy walked Conner to the door.

Returning to her seat, Wendy asked, "Isn't it strange that Conner knew Mitt?"

"Yes. Could they be in the same type of business? Do you know what Conner does for a living?"

"He's president of an investment company."

"And Mitt ran a property management company."

"That's the connection—like a bank and a lender. Mitt must've gone to Conner for financing on some property deals," she said, sounding pleased that she had figured it out.

A disturbing thought sprang into my head. "What time is Conner picking you up for dinner?" I asked, hoping it wasn't the same time Mason would be here.

"Seven-thirty."

I took a calming breath. Having Conner and Mason bump into each other at the apartment wasn't anything I wanted to happen.

The doorbell rang, and Wendy hurried to answer it. I swallowed hard, briefly closed my eyes, and felt a tightening sensation in my chest, thinking Conner had returned and my resolve became harder to bear with each encounter. Then I heard Detective Karl Gilbert's voice, and a gust of air rushed through my lungs as my body relaxed.

"Good afternoon, Miss Jablon," Gilbert said, walking into the living room.

"Detective Gilbert." I shook his hand, and then Detective Moss's hand. "More questions?"

"Actually, we're here to talk to your cousin," Gilbert said.

I suspected they might prefer to talk to her alone, but I wasn't going to volunteer to leave the room. "Please have a seat."

Wendy grabbed a chair and sat next to me. When the detectives were settled on the couch, each holding a notepad and pen, Gilbert began, "Miss Wendy Jablon, were you here Wednesday night?"

"Yes." She nervously fidgeted with her fingers.

"Did you see Mitt Thurman leave the apartment?"

She nodded.

"Do you recall the time he left?"

"No, not exactly," she said, through shaky breaths. "It was late, probably after one. Voices woke me up. I peeked out my bedroom door and saw him saying goodnight to Sally." Wendy rubbed her palms together as her right knee jittered.

"Was anyone with Mr. Thurman?"

Pressing her lips together, she shook her head.

Detective Gilbert stood up. "That's all we need for now. How long are you planning to stay in Baton Rouge?"

"A week or so," Wendy replied.

"Call before you leave," Gilbert said, handing Wendy a business card.

Wendy closed the door behind the detectives, wiped away the sweat beads from her forehead and asked, "Did I do okay?"

"You did great," I said, forcing a smile, thinking she'd never hold up if she was exposed to any harsh questioning.

22

MASON'S PLACE

At 7:15 p.m. the doorbell rang. With a fake sad and gloomy expression on my face, I opened the door for Mason. He caressed my arm. "Rough day?"

"Yeah."

He walked into the living room, and glanced around. "Where's your cousin?"

"In her bedroom." His eyes moved to the closed bedroom door and his eyebrows furrowed, giving me the impression he doubted that someone was staying with me. "Would you like to meet her?"

"Yep. I want to see if she's as gorgeous as you." He gave me a crooked smile.

"Prettier." I tapped on Wendy's door.

"Come in."

I peered into her room. "Mase wants to meet you."

"Oh, I'll be out in a sec," she said, sounding surprised, as she buttoned her blouse.

After I closed her door, I went to the table and picked up the folders I retrieved from Mitt's apartment. "These are the folders Mitt left here. I don't know what to do with them. Can you give them to his mom or dad?" I stretched out my arm to hand them to Mase.

He took the folders without looking at the contents inside. "I'll take care of it."

Wendy came out of her bedroom, and I quickly made introductions since Conner was expected in less than fifteen minutes. Then I snagged my purse and left the apartment with Mason.

Stepping into the elevator, Mason said, "You seem anxious. Are you okay?"

"I just couldn't stand being in that living room one more minute. The image of Mitt standing by the door with a smile on his face, the same night he was murdered, keeps flashing into my mind. I can't shake the vision," I said with trembling lips. "So I've tried to stay out of the living room since I got back from the police station."

When we reached the lobby, Mason took my hand. "It'll take time," he said, walking out of the building. "We're all mourning him." He opened his Mustang's passenger door. I slid in and looked across the street, searching for Kendall. He was nowhere in sight.

As Mason climbed into the driver's seat, his eyes darted to something behind me. I glanced in that direction and saw Conner on the sidewalk, heading toward the Baxter Building. "What's he doing here?" Mason asked with a sharp edge in his voice.

I swung around and faced Mason, leaving only the back of my head visible through the passenger window. I figured Conner had already seen me sitting in the Mustang, but I wanted to avoid the possibility of eye contact. "He's dating Wendy."

"Wendy, your cousin?" he asked, squinting and looking past me, focusing his eyes on Conner.

"Yes," I replied with a nod.

"Does she know anything about his business?"

I shrugged. "I don't know. She's a very private person. It takes a lot of effort to get her talking about guys she's dating. But I do know she hasn't been dating him long. Is there anything you know about him that I should tell Wendy? If he's a womanizer or something like that, I want to warn her."

"No, he's not a womanizer. How long has he been dating her?"

Not knowing when Conner arrived in town, I needed to answer carefully. "They've only gone on a few dates. They met in the building when Conner visited a friend on my floor."

"When was their first date?"

"Thursday."

"Yesterday?"

"Yes," I said, wishing I could have given an earlier date without worrying about being caught in a lie.

"Crussett arrived in town on Wednesday, saw you that night, and then dates your cousin the following day." With a creased brow, he glanced at me. "Doesn't that seem suspicious to you?"

"He hasn't seen me since that night. I doubt he knows I'm Wendy's cousin."

"That's not how I see it," he said, staring out the windshield. "He's interested in you and he's using your cousin."

"Well, I'm not interested in him," I said, firmly.

"Crussett wouldn't still be hanging around Baton Rouge unless there was something he wanted, and I suspect what he wants has to do with you."

Changing the subject, I asked, "How did it go with Mitt's mother?"

"Fine," he said, pulling away from the curb. "Most of the funeral arrangements have been locked in."

"When is it?"

"Tuesday. At the Chapel in Westland's Funeral Home."

Still wondering why he clammed up when I mentioned Mitt's dad on the phone, I decided to ask again. "And how is Mitt's dad doing?"

"I forget to ask you what type of take-out—Chinese, pizza, hamburgers. Any special kind of food you'd like to eat?" he asked, avoiding answering my question.

Obviously, whatever was going on with Mitt's dad, Mason wasn't going to talk about it. "Chinese sounds good."

Mason stopped at a Chinese restaurant, went inside and brought out a menu. It didn't take us long to decide what we wanted to order. When he was in the restaurant waiting for our order, I noticed a black Escalade parked a few stalls away from me. I had already guessed it would be close by, but the fact that it followed openly, not making any effort not to be seen, irritated me. I felt like Conner was telling me, "I'm watching you." As if I wouldn't have spotted the vehicle without him giving me that extra nudge. The more I thought about it, the more my temper rose. I couldn't take the anger building up inside me any longer and I opened the car door, ready to go and have a word with the driver of the Escalade. Stepping out of the Mustang, I saw Mason heading toward me carrying a stuffed large white sack with food container lids protruding over the top edge.

"Did you get tired of waiting for me?" he asked, lowering the sack to the floor behind the driver's seat.

"No, I just wanted to stretch my legs."

Cocking an eyebrow, he scanned my face. "Are you okay?"

"Yeah," I said, climbing back into my seat. "Why?"

"You look flushed." He sat down, leaned toward me and placed his hand on my forehead. "Well you're not running a temperature. Are you sure you feel okay?"

"Maybe it's because I was thinking about Mitt. I can't get over that's he's gone." I laid my hand on his. "You were close friends. How are you holding up?"

"I'm coping," he said, pressing on the gas pedal and steering the car out of the parking lot. "I sure as hell hope that whoever shot him is apprehended soon."

"Do the police have any suspects?"

"Mitt's mother said they have a couple of leads they're following up on."

His eyes drifted to the rear view mirror for a few seconds, probably checking out the black Cadillac three cars behind us. "Who knows, maybe the cops don't have any leads at all, and they told her that to make her feel better."

He slowed down as he approached a high rise building. It was the same building I had followed him to the week before and, after foolishly relying on his Facebook page that said he lived elsewhere, I had waited in my car most of the night for him to go home.

Mason escorted me to his seventh floor apartment.

"Nice apartment," I said, as my eyes drifted over the paintings hanging on the walls and the dark brown leather sofa and walnut furniture. The place had a similar layout to my place, but it only had one bedroom and everything appeared new.

"Yeah, I like the place. The kitchen was remodeled a few months ago," he said, tilting his head toward dark wood cabinets and stainless steel appliances.

He sat the sack on the table and put the folders in his bedroom. "What would you like to drink? Wine, beer, pop?" he asked, setting out placemats and silverware.

"Wine."

Mason took a wine bottle out of the fridge. "Sauvignon Blanc?"

"Yes. I'm surprised you remembered," I said, recalling I had ordered that when we went to a bar the night he drove me home from Sammy's.

"That's not all I remember about you." He uncorked the bottle.

"What else do you remember?" I asked while I emptied the sack of Chinese food containers.

Raising an eyebrow, he gave me a coy smile without answering my question. His cell phone beeped as he handed me a filled wine glass. He glanced at his phone and then the ringing stopped. "I need to return the call, but go ahead and start dishing up."

"No. I can enjoy the wine until you're ready to eat." I took a sip and eased down in a chair by the table.

Mason went into the bedroom and closed the door behind him. When I heard him talking, I sneaked over to the door and strained my ears to listen.

"...track...Not a clue...Could be...We don't know who knocked off Mitt...Yeah, I know she thinks it's him...Monique...Doubt it...No, it's not Crussett's style, leaving a body out in the open like that...Find out about the Cadillac...Call later." Hearing movement on the other side of the door, I quickly tiptoed back to the chair and gulped down my wine.

Mason strolled out of the bedroom and gestured toward my empty glass. "Was it good?"

"To the last drop." I gave him a warm smile.

"There's plenty more." He picked up the wine bottle, poured, and then began opening the food containers. "Do you think we have enough?" he joked since there was enough food to serve four or five people.

"Boy, I hope so," I said as we loaded our plates. For the next fifteen minutes, we ate in silence. Gazing at him while I chewed, I watched as a grave, worried expression flashed on his face and he appeared to be in deep thought. Maybe he was concerned that he might be in danger from Mitt's killer.

"Do you want to talk about Mitt?" he asked, dishing up more food. "Or would you rather watch a DVD and get your mind off him?"

"I don't know any of Mitt's friends except you. The police asked me if I knew anyone that might want to harm him—enemies. When we went out, it was just the two of us, except once he took me to a party at his folks' house. Everyone there was so pleasant. No one seemed like they didn't like him. Anyway, I couldn't give the police even one name." I lowered my eyes and feigned a sad expression. "I wish I could do something to help the police solve the crime, but I can't think of anything."

"The cops asked me the same question. I managed to give a few names." He reached across the table and took my hand. "Sally, I've known Mitt for ten years. I've met most of his acquaintances. You only knew him for a short time. The cops don't expect you to be able to identify everyone that might have had a grudge against him."

"Well, I suppose not, but I just feel so helpless."

"You need to relax." He put the leftovers in the fridge, and then filled our wine glasses. "Let's pick up our spirits with a movie." Mason popped *Ghostbusters* into his DVD, sat next to me on the couch, hit the remote, and rested his arm above my shoulders. Then something caught his eye, and he immediately lowered his arm, reached over to the end table and grabbed it. Whatever it was, it was well hidden in his hand. With his other hand he slid open the end table drawer, put the object in it and closed the drawer. His movement was so swift that I didn't get a glimpse of it. Mason resituated himself beside me, but this time he placed his arm on my shoulders.

During the movie, I discovered he had a good sense of humor as he continually spouted out funny remarks.

"Can't they see the poor fella is just hungry?" he said as an evil, dog-like character growled outside a restaurant window.

When a possessed character acted amorously, Mason caressed my shoulder. "Sure wish I had that kind power over women." He looked at me, floated his hands in front of my face. "Listen and follow my orders. Move closer," he said in an eerie tone.

I gave him a half smile, but didn't budge.

"Oh come on, go with the…" He stopped when his cell phone chirped again, snapping me back to the reason I was there—to find information I could use to help destroy the illegal business in which he worked.

Mason rolled his eyes. "Bad timing." He yanked his phone out of his pocket and glanced at it. "I'd like to ignore this, but duty calls." He rose to his feet and headed into the bedroom.

After he closed the door, I crept to it and tried to listen. The movie sound track muffled out everything, making it impossible for me to pick up Mason's voice. Wondering what he had slipped into the end table, I scampered to the couch and opened the drawer. Inside was a cell phone, manuals to the television and DVD player. Nothing else. I kept track of the bedroom door while I lifted up the phone, pushed a button on it to light up the screen, and searched for its number. It looked familiar, but I couldn't place it. Wanting to write down the number, I quietly pushed the drawer shut, held the phone behind my back, and hurried across the room to grab my purse. Settling back on the couch, I took out a notepad and scribbled down the number. The door sprang open and I dropped the notepad and phone into my handbag, pulled out a tissue and wiped my eyes.

"What's wrong?" Mason asked, strolling toward me.

"I don't know. I was laughing, and then suddenly I started to cry."

He wrapped me in his arms. "This has been a trying day for you—learning about Mitt, and the police questioning you. You're entitled to have emotional flare-ups. Do you want a glass of water, more wine?"

"Water would be nice."

"Coming up," he said, going to the kitchen.

I placed my purse on the end table, so I could put back the cell phone next time he stepped out of the room. Did I turn it off before I stowed it in my purse?

When Mason handed me a glass of water, I asked, "Can I use your bathroom?"

"Sure. It's right through there." He pointed to the door.

Picking up my purse, I went into the bathroom, locked the door, and reached in my handbag for his cell phone. A soft ringing sound came from it while I raised it up. I flipped on the faucet to drown out the noise, saw the initial "T" displayed on the phone monitor and figured it stood for Thurman, Mitt's father as I turned it off. Why was he calling on this cell phone and not Mason's other phone?

A phone rang in the other room.

When I walked back into the living room, Mason's bedroom door was shut, and assumed he was in there talking on his cell. Keeping a watchful eye on the closed door, I pulled out his other cell phone, wiped off my fingerprints with a tissue, and put it back in the drawer.

I scurried to the bedroom door and perked up my ears to listen, but no movement or sound came from the other side. I knocked. "Mase?" No response. I knocked again. "Mase?" I inched the door open. "Mase, are you in there?" I poked my head inside and looked around. Not seeing him anywhere, I checked the floor on the other side of the bed. Feeling puzzled about his speedy departure, I decided to search his place, headed to the apartment door, and secured the lock.

I checked all his bedroom drawers. No drugs or documents. Then I made a quick sweep of his closet. A stack of boxes stood in the corner, but I hesitated to go through them since he could unlock the door any minute. I made a mental note to search them when I was tracking his car on my laptop.

In the other room, I rummaged through the drawers in the kitchen and living room. Not finding anything important, I sank down on the couch, got out my cell phone and called his number. It went straight to voice mail. "Mase, I'm still at your apartment. Did you forget I was here? If you're not back in ten minutes, I'm taking a taxi home."

While I waited, I took the cell phone out of the drawer and scanned the contact list. Only four names appeared—Mitt, Don, Reese, and T. Strange. I scrolled through the calls made and received. All the calls came from or went to one of those four people, and they all occurred in the past two months. Mitt's phone number didn't look right. I pulled out my pink cell phone, clicked on his name, and saw a different number. Did Mitt also have another cell phone? Why?

Thumbing through the calls again, I noticed Mitt had placed a call to Mason from a different number, the one I had for Mitt. The date and time—the night Mitt became concerned about my ring. He had made two calls that evening, the second one less than a minute after the first. Earlier, I had assumed the second call went to the guy I stabbed, to get a description of the ring. Was it to Mason instead? Both numbers were in my apartment, and I planned to check it out later.

If Mason suspected I was the woman who had prowled around the shed behind the warehouse and stabbed Greg, was he using me the same way I was using him—to obtain information? The shed concealed a Crussett delivery van, a van that showed signs of a struggle. Mitt thought I was working for Conner. Had he shared his suspicion with Mason? Did Mason think I was searching for the lost cargo and those responsible for it being seized?

Assuming I was on target with my suspicions, I knew there wouldn't be anything at Mason's place for me to find or he never would've left me alone. I called for a taxi, unlocked the door, and left his apartment as I contemplated how to proceed.

·

23

CONSTANT SURVEILLANCE

Scooting out of the taxi, I saw Conner emerging from my apartment building. His face lit up as he strolled toward me, and my heart began fluttering in my chest. "You're home early," he said, standing only a foot from me.

I inhaled his pleasant, powerful scent as his warm breath wafted along the side of my cheek, causing heat to cascade through me. Attempting to ward off my feelings for him, I crossed my arms over my chest, determined to control the raging urge to touch him. "I might say the same about your date with Wendy."

His eyes drifted over my face. "I have a business meeting."

"This late?"

"They can happen at any hour." He wrapped his hand around my arm and drew me closer to him.

I unsuccessfully tried to shove his hand away. "Mr. Crussett, you're dating my cousin."

"Dating isn't the right word," he said, still holding onto me as he pulled me into a dark shadow at the side of the building. "We need to talk."

"About what?" I asked as our breath mingled in the cool night air, making it harder for me to maintain my resolve.

"Sara." He raised my chin.

I saw tenderness and desire in his light brown eyes as he lowered his lips to mine, and I quickly backed away. "My name is Sally."

He straightened his spine while his hand remained firmly around my arm. "You remind me of her." His eyes dimmed a little and his face lined with sadness.

146

From his expression, I assumed he still had some doubt that I was Sara. He probably couldn't fathom me escaping the blazing warehouse inferno that left burnt corpses, especially since charred remains of one were identified as Sara Jones. My heart ached for him, but I needed to maintain my role—Sally Jablon.

Silence fell between us while we continued studying each other's faces. Finally, I asked, "What did you want to talk to me about?"

"You're in danger."

"Danger? From who?"

He stroked my cheek. "Some men think you work for me."

One of Thurman's or Buckley's men must be working for Conner and told him that. "Work for you?" I asked, wondering if I had met the man on Crussett's payroll.

"I'm afraid I'm to blame for their suspicion. The night I saw you at Sammy's, I kept my eyes on you too long."

"Even if I worked for you, why would that put me in danger?"

"A woman your size was seen creeping around a warehouse, and she stabbed an employee. Would you know anything about that?"

I shook my head. "No. Why would I? You suspect I'm a gangster or something like that? Before I came back to Baton Rouge, I was a bank teller, not a thug."

"Two envelopes containing business pictures were sent to my home," he said, emphasizing the word 'business.' "Do you have any idea who might have sent them?"

"No," I said through a lump forming in my throat.

"My colleagues and associates would never send that type of documentation to my home. In fact, most of them don't have that address."

Feeling my stomach churning, I said, "I have no idea what you're talking about."

"Well then, maybe you can answer my next question. Why did you and Wendy take Mitt to Monique Torren's house and execute him? And on that same line of questions, what did you do with Monique?"

I had assumed Conner was responsible for Monique. Could I have been wrong? "Monique? I don't know her."

"And Mitt's execution?"

"I was dating him. Why would I want him dead?"

"That's what I'm asking you."

"I did not kill Mitt," I said in a firm tone. Mitt died when Wendy scratched him, though blood still flowed through his veins long enough to take him to Monique's place. The cause of death was the poison that had invaded his body, not the bullet that penetrated his head.

"Wendy fired the shot?"

"No," I snapped.

"Then who else was with you?"

Unable to come up with a reasonable answer about Mitt's death that would appease Conner, I changed the subject, "Are you having us followed?"

"Yes. For your protection."

"Protection? And why do I need your protection?"

"Like I said before, some men believe you are working for me."

"Can't you set them straight?"

"If I tried, they would be more convinced."

"Who are these men?"

"Your date for one."

"Who else?"

"Mitt's employees."

"But Mitt's dead."

"His employees aren't. They're just being paid by someone else."

"Who?"

A hint of a smile crossed his face. "The Sara I used to know didn't like talking about business."

"I'm not Sara," I said sharply. "Besides warning me about Mason and accusing me of killing Mitt, was there anything else you needed to talk about? And did you discuss this with Wendy?"

He rubbed my hand. "I didn't ask Wendy about your early Thursday morning drive to Monique's or about her driving Mitt's car, but I must admit one of my men did chuckle when she dented the Maserati."

Was there anything Wendy and I did that night that hadn't been observed by one of Conner's men? "You're talking gibberish. Wendy doesn't even know how to drive a stick shift."

"That's exactly what one of my men said. The way she continued grinding the gears, he wondered how far she was going to make it. That's probably why you drove it the last stretch."

Recalling how I thought we had lost the Cadillac tailing us, I now knew it would take more work to ditch Conner's men than I had realized. Was it an impossible task? "Mr. Crussett," I said in a formal tone. "I would appreciate it if you would call off your men and allow Wendy and me to go about our business without constantly being tailed."

Conner squeezed my hand. "Not a chance."

"Do you also have spies inside the apartment building?"

"What do you think?"

"Since you apparently have me well protected, I know I'll sleep well tonight," I said with a sarcastic edge to my voice while I enjoyed the feel of his hand touching mine.

"My men are only watching over you for your protection, they won't interfere with your plans unless you are in imminent danger."

"Exactly what does that mean?"

"Wednesday night when Mitt stopped by for a visit, we had anticipated you'd be leaving the apartment at gunpoint. Had that occurred, my men would have come to your aid, but since you or Wendy were able to handle the situation, very admirably I might add," he gave me a big smile, "it wasn't necessary for them to interfere."

"So, unless someone is pointing a gun at me, I don't need to worry about your men getting in my way?"

He nodded, but I doubted he was being truthful. Knowing him, it wouldn't be that simple. "Are you planning on relaying our discussion to Wendy?"

"No. She believes you are interested in her and I'd hate to be the one to erase that illusion. But now I'm going to warn you. Wendy has temper tantrums and is capable of inflicting serious pain when she's in one of those moods," I said, hoping he'd be careful around her. If she thought Conner was stringing her along because of me, I wasn't sure how she would react and I worried about his safety. At the same time, I assumed she knew I wouldn't hesitate to contact Brett if she broke the Tegen rule again.

"Sara…I mean Sally, I haven't even held her hand."

"You've taken her out. Some guys are a little slow in showing affection. She probably thinks you're one of them. If she was looking out the window when you started talking to me, she's probably wondering what's going on, so I better get up there."

He pulled me into his arms. My breath hitched as his body pressed against mine, and it took all my strength not to return his embrace. "Conner, let go of me."

He released me, but seeing his shimmering eyes and a satisfied look on his face, I was certain I hadn't managed to hide my identity well enough. How long could I pretend to be Sally Jablon and not succumb to the burning desire that bubbled up inside me whenever I saw him?

24

THE BURGLARY

As I stepped into the apartment, Wendy rushed out of my bedroom. "Why didn't you answer your phone?" she said with trembling lips. "I've called you at least five times in the last hour."

"Sorry, I had it on vibrate and it was in my purse. What's wrong?" I said, fearing she had seen Conner and me.

Her hand jittered as she pointed to my bedroom. "In there." With a quivering voice, she added, "I didn't know what else to do."

Rushing through the doorway, I gasped and covered my mouth as I stared at a man's body, wrapped in tightly spun cobwebs, lying on the floor. Did I know him? I pressed my lips together and reeled in my emotions, and then I leaned forward and studied his face through the web. Relief washed over me when I didn't recognize him. After all the problems we had dealing with Mitt, I thought she would've refrained from poisoning another person. "Wendy, why?"

She held up her hands with her palms facing me. "It wasn't me. But I couldn't reach you. So I preserved the body. What else could I have done?" Her eyes fill with water and a few tears trickled down her cheeks.

Bewildered, I asked, "It wasn't you?"

She shook her head.

My eyes darted to the nightstand. "My spiders!" I yanked open the second drawer and saw the lid on the spider cage ajar. Inside were only six spiders, two were missing.

"Are they all there?" she asked.

My eyes became moist. "No. I hope they're still in the apartment." After securing the latch, I raised the cage and sat it on the bed. I pulled a two-inch disk-shaped device out of my purse. It was white on one side and black on the other. Each side had a button in the center. The button on the black side was used to call Tegen spiders. It sent out a soft, deep, resonant sound, but the spiders had to be within thirty feet to pick up the signal. The button on the white side was only used if a Tegen was in danger. It was programmed to other Tegens' cell phones and gave the GPS location of the device.

I held down the button on the black side and waited anxiously, hoping my spiders would appear. Then I noticed the spiders in the cage were crawling up the inside wall, trying to reach the signal. I immediately released the button and said, "This won't work." I pulled off a pillow case, placed the spider cage in it and handed it to Wendy. "Take this and your spiders out to my car. Stay there until I come for you."

She nodded. "Okay. Keys?"

When Wendy left the apartment with all the caged spiders, I pressed the button again. A few minutes later, I smiled at the spider scurrying up my leg toward the device. I gently cradled it in my palm while I took a small container with pin-like holes in the lid out of my top drawer and slipped the delicate creature in it. Carrying the container, I pressed down the button and searched the room for any sign of the missing spider. Nothing. I moved to the living room and continued the process. Still nothing.

After thoroughly sweeping the device around the apartment, I went into the apartment building hallway, fearing I might stumble across another victim as I held down the button and scoured for the spider. I caught a glimpse of dark spot gliding toward me from under the door across the hall and gathered up my sweet arachnid. A chill washed over me while I stared at the closed door and worried my spider might have bitten someone on the other side.

Slipping the container in my pocket, I glanced at my watch: 11:45 p.m. I decided I'd wait until tomorrow to knock on the neighbor's door to verify everyone inside was okay, or someone wasn't. If it was the latter, time was not of the essence since no one could save them.

I took the elevator to the first floor and headed toward the parking lot. On the way, I passed a man dressed in gray, stripped coveralls and carrying a tool box. He strolled by me and never looked my way. Since it was doubtful any maintenance occurred in the building around midnight, I suspected he worked for Conner. I smiled to myself as I thought the guy and his co-workers were probably trying to figure out what Wendy and I were up to.

When I reached the car, Wendy climbed out. "Did you find them?"

"Yes. They're safe and sound and I hope the neighbors are too."

"Neighbors?"

"I'll explain later," I said, thinking one of Conner's men could be within earshot.

Back in the apartment, I moved the two spiders from the small container into the cage, and put it back into my nightstand drawer while I answered Wendy's questions about the neighbor. Then, it suddenly hit me—my ring and Mitt's cell phone weren't in the cage. I motioned toward the preserved body. "Wendy, is this where you found him?"

"Yes. I didn't move the guy. I wrapped him up right there."

I bent down and looked under the bed, the nightstand and the dresser for my ring. "Was the apartment door locked when you got home?" I asked, guessing he didn't come alone.

She squinted. "You know, thinking about it, when I turned my key I locked it. It must have been unlocked, but I locked it when I left. Honest. You can ask Conner. He saw me."

"Besides the guy lying on the carpet, did you see anything else out of order in the apartment?"

"Well, your computer and backpack were on the floor next to the guy. I put them back in your closet. Was that okay?"

"Yeah," I said, taking my backpack out of the closet and dumping the contents on the bed, hoping the victim stuck my ring and the cell phone in it.

"What are you doing?"

"Looking for my ring and a cell phone," I said, rummaging through the stuff.

"Your ring?"

Not seeing it among the stuff, "Did you see my ring anywhere?" I asked, biting my lower lip as I put everything back in my backpack.

She shook her head. "No. Why aren't you wearing it?"

"It's complicated. Anything in the guy's pockets?"

"I went through them. All I found was a cell phone and a set of keys. He's wearing a gun holster, but I took the gun."

"No wallet?"

She shook her head.

"Where did you put his stuff?"

"Well," she hesitated. "The gun is in my suitcase."

I wondered why she wanted it, though I didn't have time to dwell on it. "How about his cell phone and keys?"

She swallowed hard. "In the dumpster."

"Dumpster? When did you throw them away?"

"That was the first thing I did when I couldn't reach you. His cell phone might have GPS so I had to get rid of it and I didn't know who had poisoned him. I thought you always carried your spiders with you, like I do."

Most Tegens away from their domicile carry a small, black ovoid container with their spiders in it at all times in case they need to make a quick departure from their current location. Leaving any of our spiders behind would not be acceptable. "By any chance, did you turn it off before you dumped it?"

"No. It could've been turned off. I didn't check it. I just wanted it out of here."

"You don't think leaving it in our dumpster would guide anyone searching for the victim to our apartment building?"

She scratched her forehead. "Well, I guess it would. But, they wouldn't know which apartment."

Feeling irritated with her reasoning, I said, "I doubt that whoever sent the man to our apartment would've had him search every apartment in the building. What do you think?"

"Maybe he was just a burglar and no one sent him."

She had a good point, but I knew that wasn't the situation. "Mitt's cell phone and my ring were in the spider cage. They're both missing, so our victim had an accomplice."

"A guy got away?"

"That's what I suspect."

She glanced at her black ring. "These rings are real valuable. Do you think whoever took yours will come back and try to get mine?"

"I don't know."

"Let 'em try," she said, clenching her teeth and narrowing her eyes. "They have no idea what will be in store for them."

"We need to do some dumpster diving for the man's cell phone. Without his name or something, I don't know how I'll find my ring."

"Dumpster diving? Yuck." She wrinkled her nose.

"Help me get him to the other side of the bed, so he can't be seen from the doorway."

As we pushed and pulled the preserved body, Wendy asked, "What are you planning to do with him?"

"I'll make some calls."

She looked panic-stricken. "Not to Brett."

"No. I won't call him."

Wendy exhaled as a relieved expression flashed across her face. Gazing at her, I felt overwhelmingly sad, knowing it wouldn't be long before I'd have to divulge her location to Brett and I feared the consequences.

As we neared the back exit to the apartment building, voices drifted through the door. Wendy grabbed my arm. "Someone's out there."

"It's Friday night. Maybe some tenants are getting home late," I said, walking at a slower pace.

"Why don't we go out the front door and sneak around the side of the building?"

Knowing as soon as we stepped out the entrance, one or more of Conner's men would follow us around the building, I did not want to explain our dumpster diving. "No. If whoever is out there doesn't go into the building, we'll get in my car and head to an all night diner. I could use a cup of coffee and a donut."

"So could I."

Loud clanging sounds, like something striking metal, came from outside.

Wendy and I stopped in our tracks and looked at each other. "I hope that noise isn't coming from around the dumpster." I pushed the door open. "Walk normally and go straight to the Dodge. Don't look at the people out there until you're in the passenger seat."

Out of the corner of my eye while I trotted to my car, I saw two men milling around near the dumpster. One carried a large garbage bag and wore coveralls. He was the guy I saw earlier in the hallway. The other man was nicely dressed in a suit. He probably worked for Conner.

Footsteps pounded against the pavement behind me as I pulled out the car key and pushed the unlock button.

Wendy had already fastened her seatbelt before I got situated behind the steering wheel. "Do you think those guys were dumping stuff?" she asked.

"I hope so. Otherwise, they've beaten us to the dumpster diving. Was anyone in the parking lot when you threw in the cell phone and keys?" Tracking devices and bugs suddenly sprang through my head.

"No, I—" she began

"Stop," I said, leaning toward her. I cupped my hands around my mouth and whispered in her ear. "I think the car might be bugged."

She squinted. "Really?"

I nodded and pressed together my thumb and index finger and glided them over my lips like I was zipping it up.

She nodded.

After we had driven a couple of miles, I stopped by the side of the road and combed my fingers through my hair, searching for a bug.

"You think you have—"

I held up a hand. "Shhh," I mouthed, "Yes. Open the car door," I gestured toward it, "and get out." Climbing out of the car, I bent over and shook my hair while I continued raking my fingers through it. Both Wendy and I had changed clothes before we headed out of the building, so no bugs could have been planted in our garments. Since Conner had taken her to dinner, I said, "Check your hair."

"But it looks so nice."

She was right, her hair looked perfect. "Never mind." I opened the trunk and grabbed a small bag. I rifled through it and pulled out a palm-size black object used to detect bugs. I slid a lever embedded in the side of it and a green light appeared on top of the gadget. Holding it firmly in my hand, I moved it over Wendy's hair, making sure to keep it an inch or two away. "No bugs."

She touched the device. "That is so cool. Where did you get it?"

"Online."

"Really?"

I bobbed my head. "We could have used it after we took care of Mitt, but I had left the bag in the apartment."

"Yeah, I remember looking for tracking devices. Do you want me to do that again?"

"Yeah, why don't you get started while I search for bugs inside the car?"

She began looking around the tires and I got back into the Dodge with the detector. A few minutes later, I located a bug under the dashboard, but didn't end my search until I had moved the gadget over every surface inside the vehicle.

As I climbed out of the car, Wendy hurried over to me. "I found two," she said in an uplifted voice, showing them to me.

"Shhh," I whispered, pointing to the bug in my hand. Glancing around, I didn't see any people walking on the sidewalk or hear any car engines running. Assuming one or more of Conner's men were lurking nearby, it seemed pointless to try to find something moving that I could attach the devices to. I carried the three small objects to the closest bush and tossed them into it.

"Someone might find them there," Wendy said as I returned to the car.

"Yeah, that's a possibility, but that isn't our problem."

At the diner, I found myself checking out everyone who walked through the door, even though, I probably could not recognize most of Conner's employees. Since I hadn't noticed anyone following us the night Mitt was shot, I knew he hired men who didn't stand out and blended well with the people around them, or they hid undetected in the shadows.

"You know," Wendy said between sips of her coffee. "The first time I went out with Conner, on our lunch date, he asked me about my ring, almost like he had seen someone else wearing a ring like mine." She stopped and admired the black stone.

"What did you tell him about it?"

"That I was in a club and all club members have a ring like it. That way, if he did run across someone wearing a Tegen ring, he'd just think the person was a club member. Wasn't that a good answer?" she said, looking pleased.

"Yes. It was."

"I've been trying to figure out if any Tegens I know live in Houston and I can't come up with anyone. Do you know any?"

"Not personally, but once I met a woman at a gathering who lived there."

"Are we still going to look through the dumpster when we get back?"

"Maybe. Let's see if someone is hanging around it."

A half an hour later, we pulled into the apartment building parking lot. I had to stop the car before we reached a stall because a couple of guys were hosing down the asphalt. I didn't see any garbage lying about, but at two-thirty in the morning, I suspected they were cleaning up their mess from dumpster diving especially since the one guy now wore a pair of dirty slacks and a stained dress shirt with rolled up sleeves. He certainly hadn't been dressed for the job.

The man in the coveralls, that now looked filthy and well-worn, turned the hose away from the Dodge and motioned me into the only vacant parking spot.

"No dumpster diving tonight." I turned off the car engine.

"You think the man in the apartment is one of these guys' partners?" she asked, waving her finger between the two men.

"Something like that."

"Do you think they found the guy in your room?"

"We'll see. I just hope no one went snooping in the nightstand or we're bound to run across another victim."

25

HARBORING A TEGEN

Pleased we didn't have any uninvited guests while we went to the diner, Wendy and I said goodnight. In my bedroom, I glanced at the body on the other side of my bed, and then pulled my notepad from my backpack, searched through it for the numbers Mitt had dialed the night he became concerned about my ring, and compared them to Mason's second cell phone number. Just as I suspected, Mitt had called that number. Mason knew about my ring. Since I wasn't wearing it last night, had he sent someone to my apartment to retrieve it so he could show it to Greg, the guy I stabbed? Or was Mason the accomplice? Was that the reason he rushed out of his apartment in such a hurry without telling me he was going?

I stepped into the closet and removed the loose board under my shoe boxes, revealing the place I had hidden my black cell phone before I went out with Mason. I turned it on. Within a minute, it registered two voice messages. Flipping to the missed calls, I saw one was from Brett and the other one from Father. I dialed voice mail and listened to the messages. Brett said he had something important to talk to me about without giving any details. If he didn't answer his cell, he wanted me to contact him through the office. Father's message was brief. He wanted me to return his call. At 3 a.m. in the morning, I was certain they were both sound asleep. I left the cell phone turned on, placed it on top of my nightstand and crawled into bed.

I awoke to the beeping of a cell phone. Feeling groggy and disoriented, I grabbed the pink one, pushed the button and said, "Hello," but a phone continued ringing. Then I discovered it was the black phone and answered it.

"Sara," Brett said.

"Yeah."

"You sound like you're only half awake."

"Well, then there isn't anything wrong with our connection." The sun streamed in through the window, and from its angle, I guessed it was late morning. Glancing at the clock, I knew I was right.

"It's almost eleven and you're still in bed?" he grumbled.

"Calm down. I got into a late night movie on television and stayed up. That was all."

"You didn't go out last night?" His tone suggested he wasn't buying my excuse.

"Nope. I was home alone."

"Then why didn't you answer your cell phone?"

"It ran out of juice and I didn't discover that until I was getting ready for bed. Is there a problem?"

"We finally got permission to exhume Marilee Kent's body."

A terrible foreboding crept over me and I closed my eyes while I waited for him continue.

"Sara, why didn't you call me?"

"Call you about what?"

"Wendy. She's been staying with you."

"She begged me not to. And you don't know if she broke the rule, do you?"

"No. But if she wasn't worried about something, why didn't she want you to call me?"

"Who knows? She didn't tell me why," I lied since I wasn't ready to tell him about Wendy's confession yet. "Sometimes she just doesn't want to talk to you."

"True." He paused. "Can you keep an eye on her until we get the results of the autopsy?"

"Yes. When do you think you'll have them?"

"Probably the first part of next week. If Wendy talks about going somewhere else, will you call me?"

"I promise," I said and meant it. Regardless of how often I had talked to her about not using her poison unless she had no other recourse, I suspected it had fallen on deaf ears. I thought Wendy could easily be driven to use it and I didn't want her roaming around without a Tegen watching over her, someone she couldn't poison. "You're no longer in the field? Or do you have cell coverage there?"

"I'm still working in the field. No cell coverage. The crew is staying a couple of days in a nearby town to catch up on a few things and to wait for some additional supplies. I'm not sure how long I'll be reachable on my cell."

"If you're not, I'll call the other number."

After we said our goodbyes, I clicked off the phone and speculated about who told Brett Wendy was here. Besides Conner's men, was a Tegen also spying on us? Kendall? Assuming Father had called about the same thing, I tapped in his number.

"Hello, Sara," he answered with an edge in his voice.

"Father, I'm sorry I didn't return your call earlier. My phone was off last night. Anything urgent?"

"Brett called."

"About Wendy, right?"

"Yes. You never mentioned she was there when we talked yesterday morning. How long has she been staying with you?"

"Since Wednesday night. I was out when she got here."

"Are you harboring her?"

"Brett doesn't know for sure she broke the rule."

"Do you?"

As much as I wanted to, I couldn't lie to my father. "Yes. She confided in me."

"When?"

"Thursday, but things got complicated. I was busy dealing with another problem," I said, thinking about Mitt.

"Mr. Thurman?"

"Yes. How did you know?"

"Sara," he said in a harsh tone. "The reason I want you to call me each morning is to make sure you're okay. When you neglect to mention you're involved in a murder and I learn it from someone else, don't you think that rather defeats the point of the daily call?"

"Well...I didn't want you to worry."

"I'm used to worrying about you."

I knew he did, especially since during the first year a person changes from being a human to a Tegen can be difficult dealing with the transition—our senses are enhanced, we can climb without the aid of ropes, and we become lethal. Being lethal was the reason for the number one rule—no killing for revenge or sport. I had been a Tegen for less than a year and Father trusted me, though he still wanted me to check in with him each day. Feeling guilty for not telling him Wendy was at my place, and for hiding the murder from him, I said, "I know. But no one suspects he was poisoned before he was shot." The words flew out of my mouth, and then I wished I could get them back—Father hadn't said anything about Mitt being poisoned.

Without skipping a beat, like he already knew, he asked, "Was Wendy responsible?"

"Yes, but she thought I was in danger."

"Danger?"

"Mitt was brandishing a gun."

"Why?"

"Well… he thought I worked for," I swallowed hard, "Conner."

"Yes. I heard he was there. What I meant was why didn't Wendy think you could handle the situation? We heal from gunshot wounds."

"Beats me. But I do believe she thought she was coming to my aid."

"Then she didn't break the rule that time, but it doesn't matter since she had already broken it."

"I don't think she planned to kill Hank," I said, trying to help Wendy. "She got upset and it just happened. She had only been a Tegen for eight months. Isn't there anyway she can have a second chance?"

"How about Marilee Kent? Wendy had been a Tegen for over a year when Marilee died."

"She never confessed to me that she killed Marilee."

"Let's see what the autopsy shows."

"So there is a chance for Wendy?"

"Slim. Dr. Driggs would have to verify she didn't know what she was doing at the time Hank Davidson was poisoned. Did she tell you the location of his body?"

"She mentioned a lake. She never specifically said that's where he was, but she inferred it."

"What lake?"

"Don't know. It has to be in or around McComb since she used to swim with Hank there."

"We'll get someone to start combing the lakes. But Sara, I am very disappointed you didn't call me after she confessed. It's your obligation as a Tegen to report that, and you'll be punished for harboring her."

"Punished? How?"

"You know the rules. Only one rule requires the ultimate punishment, but they all are enforced. Punishment will be determined by the colony council and individualized to the Tegen who committed the offense."

"How have other Tegens been punished for breaking that rule?"

"Sara, we'll discuss it when you get home."

"I just wanted her to have a few days before I turned her in. I planned to call, but now she's my alibi in Mitt's murder."

"I already knew that from your interview at the police station."

"How did you get that information?"

"From a reliable source," Father said, giving an ambiguous answer. "However, it would be more accurate to say, you were her alibi. She committed the crime."

"She didn't shoot him. I did, to cover-up the poison."

"Good thinking. Last time she stayed with you, you mentioned she didn't care for Agnes. Are they getting along better this time?"

"When Wendy arrived here, Agnes went to stay with her sister, so that isn't a problem."

"We'll hold off doing anything about Wendy until we get the results of Ms. Kent's autopsy or we locate Hank's body. Without physical evidence, she could claim you were out to get her for some reason and she never confessed or killed for revenge."

"She wouldn't do that."

"Tegens, like humans, sometimes act in unexpected ways when they're backed into a corner. Proof of guilt makes the process go smoother. Can you watch her for a few days?"

"I already told Brett I would."

"Did you tell him about the confession?"

"No."

"If Wendy becomes a threat to anyone, you need to contact me immediately," he said firmly.

I wanted to tell him I didn't always carry my black cell phone, the one I used exclusively to call Tegens, with me, but I realized he knew that. Obviously, I better have it on me all the time from now on or easily accessible. I didn't have a clue what my punishment would be if I disobeyed his order nor did I want to find out. After all, I already had one punishment waiting for me. "Father, the vaccine you developed for Mother, the one that made her immune to our spiders' venom, did that also work if she would've been scratched by a Tegen's needles?"

My biological mother was not a Tegen. She died when I was born. Mortals who bore a Tegen's child didn't survive after giving birth. Mother knew that, but she was aging and my father never would. Father deeply loved her and still does. She wanted to see me, and Father managed to keep her alive for a day.

"Yes. Why?"

"Conner's been seeing Wendy. Not romantically, but I think she's seeing it differently."

"And since you know how she handled her prior ex-boyfriend, you're concerned what she might do to Conner when she realizes he's not romantically interested in her. Or worse, if she believes he was using her to find out about Sally Jablon, a woman who bears a remarkable resemblance to Sara Jones."

"You got it. I think she might overreact."

"Sara, we could pick her up now and keep her in our custody until we get verification."

"No. The police here might want to ask her some more questions about Mitt and I don't want to leave Baton Rouge yet."

"That vaccine was developed just for your mother. It took into consideration her weight, blood type and DNA. I'm sorry, but it won't work for anyone else," he said sadly.

Though I was disappointed, I believed he would have given it to me if the serum would've helped. Father knew I still longed for Conner. He had comforted me often when tears flowed. A buzzing sound came through the cell phone.

"I have a patient waiting."

"Before you go," I said. "I did want to talk to you about...a body."

"A body?"

"It's been preserved."

"And where did this body come from?"

"We had an intruder last night?"

"Did Wendy handle him?"

"No. He was snooping in my drawers and ran across my spiders."

"Your spiders? Are any missing?"

"Two were, but they're back now."

"Any other casualties?"

"No," I said, hoping I was right.

"Where's the body?"

"Next to my bed."

"I'll have it picked up today. Don't leave your apartment before it's gone."

"One more thing."

"Yes."

"The victim had an accomplice. My ring is missing."

"Your ring?"

"Yes. I have an idea who might have taken it," I said, envisioning Mason.

"If you feel like you need the comfort your ring provides, touch or hold Wendy's, but don't put it on. It's bonded to her and you'll receive a very unpleasant reaction. Sometimes Tegens have misplaced their ring. Your senses could help you locate it."

"How?"

"Close your eyes and think about it. If it is within thirty feet of your location, a soothing, peaceful feeling will run through your body. If you have been without it for more than forty-eight hours, your ring finger will tingle and jerk when you're close to it."

"What if I can't find it that way, or find it at all?"

"You'll get another ring, but in order to bond to it, you'll need to spend a few days in the cave. And, you can't go without a ring for more than a week."

"What happens if I do?"

"Don't let that happen. If you haven't found your ring in five days, get on a plane and come home. You can return to Baton Rouge after you've bonded with a new ring." The buzzing sound came through the airwaves again. "Sara, I need to go. Anything else?"

"No. That takes care of everything."

"I love you, Sara, and don't hesitate to call if you run into any more problems."

"I won't, and I love you too, Father."

I headed to the kitchen and poured water into the coffee maker as the throbbing sound of a siren came from off in the distance and continued getting louder. Then it seemed like the noise ended close to the apartment. I went to the window and saw an ambulance with its strobe lights flashing parked next to the curb. I watched two paramedics take a gurney out of the vehicle and move toward the apartment entrance.

Fearing my spider had left another victim in the apartment it had visited the night before, I cracked open the hallway door.

26

PACKAGE PICK-UP

When I didn't see any activity in the hallway, relief washed over me as Wendy's door sprang open.

"I heard a siren. Is the apartment building on fire?" she asked, terror stark on her face. Fire destroys Tegens. It was the only thing that could.

"No," I said, closing the apartment door. "It's an ambulance."

"For someone in the building?" she asked, anxiety evident in her voice. I assumed she was concerned about the same thing I was—another spider victim.

"Yes, but the paramedics didn't go to our floor. Since a spider crawled out from under the neighbor's door, I'm going to check to make sure everyone is okay in that apartment. I opened the door again, walked across the hall, and knocked.

After a heavyset woman with silver hair answered, I said, "Hello, I'm Sally Jablon from across the hall. My cousin is staying with me and she can't find her necklace with a crystal pennant. She thinks the clasp might have broken on her way to my apartment. Have you noticed a necklace on the hallway carpet?"

She shook her head. "No. Have you checked with the Super?"

"I'm planning to do that. Can you ask everyone else in your apartment if they've seen it?"

"Dear, I live alone."

"Sorry to have bothered you."

"Not a bother. I hope your cousin finds it."

When I returned to my apartment, Wendy asked, "How's the neighbor?"

"Fine. I guess my spider just wanted to check out the apartment. No harm done." Then I told her Father would be sending someone to pick up the body by my bed. Feeling uneasy about the events of the prior night, I asked, "Can I hold your ring for a while?"

She cocked her head and her eyes narrowed. "Why?"

"I'm not going to steal it. In fact, I'm not even going to slip it on," I said, and proceeded to tell her what Father had said about Tegen rings.

"Sure." She took off her ring and gave it to me.

"Thanks." I gripped it in my hand and briefly closed my eyes as a soothing sensation streamed up my arm. I had no idea I could derive this type of comfort from someone else's ring.

"Any idea when the body will be picked up?"

"No. He never said, but we have to stay in the apartment until it is," I said, though I hadn't been told she needed to stay, but I couldn't keep track of her if she left.

"What about Conner? We're going out tonight. Do you think I should break the date?"

I looked at my watch and saw it was already past two. "I don't know, but he can't be here when they come for the body."

"Couldn't I go with him and you stay here?"

She had been out with him before and there wasn't a problem, but I had a nagging feeling that he was no longer safe with her. "No, Father wants us both to be here," I lied. "Maybe the body will be picked up in time so we can still go. I just don't know."

"Then I won't call him yet. Tell me, do you think he really likes me?"

"Yeah. Why?" I asked, wondering where this was going.

"Well...I have to take his hand; he never makes a move to hold mine. It's almost like he's a little standoffish. Maybe he's just shy. What do you think?"

"He seemed like an okay guy when he came here to talk about the neighbor, but outside that, I've never talked to him. You know him better than I do, but some guys are a little slow in showing how they feel about a woman," I said, trying to justify Conner's behavior toward her.

She came and gave me a big hug. "Oh, thank you, thank you. I was worried he didn't like me that much, but now that you said he's a little slow, I'll have to let him know how I feel."

How she managed to put that interpretation on what I said, was beyond me. Though, it probably was good she had misconstrued my words since I feared her reaction if she discovered the truth.

As we were eating a late lunch, the landline rang. Wendy leapt to her feet and grabbed the receiver. "Hello....I'll get her." Handing it to me, she said, "It's a guy."

Since the person had called on the landline, I thought it was the police detective calling, and felt surprised when I discovered Mason was on the other end of the line. Still irritated that he had left me the night before, I huffed, "Mase, how could you leave me in your apartment without saying a word you were going?" Then I noticed Wendy's eyes narrowing and her lips becoming a thin line as her face contorted into an angry expression. I wished I was talking to him out of her earshot since I suspected what I had just said about being abandoned in an apartment had caused her temper to rise.

"It was an emergency and I thought I wouldn't be gone long," he said, sounding a little jittery.

"Emergency? What?"

"The police called. Someone had broken into my car."

Unable to recall seeing his Mustang, or for that matter even looking for it, when I got into the cab, I said, "But your car was parked out front."

"That's why I didn't think it would take long, but the perpetrator had stolen it. The cops stopped the guy for erratic driving. He was drunk. That's how they discovered the guy didn't own the Mustang. I tried calling your cell, but you must have turned it off. I spent a couple of hours at the police station doing paperwork."

Picking up my pink cell phone, I saw it was off, but it was on when I was at his apartment. I pushed the "on" button and scrolled to missed calls. Mason had called twice—once at 10:15 a.m. and again at 1:30 p.m. There weren't any missed calls from him the night before. I wanted to ask him how he got to the police station, but decided to let it go. Though I wasn't buying his story, I needed to maintain a good relationship with him at least long enough to determine if he had my ring or if he had information that would lead me to it.

"Sally, you still there?"

"Yeah. Sorry. I was getting a Coke out of the fridge."

"How about giving me another shot? Dinner tonight?"

"I've got other plans. How about tomorrow night?" Sally Jablon would've waited for him to ask about another day, but Sara Jones was anxious to find her ring and soon.

"Pick you up at seven?"

"Sounds good."

Hanging up the phone, I thought about Wendy and wondered if I dared leave her alone. I had promised Father and Brett I'd watch over her. Could she get into trouble while I was gone for a few hours? As much as I wanted to believe she'd behave herself, I didn't.

"The way Mase looked at you when he picked you up last night I thought he was crazy about you. He just up and left you at his apartment?"

"Yep. His car had been stolen."

"Leaving you like that…for a car? I wouldn't have forgiven him. He'd have to deal with me," she snarled through clenched teeth, reinforcing my suspicion that she couldn't be trusted.

At 6:30 p.m. Wendy still hadn't called Conner to cancel her date. She had been pacing back and forth, playing with the remote control and looking out the window every ten minutes. Every time a van or truck parked out front, she announced the vehicle was here for the body. After my fourth trip to the window to check it out, I no longer went. With all of Wendy's fidgeting around, I couldn't even think about a scheme to locate my ring.

As much as I didn't want her to be alone with Conner, I thought it might be worse if I went with them. If Conner focused on me and not her, I suspect she wouldn't handle it well and he could easily end up being poked or scraped by her needles. Though, I knew Father and Brett wouldn't approve allowing her to go out without me by her side, I wanted to keep Conner safe and decided it would be better if I stayed home. I gave Wendy the lame excuse that I wouldn't be going out with them because I needed to catch up on my sleep after the prior night's excitement. She never pressed me to change my mind, probably because she wanted Conner to herself.

A few minutes to seven, the doorbell buzzed. "I knew that blue van was for us," Wendy said, charging to the door. Opening it, she flinched and stepped back. From where I sat in the front room I couldn't see who was standing in the hallway. Wendy turned toward me as a fear gripped her features.

"Wendy," I said, rising to my feet. "What is it?"

"Naa...na," she mumbled, unable to spit out a word.

I quickly moved to the doorway and pulled her aside. That was when I saw Kendall, the Tegen enforcer. A wave of terror crept through me as I stared at his piercing deep-set black eyes and muscular arms protruding from his black t-shirt. Why was an enforcer at my door? Had he been sent for Wendy?

"Miss Jablon," he said, not showing any sign that he recognized me.

"Yes," I replied, looking at him, but avoiding his eyes.

"We've come for the package."

We. I hadn't even noticed the average-sized, well-built man standing next to him. "Please, come in." I opened the door wider. Then I spotted Wendy going into her bedroom, closing the door behind her.

The average-sized man entered, stopped and pressed his arm against mine. He kept it in place for a few seconds so he could verify that I was a Tegen since I wasn't wearing my ring. When Tegen's arms touch, pheromones are secreted. That was another way for Tegens to identify each other without relying on the ring. As far as I knew, no one had ever tried to imitate a Tegen ring, but that didn't eliminate the possibility.

The two men carried a large box with the name "T's Fine Furnishings," on the side along with sketches of bedroom furniture. I smiled to myself guessing the "T" stood for Tegen. Leading them into my bedroom, I said, "The package is on the other side of the bed."

They didn't speak a word while they removed the lid on the box and enveloped the preserved body in bubble wrap. Wondering if they planned on shipping it somewhere, I watched them lower the body into box, tightly seal it and attach a label.

When the men picked up the box, I hurried to the apartment door and opened it for them. "Thanks," I said as they carried the concealed body into the hallway. Kendall nodded and then headed toward the elevator. I tapped on Wendy's door. "They're gone."

She stepped into the living room. "Thank goodness. Did you see that guy? If looks could kill, we'd both be dead. Is he a Tegen?"

"Yes."

"I've never seen him at a gathering. Your dad must know him, huh?"

I shrugged my shoulders. "Don't know. The guy might have been the closest one who could pick up the body. He had another man with him. I didn't recognize him either," I lied, assuming if I told Wendy anything about Kendall, she'd be out the door and disappear before I could call Father.

"Did he look just as dangerous?"

"No. He appeared like a regular guy."

Her eyebrows bounced and a wide smile flashed on her face. "Now, I can go out with Conner. Too bad you're too tired to go," she said in a tone that clearly indicated she was thrilled about my decision.

.

27

TRESPASSING

"I'm going to lie down and read. Will you explain to Conner why I won't be joining you this evening?" I asked, standing in the doorframe leading into Wendy's room.

"Don't do that yet. He'll be here in fifteen minutes and I'm not ready," she said, working on her make-up. Before I could respond, the doorbell rang. "He's early. Can you let him in?"

Based on living with Conner for three years, I couldn't remember him ever being early for anything. Walking toward the door, I hoped it was someone else. I pulled open the door and found myself facing Conner, impeccably dressed in an Armani navy blue suit and a blue-and-white striped dress shirt. I felt an emotional jolt and a tightening sensation in my throat, as I gazed at the red, monogrammed tie he wore. A tie I had given him.

He glanced at my jeans and t-shirt. "I guess I overdressed."

"No," I said in my normal voice, forgetting to use my southern twang. I coughed, inhaled deeply, and then I proceeded, emphasizing the twang, "No. I got to bed late last night, so I'm going to take it easy tonight and go to bed early."

The corners of his mouth curved up as his eyes met mine. "We could stay here and order take-out."

"No. No. You two should go out and have a good time," I said, attempting to sound sincere while I wished I could take Wendy's place as my desire for him churned through my body.

"Sally," he said, reaching for my hand.

Hearing Wendy's door opening, I quickly pulled my hand out of his reach. I turned as she hurried toward Conner. She wore a short, light pink, silk dress that hugged her curves, and five-inch stilettos a shade darker.

"I'm ready," she announced, her face glowing.

Conner gave her a pleasant smile. "Sally mentioned she was tired and wouldn't be accompanying us. I've had a busy day. How would you feel about staying here and ordering take-out?"

Disappointment etched her features. "Huh?"

"No. No. You two should go out," I said.

"See. Sally wants to go to bed. Maybe, if we're quiet, we could come back here after dinner and watch a movie. Then you could relax." She caressed his arm and looked at me. "Would that be okay?"

"Yeah. I sleep pretty soundly. I doubt you'll wake me up."

A sad expression flickered on Conner's face as he escorted Wendy out of the apartment. I leaned against the wall next to the window, discreetly looked out, and my pulse quickened as I watched the man I couldn't forget sliding into the backseat next to Wendy, the woman I didn't trust. Then a tinge of guilt washed over me. I had promised both Father and Brett I'd keep track of her and I was letting her out of my sight in order to protect Conner. He'd be safer without me tagging along.

After the car drove away, I laid the laptop on my bed and flicked to the tracking program. Pulling up the screen for Mason's Mustang, I saw the blue blip. I smiled, knowing the tracking device hadn't been discovered. The Mustang was parked at the warehouse. Could my ring be there?

Suspecting it wouldn't be long before Conner and Wendy returned, I stuffed pillows under my bed covers for a sleeping body illusion, grabbed my laptop and purse, opened my bedroom window and then headed to the Dodge.

Once I was settled behind the steering wheel, I thought about the Escalade that would be following me. Since I hadn't managed to lose the tail Wednesday night, though I believed I had, I doubted I could escape Conner's surveillance. I decided not to even try and drove out of the parking lot with my computer sitting on the passenger seat, showing the blue blip had not budged.

Exiting the freeway, I glanced at the blip and saw it moving away from the warehouse, but my ring could still be there. A dark gray Ford truck was parked in front of the structure. I knew it belonged to Jeff, a guy who attended the meeting at Buckley's house and the guy in some of the pictures I sent to Conner.

A few hundred feet from the warehouse, I stopped by the curb, got out of the Dodge and glanced up and down the street. Not seeing any headlights or people, I slipped on a ski mask and crept through the woods to the fence surrounding the warehouse. There, I closed my eyes and concentrated on my ring. Nothing came. I stealthily moved along the fence line, stopping about every thirty feet and focusing on my ring. Nothing. I made my way to the fence on the other side of the building and continued the process. Nothing.

Then I climbed into my car, checked my laptop for the blue blip and saw it was still moving. Glancing at my watch, I figured Wendy and Conner were back at the apartment, but I wanted to continue looking for my ring and headed in the direction of Mason's car.

The blip led me to Orson Thurman's estate. The Mustang was somewhere behind the wrought-iron gate and couldn't be seen from the street. I stopped at the side of the road beyond the perimeter of Thurman's property.

When I attended Thurmans' garden party with Mitt, I saw blowtorches. He told me they would be used if an intruder carried spiders onto the estate, but they didn't have any way of knowing if a trespasser had spiders. In case a blowtorch was their chosen weapon to handle all unwelcome visitors, I needed to be prepared for a quick escape and didn't want to be weighted down with my backpack. I fished out my ski mask, slipped it on, and left the backpack in the car. I climbed over Thurmans' stone wall and gazed around for surveillance cameras. Not seeing any, I cautiously moved toward the house.

A moment later, the sounds of dogs barking and rustling of leaves drifted through the foliage. I sprinted to the nearest tree and scrambled up it. Perched on a branch twelve feet above the ground, I surveyed the area and listened to the yelping dogs running. Four hounds pounded toward the stone wall I had just climbed over and began sniffing around. One broke away from the pack and sniffed its way to the tree I occupied. The animal scratched the bark at the bottom, lifted its head, and snarled as if it could see me.

My eyes darted around, looking for the closest branch in another tree. I spotted one touching a limb a few feet above me. Before the barking drew the security guards to the tree, I needed to quiet the dog. I rubbed my hands together and spun a piece of webbing. Making sure to remain hidden in the branches, I climbed down five feet and dropped the sticky web on the vigilant animal. The hound shook its head, but continued growling.

Since that didn't work, I retreated higher into the tree, gripped the limb touching another tree and vaulted over to it, sending leaves floating through the air. To my dismay, the hound charged to the other tree. Looking at the three sniffing dogs by the stone wall, I wished my pursuer would go and join his buddies. I heard voices off in the distance and assumed guards were headed this direction to find out what had excited the hounds. I snapped off a small branch and threw it into a cluster of bushes about forty feet away. The three dogs charged toward the bushes, but the hound below me remained in place. If I wanted to reach the house, I needed to do it on foot since no other tree was within my grasp in that direction. Doubting I could reach my destination without avoiding a confrontation with the animal on the ground, I began inching down the trunk of the tree. I stopped the instant I spotted two security guards approaching, one held a blowtorch, positioned so it was ready to use.

As I scooted higher into the tree, a guard with a raspy voice yelled, "Ajax, whatcha got?"

Staring at the blowtorch, I reluctantly leapt back into the first tree, the one closer to the stone wall. When I landed in it, leaves swayed and a few twigs snapped, but the barking drowned out the noise. Feeling relieved Ajax stayed at the tree I had just left, I watched as the guards looked up and moved around the tree trunk while Ajax bounced against the bark and yelped.

The guard patted the hound. "Boy, don't see anything. Probably a squirrel." He gripped the animal's collar. "Come on, back to the house."

The other guard gathered up the three hounds near the stone wall and retreated with them in tow. When the guards and dogs were out of sight, I shimmied out of the tree and headed to the wall. Preparing to climb back over it, I ejected hair clusters on my hands and placed them on the stone structure. A soft snapping sound caught my attention. I glanced over my shoulder and saw a security guard, the same guy who had escorted the hound away from the tree, less than ten feet from me.

"Hands up," he demanded, aiming a pistol at me.

Planning my next move, I complied with his order and raised my arms, retracting the clusters at the same time.

"Ajax only barks when there's an intruder. I knew someone was lurking around. A woman? You the one that stabbed a fellow at Buckley's warehouse?" He paused as if he expected an answer, but I didn't utter a word. "Take off the mask."

Grateful he wasn't carrying a blowtorch, I stood still and ignored his request. Then he made a deadly mistake. Keeping his weapon pointed at me, he leaned toward me, ready to yank off my ski mask with his other hand. "I'll do it," I snapped, ejecting the lethal hairs and scratching his hand as I gripped the mask.

He flung the back of his hand across my covered face, sending me backwards into the stone wall. "You bitch. What have you got?"

I retracted the needles and showed him my hands, flipping them over so he could see both sides. "Sorry. My fingernails are a mess."

The guard ran his fingers over my smooth hands and around the arms of my long-sleeve black t-shirt. "This way." He gestured toward the house.

Waiting for the venom to take effect, I said in my normal voice, "Can I ask you a question?"

"We'll be asking the questions," he hissed.

"Please, just one."

His eyes narrowed. "What?"

"Are you immune to poisonous spider venom?"

A shocked expression flashed on his face. He held his bleeding hand up in front of his eyes, and inhaled deeply. "That's not a spider bite," he said with a smirk, and then his body swayed. "What the…" His pistol tumbled out of his hand. He bent to retrieve it and his body toppled over. He staggered and attempted to stand, but he was no match for the venom surging through his veins.

While I watched him struggling on the ground, I lifted up my pant leg and pulled my knife out of the sheath. Then I tried to decide between shooting him with his pistol or stabbing him. Since I had stabbed Greg at the warehouse and didn't want anyone to suspect the same assailant had been snooping around Thurman's estate, I tucked away my knife and wrapped the bottom of my t-shirt around the pistol's handle. I pointed the barrel at the motionless man lying by my feet and knew the gunshot would bring guards rushing toward the noise, but I'd be long gone before they could get here. Without a second thought, I pulled the trigger. Blood squirted and streamed from the wound. Some splattered on my sleeves and pants. I dropped the gun and clambered over the stone wall.

A few minutes later, I was driving away from the scene of the crime. Stopping at a red light, I rolled up my sleeves, hiding the blood stains. As I continued toward my apartment, I wondered about Conner's surveillance team. Though I couldn't see an Escalade, I felt certain I had been tailed to Thurman's estate and someone was watching me now. Yet, I doubted any of Conner's men could have observed me behind the stone wall.

Even if Conner knew I hadn't stayed in my apartment, I didn't want Wendy to know. She might ask questions, questions I wouldn't answer. I began contemplating how to get back into my bedroom undetected. Earlier I had intended to climb up the exterior of the building, but since I had gone to the warehouse and Thurman's place, I'd probably be under close scrutiny and tracked until I entered the apartment building. I mulled over its floor plan and my mind drifted to the laundry room in the basement. It was on the side of the building that didn't abut the driveway leading to the parking lot.

Turning onto my street, I saw two black Escalades, one in front of my building and one across the street, and wondered what type of vehicle had been following me. The traffic was light and I had constantly checked the mirrors, but I never spotted the same car twice as I maneuvered through the various streets to get to my place.

I pulled into the parking lot behind the building and glanced at my watch. It said 12:30 a.m., and I wondered if Conner was having a hard time keeping Wendy at bay.

Entering the apartment building through the back door, I gasped and a spasm of panic surged through my body when I saw the hard, cold face staring at me.

28

A TEGEN WEB

The Tegen's unblinking black eyes were fixed on me. A cold chill washed over me as I noticed Kendall had a rolled-up carpet draped over his shoulder and sensed something was concealed inside. My mouth and throat became dry when he closed the basement door behind him and sauntered past me without saying a word. I remained motionless while the exit door near me creaked open and closed. I exhaled and inhaled short breaths, relieved Kendall was gone. He exemplified Father's description of a Tegen enforcer—a man who could cause fear to run through the veins of any Tegen. Had he been sent to check out Wendy? Was he looking around the building for possible escape routes—places she could run to if someone came for her? Thinking about the carpet he carried, I went to the basement, the place he had just left, to investigate.

I stood next to a row of washers and dryers and looked around. On the opposite wall was a door I had never opened before. I turned the doorknob and walked into the furnace room. The humming sound of the fan driving cool air from the air conditioner echoed against the cement walls as I slowly moved around the dark space. In the corner furthest away from the door, rags and blankets were strewn around, like someone had slept there.

Crouching in darkness, I began rummaging through them to check if they were hiding something. I came to an abrupt halt when remnants of a cobweb stuck to my fingers. I raised my hand to my nose and smelled the luscious scent of a web spun by a Tegen. Gazing at the pile of rags, I worried if there had been another spider victim. Had the accomplice been bitten and managed to stumble in here? With the poisonous venom running through his system, it was unlikely, if not impossible, that he could have walked this far. Could someone have dragged him in here? But who? To no avail, I shook each rag and blanket as I frantically searched for my ring. I closed my eyes and concentrated on my beautiful, black ring. Nothing came. Still, my eyes darted back-and-forth over the floor, trying to find it somewhere, as I left the room. The clock hanging on the wall above the washing machines said 1:05 a.m.

Suspecting some of Conner's men were looking for me, I pulled a chair over to the basement window, climbed on it and unlocked the window. Using all my strength and lots of time, I finally opened the window enough to squeeze through. To my chagrin I heard male voices at the back of the building. Hoping I wouldn't be spotted, I quickly took off my shoes, ejected climbing hairs on my hands and feet, and hustled up the side of the building. Within a minute, I had reached the fifth floor and made my way around the structure to my opened bedroom window. I slipped in, chucked off my clothing and put on pajamas. After rearranging my pillows, I crawled in bed and faced the door, expecting someone to knock or peek in.

"I checked on her fifteen minutes ago," I heard Wendy say through the closed door. "She's sound asleep. Why are you so worried about her?" she asked, irritation audible in her voice.

"With the...," Conner began, and then his voice trailed off. I assumed he was further away from the door than Wendy. Suspecting he wouldn't let it drop and Wendy's temper would rise each time he asked about me, I climbed out of bed and threw on a robe.

Opening my bedroom door, I said, "Can't you two keep your voices down? I'm trying to sleep."

Conner sat on the couch. His eyes zeroed in on mine and a faint smile crossed his lips.

"See," Wendy said, walking away from my door. Conner most likely had swayed her into checking on me again, and she was preparing to do just that. "She's fine. Like I told you, we don't have burglars around here climbing in windows. We're on the fifth floor."

"Burglars?" I said. Did Conner know about the prior night's theft?

Wendy waved her hand at me. "Go back to bed. Conner should probably be a cop. He thinks about crime all the time."

I had to force myself not to laugh, picturing "Conner the cop." The first guy he'd have to arrest would be himself. "Goodnight," I said, closing the door. I slipped under the covers and softly giggled while the image of Conner carrying a badge and arresting his employees twirled through my head.

"Sorry we woke you last night," Wendy said, pouring coffee. "I just don't know about Conner."

"Know what?"

"I tried everything I could think of to show him how I felt about him. You know, snuggling, stroking his hand…I wanted to touch his arm, but his long sleeve stopped me. Besides taking off his suit coat, he stayed completely dressed. He didn't even loosen his tie. I kissed his neck, but whenever I moved my mouth closer to his, he backed away. Then he acted like he was concerned about you—the burglar thing, but I think it was just an excuse to distract me. I'm starting to think he's already got a girlfriend, or maybe he doesn't like girls. What can I do?"

"You told me he lives in Houston. Maybe he doesn't want to get involved with a woman who lives elsewhere. Long distance romances don't work out for some people."

"Don't you think he'd still go for a one night stand? Come on, I doubt he's above that."

I shrugged. "I don't know. Is that all you want…a one night stand?"

"No, but it would be a start." She held up her hands and looked at her fingers. "I wish I could use my needles to just numb someone without them dying."

"Numb someone? You want to numb Conner?"

"Yeah, sure. He's gorgeous. I'd love to see him without a shirt on, and—"

The ringing of my pink cell phone interrupted her. I glanced at the caller ID and answered, "Hi, Mase."

"Something has come up and I'm going to have to break our dinner date. How about lunch? And bring your cousin."

"Wendy?"

"Yeah. I thought she might like to join us."

That struck me as being a little odd, but it meant I wouldn't be leaving Wendy at the apartment without my supervision. "Okay. Hold on," I said and moved the cell phone away from my ear. "Would you like to go to lunch with Mase and me?"

"I'd feel like a third wheel."

"No. I want you to get to know him."

Reluctantly, she nodded.

"We're on."

As soon as I disconnected, Wendy wanted to know more about Mason. I told her he was a friend of Mitt's and he had helped Mitt's mother plan the funeral. As she pried for more information, I pretended I didn't know what he did for a living.

"Since he ran out on you at his place Friday night, I already don't like the guy, but I'll try to be nice."

"The lunch probably won't last more than a couple of hours," I said with mixed emotions. I breathed a sigh of relief that I wouldn't be leaving

Wendy alone, but at the same time, I might have been able to weasel some information out of him during a dinner date. A lunch date with Wendy along, wouldn't allow me to do any prying.

As I started to dress for the date, I couldn't find my navy blue slacks or the pink sweater I wore with them. I doubted Wendy could fit into my slacks, but she had admired my sweater last time I wore it and knew it was her size. I went and tapped on her door.

"Yeah," she yelled from inside.

"Have you seen my pink sweater?"

She opened the door and stuck her head out. "No."

"It's missing."

"You think I stole your sweater," she huffed.

"No. No. I just can't figure where it could be."

"Maybe it's in the laundry," she said and shut her door.

My sweater was a "dry clean only" garment, but I still looked for it in the hamper. "Muh," I mumbled, strolling back into my bedroom empty-handed.

29

THE KIDNAPPING

Shortly after one, Mason escorted Wendy and me to a black limo parked near the apartment building entrance. "We're not going in your Mustang?"

"No. When it was stolen it sustained some damage to the steering column. I'll be without those wheels for a week. Jeff's been driving me around," he said, gesturing toward the man opening the back door.

With Jeff behind the wheel and Mason lying about the Mustang he had driven the night before, I knew something was up. And, unlike the Crussetts, I hadn't seen any of the Buckleys being chauffeured around. My eyes darted to the other side of the street, searching for the Escalade. It was gone.

As the limo pulled away from the curb, I hoped I'd have an opportunity to warn Wendy not to use her poison if someone aimed a gun at her. Dead guys can't talk about my ring. I also hoped Mason was taking us to the place where I could find my precious jewel.

It surprised me when the limo stopped in front of a French restaurant, but I suspected that was just our first stop.

After lunch, we headed back to the waiting limo. When Wendy and I were seated in the vehicle, Mason peered in and said, "I need to talk to Jeff, so I'll be riding up front." He closed the back door.

Watching him climbing into the front passenger seat, I heard the click of a lock and assumed Wendy and I were now secured inside the limo. I leaned closer to her and whispered, "If anything strange happens, don't use your needles. Understand?"

She squinted. "Strange?"

"Like someone pulls a gun. Just go along. Pretend you're scared."

She wrinkled her nose, "Huh?" and mouthed, "Gun?"

I bobbed my head.

After we had driven a few miles, I tapped on the window behind the front seat.

Mason edged it open an inch. "Yeah."

"This isn't the way back to my place," I said, though I had already concluded he had no intention of taking us there. Still, I wanted to hear his excuse.

"I need to pick up something so we're making a little detour." He slid the window shut.

"Hide your spiders," I whispered, "but don't let them see you. Watch me." I put my purse on the floor, leaned down and pulled out my black cell phone. I stuffed it in my bra and sat up straight. Wendy followed my lead and hid her spider case in her bra. My spiders were still in my nightstand drawer, and I hoped we wouldn't find another victim when we got back to the apartment. I knew if Mason frisked Wendy and me, he'd run across our hidden items. Then I might be forced to use my needles, but until that happened, I was determined to pretend I was vulnerable.

"You never finished telling me about the movie you saw last night," I said to Wendy, hoping to keep things calm.

Wendy proceeded to fill me in on all the details. When she finished, she asked, "Do you think it would be safe for me to go and see my folks?"

"Safe?"

"Brett wouldn't be hanging around, would he?"

"Let's talk about it when we get back to the apartment," I said, thinking Mason and his buddy, Jeff, might be listening to every word we said. Looking out the window, I saw we were on a narrow deserted road, and only a few dilapidated shacks could be seen from the limo. Expecting a larger, intact, structure to appear soon, my eyes scanned the area as we continued moving along.

The limo pulled over to the side of the asphalt. I still couldn't see any buildings and wondered if Mason had decided to get rid of Wendy and me without any type of interrogation.

Mason stepped out of the vehicle and yanked open the back door. "Give me your purses," he ordered. His demeanor had changed. His blue eyes bore into mine, and I saw no sign of anything but contempt streaming through them.

"Mase, is something wrong?" I asked, sounding innocent and naïve.

"Purses," he said with an outstretched hand.

Brandishing a pistol, Jeff approached and stood beside Mason.

I sucked in a ragged breath, popped my eyes wide open and attempted to look terrified. "A gun! Mase, why?"

Without answering my question, he clenched his teeth and his face hardened.

Playing the role of a defenseless captive, I chewed on my lower lip, handed over my purse, and clasped my hands together.

Mason nodded toward Wendy. "The purse."

Wendy's eyes narrowed and she snapped, "You can't have my purse."

Jeff aimed the barrel of his gun at her. "Give up your purse or your life. What will it be little lady?"

I tugged on Wendy's arm. "Come on. Give him your purse."

"It cost me a lot. He can buy his own."

"I'll buy you another one," I said, pulling it out of her grip. "Come on Mase, what's this all about?"

"As if you don't know," he growled, holding onto the handbags and slamming the door shut.

Wendy scooted over to my side of the backseat, and we both stared out the window.

Mason reached into the front seat of the limo, took out a pair of thick rubber gloves and tugged them on. He dumped out the contents of the purses, picked up the cell phones and handed them to Jeff. Jeff disassembled them, took out the batteries and tossed the phones into a cluster of oak trees. Mason thumbed through my wallet, took out my cash and pushed it into his pant pocket. He dropped my wallet, picked up Wendy's and started going through it. He plucked out her driver's license. "Wendy Adams. McComb, Mississippi. Remember that, Jeff."

Mason pulled out her money, handed the bills to Jeff and flipped her wallet back into the pile. He stooped down and grabbed the disk-shaped, black-and-white devices. "What do you suppose these are?"

Jeff shrugged and shook his head.

Mason pushed the button on black side, and I held my breath, fearing he'd push the one on the white side. The one used if a Tegen was in danger; the one that called other Tegens for help. Wendy and I didn't need any help, and I wanted to see where this little adventure out in the countryside was going, hopefully to my ring, before reinforcements showed up.

"I thought they might make a loud noise—something a woman would use to scare off a would-be assailant," Mason said, then opened the car door. "What are these?"

"Remotes," I answered. "They unlock a storage shed we have outside Alexandria."

"What's in the shed?"

"Furniture, albums, keepsakes, mostly Granny's stuff."

"We'll see," he said, closing the door and putting the gadgets on the limo's front passenger seat. Looking at the remainder of the items scattered on the ground, he asked Jeff, "Do you see anything else we need to be concerned about?"

"Nope."

"Burn the rest."

Wendy grasped onto my arm as Jeff took a small blowtorch out of the trunk. "He's going to burn our stuff."

I patted her arm. "As long as he's not pointing that thing at us, we don't have anything to worry about."

"But my make-up, comb, wallet."

"They can be replaced." I watched Jeff torch our belongings and wondered why they hadn't just thrown them into the bushes. In this deserted place, they would probably never be found.

When the pile had turned to ashes, Jeff climbed into the driver's seat, and we headed further into what appeared to be a more isolated territory, not even an occasional shack popped up in the horizon. The pavement ended and we continued on a dirt road riddled with potholes. Wendy and I jerked against the seatbelts that were preventing us from bouncing onto the floor. I noticed we were approaching an abandoned three-story building with large pieces of broken equipment surrounding it. A worn out sign hung lopsided from the flat roof of the structure. Only a few letters were readable, but I could make out the name "Cement." Seeing the coating of white dust on everything in sight, I assumed it used to be a cement plant. Three men with holstered rifles over their shoulders paced in front of the structure. One was Don, Mitt's friend I met at Sammy's. Mason's Mustang, Don's Corvette, and a black SUV were parked next to a concrete archway that I took to be the entrance. The limo stopped by it.

Mason walked toward the building and chatted with Don, but I couldn't make out what he was saying. Don walked away from Mason and talked to the other two men. Mason stepped closer to the structure, took out his cell phone and turned so he was facing the limo as Don climbed into his Corvette and drove away. Then I spotted two blowtorches leaning against the wall behind Mason.

"Should I get them out?" Jeff yelled.

Mason held up his hand, gesturing Jeff to wait.

"What's going on?" Wendy asked.

"No idea, but I sure would like to know who Mase is talking to."

"Let's get his phone," she said, gripping the door handle.

"No. Maybe my ring is around here, and I might need Mase to help me find it."

"You think he broke into the apartment?"

I shrugged. "Maybe. He wouldn't have brought us here and burned our purses if he wasn't up to no good."

"Yeah. He's kidnapped us. Why? Sara, are you keeping something from me?"

I held my index finger against my mouth. "Shhh. Remember, I'm Sally."

"Sorry. Forgot."

"Wendy, just pretend you don't have any special abilities until I figure out what's going on. Okay?"

"Does all this have to do with why you came to Baton Rouge? Is this part of your project?"

"Something like that."

"Tell me—" Wendy said, and immediately stopped when Mason opened the car door.

"Get out."

I stepped onto the ground, and Wendy climbed out right behind me. I held her hand and attempted to look scared. "Mase, why are you doing this?" I asked through trembling lips. "I thought you liked me."

He touched my cheek. "It's not that simple. You can't have friends on both sides of the fence."

"Is this because I dated Mitt? Wasn't he your friend?"

"Not Mitt. Crussett."

"Conner?" Wendy asked, wrinkling her nose. "This is because I'm dating Conner?"

Mason's eyes moved from Wendy to me. "Sure," he said with a crocked smile. "She doesn't know what you've been up to. Does she?"

"What are you talking about?" I asked.

"Inside," he said, nodding toward the entrance.

Mason and Jeff, armed and ready, walked behind us as we headed into the building. The interior was a large open space with rusty equipment, broken chutes and piles of white sand scattered along the cracked, cement floor. It appeared the facility had been abandoned for several decades. Two doors were in the center of the far wall. A scruffy-looking man with an unkempt beard and shaggy hair, dressed in a pair of grease-stained jeans and a t-shirt, stood next to one of the doors. He was the only guy at the facility who appeared to be out of touch with personal hygiene. Eyeing the area around him, I bit my lower lip when I saw another blowtorch hanging from a steel pole two feet from him, easily within arm's reach.

Wendy grabbed my hand. "Look...look," she whispered, a quaver in her voice, gesturing toward the blowtorch. "We need to do something now."

"No," I said firmly, lowering her pointed finger and assuming she hadn't noticed the two other blowtorches standing outside. "Let's see—"

Mason poked me in the shoulder with the barrel of his pistol. "No talking."

Attempting to calm Wendy down, I squeezed her hand and gently rubbed it. I wanted to know who had sent Mason to fetch us, and the location of my ring. If Wendy went berserk, I couldn't get the answers. Instead, we'd be surrounded by poisoned victims, and the danger of one of us going up in flames was clearly present.

Mason led us through the guarded open door. The room looked vaguely familiar. Gazing at the cement wall smeared with black stains and chains dangling from it, I remembered where I had seen it. A picture. Orson Thurman's mistress had been tortured in here. The black stains were the woman's dried blood. Outside, I thought Mason might've been talking to Thurman on his cell phone, now I figured it must have been someone else. Who?

"Frisk them," Mason ordered the scruffy-looking man.

As the man strolled toward Wendy, she yelled, "He's not touching me."

I glanced at her hands and saw the needles protruding from her fingers. "Wait!"

"Wait for what?" Mason asked. "Your boyfriend to rescue you?"

"I don't have a boyfriend," I replied, watching Wendy out of the corner of my eye and preparing myself if she made a sudden move toward the man standing four feet away from her.

Mason shook his head. "Was he that easy to forget?"

Knowing he was referring to Conner, I wanted to scream, "No," as sadness and regret crept through my body just thinking about him.

"Sally doesn't have a boyfriend," Wendy said.

"Yes, she does," Mason huffed. "He and his goons are trying to track down a strawberry-blonde wearing Sally's slacks and her pink sweater right now. A woman with Sally's build who, from a distance, could easily be mistaken for her."

Wendy's head swung toward me. "Your missing sweater," she said, gritting her teeth and narrowing her eyes. "Those creeps stole your sweater."

The scruffy-looking man raised his weapon and aimed it at Wendy. "Want me to shut her mouth?"

"Not yet. Frisk her."

Anticipating Wendy wouldn't allow the man to take her spider case, I braced for action. My eyes darted between Mason and Jeff. Jeff stood slightly behind Mason, closer to the doorway. He was also the one closest to the blowtorch and therefore the one I would have to deal with first.

The scruffy-looking man holstered his weapon and put his hands on Wendy's shoulders.

Her eyes bore into him, and her jaw tightened. "You touch my boobs and you're a dead man."

"Your cousin certainly is feisty," Mason said. "Threatening Steed as if she could take him. Delusional, but feisty." He eyed her up and down. "Steed, leave her boobs alone for now."

Mason moved closer to me and his eyes dropped to my chest. "You hiding anything there?"

I stared at him, thinking if he took my black cell phone, he'd probably put it aside while he questioned me. Then I would find a way to retrieve it before he had a chance to check out my contact numbers.

"The silent treatment," he said in a cocky tone. "I guess I'll have to check." He slid his hand over my body.

My hands began pulsing with the need to release the needles. It took all my willpower to keep them at bay while he continued pressing against the thin, soft clothing covering my body. I felt violated as his hand explored every curve.

"What do we have here?" he asked, unbuttoning my blouse. I stayed motionless as he stuck his hand in my bra and pulled out my cell phone. "You planning on making a call?" He paused and studied it. "Or have you already done that?"

I cringed when he clicked through the menu. "Muh. Don't recognize the area code. You called it this morning, before we went to lunch. No calls after that." He turned off my cell phone and dropped it in his sport coat pocket. "Wendy, hiding something in your bra?"

"No," she snapped.

"Want me to check?" Steed asked.

Mason nodded.

Wendy's lips clamped together and her face darkened with rage. I needed answers before she unleashed her hostility and left bodies in her wake. At the same time, I couldn't allow these thugs to destroy Tegen spiders. "Wendy, it'll be okay," I said, hoping Mason would put the container aside and not order anyone to burn it.

She squinted as she looked me. "But—"

"I know," I interrupted her. "Let's see how it goes."

"How it goes?" Mason asked, his eyes fixed on me. "What she got?" He turned to Steed. "Find out."

Wendy stared at me as she dropped her hands to her side.

Steed ran a dirty hand over her sweater. "She's got something," he said, reaching into her bra and pulling out the small ovoid black container. "What's this?" He gripped the pinhole-covered lid, prepared to raise it.

Mason flinched. "Don't! Spiders!"

"Huh?" Steed said, focusing on the container.

"I've heard about containers like that with pin-like holes, filled with deadly spiders. Sally has spiders in a cage."

Earlier, I had thought that whoever had been in the apartment's furnace room was an accomplice to the poisoned man found in my bedroom, now I wasn't sure. Since Mason knew about the spiders, either he was the accomplice or the accomplice survived long enough to give him a call.

Steed stretched out his hand, gingerly holding the container as far away from his body as possible.

"Don't drop it. Set it on the floor," Mason said, gesturing to the corner behind him.

Steed slowly moved to the spot and eased the ovoid container down. "Want me to burn it?"

"Yes," Mason said, and then he held up his hand in a stop motion. "No. No. I've got a better idea."

"What?" Jeff asked, standing a foot outside the door with fear gripping his features and his eyes fixed on the black container across the room. He must have retreated to the large open space when he heard Mason say, "spiders."

"We can use the spiders. They don't know who their master is. If we don't get answers, we can drop them on these two." He nodded toward Wendy and me. "No bloodshed. A clean kill."

"You think they're safe in the container?" Jeff asked.

Mason tilted his head toward Wendy. "She had it next to her chest. She'd be dead if those spiders could penetrate that container."

Wendy turned toward me so Mason couldn't see her face. She grinned and bounced her eyebrows. She mimicked exactly what I was thinking, "We'd love to feel spiders crawling over our bodies." Though, I surmised flames from the blowtorches wouldn't be far behind the spiders being released since I doubted Mason would rely on pesticides to deal with the deadly arachnids after the poisonous venom had been injected.

"Do you also have spiders with you?" he asked me as he slowly moved his hands over my hips and down my legs. Had I suspected before Mason picked us up that he wanted more than a lunch date, a sheath with a knife tucked inside would be strapped to my calf. But then, I'd have a harder time denying I had anything to do with Greg's stabbing.

"You're clean," Mason announced, his face six inches from mine. "Can I get you something to drink?"

"Sauvignon Blanc," I said with a lopsided smile.

"No booze. Only water."

"Get me a bottle," Wendy demanded.

Mason looked at her. "Feisty Wendy." He turned around. "Steed, get a couple of bottles." As Steed left the room, he continued, "Might as well make our guests comfortable before we get started. Have a seat." He motioned toward a row of folding chairs lined against the side wall.

When Wendy and I were seated, Mason stepped out of the room and chatted with Jeff.

"I don't know anything about Conner's business," Wendy said, "and why does he think you're his girlfriend?"

I shook my head. "Don't have a clue."

"What do you know about Mason? Why does he hate Conner?"

Suspecting she wouldn't believe me if I played dumb about everything, I said, "He's involved in some kind of illegal activity."

"Yeah, he kidnapped us. What else?"

"I think drugs."

"Drugs? Heroin—stuff like that?"

I shrugged. "Possibly."

"I get it now. He's worried Conner is going to turn him into the police. That must be why Conner has bodyguards. I wonder why he hasn't done it yet."

"Maybe he needs more evidence," I lied, keeping my face from showing any emotion as I hid the urge to laugh.

Steed strode through the doorway. "Here," he said, handing Wendy and me each a bottle of water.

She removed the cap and took a big gulp before I could stop her. "It could be drugged."

"Huh?" she said. "But I'm still thirsty."

I slowly twisted the cap on my bottle and heard a whooshing sound and a snap from the plastic band separating, signs it hadn't been previously opened. "This one is okay," I said, handing her the bottle. I noticed Steed's eyes narrowing, which made me surmise the bottle he had given her probably had been drugged. I hoped she hadn't consumed enough to affect her.

"Do you want to share?" she asked.

"No. Go ahead. I'm fine." I kept an eye on Steed, trying to come up with a reason why Mason would want Wendy drugged. There was a slim chance that bottle hadn't been drugged, but I never heard a snapping sound when she opened it.

Jeff's voice floated through the doorway, "I still think it was Monique."

"Let's find out," Mason said, strolling back into the room along with Jeff. Both men glanced at the spider container on the floor as they headed to the metal chairs. "Steed." He tilted his head sideways toward the door, and Steed trudged out of the room, closing the door behind him.

"I don't feel well," Wendy said, slumping. She began sliding out of her chair.

I leaned over and held her awkwardly so she wouldn't land on the floor. "What did you give her?" I snapped at Mason. Since Wendy was a Tegen, she wouldn't be out long, but the fact Mason had drugged her, irritated me.

"It'll put her to sleep for a while. No lasting effect. You can't keep holding onto her like that. She'll be okay on the floor." With Jeff's help, they laid her on the floor. Mason lifted her hand, gripped her ring and tried to remove it.

"What are you doing?"

"I want her ring," he said, pouring water over it. He grabbed the ring again. "If it doesn't come off this time, your cousin is going to be missing a finger."

There was no way I would allow him to chop off one of her fingers, but I decided not to bring out my needles until he brought out a knife. Curious about why he wanted her ring since he probably already had mine, I asked, "Why do you want it?"

"It's like yours."

"So?"

"Apparently, no one else can wear your ring. We want to know if all black rings like that have something strange about them. We're having yours analyzed. You practice witchcraft or something like that?"

"No," I said, shaking my head and thinking what a bizarre twist someone has attributed to my ring. Though, I was grateful they were searching along a strange path, far from the truth.

Twirling around her ring, he forced it off her and slipped it on his little finger. "Weird." Mason yanked it off and rubbed his finger. "Awful sensation. What's with these black rings? Another one to be analyzed." He dropped it in his sport coat pocket. "Before feisty Wendy joins us again, let's begin." He pulled a chair in front of me and sat down so close our knees were touching.

Jeff stood by the door with his hand under his jacket, and I assumed he held the handle of his pistol, a worthless weapon against Tegens.

"How long have you been working for Crussett?" Mason asked.

"I don't work for him."

"Right? Then how do you know him?"

"He's dating Wendy," I said, eyeing her stirring on the floor.

"No. That's not it. Crussett seldom stays overnight when he comes to town, but he's been here four nights. We're convinced it's because of you. Are you a former girlfriend? As far as we know, he hasn't seriously dated anyone since his girlfriend was murdered."

"Who's we? You, your dad and brother? Orson Thurman?"

"You haven't figured it out yet?"

"Figured what out?"

"Who's running the show."

Wendy jerked around and murmured, "Wha...what happened?"

"You must not have drank very much of it," Mason said, looking down at her.

She held onto the rim of the chair, staggered to her feet, and snarled, "You drugged me."

I clasped my hand around her forearm and pulled her down into the chair. "You're okay. Wait for your strength to return."

Her eyes met mine. "How long do I have to be good?"

"Not long," I said.

"You planning to take on Jeff and me?" Mason asked with an amused expression.

She nodded.

"Can we finish asking our questions first?" he said in mocking tone.

She glared at him. "As long as you can make it quick."

Mason looked at Jeff, a brief smile flickering across his lips. "Ready to take on feisty Wendy?"

"I think I can handle the little lady."

"Then let's get these questions out of the way. Sally, if Crussett isn't here because of you, why's he here?

"What's he talking about?" Wendy asked, scrunching her face in confusion.

"Mase is under some kind of delusion that Conner and I are somehow involved."

"Why do you think that?" she asked Mason while she rubbed her hands together.

"Isn't it—" he began.

Wendy interrupted him. "My ring! Where's my ring?" She stared at her hand.

"Mase has it in his pocket," I said.

She pressed her lips together and scowled at me. "You let him take my ring?"

"Sally didn't have a choice," Mason explained.

"Don't worry," I said, patting her arm. "We'll get it back."

Mason rolled his eyes. "Jeff, it sounds like we'll have to defend ourselves against both ladies."

Jeff grinned. "Whatever."

"Let's move on," Mason said, leaning toward me and placing his hand on my knee. "Since you arrived in our fair city, a valued associate has gone missing, an employee has been stabbed, Mitt has been killed and a security guard shot to death with his own gun. Did you do all that by yourself?"

"Mase, I haven't the foggiest idea what you are talking about. Do I look like a skilled assailant?"

"Looks can be deceiving. I can see we're not getting anywhere. Maybe a little forceful persuasion will help loosen your tongue." He turned to Jeff. "Get Steed."

"Mase, they have a lead on Monique," Jeff said. "Aren't you going to wait and see how that goes?"

"No. My orders were to get answers."

Wendy nudged my arm. "Time?"

As I held up my index finger, a burst of gunfire, loud banging and clanging sounds erupted from outside the building.

30

THE RESCUE

The door flew open. "You want me to stay here or go find out what's going on?" Steed asked.

"It's got to be Crussett," Mason said. "Go check it out." He stayed by the doorway and watched Steed rushing toward the entrance as the gunfire continued off in the distance. Then Mason turned back to Wendy and me. "Ladies, it sounds like a rescue team has arrived, but they won't find you. Jeff, keep an eye on them while I unlock the passageway."

"You're not leaving here with my ring," Wendy shouted.

"Feisty Wendy, you'll get an opportunity to fight for it later."

Wendy leapt to her feet and rushed to the doorway, blocking Mason.

"Move," he said, hitting her with the back of his hand.

There was no way I could prevent her from going after her ring nor did I want to. I'd be doing the same thing if he had my ring. My black cell phone suddenly popped into my head. It was also in his pocket. I jumped up and charged toward Mason while Wendy struggled with him.

"Aaah…What other weapon have you got?" he asked Wendy, grabbing her hands.

Though I couldn't see a scrape mark on Mason, she had scratched him someplace. I stuck my hand in his pocket and fished out my cell phone and Wendy's ring. "I've got them," I said, holding the items up so Wendy could see her ring.

"Jeff," Mason yelled. "Do something."

Jeff didn't budge. He stood motionless and observed Mason attempting to fight off a skilled opponent. I also watched feeling pleased how well Wendy was doing against the man who had abducted us. Of course, the poisonous venom running through his veins gave her a definite advantage.

My attention turned to Jeff and I wondered if he worked for Conner since he hadn't made a move to assist Mason. While I waited for Mason to collapse, I pushed on my cell phone and saw I had one missed message. I stepped away from the fight and listened to Father, anger evident in his voice. His message said, "Sara, why didn't you answer your cell phone? Get to your apartment with Wendy as soon as you can."

I stared at the cell phone, wondering if Father would accept the excuse that I couldn't answer it because Mason had taken it. Did he expect me to use my Tegen ability if someone threatened to take my cell phone? Even though it wasn't in my possession, it was close by all the time, and I never would have left the abandoned cement plant without it. Would Father agree with how I had handled the situation? I knew a punishment was already waiting for me when I got back to his house since I didn't immediately notify him about Wendy's confession. Would not having my cell phone accessible at all times be grounds for another punishment? I cringed as I wondered what was in store for me, and I'd find out real soon if didn't locate my ring and had to go home.

A loud thud echoed through the room. I looked over my shoulder and saw Mason's body stretched out on the floor in front of Wendy, a big smile on her face.

"That's what happens when someone tries to swipe my ring," she declared, taking it from me and easing it onto her finger. Gazing at the ring, she said, "I've missed you." Wendy looked at Jeff. "You're next."

"I think he works for Conner," I said, moving toward Jeff.

"Really?" she asked.

His eyes darted between Wendy and me, but he didn't utter a word. He knelt down beside Wendy's victim, reached under Mason's sport coat and took his pistol.

Heavy footfalls pounded across the cement floor. A second later, Conner along with two unfamiliar men rushed through the door. He wrapped his arms around me. "Are you okay?"

"Yes," I nodded.

"What's going on?" Wendy glared at him. "Mason was right. You and...Sss." She stopped. I guessed she was about to say, "Sara."

Fearing her next move, I pushed Conner away and leapt between them just as she charged toward him with her fingers outstretched. "Noooo!" I yelled, and punched her in the jaw as hard as I could, knocking her over Mason's body and into the chairs. They crashed to the ground with her on top of them.

"Boy, can you throw a punch," Conner said with a shocked look on his face.

I waved my hand toward the door. "Please, leave. Let me handle Wendy alone."

"I'm not leaving you here," he said.

"You don't have to leave the facility, just go while I deal with Wendy." I took his hand and ushered him out of the room as his men followed, including Jeff.

Conner pulled a pistol out from under his suit coat. "Take this," he said, handing it to me. "Use it on Mason if he wakes up and gives you any trouble."

"Thanks." I closed the door behind him while Wendy rose to her feet.

"How long has this been going on?" she hissed. "Is that why he always wanted you to go out with us?"

I contemplated telling her the truth, but seeing the rage in her blue eyes, I decided against it. If she knew, I suspected she wouldn't try to keep my true identity a secret from Conner. She'd probably be anxious to spill it to him the first opportunity she got. "Nothing is going on. I don't even know the man. I've only talked to him in the apartment, and you've been there the whole time. Mitt told me that I bore a strong resemblance to Conner's girlfriend who was murdered. That's probably the reason he shows me some attention. Nothing more."

"Do you think he was dating me just so he could see you?"

I shrugged. "Don't know, but I doubt he'd continue taking you out if he wasn't interested in you. He never asked me out."

"Yes, he has. He's asked you to go out with us."

"He hasn't asked me out on a date—just him and me. You've always been in the picture."

"Then why did he hug you when he got here and not me?"

I shrugged again. "Maybe he saw me first. He probably thinks we're close so, of course, he'd be concerned about your friends and relatives."

"We are close," she said, giving me a hug. "You really think that's why he acted that way?"

"Yes, I do." I hated lying to her, but I'd do whatever it took to keep Conner safe from her venom. Wondering how I could tell Conner to give his attention to Wendy without her overhearing me, I caught the sight of Mason's body on the floor. "What are we going to do about him?"

"Shoot him," Wendy said. "You have the gun Conner gave you."

"Okay. Stand behind me so you don't get splattered with his blood."

"Before you pull the trigger and bring someone running in here, can I drop a spider on him, and have a little taste?"

I also wanted some *venotrolia*. "Sure, but only one spider. We have to be able to find it afterwards since we don't have our disks."

She nodded, picked up her container in the corner of the room and brought it over to Mason. Carefully, she raised the lid and picked up one spider. Holding it cradled in her hand, she closed the container and placed the spider on Mason's neck. We both eyed the arachnid while it scurried under Mason's chin.

I lost sight of it when it crawled up by Mason's ear. "Can you see it?" I asked, anxiously.

She dropped to her knees, "Yeah. Yeah. I can see it. I also see two red dots." Wendy went to retrieve the spider and it scurried into Mason's hair. "Oh, great. Hold this," she said, handing me her container. She rolled over the body. "See it!" Running her fingers through his hair, she caught the spider and let it crawl up her arm. "That feels so good."

"We need to hurry before someone comes to check on us," I said, enveloping the loose spider in my hand and gently easing it back into the container. "Do you have anything sharp?"

"A safety pin," Wendy said, removing one from the bottom of her slacks. "I stepped on the hem, snagged a few threads before we left the apartment and this was my quick fix." She gouged into the side of his neck, hitting a major vein, and blood oozed from his body. She stuck her finger into the red liquid, smelled it and licked it off. "Boy does that taste good."

I hunkered down beside her, and we took turns sucking up the blood, making sure none of it landed on our clothing. While I waited for my next turn, I fished through Mason's pockets and found his cell phone. I stuck it in my bra, and then consumed more *venotrolia*. We both jumped up when we heard the shuffling of feet heading our direction. I grabbed a bottle of water and took a big gulp. "Here," I said, handing it to her. "Drink some water so they can't smell his blood on our breath."

After she downed the rest of the bottle, I stood and aimed the weapon at Mason's neck near the spot where we had enjoyed our beverage. "Get behind me." She followed my instruction and I pulled the trigger a few seconds before the door opened. Seeing Conner, Jeff and another man, I turned and wrapped my arms around Wendy so he couldn't single me out. "I had no choice," I said, quivering my voice. "Mason grabbed Wendy and put his hands around her neck. I thought he was going to choke her to death. I hit him with the gun, and then he came after me. I had to shoot him." I buried my face in Wendy's hair. "It was awful. Look at all the blood."

She stroked my hair. "You saved me," she said, going along with my excuse for plugging Mason.

"You did the right thing," Conner said, moving toward Wendy and me. "Jeff, Sam get rid of the body.

I noticed Jeff and Sam were wearing thick rubber gloves. Earlier, both men were nicely attired in dress shirts, ties, and sport coats. Now, they wore blood-and dirt-stained slacks and shirts with rolled up sleeves. Their shoes appeared to be covered with blood-speckled mud. Conner still looked immaculate; his suit didn't show any signs he had been doing any physical labor.

Conner put his arm around Wendy's back and mine. I held her hands like I needed her comfort. "I'll get these two settled in the car," he said, leading us out of the room.

A warm, soothing surge ran through my veins when I touched her ring and my lips slightly trembled as I worried about my missing priceless possession. If I didn't find it in a couple of days, I would have to leave Baton Rouge before I completed my project of destroying the Thurman drug business.

Without any warning, everything in front of me became hazy, a murky blur of black shadows with random streams of blurry light. I briefly closed my eyes in an attempt to clear my vision. Wendy swayed away from me.

"Wendy, can you walk?" Conner asked, releasing me as he caught her before she sank to the cement floor. "Kirk, need some help here."

"What's wrong with Wendy" was the last thought that swept through my mind before everything around me dissolved into a black hole.

31

UNEXPECTED PICTURES

Slowly opening my eyes, I saw Conner's face and wondered if I was dreaming. Seeing his glowing eyes and gorgeous smile was something I dreamt about often.

"How are you feeling?" he asked, caressing my cheek.

Listening to the hum of an engine, I glanced around and saw the light gray leather upholstered car seats and the back of the head and shoulders of the driver. "What happened?" I asked, realizing my head was lying on Conner's lap.

"You and Wendy drank water laced with sleeping powder from a bottle." He moved his arm under my back and raised my head, prepared to kiss me. My arms slid around his neck of their own accord, something they had been aching to do since I saw him at Sammy's. He kissed me passionately. My heartbeat plunged into a chaotic rhythm. His lips inched down my chin to my neck, kissing me as they moved. My body tensed with anticipation. My fingers raked through his hair as his cologne wafted through the air I breathed. I found his powerful, sexy scent intoxicating and I wanted nothing more than to feel his body next to mine.

An unwanted thought sprang into my mind—Wendy's revenge if she spotted us in each other's arms. His safety trumped my desire. I pushed away from his embrace. "Wendy. Where's Wendy?" I asked, gasping for air.

He pulled me back into his arms. "In the other car. I have a man watching over her. Relax, she's safe," Conner said, and I thought, but you're not. The image of her charging after him the instant her anger flared up flashed through my mind. Had I not been there, Conner would've been her next victim. I suspected if she saw the slightest indication he wasn't interested in her, she would be quickly consumed by rage.

Conner rubbed my shoulder. "Are you okay?"

"Yeah. I was just thinking about Wendy. Conner, she can be dangerous. Never be in the same room with her."

A puzzled expression crept across his face. "Don't tell me you're jealous?"

"No. No. That's not it."

"I heard how she took on Mason. I think I can handle myself against her, but if it will make you happy, I'll make sure one of my men is by my side when I'm around her."

"Conner," I said, gazing into his shimmering light brown eyes. "Wendy has spiders, and she won't hesitate using them on anyone who crosses her path."

"The same type of spiders that killed Caden and some of my men?"

"Who?" I replied, tilting my head and squinting. Sally wouldn't know about that, but Sara would. Caden was Conner's 23-year-old nephew who shot me. The poisonous venom had entered his blood stream right before the bullet pierced through my body. Since I was a Tegen, I survived. He didn't.

"Have it your way." He picked up something on the ledge below the rear window. "Is this yours?" he said, showing me the black-and-white disk Mason had confiscated before he gave the order to burn my purse along with Wendy's. "It's either mine or Wendy's." After Conner handed it to me, I looked along the edge of the gadget and saw my initials, SA, which stood for Sara Alston. "It's mine. Did you push either of the buttons?" I asked, hoping he hadn't sent out the signal that I was in trouble.

He shook his head. "No. I knew someone who had a gadget just like that," he said, pulling me closer to him, adjusting our bodies so I was seated on his lap. He held me tight and kissed me, sending desire raging through me again. Remembering the role I was playing as Sally Jablon, I forced myself to back away from him. "Conner, this has to stop. I'm attracted to you, but I don't know anything about you."

A shadow of a smile crossed his lips. "Sure. By the way Sally," he said, emphasizing "Sally," "one of your blue contact lenses has fallen out. Why don't you take the other one out so I can see those gorgeous deep brown eyes?"

I covered my eyes with my hand as I collected my thoughts and tried to figure out how to respond.

"I've had a team re-examining the medical records of the woman I buried," Conner said. "They're convinced she's Sara Jones. But I don't believe I'd be fortunate enough to run into another woman who was a perfect match for her. On top of your appearance, your smell, touch, the way your body moves, everything about you says Sara." Conner held me tight against his chest. "Sweetheart, I don't care what name you want to be called. I'll always love you. My biggest regret in life was taking you to that warehouse."

My eyes became moist as I remembered him cradling my head and kissing me "Good-bye" after I was declared dead. The hardest thing I've ever had to do was remain motionless as I felt his tears on my cheek. As much as I wanted to, I couldn't tell him what I had become. I inhaled deeply and cleared my throat. "Conner, you've mistaken me for someone else. I'm not this Sara you're talking about. And, if you truly believed I was the only one who was a perfect match for her, then how come you followed another woman because she was wearing my clothes?" I touched his cheek. "Don't you see, probably a lot of women remind you of the one you buried."

"No," he said, gazing into my eyes. "I knew the woman wearing your pink sweater, a sweater you wore a few days earlier, wasn't you, but I wanted information. I had you well protected so I allowed Mason to assume he had successfully guided us astray."

"What information did you want?" I asked as I became aware that my arm was still around his neck and I had no intention of moving it.

"Maybe the same information Sally Jablon wants."

"And what would that be?"

"Who Mason's boss is."

"Why would I be interested in that?"

"Sally. It still is Sally, right?" he said with cocked eyebrows.

"Yes, Mr. Crussett, my name is Sally."

"Sally, I don't have a clue what you're up to. Sally Jablon's prior employment as a bank teller and her current job as caregiver to her aging grandmother, that type of resume doesn't provide the skills in which you've demonstrated proficiency."

"And what are those skills?"

"The use of weapons. Specifically, knives and guns. Picking locks. Breaking in unseen. Expert at climbing walls and trees without being heard. Qualities I look for when hiring for certain positions. I can understand why Mitt thought you worked for me."

"The person you're describing can't be that good if you were able to keep tabs on her."

"It took two of my best men to keep up with you."

"Conner, you've got the wrong person. I don't know how to do those things."

"That is what I used to believe about you," he said, pulling out his cell phone, "until I saw you in action." He tapped his index finger on his phone numerous times. "Here." Conner showed me his screen, and I saw a video of myself climbing over Thurman's wall and ascending a tree. The video flickered several times, and then came the scene of me shooting a security guard.

"That woman wearing a ski mask isn't me."

"Oh, here." He clicked on another video. It showed me getting out of the Dodge and putting on a ski mask. The vehicle's license plate was clearly visible.

"Those videos don't show I have all the skills you rattled off."

"My fault. I didn't request my men to film you on your earlier exploits, but I do have a few good pictures," he said, tapping on his phone again. He held it in front of my face and flipped to an image of me next to Mitt's body behind Monique's house, then to one showing me rummaging through Mitt's desk. "I love the mischievous expression on your face on this one. I'm thinking about having it cropped and blown up. It would make a great addition to the other pictures I have of you hanging around my house." He went to the next picture. It showed me standing by the fence at the side of Buckley's warehouse.

I briefly closed my eyes. "I've seen enough. Besides the one you want to frame, what are you planning to do with the other pictures?"

"They're strictly for my pleasure. No one else will have access to them. If you were anyone else, I'd use them to get information." His lips softly kissed mine. "You never have to fear I'd ever consider using any method or force again to get information out of you. Never."

My mind was spinning. I had no defense against his proof. As I mulled over how to respond, I looked out the car window and recognized the buildings and knew we were close to my apartment.

He brushed a strand of hair behind my ear. "Sally, have you ever thought about dying your hair brown, chocolate brown?"

"Did your girlfriend have chocolate brown hair?" I asked, feigning ignorance. That was my natural hair color. I only dyed it to get Mitt's attention.

"Yes. It went with her brown eyes. But since you now have one brown eye and one blue eye, you'd look good in a wide range of hair colors."

A smile flashed across my face. I had already completely forgotten about the missing contact lens.

The Escalade pulled over to the curb. "Can I come up?" Conner asked.

"No. I don't want you anywhere around Wendy. Please, stay away from her."

"The spiders?"

I nodded as I saw another Escalade stopping in front of us. "Go now. I'll call you later," I said, sliding off his lap.

He wrapped his arms around me and kissed me without a word of protest spewing out of my mouth. "Promise?"

"Yes."

Conner's driver opened the back car door, and I slipped out, grateful his vehicle had heavily tinted windows. I stood by the apartment stoop and watched Conner's Escalade drive away just as Wendy emerged from the other vehicle.

"Was Conner with you?"

Thinking someone might have mentioned that Conner was in the other Escalade, I replied, "He was in the front seat. I was sound asleep in the backseat. He told me we drank water laced with sleeping powder."

"That's exactly what Jeff told me. I didn't even think about it when we each took a sip from that water bottle. I had emptied the good one earlier. Boy did that knock me out."

I noticed the Escalade make a u-turn and park across the street. Then I cringed when I spotted Kendall leaning on the corner of a building right behind it.

32

TEGEN ENFORCER'S VISIT

"What is it?" Wendy asked, looking at the other side of the street.

Not wanting her to see Kendall, I pointed to the Cadillac. "The Escalade that brought you here is parked right there. Are they keeping track of you?"

"Yeah," she said, beaming. Then she turned, and we headed toward the apartment building entrance. "Jeff said someone's been parked in that spot since Thursday. You know, the first time I went out with Conner. Well, they're not there all the time, only when we're in the apartment. A couple of guys follow us whenever we leave here. Isn't that sweet? Conner wants to make sure we're not mugged or anything."

"Jeff told you that?" I asked, pushing the elevator button.

"Not in that many words, but I got the drift. Did you know Conner caught me when I collapsed on the way to the car?"

"Yes, I saw. Right before everything went blurry."

As we stepped into the elevator, Wendy patted my arm. "Oh, I'm sorry. You must have landed on that hard cement floor." She hugged me. "You are the best friend I've had since I transitioned. Boy am I glad you stopped me from scratching Conner." She squeezed my shoulders. "Best friend."

When we got off on the fifth floor, I moved to the trash can standing near the elevator, looked in it and pulled out two wire hangers.

"If you needed hangers, you should have said. There's a whole bunch of empty hangers in my closet."

"That's not what these are for," I said, walking beside her as we headed toward the apartment.

"Then what?"

"Remember, we have no keys."

"Right. Do you want me to climb out that window at the end of the hall," she said, pointing at it, "and see if one of the apartment windows are opened?"

"No. I think I can manage with this." I held up one of the wire hangers.

Wendy's brow furrowed. "Huh?"

I unwound the end of the wire and straightened out the hanger. "You'll see." Bending down, I went to work on picking the lock. Two minutes later, we entered the apartment.

"When did you learn to do that?"

"Right after I became a Tegen."

"Can you teach me?"

"Sure," I said, doubting there would ever be an opportunity. Gazing at her, I feared the call I had to make to Father might be about her. Before, I placed that dreaded call I decided to spend a few minutes talking to Wendy. *Am I just stalling?* I washed my hands and opened the fridge. "Want a Coke?"

She nodded and sat down at the table. "Today was weird," she said, between sips, "but it was a little fun. Lunch, being kidnapped, and rescued by Conner. I'm still mad about my purse and the stuff in it." She pulled her black-and-white circular-shaped gadget out of her pocket. "At least Jeff gave me back my device. That isn't something I can buy at the store. You were so cool through the whole kidnapping thing. I wanted to take care of Mason right away, but then Jeff would've told Conner about it. Huh?"

"Yes. That isn't anything he'd keep from his boss." I took another swig of Coke. "Wendy, you always have to remember you can't use your poison unless you are in imminent danger, and then you can't leave any witnesses."

"They had a blowtorch. That's imminent danger."

"They never threatened us with it."

"But I thought they might use it."

"*Might* doesn't cut it."

"Well, anyway, it's over." She drained the rest of her bottle. "After I get cleaned up, I'm going to call Conner, see if he wants to come over and watch another movie."

"I'm beat. I think I'll crawl into bed and read," I said, but intended to call Father as soon as I got out of the shower.

"You slept pretty good last time Conner and I watched a movie. I'll make sure not to have the volume up too high."

While I waited for Wendy to finish showering, a siren blared off in the distance. The throbbing noise continued getting louder, and louder, and then it sounded like it stopped nearby. Wondering if it had been called for someone in the apartment building, I looked out the window and saw the ambulance's flashing light five stories below.

"Your turn," Wendy said, stepping out of the bathroom.

I crossed the living room and went into my bedroom to grab my robe when my black cell phone rang. Suspecting it was Father with angry words, I grabbed it off the table and glanced at the caller ID. "Father, I'm sorry I didn't answer earlier, but—"

He interrupted, "We'll talk about that later. I'm calling to tell you to expect a visitor soon."

"Who?"

"We have enough evidence."

"Wendy?"

"Possibly three victims."

"Three? It was my spiders that killed the guy in my apartment. And she was trying to help me when Mitt got scratched. She can't be blamed for those!"

"She isn't. The three are innocent victims."

"Hank and his girlfriend. Who's the third?"

Before he could answer, the doorbell buzzed. "Your doorbell?"

"Yes."

"You need to answer it. We'll talk later."

Wendy peeked out her bedroom door with a towel draped over her shoulders. "You getting that?"

"Yeah." I laid my phone on the table as the doorbell buzzed again.

"Maybe it's Conner. I'll hurry and dress." She closed her door.

I knew it wasn't him as I turned the doorknob. Fear and sadness rippled through my body when I found myself staring at Kendall's taut face and his cold, black piercing eyes. Just like the time he had passed me in the downstairs hallway, he didn't give even the slightest indication that he recognized me. Next to him stood a tall, broad-shouldered woman with long black hair tied behind her head. Her eyes had the same quality as Kendall's—cold and piercing. Kendall and the woman were dressed in sage green scrubs. Without being invited, they strode into the apartment, pulling a gurney behind them. The woman went and stood in front of the window.

"Can I help you?" I asked, my voice quivering.

"We're here to see Wendy Adams," Kendall said in a firm, formal tone.

I assumed the Tegen enforcer standing in my living room was the visitor Father told me to expect. Gazing at Kendall's sinister-looking face, I had the urge to warn Wendy, but I couldn't go against Tegen rules. As my Tegen duty, I knocked on her door, dreading each tap.

"Tell Conner I'll be out in a minute," she yelled, cheerfully, from behind the closed door.

"Wendy, it isn't Conner," I said, choking on each word.

"Brett?"

"No."

"Thank goodness. Just give me a minute."

"She'll be out soon," I said, my voice just above a whisper as my eyes filled with water. "Excuse me." I headed into my bedroom to get some tissues and had the urge to shut my door so I couldn't witness the event about to unfold. If I displayed that type of cowardly behavior, I knew Father would hear about it. I dabbed my eyes with a tissue and marched back into the living room. Biting my lower lip, I waited for the impending scene. Kendall and the woman stood stoic, their eyes fixed on Wendy's door.

As her door opened, my hands trembled. I flinched and felt a sickening sensation in my stomach. I caught a glimpse of a smile on Wendy's face that immediately vanished when she saw the woman standing by the window. "No!" she screamed and backed up into her room. In a split second, Kendall was there, blocking her from retreating.

Wendy charged to the window. The woman stretched out her arms, preventing her from escaping through it. Wendy swung around. She pushed the gurney away, looped around it and rushed toward the apartment door. Kendall got there first. Panic covered her face as her head moved back-and-forth, searching for an escape route. She started to push the gurney in the opposite direction to clear a path to my room. Kendall gripped its bottom rail. Wendy gritted her teeth, firmly grasped the side of the gurney and used all her strength to try to get it to move, but she was no match to the huge, muscular Tegen enforcer.

"No!" She ran to me and threw her arms around me waist. "Tell them…tell them it wasn't my fault."

I stood frozen in place. Wendy clung to me so hard I found it difficult to breathe. Kendall pulled a syringe from his pocket and plunged it into her neck.

"Ow," she moaned. "I'll be good. I promise."

"No second chances," the woman said, her voice raspy and cold.

I didn't budge as Wendy's arms became limp around me, and she sank to the floor.

Kendall lifted her to the gurney and secured the straps over her body. No one spoke. The woman opened the door. They wheeled Wendy out and shut the door behind them.

Staring at the closed door, I felt numb and knew I'd never see Wendy again and neither would anyone else. The image of her mother sprang into my mind, and I thought of my own mother. How she would've mourned if I had died before her. Poor Wendy's mother wouldn't even know what had happened to her precious daughter. Wendy would be missing without a trace, just like Hank. Tears welled in my eyes as I pictured Wendy's mom hanging up posters everywhere with a photo of her missing daughter and a phone number for people to call if they've seen her.

Someone knocked on my door, but my legs refused to take me to it as I feared Kendall had returned. Though I hadn't broken the same rule Wendy did, I had broken a Tegen rule by not telling anyone she was at my apartment immediately after her confession, and a punishment was waiting for me. Will Kendall also deliver that punishment? The knocking continued, and my eyes remained focused on the door.

33

A STRANGE ALLIANCE

The knocking on my door turned into pounding, I wanted to scream, "Go away," but I couldn't utter a sound. The doorknob jerked and the door flew open. In walked a man I recognized. He had accompanied Conner into the room at the abandoned cement plant, the place where Wendy and I had been held just a few hours earlier.

"You okay?" he asked, sounding breathless, as he flipped out his cell phone.

I shook my head.

He punched in a number. "She's here, but she doesn't look so good… No, don't see any blood… No bruises…Pale…okay." He put away his cell phone and took my arm. "Mr. Crussett will be here soon." He guided me to the couch.

The vision of Wendy's mother withering away while she searched for her daughter kept running through mind. Tears drizzled down my cheeks. There was no way I could lessen the pain the woman would suffer when she learned Wendy was missing. If she asked me about Wendy, I'd have to lie to her. Suddenly, the horrified expression on Wendy's face when she ran to me for protection flashed into my mind. The same expression appeared on Mandy's face after Kendall dropped a spider on her chest. Terrified faces of other victims began floating around me. I sensed I had drifted into a dark place, and I couldn't move a muscle or hear a sound as more images invaded my head.

Through the fog, I heard, "Sara, talk to me."

My eyes flickered and slowly Conner's face came into focus replacing all the others, and I felt his hands on my shoulders jerking me back and forth.

"My name's Sally," I mumbled.

He pulled me into his arms. "Okay, Sally. Can you talk about what happened?"

"Not now." I leaned my head against his chest.

"Do you want me to track down the ambulance that took Wendy?"

I shook my head. "No."

He brushed my hair away from my face. "Kirk, get a glass of water." Conner gently kissed my forehead. After the man handed it to Conner, he held it against my mouth. "Drink."

I took a sip, and then I wrapped my fingers around the cold glass and downed the liquid in two large gulps.

"Feeling better?"

I nodded.

"Can you answer one question for me?"

I nodded again.

"Was Wendy bitten by one of her spiders and are any loose in your apartment?"

I raised two fingers. "That's two questions. Which one do you want me to answer?"

Conner's head moved back and forth like he was checking the apartment. "The second one?"

"There aren't any spiders wandering freely around the apartment. They're all contained." I inhaled deeply, relieved Wendy was gone; at the same time I didn't want her to receive the ultimate punishment. Maybe if she would've had more help learning how to deal with her emotions, the whole problem could have been prevented. Poor Wendy.

"Have you had anything to eat since you got back?"

"No, but I don't feel hungry."

"How about a pizza?" Conner asked, ignoring what I had just said.

Seeing the concerned look in his light brown eyes, I said, "Okay, but I want to shower first."

"Can I stay here while you do that?"

"I need a little alone time." I wanted to talk to Father without him being within earshot.

Conner didn't push it, instead he kissed my cheek and rose from the couch. "I'll be back in an hour. Will that give you enough alone time?"

I gave him a small smile. "Yes."

As soon as he walked out the door, I rubbed my forehead and gathered my thoughts. What am I doing? I had to pretend I died so he wouldn't come looking for me, but I never expected Conner would show up in Baton Rouge when I planned my project. I had no idea he was having business problems in this city. What kind of a mess had I stumbled into? Mulling it over, I headed to the bathroom.

Fifteen minutes later, I was showered and on the phone talking to Father.

"Who's the third victim?" I asked.

"Sara, of the three potential victims, only one has currently been confirmed. That was enough to have her picked up. We should have the test results on the other two sometime tomorrow."

"Maybe she's not responsible for the other two. She said she didn't know what she was doing when she poisoned Hank. I thought Dr. Driggs was going to see her, and verify if that was the case. Can't he do that?" I asked, unable to understand why I was defending her. She would have killed Conner, but I couldn't get the look on her face out of my mind as she clung to me to help her. I'd probably have a similar expression if Kendall came for me.

"Sara, the confirmed victim is Merilee Kent."

"Oh," I said, absorbing the impact of his statement. Hank might have been an accident, Merilee wasn't.

"Are you handling this okay?" he asked, concern evident in his tone.

"It might take me some time to get over the terrified look on her face, but her mood swings seemed to be getting worse. Today I had to punch her so she couldn't scratch Conner," I said, and then filled him in on the day's events.

"What do you want to do about Conner?"

"I don't know. Part of me desperately wants him, and part of me wants him out of my life forever. And then, there's Brett. What am I going to do?"

"My darling girl, I can't make that decision for you, but never forget I'll always be on your side. Does Brett know Conner is in Baton Rouge?"

"I haven't told him. Do you think he'd go after Conner?"

"Absolutely not. That's one thing you don't need to worry about. Brett's been a Tegen a long time. He knows the rules well. He'd never put himself in a situation where an enforcer would be hunting him down."

"So, he'd be mad and probably never want to see me again."

"I didn't say that. That's something he'll have to work out."

"Does he know Wendy was picked up?"

"Not yet. I tried calling him earlier and his phone went to voice mail."

"Last time I talked to him, he mentioned that he'd be working out in the field, and there was a chance he wouldn't have cell phone service. I have an emergency phone number for him that goes through the company. Do you want it?"

"I've got that number."

"Can you let me know when you've talked to him?"

"Yes, I'll give you a call."

The doorbell buzzed.

"That must be pizza."

"Remember, you have to fly home on Wednesday if you haven't found your ring."

"I know. Now with Wendy being gone, I can't hold her ring. Better go. I love you, Father."

"I love you too, Sara."

Opening the door, I saw Conner had changed into a pair of casual slacks and a short-sleeved red-and-white striped shirt. No tie. As he strolled in with the pizza and a bottle of wine, I noticed a man standing by the door, dressed in a suit. He stayed in the hallway as I closed the door behind Conner. "Bodyguard?"

"He came with me earlier and remained by your door while I was gone."

"Do you think I need constant protection?"

"Yes, I do." He pulled plates out of a kitchen cabinet.

Taking utensils and napkins out of a drawer, I said, "Conner, I am quite capable of taking care of myself."

"So it would appear. But until we know the name of Mason's employer, I'm not going to take any chances with you." He uncorked the wine and filled two glasses. "Sauvignon Blanc, chilled. I hope Sally likes this as much as Sara did."

"I don't know how much Sara liked it, but this," I held up the wine glass, "is Sally's favorite."

He raised the lid on the pizza box. Inside was a thin crusted pizza smothered with almost every topping available. "Your favorite?"

I smiled, "How did you know?"

"Just a wild guess." His face lit up when his eyes met mine. "Now I can see both those gorgeous brown eyes."

Since Conner had already realized I had been wearing blue contact lenses and I couldn't find my spare pair, I decided it would be better to take the other one out rather than going around with one blue eye and one brown. I knew there no longer existed the slightest doubt in his mind that I was Sara. Still, I continued using my southern twang. It was a silly attempt at pretending I was someone else, but it was all I had left to keep a small barrier between us.

He leaned across the table and stroked my cheek. "It's okay Sally. Sara isn't the only person who has brown eyes," he said, and I assumed he must've seen a worried look on my face.

Gazing at him, I took another bite of pizza as I pondered how to tackle the way I felt about him. I wanted him to be the man I thought he was when I fell in love with him, a man who was an officer in a national investment company. Believing that, I had lived under his roof for three years. Then, I discovered the truth. He was a member of an organized crime family. Now, to make matters worse, he ran the family business. They kill, maim, and destroy people. How can I still want him? Yet, my heart ached for him.

An idea sprang into my mind. With Conner's connections, could I use him to help me get back my ring? Or was that just another excuse to be near him? "Can I ask you some questions?" I asked, the words spewing from my mouth before I thought it through.

"Absolutely, if I can ask you some."

Thinking about how to respond, I sipped my wine. "You can ask, but I can't promise I'll answer all of them. Will that work for you?"

"Will that scenario also work for you?"

"Well, let's give it a try. Can I start?" He nodded, and then I began, "If you hoped to acquire information today after Mason kidnapped me, why did you rush in when you did?"

"I can answer that one. Jeff was wearing a bug. Mason called Steed into the room to help him persuade you to answer his questions. No way would I allow that maniac to touch you."

"Next question—"

He interrupted, "Isn't it my turn?"

"I thought I'd finish mine first," I said, dishing up another piece of pizza.

"No. Let's alternate."

Lifting an eyebrow, I doubted he'd cooperate if I didn't give him a little leeway. "What do you want to know?"

He drank his wine as his eyes scanned my face. "I have a slew of questions, but suspect you might decline to answer them. In order to avoid having this questions and answer session go immediately south, I'll start with an easy one. "Had Wendy been bitten by one of her spiders when she left here?"

"Yes," I lied, not wanting him to pry any further into Wendy's departure.

"Then why did she—"

I held up my hand in a stop gesture. "My turn. Mitt mentioned one of his associates had something stolen out of a vehicle. Was he referring to you?"

"Interesting you should bring that up. It wasn't just the contents that were stolen, it was the entire vehicle. Someone recently sent me pictures of that vehicle in a wooden storage shed. Was that by any chance you?"

"That's one of the questions, I'm not going to answer. But on that same line of questioning, did you know about the van being in that building before you received the photos?"

He chewed and swallowed the food in his mouth. "Van. I don't recall saying it was a van. You must be clairvoyant. The answer to your question is yes."

"Then why didn't you go after it earlier?"

"The person who appeared to be giving the orders was not the one calling the shots. Mason's boss."

"How do you know that?"

"That wasn't the first shipment that vanished before it reached its destination."

"How long has Jeff been pretending to be a Buckley employee?"

He shook his head. "I never would have thought you'd be this interested in my business. You know the names of the players, where they live, business locations. I must admit I'm impressed. I'll answer that question, and then if I've been counting correctly, I get to ask you four questions in a row. Jeff's been working for Buckley over six months. Before that he worked for me, but he had some family issues that made him want to relocate to Baton Rouge." Cocking his brow, he went on, "Like you, Sally, returning to Baton Rouge to take care of your elderly grandmother."

I rolled my eyes. "Stay with the question."

"I've answered it." He filled our wine glasses and took a sip. "Are you ready for more questions?"

I bobbed my head as I finished devouring my second piece of pizza.

"Why did Wendy carry around spiders with her when unlike Sara, she wasn't immune to the deadly venom?"

Even before I became a Tegen, I was immune to the poisonous venom. When I was five, I had been bitten by a poisonous spider, and I had shared that story with Conner. I needed to stir him away from asking questions about her. "Another Wendy question. I must've mistaken the relationship you were forming with her. When we talked in front of the building on Friday night, I had the impression you weren't all that interested in her. Was I wrong?"

"There you go again," he said with a smile, "sneaking in another question when it's not your turn. You got the correct impression. I'm only asking questions about Wendy because of her ring. An identical ring to one Sara had." He took my right hand that felt naked without my ring. "Instead of asking you directly about it, I was building up to it. Forget the last question. The assailant who stabbed a man near Buckley's warehouse, an incident that occurred before I arrived, wore a black ring. Did you give your ring to Wendy?"

"No." I noticed Conner squinted and suspected he didn't believe me. Since I wanted him to help me track down my ring, I added, "I had a ring just like it. It was stolen from my nightstand Friday night."

"The night Mason left you at his condo?"

"Yes."

He drained his glass and sat quietly studying me for a minute. "Sally, why are you here?"

"This is my apartment," I said, playing dumb.

"You know that's not what I'm talking about."

"Conner, I could ask you the same question. Why would a man who runs an organized crime family come to Baton Rouge to track down some missed shipments? He'd send an employee to handle that."

"How do you know about my business?"

I swallowed hard. "Mitt told me."

"The night you killed him?"

I couldn't deny I was involved with Mitt's death since Conner had pictures of Wendy and me at Monique's. "He started manhandling me, and one of Wendy's spiders ended up on him," I said, hoping that explanation would satisfy Conner.

"You're right. I wouldn't deal with stolen shipments. I'd send an employee, but then I received a picture of Mitt's new girlfriend. That's why I'm here. How about you, Sara? I mean, Sally."

"I'm not going to answer that question."

"I didn't think you would." He rested his elbows on the armrests and tapped his fingers together. "Do you have Mason's cell phone?"

"Why would I have that?"

"Sally, you can't answer a question with another question. Let me rephrase it. The hard object in your bra, was that a cell phone?"

"How do you—"

He shook his head. "You're doing it again."

"Yes. It was a cell phone."

"Yours was in your pant pocket. So whose was in your bra?"

Did he search me before the drugs wore off? "Conner, when I woke up in your car, I had no idea you had frisked me."

"I didn't. Jeff saw you put your cell phone in your pocket. When I embraced you, I noticed a hard object around the location of your bra. You have my word I did not in any way take advantage of you when you were unconscious."

He had to be telling the truth, otherwise, I wouldn't still have Mason's cell phone. "Why do you want his cell phone?"

A big smile crossed his face. "Sally, you need to learn how to play this question-and-answer game. One person asks the question, the other person answers or doesn't answer, but you can't answer with a question."

"Got it."

"I suspect I want the cell phone for the same reason you do. I'm just as curious as you are who Mason called at the old cement plant while you and Wendy were in the limo."

An empty sensation surged through me. I felt weak, like I needed to eat, but I just consumed three pieces of pizza. Before I talked to Father, I drank two glasses of *venotrolia*, so that couldn't the reason. It had to be my ring. I should have held Wendy's before she was taken away. Wondering if I could survive a few more days without it, my eyes became moist and I asked, "Conner, will you help me find my ring?"

He came around the table and wrapped me in his arms. "Hey, it's okay. I'll help you." He picked up a napkin and wiped my face. "Let's sit on the couch." He led me to it. After I was seated, he got the wine and the glasses. "Why don't we start by comparing notes? That might narrow down the potential culprit," he said, sitting beside me. "Since you seem a little hesitant to divulge very much, I'll begin. At the table you seemed to be curious about Jeff's employment status. I'll fill in the holes. He was no longer one of my employees when he took a position with Buckley. About six weeks ago—that was when the first shipment was stolen—he wasn't involved, but he heard rumors about it and suspected that either Buckley or someone associated with Buckley was. He probably figured the situation could get rough and not wanting to be on the losing end of the stick, he contacted me. The following day he had been reinstated on my payroll." He put his arm around me shoulders. "Anymore questions about him?"

"Why did he help Monique unload the second stolen shipment?"

"Interesting that you know he did that. Did Mitt discuss business with you?"

"No. I eavesdropped on a conversation."

"Chalk up one more skill on Sally's growing list." He kissed my forehead. "In one of the packages I received in Houston were documents applicable to Monique Torren. What do you know about her?"

"She wanted to sell Thurman drugs at a price cheaper than yours. Is that what you mean?"

"Anything else?"

Finding my ring had become more important than keeping information from him. "I visited Monique's house last Sunday night, and found no one at home and the scene of a struggle in her living room."

"As an uninvited guest, did you stay long?"

"Long enough to briefly look through her files before headlights moved down her driveway and shined through the windows."

"Whatever happened to Monique, I wasn't responsible for it. In fact, I had hoped she would lead one of my men to her employer," he said, but I doubted he was telling the truth. Conner had lied to me often when I lived with him, and he could do it without showing the slightest sign of deception.

"How are you so certain she had an employer? I saw purchase invoices, sales invoices, names of customers, and a lab folder. It looked like she was running her own show."

"By following the money trail. Two years ago, her total assets, including a used Honda, were worth less than $12,000. She received a large influx of funds from various accounts, but we haven't been able to trace the true identity of the owner. I never would've looked into her finances or for that matter anything she did, had she not stolen shipments. It appears her backer wanted a better rate of return."

"She could've decided to steal the shipments on her own and not been coerced by some backer."

"Jeff overhead her chatting on her cell phone the night the second shipment was heisted. That conversation led him to believe she had a boss. On Monday, the day after you were there, Jeff went to check out her house since Buckley couldn't reach her on the phone. The house looked orderly, but all her files, her computer, and answering machine were gone. Her black Porsche still stood in front of her house. Let's assume she didn't have a boss, an unsatisfied customer might have knocked her off, made sure they didn't leave any fingerprints behind, but I doubt they'd bother cleaning up." He sounded like he had nothing to do with her disappearance, but I knew better than to trust every word he said.

"I saw the clean-up crew."

He raised my chin and his eyes met mine. "Amazing Sally. How were they dressed?"

"Suits. It didn't seem like they were prepared for that type of work. They didn't have enough brooms or garage bags. They had to rummage through the kitchen to get the supplies they needed."

"Names?"

"I did catch a few. I need to check my notebook." I went to the bedroom, pulled it out of my backpack and took it along with Mason's phone into the living room. I sat down and thumbed through my notes. "Here it is, Andy, Jim and Leon—no last names."

Conner gave me a crooked smile, and I wondered if I had screwed up by giving him those names. Leon was an unusual name. The guy was, or at least used to be, a Crussett employee. Had Conner guessed that I recognized him? Yet my ring dominated my thoughts, ruining my judgment, and I probably was giving up more information than I needed to in order to locate it.

"But I only got a quick look at one of them. A tall, beefy looking guy who answered to the name Andy," I said, trying to steer Conner away from thinking about Leon. I had to tread carefully around him since I felt vulnerable and my defenses were no longer intact. The project that brought me to Baton Rouge certainly wasn't turning out like I anticipated. I came here to ruin Thurman's illegal crime business, and in the process, I had hoped it might damage some of the Crussett family business. Now, I found myself in the precarious position of not only trying to locate my ring, but also helping Conner determine who gave the order to steal some of his drugs.

"You look beat," he said, caressing my arm. "Why don't you go to bed, and we'll finish talking about it in the morning. The word will be getting out soon about Mason and his men, if it isn't already out. Whoever Mason talked to on the phone knew you and Wendy had been taken to that abandoned cement plant. There will be no further communication with Mason or his men and no bodies will be found, but they'll know something went down. Someone could be sent to see if you made it back to your apartment. I don't want to leave you alone. Is it okay if I sleep on the couch?"

"Conner, I can take care of myself," I said, fighting off the urge to tell him he could share my bed.

"Please, Sally, let me stay. I promise, I won't go anywhere near your bedroom."

"Well, okay, but you don't need to sleep on the couch. You can sleep in Granny's room. It won't take me long to change the sheets." I got some linens out of a cabinet.

"Let me do it," he said, reaching for the clean sheets.

"You know how to make a bed?" I asked, recalling never seeing him do any domestic chores except cooking eggs a few times.

"Come on, Sally. I've watched people make beds. It can't be that hard."

"Thanks, but this won't take me long," I said, wanting to make sure Wendy hadn't left anything incriminating behind. "That's Mason's cell phone on the coffee table, you can check it out while I'm making up the bed."

He eased down on the couch again. "But remember I offered."

Walking into Granny's bedroom, I saw Wendy's spider container on the dresser and felt a lump rising in my throat. The lid stood ajar.

.

34

A SURPRISING FIND

Fearing the worst, I hurried to the spider container and carefully removed the lid, trying to keep the spiders inside still contained. A spider dropped out. I caught it and gently held it while I counted the spiders. I sighed with relief knowing none were missing.

After I finished making up the bed, I stuck the dirty linens in the hamper, and put Wendy's spiders and disk in my nightstand. I returned to Granny's bedroom and glanced around to check everything was in order for Conner. Then I noticed a piece of light blue fabric, probably from a blouse or dress, protruding from the closed closet door.

Opening the door to push it inside, a lump formed in my throat when I saw Agnes's walker, something she couldn't manage without. Tears drizzled down my cheeks as I dropped to the floor, pulled it to my chest, and clutched the hard metal. "No...not her...please...she can't be the third victim."

Conner rushed into the bedroom. "Sara, what's wrong?" He knelt next to me and caressed my arm.

"Ag..Agnes," I stuttered and pressed my lips together. "Wendy ki..killed her." I grabbed Conner's shirt and swallowed hard, trying to get my emotions under control. "Why did she do it?"

"I don't know." He led me to the couch, and I sat down. Conner took a box of tissues from the bathroom and wiped my face. "Why do you believe Wendy killed Agnes?"

Dapping at my eyes, I tried to figure out how to answer his question. "Remember, I told you Wendy was dangerous. If someone irritated her, she had no scruples about letting one of her spiders handle that person. Wendy arrived here when I wasn't home, and told me Agnes had gone to her sister's. From Wendy's last visit, I knew she didn't care for Agnes."

"So when you saw Agnes's walker, you assumed the worst."

"Yes."

"How about Agnes's sister, wouldn't she have called?"

Could I be wrong? Agnes talked to her sister every day. "Her sister always called on the landline." I stood up. "I'm checking the answering machine." I walked to it with Conner right behind me.

The light wasn't blinking, but I still pressed the play button. "No messages," came from it. "In case Wendy gave Marsha some kind of excuse why Agnes couldn't talk on the phone, can you call Marsha and see if Agnes is there? I'd do it, but Marsha will recognize my voice."

"It's almost ten. Will she still be awake?"

"Agnes always watches the eleven o'clock news."

"Give me her number."

"Press pound one. And only ask for Agnes, no last name." He didn't seem at all surprised by my request. I guessed he had investigated Agnes while he was doing a background search on Sally Jablon.

I stopped speculating when Conner said, "Can I please speak to Agnes Webster? …Good evening, Agnes."

As I inhaled deeply, a warm sensation spread through my body and blood rushed to my cheeks. "Give it to me," I said, motioning for the receiver.

Conner handed it over with a smile on his face.

"Agnes, I missed you," I said, feeling overwhelmed she wasn't the third victim.

"I've missed you too, dear. Has your cousin left?"

"Yes. I just noticed your walker in the bedroom. Was there a reason you left it behind?"

"Well. I'm afraid your cousin doesn't care for me. She practically threw Esther and me out of the apartment."

"She what?"

"I hate to talk badly of your relative. Why don't you ask her?"

"Agnes, it's okay. She isn't prone to be truthful when I ask her questions. Why don't you tell me what happened?"

"Well, trying to be nice, Esther asked her a few questions. You know, where she lived, how long she planned on being in town, stuff like that. I'm afraid your cousin took it as prying, and ordered us out. I must have taken too long getting out of my chair, because she pushed me to the door. I stumbled. Esther caught me. I told Wendy I needed my walker, and she threw it across the room, breaking off the wheels. Esther helped me get situated on the sidewalk and while I held onto a signpost, she called a cab. Esther was real upset with Wendy and headed to the apartment to get my walker. The taxi came before she got back with the broken thing. She probably gave your cousin a piece of her mind."

"How are you getting along without it?"

"Using an old one."

"Agnes, I'm glad you're okay, and I'm sorry about the way Wendy treated you. I'm not going to let her visit anymore."

"Good. Do you want me to come back tomorrow?"

"I have some things I need to take care off. Can you stay with your sister a few more days?"

"Not a problem. Just call when you want me there."

"I will. See you soon, Agnes."

Putting the phone into the cradle, I sank down into Agnes's chair. Who could be the third victim? Whoever it was, I was glad it wasn't Agnes.

"Feel better?" Conner asked.

"You have no idea."

"I think I do," he said with glowing eyes focused on me.

"I guess I overreacted."

"No, not at all. I'm just grateful your misery didn't stem from me."

"Are you planning to give me some misery?" I asked, recalling all the sleepless nights I had already suffered thinking about him.

"Never." His eyes dropped to the floor and he tapped his fingers on his thigh.

"I feel beat. I'm going to bed."

Waking up, I found myself snuggled against Conner's chest and his arms encircling me. My pulse quickened as I breathed him in. A torrent of emotions invaded my thoughts. I had dreamt about a moment like this. He still lingered in my heart, but I had to escape from him before the sensible part of me could no longer win the battle raging inside me between my heart and mind. Sitting up and pushing away from him, every fiber in my body ached to remain snuggled against him. "What are you doing here?" I snapped in the harshest voice I could muster.

"Hey, hey," he said, stroking my arm. "You were moaning in your sleep. When I came in to check on you, you asked me to stay." He leaned on his elbow. "Look, you're still wearing your pajamas."

My eyes dropped to them. "Oh."

He studied my face and tucked an unruly strand of hair behind my ear. "Are you okay?"

"Yes. Give me a minute to get dressed and I'll make us some coffee."

"I'll do that," Conner said, climbing out of bed, dressed in his wrinkled clothing.

While we ate breakfast, my black cell phone rang. I excused myself, hurried into the bedroom, and closed the door behind me, thinking Father was calling. When I saw Brett's name on the screen, a rush of guilt swept through me. "Hi," I answered, hoping my voice didn't betray me. "I guess you heard about Wendy."

"Yeah. Just got off the phone with Lance," he said, referring to my Father. "I'm so sorry you were there. Sara, believe me, I had no idea Wendy had broken that rule when I asked if she could stay with you. Was it terrible?"

"Kendall makes me shiver just seeing him."

"We all can relate to that. Was he alone?"

"No. He had a woman with him. I think she must be his twin."

Brett chuckled. "Misty."

"Misty? That name sure doesn't suit her. It should be something like Cruella de Vil. Her eyes were as dark and penetrating as Kendall's."

"Kendall's been training her for years. I guess his mannerisms are rubbing off. Have you found your ring yet?"

"No."

"Do you want me to fly out there and help you look for it?"

"No, I think I can manage. I've got a couple of leads," I lied, not wanting him to know Conner was in town. "And if I haven't got it on my finger by Wednesday, I'll be going home." Worrying about the unknown punishment waiting for me there, I asked, "Brett, have you ever broken any of the rules?"

"I came close one time—not the number one rule—one of the others. But then, I heard about a punishment handed down to a friend. That swayed me never to contemplate it again."

"What was the punishment?"

"Sara… are you going to be punished for not revealing Wendy's locations?"

"Uh-huh," I mumbled over the lump forming in my throat.

"It's my fault. Wendy was my responsibility. Not yours. What can I do?"

"Nothing. Unless you have some kind of power over the Council."

"Sorry. I'm powerless. But your father?"

"No use. He was pretty mad when he learned Wendy was staying with me when she might have broken a rule, and I neglected to mention her whereabouts to any Tegen. Father told me the punishment would be handed down when I got home. So how was your friend punished?"

After a notable pause, he reluctantly said, "The punishment is individualized to the guilty party. Did you ask your father about it?"

"Yes. He wouldn't even give me a hint."

"Then I better not say anything. But Sara, I'll be there for you, and I know you'll get through it—whatever it is."

Staring at the floor, I sat quietly pondering the possible ways I might be punished, but all that came to mind were prison time, torture, and being chained to a wall for some specific period. I couldn't imagine my father would be involved with sentencing me to be tortured.

"Sara, you still there?"

"Yeah," I said, as my cell phone made a soft chirping sound, indicating someone was calling me. Glancing at it, I saw Father's name. "Father's trying to reach me. I better talk to him."

"Let me know when you're flying home. I want to meet you there."

"I will."

"Love you, Sara."

"See you soon."

After I disconnected, I found Father was no longer waiting on the line. I punched in his number. He picked up on the second ring. "I take it you were talking to Brett?"

"Yes. Father, is it over?"

"Wendy?"

"Yes."

"Not yet. We're waiting for the identification of the third victim before we proceed."

"Will it make any difference?"

"Not in terms of the punishment, but we don't like to leave any loose ends. If we can't make a positive identification, Wendy will have to be swayed to help us."

"Given her impending punishment, why would she want to help?"

"We have proven methods of persuasion."

I wanted to ask what they were, but at the same time I didn't want to know. "Do you think the third victim might be someone I know?"

"Until that victim has been identified, I have no way of speculating. We should have that identification in a few days. Sara, I heard you handled yourself very admirably when Wendy was picked up. Are you feeling okay with it today?"

"I'm worried about Wendy's parents. So they don't spend the rest of their lives searching for her, isn't there some way they can be told their daughter is dead?"

"No," he replied without hesitation. "Sara, remember the rules. Don't put yourself in a position to be sentenced for two infractions."

"I wasn't going to say anything to Wendy's parents. I was just hoping there was some way they could be told."

"Since she has Tegen DNA, her remains will never be found. I'm sorry you had to be a party to this unfortunate situation. Most Tegens don't see firsthand another Tegen being taken away by an enforcer, and those who have experienced it have been Tegens for more than twenty years. The first few years after the transformation can be a difficult time establishing a new life style. In your case, you lack the comfort your ring could bring while you deal with this added stress. If you sense you're not handling it well, you need to spend some time in the cave."

"I think I'll be okay if I can find my ring soon."

"Sara, drink plenty of *venotrolia*. That will help. But if you start feeling dizzy or disoriented, call me immediately and I'll get you home."

A soft beeping sound echoed through the airwaves.

"A patient is being prepped for surgery, I need to go," he said, and then I remembered Conner was in the other room waiting.

"I love you, Father."

"I love you too, Sara. Talk to you tomorrow."

I clicked off my phone, opened the small fridge, and drank half a bottle of *venotrolia*, savoring its exclusive flavor.

.

35

SHARING

Conner sat tapping on the cell phone in his hand. "That took a while," he said, looking up.

"I'm sorry. Is that Mason's phone?"

Conner nodded.

"Find anything?"

"The last person he talked to is listed as T. I had a tech working on locating the owner of that number last night. It appears that phone has been discarded. It was purchased with cash at a store downtown. Untraceable. This phone," he said, holding it up, "only sent and received calls from four people. Mason has another phone."

From my visit to Mason's condo, I already knew he had two cell phones, but now that I was feeling better, I didn't want to disclose any more to Conner than was absolutely necessarily to find my ring. "Are you sure? I didn't find another one in his pockets."

"Yes. The number of this phone is not the number used by his clients. Also, Mitt's number in this phone isn't the contact number I have for him. Most likely, every contact listed has another cell phone."

"What are the other names?"

"Mitt, Reese, and Don."

"Maybe T stands for Orson Thurman," I said, but doubted it was him. Based on what I overheard at Buckley's house when they were discussing Conner's employees' visit to the warehouse, Mitt had some kind of a gripe against his father. It also sounded like whatever accusation Mitt had made against his father, Reese believed it. Would they still want Thurman in this close circle? Then a thought occurred to me—unless they were somehow trying to set up Mitt's father for a fall.

Conner shook his head. "No."

"Are you sure?"

"Yes."

"Can you fill me in more than that?"

"Without going into details, let me just say... something outside Thurman's control happened at the dilapidated cement plant in the same room you were being held."

"To his mistress?"

Conner's eyes narrowed, and he rubbed his chin. "I can't imagine Mitt would discuss that with you, or leave documents laying around that anyone could stumble upon in his condo. Who told you?"

I wasn't about to tell him that I had stumbled upon the first set of pictures when I lived with him and rummaged around in his den. On the back of those pictures, it clearly stated the identity of the people in the photos. "No one. I found a disk containing pictures in Monique's file cabinet with a sticky on it that said, 'Thurman's mistress.' Since the woman appeared to be older than Mitt, and he seemed to be enjoying himself in the photos, I assumed it was Orson's mistress." Then recalling how Conner had me bound and electro-shocked to obtain information about his brother's death, I added, "Of course, Mitt wouldn't be the first man who tortured his girlfriend, so I might have it wrong."

Conner looked at me with his eyes fixed on mine without saying a word, and I worried that I might have ended our sharing of information too soon. My ring was at stake. I couldn't let him leave before he divulged everything he had learned about Mason and the group. Finally, he spoke, "Sally, I'm not infallible. Sometimes I make bad decisions, and sometimes those decisions are irreversible. Haven't you ever made a wrong decision?"

Sitting across from him, I couldn't count how many bad decisions I had made during my life, and I felt confused about the decisions I had made regarding Conner. Were they good decisions or were they bad decisions that would haunt me forever? "I'm sure I have," I said, reminiscing about the way we were.

Conner and I sat silently gazing at each other while I continued thinking about the good times we shared, a life that seemed so full of promise and happiness. A life that had vanished in the chaos of discovering he was a member of a crime family, and me becoming a Tegen. We lived in two different worlds.

His cell phone rang, snapping me out of my reverie. He jerked and fished it out of his breast pocket. As he answered it, I wondered what had consumed his thoughts while I had revisited the past.

"What have you got?...When?...Follow the routine." He laid his phone down on the coffee table. "Let's get out of here before company arrives."

"Who?"

"Probably Reese and a few others."

"They know what happened at the cement plant?"

"No. They're having a meeting at Buckley's and speculating about it. Buckley thinks his son has been captured and is being held someplace to answer questions. They know you and Wendy made it home. They also know Wendy was taken away in an ambulance and are assuming she had been injured at the cement plant."

"Is Jeff at the meeting?"

"No." Conner rested his elbow on the armrest and scratched his forehead. "As far as Buckley is concerned, he disappeared along with everyone else."

"How about Dan?"

"Dan?"

"Mitt's friend. I saw him outside the cement plant? His car was there, too. A red corvette with white stripes."

"That guy. Mason had sent him on some kind of errand right after you arrived. He wasn't around when the shooting began."

"Lucky guy," I said, guessing that none of Mason's men at the plant had been left alive. "You keep mentioning 'they'. Who are 'they'? The people meeting at Buckley's?"

"There are eight there. Reese, Buckley, the Corvette driver, Buckley's wife, but it appears she's just there to serve coffee and pastries. Besides voicing her concern about her son, she isn't contributing to the discussion. The others in the room aren't major players."

"How are you eavesdropping?"

"Several ways."

"How?"

"That's one question I'm not going to answer."

I suspected he didn't want to reveal that information since he had been using the same methods to keep track of me. "T isn't at the meeting?"

"Buckley's running the show. It doesn't appear T is there, but he could be someone pretending to be an ordinary employee, nothing more. I'm having the other three checked out."

Interesting. He said three, not four. Conner must have already checked out one person, or swayed that person to become a member of his team. A thought bounced into my head. "Could T stand for Torren, Monique's last name?"

He tilted his head and squinted. "You think she's still alive?"

"Has anyone found a body?"

"No, but there are endless places were a body could be hidden and never found," Conner said, and I knew he was talking from experience. "Do you have a theory?"

I hated sharing my thoughts with Conner, but my ring took precedence. "Maybe she staged the whole struggling scene because she suspected someone was on to her—like you."

"Besides me, anyone else?"

"Did you know Mitt and Monique were business partners?"

"Yes. They had recently acquired a warehouse. They planned to put Buckley out of business—not all his business, but his drug storage business."

"How do you know that?"

A sly smile flashed across his face. "Sally, you led us to the documents. Had my men not been tailing you, I wouldn't have known about Mitt's scheme. Had Buckley seen those documents, he probably would have knocked off Mitt, but you beat him to it. By the way, what did you do with the documents?"

"Gave them to Mason."

"Interesting. Mason's place has been searched. The documents weren't there."

"Maybe he handed them over to T."

"Then T can't be Torren, unless for some reason Mason wants to put his father out of business."

"That's a—" I began, and abruptly stopped when Conner's cell phone chirped.

"Maybe the meeting's over." He raised his phone to his ear. "What's new? …Now…Bring ten." He pocketed the phone and stood. "Reese and two guys are on their way here. Grab what you want to take and we'll go to a safer place."

"No. I'm staying here." I thought about my spiders, the *venotrolia*, and knew I could easily handle anyone coming to give me a bad time, unless… "Do they have blowtorches with them?"

"Never asked. You worried about Wendy's spiders?" Conner took my hand and urged me to stand up.

"Wait," I said, not budging. "Conner, I need to find my ring and think I can convince Reese I had nothing to do with whatever went down at the cement plant. I doubt he'll come in here shooting since he wants information first. Please make your guys scarce or completely obscure, move the Escalades from the front, stuff like that."

"Sally, I'm not going to leave you," he said, his hard tone matched his stern expression and defiant demeanor.

"Okay. You can stay in the bedroom. Will you be upset if I mention your name?"

"What are you planning to say?"

"I'm not going to tell him Mason and his guys are dead and buried if that's what you're worried about. But Conner, do you think there is any chance they don't already suspect you were involved with what went on at the cement plant?"

"They know I was there along with some of my men, and they suspect I'm holding Mason."

"How do they know that?"

"One of Mason's guys took off when he saw us approaching the cement plant. Of course, he told them he managed to get away after he put up a gallant attempt at defending us off," Conner said sarcastically.

"So if I mention your name, I won't be telling them anything they don't already know, right?"

"Are you planning to use your charm to captivate Reese?"

"I might be able to get information from him that way. Do you think it will work?"

A boyish smile crossed his lips. "I'd be surprised if it didn't. But, if I sense it isn't working, he'll be a dead man along with his buddies."

"No. Don't do that. You can capture him, but don't kill him. I need to know where my ring is."

He briefly studied my face as he tapped his index finger against his bottom lip. "I'll play it your way." He picked up his cell and made a call.

I went into the bedroom, changed into a more flattering outfit, a soft blue sweater that showed a little cleavage and a pair of jeans that emphasized my derriere. Then I frantically searched through my drawers for the extra pair of blue contact lenses. I was relieved to find them tucked in the corner next to my folded t-shirts. After putting them on, I returned to the living room.

Conner eyed me up and down. "Your charm is well displayed." He moved closer to me, wrapped his arms around me and kissed me. I tried not to kiss him back, but my lips had another agenda that my mind couldn't control.

"Let me take you away from Baton Rouge for a few days." He held me tight against his chest. "I could fly you to an island Sara loved."

Hearing him say Sara gave me just enough strength to push away from him. "Conner, I'm not Sara."

He gently touched my cheek. "I think Sally would also love the island."

The corners of my mouth curved up. "She probably would, but right now Sally has work to do." I went to the window, glanced out and looked up and down the street. The Escalades were nowhere in sight.

"Reese is less than five minutes away. He won't see any of my men, unless someone comes marching this way with a blowtorch. Then they'll never make it to your apartment."

"Reese...I don't want anything to happen to him before I have answers."

Instead of responding, Conner moved to the window and peered out.

Doubting he had given the order to keep Reese alive, I said, "Conner, promise me your guys won't shoot Reese."

"Sally, I can't make that promise. If he can't be disarmed, there won't be an option."

"Then let's hope it doesn't come to that, and I can't imagine they'll charge in here with blowtorches. Did the guy who escaped know Wendy had spiders with her?"

"No. None of the guards patrolling the exterior perimeter of the cement plant had been alerted to that." He peeked out the window. "Hmm. Interesting. Reese is driving Mason's Mustang."

I wondered if the tracking device was still attached to that vehicle and decided to keep that piece of information to myself. At least until I found out if Reese would buy the story I planned to tell. "Promise me you'll stay in the bedroom."

"I will unless I sense you are in imminent danger."

"Conner, I can take care of myself. Even if Reese wants me to accompany him to another location, I'd rather you not interfere. He could be leading me to my ring."

"Sally—" he began, and stopped when someone knocked on the door.

36

THE INNOCENT ROLE

Conner instinctively ducked into the bedroom and pushed the door almost closed, leaving it slightly ajar.

I secured the chain on the apartment door, and inched it open. "Reese, is Mase okay?" I asked as I checked out the two men who were with them. They weren't dressed in suits, like Conner's men. Instead, they wore jeans and short sleeved shirts, exposing their muscular arms.

"Huh?" Reese said, squinting.

"Mase took my cell phone. His number was in it, but I hadn't memorized it. I need my cell phone back."

"Can we come in?"

"Sure. Let me unhook the chain." I closed the door, took care of it, and opened the door for my guests. "Please, take a seat," I said, gesturing toward the living room.

Reese sat down on the couch. The two men with him stood stoically next to the door.

I eased down next to him. "Where's Mase?"

"I came here to ask you that same question." He furrowed his brow as he drummed his fingers on the armrest. "What happened yesterday?"

"You know, for awhile, I thought I was in a lot of trouble. Mase kidnapped Wendy and me and he burned our purses. Did you know that?"

"No," he said as he clutched his hands together and his jaw tightened. He certainly didn't possess Conner's ability to lie without showing any signs. "Aah..aah," he stammered. "Where did he take you?"

"To some deserted plant miles from the city."

"And how did you and Mase get separated?"

"Oh, it was terrible. Really...terrible." I placed my hand on his arm. "Mase thought I worked for Crussett—like I'm a spy or something. I've never owned or shot a gun, and I hate such dangerous weapons. I don't know what got into him. Next, he accused me of stabbing some guy, and then asked about a black ring I wore once with Mitt. A beautiful ring I borrowed from my cousin, Wendy. Now her ring's missing. She thought I stole it until Mase told her he knew where it was, but he wasn't giving it back. She punched Mase with such brutal force, he could barely fight her off. I didn't know Wendy could attack so viciously. A couple of Mase's guys were in the room when she tore into him. Didn't anyone mention it?"

He shook his head. "No. Where is your cousin?"

"I wish I knew. She fought off a couple of guys to get us out of there, and one of them cut her arm. When we got back here, I kept asking her questions, but she just ignored me. Anyway, she made a call, and then an ambulance came for her. She wouldn't tell me what hospital they were taking her to or anything. I've called all the local hospitals and haven't been able to find her. I just don't know what to do. Do you think I should call the police?"

He patted my hand. "Let me work on it. I'm still confused as to what went on at the plant. What happened between the time Wendy fought with Mase and you two escaped? Did Mase leave you alone?"

"Mase ordered a guy named Steed to tie Wendy to a chair. I screamed for him to leave her alone, but Mase directed another guy to take me to the car. I didn't want to leave Wendy, but got yanked away, and just as we were leaving, noise erupted around us. Blasts of gunfire, shouting, yelling, everyone rushing about. When Mase and Steed left the room, the guy released me, pulled a pistol from his holster, and followed them. I untied Wendy, as she pointed to a window high off the floor. Then she stacked chairs to climb, and we escaped."

"Who brought you home?"

"Shortly after we reached the gravel road, we saw a cloud of dust heading our way. Assuming it was a car, we ducked behind a pile of rocks. She recognized the car and ran to the road. It stopped and Mr. Crussett got out of the backseat. He put his arms around Wendy and she said, 'It's about time.' I figured he came there to rescue her." I cupped my head in my hands and a few tears trickled down my cheeks. "Reese, what's going on? I couldn't sleep a wink last night. I wanted to go to the police, but I don't want Wendy to get in trouble. She stabbed a guy as we were leaving. He didn't move. I think she might have killed him. And there's Mitt. Someone killed him. I'm just glad Granny is staying with her sister for a few days. I'm thinking I need to take her away from here. Guns, killing, aren't anything we're used to. Does everyone in Baton Rouge have a gun?"

He put his arm around my shoulders, and I knew he was buying my story. "Sally, I'll get to the bottom of this."

Wiping my eyes with my fingertips, I sat up straight. "Tomorrow is Mitt's funeral. I just can't believe it. He was such a wonderful man. Are you going?"

"Yeah."

"I don't know if I can handle it alone. Can I go with you?"

"Of course." He reached into his back pant pocket, pulled out his wallet and took out two hundred dollars. "Here," he said, handing me the money. "Sorry I don't have more cash on me. This won't be enough to get you a fancy cell phone, but you'll be able to get something."

"Reese, your brother took my phone. You shouldn't have to pay for it. That's not right. I'll wait until I see him."

"No," he said, squeezing my hand around the bills. "I want you to get something now. Make sure you get the same number. It's saved in my phone."

Since I had never talked to Reese on the phone, I wondered why he would have my number, but I refrained from asking him about it.

"After you get the phone, could you give me a call?" he asked, sounding concerned.

"Yes. Maybe you'll know where Wendy is by then. I'd like to visit her at the hospital."

He stood and I followed him to the door. "Thanks again for the money for a cell phone. I have a limited budget, and didn't know how I was going to replace it."

"You're welcome." He opened the door. "When you're here, keep the door locked."

"I always do."

He caressed my arm. "I'll pick you up at eleven," he said, and then left with his two friends. I stayed next to the door and listened to the footsteps until they faded away.

Conner stepped out of the bedroom. "Smooth. Very smooth. Had I not known better, I probably would have bought your story. I have no doubt that Reese fell for it lock, stock, and barrel. However, I don't like the idea of you going with him to the funeral."

"Conner, Mase knew where my ring was and I suspect so does Reese. On top of that, I couldn't show up with you after what I told Reese, and the Buckleys think you're holding Mase."

"True, but you could've gone alone."

"Nope. I want to get close to Reese. Conner, I'm safe now. You and your men don't need to protect me."

Conner took his cell phone out of his pocket and raised it to his ear. Since I never heard it ring, it must have been on vibrate. "What?" he said into the phone, sounding irritated. "When... how many... ten minutes." He disconnected, dropped the phone in his pocket, and strolled to the window. "I don't like leaving you alone, but there's a problem I need to check on."

I glanced out the window and saw the Escalade parked across the street again. My eyes popped wide open as I noticed Kendall walking along the sidewalk on the other side of the Escalade.

"What's wrong?" Conner asked, putting his arm around my shoulders.

"Aah… aah… nothing," I stammered. "It's your car. It's already back. How did your guys know Reese was gone? Did you call from the bedroom?"

"No, but they're good at their jobs." He took my hand and led me to the apartment door. "Since we still don't know who T is, I don't want you to leave your apartment. I'll have one of my men buy you a new cell phone and drop it off."

I had no intention of following his request, but there was no point in discussing it with him. "Thanks. After my restless night, I'm going to take a nap."

"Good idea." He wrapped me in his arms and kissed me. "I'll be back later."

Locking the door behind him, I pondered if I should call Father about Kendall. I peered out the corner of the window, hidden from the Escalade, and scanned the area as I searched for Kendall. I couldn't spot him anywhere. I sat down on Granny's chair and wondered if Father had asked Kendall to keep an eye on me since he was worried about how my body would react the longer it went without touching my ring. Or maybe, Kendall was working on trying to locate the identity of the third victim. Do they think it was someone that lived in the apartment building? Recalling Agnes saying that Esther was going to have words with Wendy—could Esther be the victim?

Mulling that over, I headed out my apartment and ran face-to-face into Leon, Conner's guy who was guarding my door. He was the man I had recognized at Monique's. Either Leon was working for two people, or Conner was involved with Monique's disappearance. I tended to believe it was the latter. Conner had lied to me again. I didn't say a word to Leon as he watched me walk down the hallway and knock on Esther's door.

The door opened. "Is Agnes back?" Esther asked.

"No. I just wanted to know how you were getting along."

She held up her bandaged hand. "Fine, except for this. Is your cousin still staying with you?"

"No. What happened to your hand?"

"Your cousin," she said, shaking her head. "She slammed the door on it when I tried to get Agnes's walker. If the super hadn't been close by when I screamed, my hand would probably still be stuck in that door frame."

"Oh, I'm so sorry, Esther. Is there anything I can do for you?"

"It's much better now. You want to come in and have a cup of coffee?"

After I declined her invitation, I went back to my apartment feeling relieved Esther wasn't the third victim, but at the same time, upset about the way Wendy had treated her and Agnes. I gave Conner's guy an awkward smile as I stepped through my doorway. I picked up my landline phone and ordered a bouquet of flowers to Esther. It wouldn't take away the pain she had suffered under Wendy's anger, but it was all I could think of doing.

I put my laptop on the kitchen table and checked for the location of the Mustang. The tracking device hadn't been removed. It appeared the blue bleep was heading toward Monique's house. I continued staring at the screen as I wondered why they would be going there. Did they think Monique could have returned? The blue bleep flipped a u-ey before it reached her street. While it traveled along the highway, I went into the bedroom and got a bottle of *venotrolia*. I quickly devoured it.

Sitting back down in front of the computer, a loud knock on the door sent it rattling on its hinges. Jumping to my feet, I said, "What the...." I hurried to the door. Without opening it I yelled next to it. "Who's there?"

A cold gruff voice blurted out. "Kendall."

I stood frozen in place. What does he want? Knowing he'd come busting through the door if I kept him waiting out there long, I edged the door slightly open. "What...what can I help you with?" I asked with a trembling voice.

"Wendy's spiders."

"Oh," I sighed. "They're in the bedroom. Let me get them." I opened the door wider and rushed into the bedroom. A few seconds later, I handed her spider case over to Kendall. He raised the lid, and I assumed he was counting them. "They're all there," I said, irritated about his distrust. If I wanted more spiders, all I needed to do was ask Father.

"Yes, they are," he said in a formal tone.

Then I wondered why Leon hadn't tried to stop Kendall and glanced around Kendall. There, slouched on the floor was Leon. "You didn't?" I said, pointing at Leon's body.

"No," he answered bluntly, his eyes fixed on my face.

Chills swept over me as he continued staring at me. Every muscle in my body tensed while I quietly waited for him to depart. My eyes dropped to his ring and a longing emerged through me. I had to touch it. Without another thought, I grabbed his hand and caressed his ring. He raised it toward me. I held onto it tighter and closed my eyes, savoring the sensation swimming through my organs. I bent my head and ran my tongue over the precious black stone. Kendall didn't say a word as I slowly moved the back of his hand up my arm, around my neck and over my face, wanting the ring to touch every inch of my exposed flesh. I don't know how long I had enjoyed the feel of his black stone, when the ringing of phone snapped me back to the present. I opened my eyes and looked at the piercing eyes glaring at me. "Sorry," I muttered, not knowing what else to say. The phone continued ringing. "I better get that." I hurried to the landline and grabbed the receiver as Kendall turned on his heels and strode down the hall.

"Hello."

"Hello, Sara. This is Wendy's mother, Beth Adams."

"Hello, Mrs. Adams," I said as my stomach churned.

"Is Wendy staying with you?"

Suspecting that some of the tenants had seen her in the building, I couldn't completely lie to her mother. "She was, but she left last night."

"Did she say where she was going?"

"To Florida to visit a friend."

"Oh. She must be at Sheila's. Thanks, dear."

Feeling sad and guilt ridden, I hung up the phone. Poor Mrs. Adams, she'll never find her daughter. I desperately wanted to tell the woman the truth, but there was no way I could save her from the pain of losing a child. If I disclosed anything, it might hurt all Tegens in the process and I'd be breaking another rule. Tegens would always be part of my life and I had to protect them. I noticed my apartment door still stood wide open and moved toward it as Kendall's sinister face flashed into my head. I closed the door, leaned against it and felt my limbs shuddering as I recalled holding his hand. Yet, I couldn't deny that I'd do it again just to touch his ring. At the same time, I couldn't understand how he managed to captivate Mandy's heart, the 19-year-old who attended the gathering and became his victim. Just seeing Kendall across the street had sent a surge of fear up my spine. How could she have not sensed the sinister force his body emitted? Maybe, it was because her evil nature out-masked his.

Sitting at the table, I saw the blue bleep stopped in front of a small structure at the end of a long dirt lane surrounded by trees and shrubs. I moved the curser away from the Mustang to the street and jotted down the first address I spotted. Could drugs be hidden inside that structure? The more I dwelled on it, the less likely it seemed since drugs could be guarded twenty-four-seven at Buckley's warehouse.

I wanted to check out the structure, but I needed a plan first. Getting into my car and driving to the destination was not an option with Conner's men lurking about. Mulling over other potential ways I could leave, I grabbed a fresh towel and took a shower.

Stepping out of the bathroom, I saw a package on the table. Irritated that someone had entered my apartment without an invitation, I opened the package. Inside was a new pale green cell phone with a note attached. It read: "Your cell phone number has been installed." I didn't recognize the penmanship, figured it had been written by one of Conner's men, and opened the door prepared to snap at whoever stood in the hallway for intruding on my privacy. To my surprise, no one was near my door. I moved outside and checked both directions of the hallway without seeing anyone. Strange.

I returned to my apartment, locked and bolted the door. Though I wasn't concerned about my safety, I still wanted a little warning if unexpected visitors showed up. As I wondered if I had misjudged Reese about buying my kidnapping story, a sharp, clanging sound echoed behind me.

37

THE SHACK

Expecting to see someone there, I slowly turned around. No one was in sight. My eyes darted around the room looking for the source of the noise. A mug on the kitchen counter was tipped on its side. Outside of that, nothing appeared out of place. Since the mug wouldn't have moved under its own accord, I picked it up and saw a small object, a bug, lying next to it. Guessing the listening device had fallen off the cabinet, I contemplated searching for other bugs, but decided against it since I assumed somewhere in my apartment a surveillance camera had also been installed, probably when the new cell phone was delivered. If I removed and destroyed all of Conner's surveillance equipment, it wouldn't be long before his men stood guard at my door again. Then Reese would know I hadn't told him the whole truth, and hoping he could lead me to my ring, I needed him to trust me. Also, I doubted a camera had been installed in the bedroom. Conner wouldn't want his men seeing me undressing.

I clicked on my computer, entered my password, and saw Mase's Mustang was still parked by the small structure. Recalling Reese wanted me to call him, I punched in his number. On the fifth ring, it went to voice mail. I left message telling him I had purchased a new cell phone. Next, I called Conner.

He answered after the first ring. "Feeling rested?"

"Yeah. Thanks for the cell phone," I said, though the delivery method still irked me. "I need to go shopping for something to wear to Mitt's funeral."

"Let me get you something. It's not safe for you to be out of your apartment."

"Conner, I'm not going to let you buy me clothes," I said. Then he went on for about ten minutes pointing out how dangerous it would be for me to go out, and my temper rose. "I want to go shopping, and you can't stop me." I disconnected and turned off the phone.

It probably wouldn't be long before his men appeared at my door. I quickly slipped my computer in my backpack and headed out of my apartment. Suspecting they would be coming up the elevator I took the stairs to the roof and scurried down the exterior of the building. Within five minutes, I was in the Dodge and driving out of the parking lot.

Since I left in a rush, I didn't check the vehicle for tracking devices. I drove ten miles to a shopping mall and parked in a visible location close to a side entrance. I went into the first department store I reached. In the dressing room, I took apart the cell phone and found a tracking device, just as I had expected. After purchasing a black dress and a blouse, I attached the tracking device to a teenager whom I overheard telling her friends she planned on shopping all day.

I ducked into a restroom near the food court and changed my blouse to the new one. I went to another mall entrance, followed a group of people out and maneuvered around parked cars until I reached the sidewalk that abutted the street. Walking at a brisk pace, but not so fast as to draw attention, I headed to a small car rental office a few blocks away.

The only ID I carried had the name Sally Jablon on it. Reluctantly, I used it and a credit card in the same name to rent a Ford coupe. I doubted I'd be able to get the car back to the rental agency before Conner discovered my credit card charge. At the same time, I knew the newly rented car was free of tracking devices.

A half an hour later, I drove by the dirt lane that led to the small structure and cut to the shoulder of the road. I checked my computer for the blue blip. The Mustang had moved to a spot in front of the Buckley house. The secluded small structure had piqued my curiosity. I climbed out of the car and looked around for any familiar cars. Not seeing any, I thought about moving the Ford to a less conspicuous place, but there wasn't one within eyeshot. I sat in the driver's seat and kept track of the stationary blue blip until the sun began to set. Then I slipped on a long-sleeved black top, tucked my hair under a ball cap and tugged on my backpack. I cautiously climbed over a four-foot high barbed wire fence and sprinted to the closest cluster of bushes as cars sped along the street.

Concealed from the street, I took off the ball cap and put on the ski mask. Recalling the video Conner had showed me in his car, I swept my eyes over the open field and searched for a reflection of a photo lens. Unable to see the faintest flicker of light except in the direction of the building, I darted to a tall tree about hundred feet away and stealthily continued toward the structure.

When I reached the last bank of trees surrounding the structure, I peered out and swept my eyes over the building that now appeared to be nothing more than a shack with a sagging roof, peeling paint and badly in need of repair. A light from the opposite side shined, illuminating the corners of the structure. From my angle, I didn't see any windows, but noticed the back bumper of a car parked behind the building. I crept toward it. It was a black Volvo. Reese's car?

Keeping low to the ground, I moved around the shack and saw the cement remains of a foundation next to it. Based on its size, I suspected a house had once stood on the site. I searched for another way to enter the small structure and discovered it was windowless. The only way in and out of the shack was through one door that had a narrow shaft of light shining around its edges. I hunkered down behind the trees, pulled the mini-directional mike out of my backpack, and pushed in an earbud. I inched closer to the building, flipped on the mike and pointed it toward the exterior wall. Static buzzed for several seconds. Then a moaning sound came through the gadget.

"So you're awake," a husky voice said. "Let me call the boss…yeah…See ya in thirty." Feet shuffled against a hard floor. "Just a sip."

The distinct sound of a slap echoed through the mike.

"Don't know," a deep, raspy voice stammered. A voice that sounded strangely familiar.

"Jeff, come clean," the husky-voiced man said. "No one's buying that you don't know where he is."

Jeff, Conner's guy? He had helped Wendy and me. And who is the "he" the other guy mentioned? Conner? Mason? From what I picked up ten minutes earlier, someone would be here in twenty minutes. Since I had only heard two voices, I figured there was only one captor inside the building. If I wanted to rescue Jeff, I had to do it now.

A punching sound, followed by a moan, reverberated through the mike. I assumed Jeff had been struck again. I quickly put away the mini mike, found a rock and threw it at the door. Hiding next to the Volvo, I yanked out my knife and waited for the door to open. It didn't budge. I grabbed a bigger rock and heaved it to the door. Still nothing.

Evaluating the situation, I wondered if the husky-voiced guy had been given orders not to open the door unless his boss called his name. I grabbed the car's front door knob and to my relief, the vehicle wasn't locked. I ran to the trees, broke off a stick and slipped into the vehicle. I turned on the lights and inserted the stick through the steering wheel, forcing it to push down on the horn.

The horn blared.

I slid out and remained hidden in the shadows cast by the Volvo. Sure enough, the obnoxious sound got the guy's attention and the door cracked open. The barrel of a gun emerged as the door opened slightly wider.

As the whining of the horn continued, I edged along the side of the building out of the gunholder's line of sight. The horn stopped, and something poked me in the back.

"Well, what have we got here?" a cold, gruff voice said behind me. "Before you climb into a car, little lady, you really should check the backseat."

"Leon, that you?" the husky-voiced guy yelled through the doorway.

"Yep. Think I got the little lady who stabbed Greg." He took the knife from me. Playing my mortal role, I didn't put up any resistance. "Let's see what you look like." Leon grabbed the top of my ski mask. As he yanked it off, I scratched his hand. "Ow, you bitch," he snapped and raised his hand, prepared to sling it across my face. He abruptly became motionless and stared at me. "Crussett's girl." Fear flashed across his face. "Boyd, we've got a big problem. I'm gettin' outta here." He pushed me into the shack and charged toward the car.

"Leon, you can't leave," Boyd yelled, pressing the barrel of the gun into my chest.

"That's Crussett's girl. He'll be here soon. We're dead men."

"Wha...wha...It can't be."

The Volvo engine roared to life. "Hey, I'm coming with you," Boyd said, pushing me further into the structure.

As he darted around me, I tripped him and scraped his arm. The pistol went off, shattering a wooden table.

"Boyd," Leon shouted from the car.

"Give me a sec," he yelled, stumbling to his feet.

Wanting to cover-up the fact that he had been poisoned, I kicked the pistol out of his hand. It slid across the floor. I scrambled to retrieve it. He lunged toward me, knocking me over. I gripped the gun and squeezed the trigger. The bullet grazed his shoulder. He struggled with me for his weapon. Then his body went limp. Knowing he wouldn't have died from his injured shoulder, I leapt to my feet and planted a bullet in the center of his chest.

"Sally," Jeff murmured.

I swung around and saw the blood-caked man tied to the chair. His eyes were almost swollen shut. His face had a long gash that ran from his temple to his mouth. His foot dangled awkwardly on the floor, probably broken. As I continued surveying his damaged body, I wondered how I was going to get him to safety.

The car engine idled outside, and I assumed Leon had succumbed to the poisonous venom. Before I went to work on freeing Jeff, I hurried outside, opened the driver's door and saw Leon's head draped over the steering wheel. I gripped his arm, braced my leg on the car's footrail and yanked him out of the vehicle. As I leaned down to search his pockets for my knife, I noticed it lying on the passenger seat. After I grabbed it, I shot Leon in the head with Boyd's pistol. Feeling confident that no one would suspect the two guys had been poisoned, I pulled a pair of rubber gloves out of the side pocket of my backpack, slipped them on and opened the back door of the Volvo.

With the clock rapidly ticking and reinforcements on their way, I rushed back into the building and cut the ropes securing Jeff to the chair. His legs buckled under him when he tried to stand. I laid his arm over my shoulders, wrapped my arm around his waist and dragged him out of the building. Using all the strength I could muster, I managed to get him into the Volvo's backseat. I stepped over Leon's body and climbed into the driver's seat.

I backed up the vehicle and swung it around, then gunned the engine and plowed down the dirt lane, leaving a thick cloud of dust in my wake. Assuming the reinforcements would be taking the same route I had taken to get to the shack, I turned the opposite direction onto the street and zoomed past my rented car. I drove two miles until I reached a crossroad and executed a right turn. I cut to the edge of the pavement and stopped the Volvo. I looked over my shoulder at my weak passenger.

"Call Crussett," he mumbled.

I didn't want Conner to know what I had been up to, but Jeff needed medical care and I couldn't take him to a hospital without being questioned. Since there wasn't another option, I pulled out my new cell phone and punched in Conner's number. It went to voice mail. Recalling, the emergency number he had given me, I tapped it in."

"Miss Jablon?" a female voice answered.

"Yes. Jeff is with me and he's been beaten. Tell Conner he can find Jeff in a black Volvo." Then I proceeded to give her the location of the vehicle. I disconnected, turned off the phone and gazed at Jeff. "They're on their way. I have to go."

"Huh," he murmured. "Don't..."

"I'll make sure they find you." I got out of the car, closed the door and wiped off the handle. My eyes scanned over the vehicle as I tried to remember if I had touched it anywhere else before I put on my gloves. Earlier I had hidden by the bumper near the passenger door. As a precaution I wiped it off. Satisfied I hadn't left any fingerprints behind I stayed out of sight from passing cars and jogged toward the rented Ford.

When I was within a hundred feet of the vehicle, two black Escalades sped by me. I suspected the vehicles belonged to Conner, but since I had only placed the call around twenty minutes earlier, I wasn't sure. After throwing my backpack into the backseat and sliding behind the steering wheel, I looked in the direction of the small building and saw bright lights shining through the trees. Wondering how many men were checking the scene, I started the engine and headed toward the Volvo.

Reaching the crossroads, I glanced to the right and saw two Escalades parked near the Volvo. With a smile on my face, I proceeded down the road a short distance, flipped a u-ey, and thought about Leon as I headed to the car rental agency. What happened to him after Kendall knocked him out? Did he think Conner was responsible? When I saw him at Monique's, was he working for Conner or whoever had given the order to capture Jeff? Conner had mentioned thugs could easily be bought. Did Leon's loyalties change on a daily basis depending on who was the highest bidder?

38

A MYSTERIOUS CALLER

Almost two hours later, I pulled the Dodge into the parking lot behind the apartment building. Climbing out of the vehicle, I was greeted by Eldon, the elderly man who lived in apartment 512, Conner's friend—probably an employee.

"How are you doing this evening?" he asked.

I suspected he had been sent out to the parking lot to watch for me to return. "Fine. Are you out for your evening stroll?" I took my shopping bag out of the trunk.

"Yes. Fresh air."

"Have a nice one," I said, walking to the entrance. As I opened the door, I turned and saw him pulling a cell phone out of his pant pocket. Definitely an employee.

I stepped into the apartment, saw the landline answering machine light blinking, and assumed a message from Conner awaited me. Wrong. Father's tone reflected irritation as he commanded me to call him.

Hurrying into my bedroom closet, I moved a floor board and lifted up my black cell phone. Since my apartment was bugged, I closed the closet door and placed the call. He picked up on the second ring. "Why didn't you have your phone with you?"

"I thought I only needed to carry it all the time when Wendy was here."

"No. I don't want you to go without it."

"Why?"

"Sara, you don't have your ring. It's been over three days. You have to call me immediately if you start feeling disoriented, time is against you. You'll need to get to the cave as soon as possible."

"What happens if I can't?"

"That's why you need to carry your phone."

"I always have my disk on me. I can signal for help that way."

"Yes, but it'll take valuable time to locate you. We can have you picked up faster if you call."

"Hypothetically, what happens if I can't get to the cave?"

"Within two days of becoming disoriented and dizzy, your body will tremble and you'll experience uncontrollable painful seizures."

"How long will that last?"

"Until you're in the cave with another ring on your finger."

"I never should have taken my ring off."

"Do you want to come home now?"

Packing up and leaving Baton Rouge before finishing my project didn't bode well with me, but the option of staying here was dwindling by the hour. "If I don't have my ring on my finger by tomorrow night, I'll come home."

"Wise decision. Keep your phone with you. I love you, Sara."

"I love you too, Father." I disconnected, leaned back against the wall and hoped somehow I could figure a way to ask Reese about the location of my ring.

I placed my black cell phone on my nightstand, and then consumed a bottle of *venotrolia*. I went back into the living room and took the light green cell phone out of my backpack. I pushed it on and saw four unheard voice messages—two from Conner, one from Reese, and the last one from a number I didn't recognize. It was received when I was on the phone to Father. Reese's call had come an hour earlier. Wondering if he was checking to see if I could've played a role in what transpired at the small building, I punched in his number.

"Hey," he answered.

"Hi. I just discovered you had called. I turned off my phone when I went out to get a dress to wear to Mitt's funeral and I forgot to put it back on. Sorry about that."

"Did you find one you like?" he asked in a pleasant tone, not a hint that he suspected I wasn't telling the truth."

"Yeah. I hope you like it. Were you able to find out what hospital Wendy's in?"

"She's not in any hospital around Baton Rouge."

"Could she have registered under a phony name?"

"Nope. No new patient matching her description was admitted. I suspect she only stayed long enough to get stitched up."

"But she's not back at my place yet and her clothes are here."

"Not all of them."

"Huh?"

"I think she left something behind at one of our facilities."

"At that dilapidated plant?" I asked, trying to figure out what he was talking about.

A loud banging and commotion came through the phone.

"Sally, I'll talk to you tomorrow," he said and clicked off.

Worried that something might have fallen out of my backpack when I was struggling with Boyd on the floor, I picked it up, unzipped all the compartments and yanked out the various pieces of clothing. Gazing over the pile on the table, it didn't appear like anything was missing. I lifted up each item, examined it for tears and put it back in the compartment where it belonged. Suddenly, it struck me. The ski mask was gone. I tried to recall what happened to it after Leon pulled it off me. Nothing came to mind.

The green cell phone buzzed. I glanced at the caller ID and answered, "Hello, Conner."

"When you told me you were going shopping," he said in a stern, annoyed tone, "why didn't you tell me you knew where they were holding Jeff?"

"I didn't know Jeff was missing."

"Then how did you happen to end up at that shack?"

"Aah...aah," I mumbled, trying to think of a reasonable explanation without telling him the truth. "Conner, I don't like discussing things like that on the phone. There are ways conversations can be overheard."

"Not your phone or mine. All anyone could possibly obtain would be the phone number I had dialed, and that would require an expert. I'd come over, but I'm not in Baton Rouge."

"Where are you?"

"I'll be back tomorrow in time for the funeral."

Wondering why he didn't answer my question, I asked, "You're going to the funeral?"

"Wouldn't miss it. Thurman is an old friend."

I doubted they were friends, but Thurman was a valuable customer and Conner probably didn't want him to suspect he was involved in his son's death. "But what about Mase's family? They'll be there."

"It'll be cool. No one will attempt to harm anyone at a funeral."

"You sure about that?"

"Yes, but after could be a different matter. Enough funeral talk. Let's get back to the shack. How did you know about it?"

I wanted to keep the tracking device on the Mustang a secret, but I still might need his help in locating my ring. A deviated course flashed into my head. "A tracking device," I blurted out.

"A tracking device? On who?"

"Reese."

"You put one on him when he was at your place?" he said, sounding befuddled.

"Yes."

"And you didn't think that was important enough to share with me?"

"I found it in Granny's room when I was straightening it up. It must have belonged to Wendy, and I didn't know if it worked."

"And the tracking software?" he asked, suspiciously.

"Wendy had used my laptop a few times, and I found the software had already been installed." I felt like I was digging a deep hole I'd have a hard time climbing out of if he asked any more questions.

"How convenient," he said in a tone that told me without a doubt he didn't buy my Wendy story. "So this software that magically appeared on your computer, directed you to the shack?"

"You got it."

"Was Reese still at the shack when you scouted it out?"

I figured Conner was just fishing for more information. Jeff would've already told him Reese wasn't there. "No, but that was the last place the tracking device registered."

His breathing with muffled sounds in the background came through the line. I waited a minute for him to say something, then I couldn't take his silence any longer and asked, "Conner, are you still there?"

"Yes. Sara, promise me that you won't put yourself in danger again."

"My name is Sally," I said firmly. "And I'm not going to make a promise I might not be able to keep. I need to find my ring."

"See you tomorrow," he said and ended the call.

I stared at the cell phone as I pondered why Conner didn't argue with me about the safety issue. It wasn't like him to give up that easily. He's up to something. What? Then I recalled I still had one message left on the cell phone from an unfamiliar number. I pulled my notepad out of my backpack and compared the number to those I had jotted down from Mitt's and Mase's phones. No match. Curious about it, I flicked on voice mail. As I listened to a crackling, disguised female voice, an uneasy sensation vibrated through my body when she said, "I know your secret. I know what you are."

Needing to know the identity of the mysterious caller, I punched in the number. After five rings, a man answered, "Mildred?"

"No. Who am I talking to?"

Slurring his words, he said, "Hey… hey, huh, laa-dee, give me a ri-ride home."

Assuming the guy on the other end of the line had consumed way too much alcohol, I asked, "Hey buddy, where are you?"

"Sammy's."

"Sammy's Place?"

"Muh huh," he muttered.

That establishment I knew well. The bar Mitt used to frequent and hang out with the Buckley brothers. A payphone hung on the wall between the doors leading to the restrooms. I envisioned the caller leaning against that wall. "Are there many women in there?" I asked, wondering if the woman who had left the message could be hanging around.

"Flam...ing Maxie...and some other broad. Hey, hey, ge-et," he said, followed by a loud thud, and then the line went dead.

My watch read 11:35 p.m. It had been less than an hour since the female called and I hoped she was still at Sammy's. If not, maybe the bartender could give me some information. I dropped both cell phones into my purse and walked out into the hallway.

I gritted my teeth when I ran into two men dressed in suits, Conner's employees, standing against the wall next to my door. No wonder he didn't argue with me about the safety issue. He had taken care of it by stepping up his security detail on me. I turned on my heels, went back into my apartment and locked the door. Without lingering on the situation, I headed to my bedroom and shut the door behind me so I couldn't be spotted by the surveillance cameras. Quietly, I opened the window, glanced down, and searched for any sign of Conner's men five stories below. Satisfied, I inched out, scampered to the corner of the building, and saw an Escalade in the parking lot next to the Dodge. A suit-clad man, with the handle of a rifle protruding above his shoulder, paced the pavement, and probably another man or two were sitting in the Escalade. Feeling irritated and defeated, I crawled back into my bedroom, sat on the edge of my bed and briefly had the urge to poison all of them, but the sensible part of me immediately squished that stupid notion. Then the woman's voice drifted through my mind. *I know your secret. I know what you are.*

A new resolve rushed into my head, and I became determined not to let Conner rule my every move. What harm would it do if they followed me to Sammy's? On that thought, I left the bedroom and headed toward my car. The two muscular men who had been guarding my door accompanied me on the elevator. No one spoke.

When I reached the Dodge, the two men were joined by the guy pacing the parking lot. He politely opened the driver's door for me. "Thank you," I said. He gave me a quick nod. The Escalade engine idled as I started my car. Pulling onto the street, I noticed the Escalade that had been parked across the street now sat in front of my building. It drove next to me while the other Escalade drove behind me all the way to Sammy's. Besides the occupants of the vehicles not letting me out of their sight, I also suspected several tracking devices were attached to the Dodge. I doubted I could have been guarded better if I had been royalty.

Arriving at my destination, I saw only a few cars were parked along the street. My buddies and I had plenty of spots to choice from. I cut to the curb and soon found my vehicle sandwiched in by the Escalades, leaving me no wiggle room to drive away until one of them budged.

A man climbed out of the backseat of the vehicle in front of me and started to walk toward my car. Expecting that he planned to open my door, I quickly scooted into the passenger seat, leapt out and hurried into Sammy's. To my chagrin, two men dressed in suits stood right inside the door. How did they know I was coming here? Then I recalled my apartment was bugged. Someone was listening when I mentioned Sammy's. Did they think I planned to drive the drunk home?

I glanced around the establishment and saw two scantily clad women playing pool with two guys wearing t-shirts and jeans. A couple holding hands sat at a small round table, a guy occupied a barstool and the bartender, dressed in a white short-sleeved shirt and sporting tattoos that covered his exposed arm, stood behind the bar. Outside that small group of people, I didn't see anyone else in the place except for Conner's men who were lingering near the far wall, eyeing everyone inside. I wondered if the guy I briefly chatted with on the phone was passed out in the hallway leading to the restrooms.

As I marched up to the bar, two more of Conner's men entered Sammy's. The bartender's eyes drifted from me to the men dressed in suits. "What can I get you little lady?"

"Information."

He cocked an eyebrow as his head swung from side-to-side, checking the location of Conner's men. His chin slightly twitched, and I suspected my escorts were making him nervous. "What kind of information?"

I checked my watch. "About an hour and a half ago, I received a phone call from a woman using your payphone. Besides those two," I said, pointing at the pool players, "did you notice any other women in here around that time?"

"Lady, a lot of women come and go from this place, and I don't keep track of the payphone."

"This woman probably came in here alone. Did you serve very many single women this evening?"

The bartender tapped his fingers on the bar and pressed his lips together as he glanced at Conner's men again. "Yeah, but," he began and looked over his shoulder at the clock on the wall, "being Monday night, almost all of them were gone by ten. Most that stuck around after that were with a fellow."

"Most? What about the others?"

"Besides my girl coming in for a drink, there weren't any single ladies sitting at the bar."

"Tables?"

"No barmaids worked tonight. Anyone wanting a drink needed to come to the bar." He shook his head. "No single ladies."

Thinking I had wasted my time coming here, I asked, "Notice anyone just come in and leave without having a drink?"

"A gal came in lookin' for a guy, a regular."

"Who?"

"Lady, we don't give out names of customers unless you're a cop. You a cop?"

I shook my head. "Was the woman also a regular?"

"Nope. Never seen her before."

"Did she stick around at all? Or just leave?"

"Don't know. I got busy filling drink orders," he said as a guy strolled up to the bar. The bartender's attention turned to the customer.

Running through other questions I could ask, I remained at the counter while the bartender filled a beer pitcher. After the customer picked up the pitcher and walked away from the bar, I asked, "Do you recall anything about the woman?"

He squinted. "Let me think. Long blonde hair. Nicely dressed. Looked like she had plenty of dough, but a lot of our customers do."

"Young? Old? Attractive?" I asked as Monique's image bounced into my head, though I still believed she was probably died.

"Lady, my girl was here when the gal came in. Let me tell you, I don't look at women when she's around. Don't need that type of trouble."

"Can you think of anything else about her?"

He shook his head.

A thought snapped into my mind. "Was she looking for Reese or Dan?" I asked, knowing they both hung out there.

He inhaled and his eyes darted between Conner's men as he grabbed a towel and started wiping the bar. "Yeah."

"Which one?"

"Lady, what do you need them for?" he asked in a jittery voice.

"Don't need either of them. I'm just trying to locate the woman."

The phone behind the bar rang. "Can't help with that," he said, answering it.

Doubting he'd tell me which one, I was mad at myself for not mentioning just one name at a time. The women playing pool most likely were here when I received the call, so I headed to the pool table.

I stood against the wall and watched them play as I waited for a break in the game. The red-haired woman, wearing a mid-rib top that revealed her well-endowed cleavage, kept glancing at me.

After her shot, she sauntered over to me. "You want something?" she asked, staring at me.

The guy I had chatted with on the phone mentioned flaming Maxie and, hoping he had been referring to her, I said, "Just wanted to ask you some questions, Maxie."

"Who told you my name?" she hissed.

"The bartender," I lied. "Hey, I'm not here to make any trouble. I just want to know if you can remember seeing a woman with long blonde hair who came in here by herself around two hours ago."

"What's it to you?"

Suspecting the woman would be friendlier if I offered her some money, I dug into my purse. "She has something that belongs to me," I said, handing her one of the hundred dollar bills Reese had given me to buy a cell phone. I thought that was too much to pay, but I couldn't exactly ask her for change.

Her eyes dropped to the money clutched in her fist. "Must be valuable."

"Only to me."

"What can I help you with?"

"Did you see a woman with long blonde hair?"

"Yeah, a few, but only one didn't have a date."

"Did you get a good look at her?"

"Only her back. She was huddling around the phone, like she was afraid I'd snatch it from her."

"Phone. The payphone?"

"Yep. I had to pee. The bitch was blocking the bathroom door. Asked her to move. Ignored me. Had to shove her to get her out of the way. What a sweetheart," she said, sarcastically.

"You didn't see her face at all?"

"Nope. Seemed like she was hiding it the way she flipped her hair around with her hand."

"Right or left hand?"

Maxie pursed her lips and briefly closed her eyes "Right."

"Any jewelry on it?"

"Oh. Did she steal your ring?"

Boy, would I like to know the answer to that question. "Was she wearing one?"

"Yeah. A big red stone—maybe a ruby. Don't know gems that well. You looking for a ring like that?"

"No," I said, shaking my head. "Was she tall, short? Slender, heavy?"

"She seemed about my height, but a little heavier," Maxie said, and my eyes scanned her rail-thin, about five-foot-eight frame. "But I don't remember looking at her feet. She could have been wearing six-inch heels for all I know."

Thinking that was close to Monique's size, I looked at Maxie's shoes, sandals with a two-inch heel. "How was she dressed?"

"Nice slacks. A blue silk blouse. Classy looking."

Maybe I had the whole Monique thing wrong. Could she still be alive? "Did you get a sense if she was young or old?"

"She wasn't a kid, but I only saw her for a couple of minutes. You know, going in and out of the restroom."

"So she was on the phone for a while."

"Can't really say. I wasn't in there long."

"Hey, Maxie, how long you goin' to keep us waiting," a burly man asked as he chalked a cue stick.

"Be right there, Hank," Maxie said, glancing at the guy. She turned her attention back to me. "Gotta go."

Glimpsing at Conner's men, I wondered if I could escape his increased security, and hurried down the hallway toward the women's restroom, but ducked into the men's instead and felt relieved it was empty. A small window above the only stall stood ajar. I climbed up the wall, opened it wider, and heard feet pounding on the ground, but didn't spot anyone moving about. I squeezed out, crawled along the wall to the roof, and checked the location of Conner's men. Two stood in front and one paced by the exit on the side of the building.

After climbing down on the other side, sprinting behind buildings and staying in the shadows while creeping through an adjacent parking lot, I crawled up an office building, looked down, and didn't see anyone around. I went down on the far side, took a path leading to the street, and hunkered down behind the parked car as I stealthily made my way toward my car. Reaching the last parked vehicle directly across the street from Sammy's, I fished out my car keys and pushed the remote door opener. Conner's men's attention abruptly shifted to the Dodge while I charged to the driver's door.

"Hey, one of you guys needs to move your car so I can go home," I said, sliding behind the steering wheel and watching the perplexed expressions on their faces. Smiling to myself, I turned the key in the ignition, and then cringed when I noticed two men dressed from head to toe in skin-tight black outfits cross the street from the same place I had been a minute earlier and climb into an Escalade. I bit my lower lip and rubbed my forehead. How did they manage to stay hidden from me?

39

THE FUNERAL

The following morning, I kept peeking out the living room window and glancing at the Cadillac parked across the street, hoping Conner would call off his hounds before Reese arrived. It would be futile to ask him to remove his guards. Conner initiated all maneuvers. I opened the apartment door only to find his men still patrolling my hallway.

After I dressed for the funeral, I looked out again and saw the Escalade hadn't budged. I sank down on the couch and pondered what to say if Reese asked questions about the men hanging around. Before I could come up with a reasonable explanation, the doorbell buzzed.

I opened the door to Reese, and didn't see any other guys in the hallway as I gave him a warm smile. "You look great in a suit. I've never seen you dressed up before."

He returned the smile while his eyes scanned my outfit. "You look lovely, But," he said, raising my arm, "you forgot to remove the price tag."

"Oh," I gasped. I had purposefully left the tag hanging to confirm my shopping spree. I got a pair of scissors from the kitchen and asked Reese to remove it. "Thanks. It would have been pretty embarrassing showing up with a dangling ticket." I put back the scissors and picked up my purse. "Has anyone heard from Mase?"

"Not a word," he said, walking out of the apartment. "How about your cousin? Have you seen or heard from her since we last spoke?"

I shook my head while locking the door. "No. I'm worried about her. I hope she'll get in touch soon, but she's been known to vanish for months at a time." I sensed we were being watched as we moved toward the elevator. "What did she leave at your place?"

"Not at my place," he said, stepping into the elevator. "At a facility owned by an acquaintance. One of the guys discovered a stocking cap there and thought it belonged to Wendy."

Interesting, he did not say ski mask. Why would he hide that from me? "I've never seen Wendy wear one of those. I doubt it's hers."

Walking out of the building, I glanced across the street and saw the Escalade. Reese took my hand and led me to his black Volvo. Wondering how he found it, I climbed into the passenger seat. "Nice car." I eyed the interior, and it seemed a little different than the one I had driven the night before. Was it the same car?

"Thanks. I like Volvos. This is the third one I've owned." He started the engine. "Got it last month."

"Were they all black?" I asked and immediately regretted it when he glimpsed at me with a cocked eyebrow and his lips pressed together in a thin line.

"Yes," he replied, his eyes fixed on the road ahead of us.

Trying to wipe out any suspicion I might have raised with my last question, I said, "A black Volvo's been parked in front of my apartment building often this past week. Was that your car?"

His brow creased, and he briefly looked at me. "A black Volvo?"

"Yeah. It was parked in the handicap spot. Thought the driver would get a ticket since I didn't see any handicap sticker or anything like that on the car. The car was in the same place the following night, so I guess the owner never got one."

"When was the last time you saw that car?"

"Mmh. Let me think…Oh, Sunday. The same night Wendy went to the hospital."

"Well, it wasn't this car."

"Could Mase have driven one of your other cars?"

"No. I've sold them."

"There's got to be thousands of people in Baton Rouge that drive Volvos. It's probably just a coincidence."

The funeral home parking lot was beginning to fill up when we arrived. Reese pulled into a stall on the first row and escorted me inside the building. I kept looking around for Conner as Reese led me into a chapel with stained-glassed windows throughout. I didn't spot Conner anywhere and with all the men dressed in suits, I had no idea if any of them worked for him.

We moved at a slow pace up the aisle as a soothing, relaxing sensation run through my body. My ring was close. The fingers on my right hand began to tingle and jerk. I gripped them with my left hand while my eyes drifted over everyone seated on the benches.

Reese stopped at the third row and gestured for me to scoot into it, but my ring was drawing me to the front of the chapel. The coffin that held Mitt's body stood next to the podium. "I want to be closer to Mitt."

"This is as close as we can get," Reese said.

The second row was already filled, but there were plenty of places to sit on the first row. "How about the first row?"

"That's reserved for the family."

My palms became moist, my pulse spiked, and an odd spasm emerged in my organs. My ring was somewhere ahead of us, and I had to get it. Adrenaline pumped through my veins, and I worried my needles would burst out if I didn't see it soon. My ring! My ring! Nothing else mattered, and the need surging inside had to be satisfied.

"I was his girlfriend. I'm sure his parents won't mind me joining them," I said and marched up to the front row. My ring finger twitched toward the right bench. I sank down beside Dwayne, Mitt's 16-year-old brother, and Reese sat on my other side.

"Sally," Reese whispered, "people are still arriving. Mitt has Aunts, Uncles, and cousins. They really should be allowed to sit on the front row."

"No. I need to be here," I said adamantly, and then my eyes swept over the five other occupants on the pew. Tessa, Mitt's mother, wearing a black long-sleeved dress, sat between Dwayne and a young woman, who I assumed was Mitt's sister. On the other side of Mitt's sister was a woman who had a striking resemblance to Tessa and appeared to be about the same age. A gray-haired, elderly man sat next to her and held the woman's hand. Orson Thurman wasn't on the bench. He sat on the one across the aisle in the middle of the row flanked on both sides by men. I briefly wondered why he wasn't sitting by his wife, but then my ring overtook my mind again.

I closed my eyes and concentrated on it as I attempted to determine who on the pew had it in their possession. That method didn't work. I slid my hand under my thigh to hid my out of control finger, patted Dwayne's arm with my left hand and asked, "How are you doing, Dwayne?"

"Okay," he mumbled, raising his head. Pain radiated from his blue eyes, and I felt sorry for the kid, not for the loss of his brother, but because he didn't have a chance for a life free of crime since his father was Orson Thurman.

If I touched the culprit who had my ring, would I sense anything? In five minutes the funeral service would begin. I rose to my feet and fisted my right hand, hiding my twitching finger, as I moved to Mitt's mother. "Mrs. Thurman, I am so sorry for your loss." I gently touched her arm and a soft breeze swirled through my body. My clutched fist sprang open with such force that my fingers smacked into the woman's leg. She had my ring.

Her head shot up, and she glared at me through swollen eyes.

"Oh, I'm sorry," I said with trembling lips and brought tears to my eyes. "It's just Mitt. I can't believe he's gone. Can I sit by you?"

"You're… Sally?" she said, brushing a strand of hair away from her face.
"Yes."

"Sally, I want to sit by my children."

The organ music stopped.

Tessa gripped Dwayne's hand. His lips pinched together and his hand twisted like he didn't appreciate her holding onto him, a typical reaction for a 16-year-old boy. Reluctantly, I returned to my seat by Reese.

"Are you okay?" he whispered.

"Yes. Seeing Mitt's mom, I wanted to comfort her."

"Ladies and gentlemen," the man behind the podium began.

As he continued, I studied Tessa's clothing and the purse sitting on the bench tucked between her and her daughter. From the sensation I received when I touched the woman's bare arm, my ring probably was also touching her skin. Besides me, no one could wear it. Still, my eyes dropped to her hands resting on her lap. She wore a huge diamond, two or three karats, on her left hand. The way her right hand was positioned, I could only see part of a gold band. My ring had a silver band with a petrified spider web embedded in it. Checking every inch of her clothing, I caught a glimpse of a chain hanging around her neck. Whatever dangled from it was concealed under her dress. Would this sophisticated dressed woman wear a ring hanging from a gold chain? If so, why? Was she afraid someone would snatch it from her? Different scenarios bounced around in my head as I pondered how Mitt's mother could have acquired my ring.

Everyone rose to their feet snapping me out of my reverie. I hadn't realized the service had ended.

Reese took my arm. "Sally, are you doing okay?" he asked tenderly, giving me the impression he thought I was indeed mourning.

Standing up, I fisted my right hand again to contain my jerking ring finger. "Yes. I still can't believe that wonderful man is gone, and the police don't seem to have a clue to the assailant. How can anyone die like that, and their killer go unpunished?" I asked, laying it on perhaps a little too heavy.

Mitt's mom moved around her son and caressed my arm. "Sally, would you like to go with us in the limo to the gravesite?"

I wanted nothing more than to remain close to my ring. Yet, it seemed strange Tessa would invite me to join her family. Was she up to something? "Thank you. At a time like this, I'd really like to be with Mitt's loved ones." I turned to Reese. "Do you mind?"

"No," he said, his eyes slightly narrowing. He probably felt as bewildered by the invitation as I did. "I'll meet up with you there."

My heartbeat fluttered when I saw Conner talking to Orson Thurman.

Tessa wrapped her arm around mine and escorted me out the side door to the waiting limo. I expected Thurman would also be riding in family limo, the first car following the hearse to Mitt's final resting place.

Goose bumps rose on my arms and a chill swept over me as I climbed into the vehicle and spotted Kendall among a group of people heading to their cars. Looming a foot taller than the crowd of mourners near him, and dressed in a suit, Kendall had obviously attended the service. Why? From the way I acted about his ring, he had to know or at least suspect mine was missing. Was he watching over me in case I had a seizure? Or was he involved in determining my punishment? Questions buzzed through my mind, but my main concern was acquiring my ring from Mitt's mother without drawing too much attention.

Tessa slipped into the limo and sat next to me. Her children sat on the seat across from us. Mitt's sister's eyes were red and puffy, like she had been crying for hours. The boy sat stoically, not displaying any emotion. Given his father's line of work, I doubted this was first gunshot victim funeral he had attended. His bottom lip twitched slightly, and I sensed he had been close to Mitt.

"Dwayne and Candace, this is Sally Jablon, Mitt's girlfriend," Tessa said.

"I'm so sorry for your loss," I said with a quavering voice, addressing Mitt's siblings. "Your brother and I had so many plans. Now they're gone." I swallowed hard and bowed my head.

Tessa slid closer to me and took my left hand that had been draped over my fisted hand. Her touch sent warmth swimming through my limbs as the energy of my ring emanating from her skin. I closed my eyes, savoring the sensation. My body yearned to have it back where it belonged, on my finger.

"I know it's hard, dear," she said, "but somehow we'll all get through this."

Opening my eyes, I saw her ring clearly, a large red stone surrounded by diamonds. Maxie didn't mention the sparkling diamonds. Could it be the same ring? I found it hard to envision the sweet woman by my side ever entering Sammy's, let alone, making a threatening call. On top of that, I couldn't imagine she'd want me anywhere near her or her children if she knew the truth about me.

The door click shut and the vehicle's engine accelerated.

"Isn't Mitt's father coming with us?"

"No," she snapped, squeezing my hand in the process while the limo followed the hearse out of the parking lot. Across from us, Candice crunched her face and gazed at her mother. Dwayne seemed oblivious to Tessa's angry tone. She looked at her children and continued, "Orson wanted to go to the cemetery with his cousin. I'm sure they're only a car or two behind us."

I swung my head around and peered out the back window. A foot away from the limo's bumper was a Cadillac Escalade. I recognized the driver, a Crussett employee. The glare of the sun hitting the glass panel behind the driver prevented me from seeing the passengers. When the limo turned right, I saw a silver-colored Camry behind the Cadillac, followed by a black Volvo, which I assumed was Reese's car. Though I had expected him to be driving alone to the cemetery, it appeared he had three passengers with him, men wearing dark suits. To no avail, I squinted trying to make out their features. His vehicle went around the corner and became blocked from my sight by the Cadillac, leaving me wondering if I'd be driving away from the cemetery in a car full of men. Had Reese planned a side trip for me similar to the one I had gone on with his brother?

40

BULLETS FLY

The hearse and the caravan of cars behind it pulled into a lush green, well kept cemetery. The pavement running through it was lined with trees and an array of colorful flower beds. The limo stopped and we climbed out as six pallbearers lifted the casket out of the hearse and carried it toward the prepared burial site. Glancing around, I saw Thurman, Conner, and two unfamiliar men step out of the Escalade. Mitt's mother, his siblings, and I walked behind the coffin up a small grass-covered incline.

I wasn't about to let Tessa out of my sight and stood close to her while pallbearers situated the coffin on a perched platform above its prepared burial site. As we waited for everyone to gather around Mitt's plot, my eyes drifted over the people, searching for Kendall. He was nowhere in sight.

The priest moved to the head of the coffin. Before he began, Tessa edged between her children, leaving me standing on the other side of Candace. Her sudden move irritated me, but she was still within arm's reach. Determined to have my ring on my finger before she climbed back into the limo, I bowed my head and stared at her shoes as I mulled over how to take it from her. My mind had been so fixed on my ring that I hadn't heard a word the priest had said when chatter erupted around me and the crowd began to disperse.

Brushing her fingers under her eyes, Tessa stood staring at her son's casket. Candace was no longer between me and her mother. She and Dwayne had joined their father, who stood next to Conner, on the other side of the coffin. After Thurman hugged and embraced his children, he walked around the platform site and strolled toward Tessa.

As he approached, I caught a glimpse of a tall figure partially obscured in the shadows cast by a cluster of trees two hundred feet away. Kendall. I

255

froze for a moment, then took a deep breath and slowly exhaled in an attempt to relieve my nerves.

Thurman grabbed his wife's arm and swung her around. "We agreed we'd drive here together," he said through gritted teeth.

"You gave the order, but I never agreed," she hissed. "Our son…is dead because of you and your whore."

Thurman's brow furrowed in apparent confusion and he asked, "Tessa, what are you talking about?"

"I saw the pictures in your den."

I knew she was referring to the photos I had sent to Thurman. The pictures I acquired at Monique's—the ones showing Thurman's lover being tortured and buried, and Mitt enjoying every minute of it.

Tessa went on in a raised, angry voice, "How can you stand so close to our dead boy and pretend you don't know who killed him."

My eyes flashed to the other side of the coffin, the place Dwayne and Candace stood by Conner. All three were staring at Thurman and Tessa. Not wanting the children to hear more, I hurried around the coffin. "Conner, please take the kids to the car."

Conner turned to the man behind him, who I assumed was a bodyguard, as I heard Thurman say, "What pictures?"

Since I was responsible for the argument ensuing between Mitt's parents, I didn't want to hear any more, yet my ring outweighed any thought I had of leaving.

"You know damn well what pictures I'm talking about," Tessa hissed.

As Conner's employee escorted Dwayne and Candace to the car, I noticed Reese chatting with some men near the paved cemetery road. While I hurried back to Tessa, I looked around and saw less than a dozen people still lingering by the coffin. Seven of them were bodyguards, judging by their rigid bodies and eye movements sweeping the area.

"Tessa, I have no idea what you are talking about." He caressed her arm.

"Don't touch me." She pushed his hand away. "You've orchestrated a phony crusade looking for your whore, when all the time you knew she'd never be found."

"Victoria?" Thurman muttered, glaring at his wife. "You know where she is?"

"Orson, your lies aren't going to work on me. You know damn well she's dead. You have the proof. Why did it take you so long to unleash your revenge?"

"Proof," he said, sounding befuddled. "What proof?"

"Those damn pictures!"

Thurman's eyes lowered and he rubbed his temple. "You murdered Victoria?" he asked as the color drained from his face.

"She was stealing from us. She had you wrapped around her little finger.

Someone had to do something. Mitt took care of it. But like always, you have spies. You killed your own son because of that whore. You're a bastard. I wish you were the one lying in that coffin rotting away." She turned on her heels and stormed away from him.

Thurman charged after her, clutched her arms, and pushed her backwards until she slammed into the coffin platform. I quickly moved to block the view from the children sitting in the Escalade.

"You...you," Thurman spat, "killed Victoria. She'd never steal from me. You stupid woman. She didn't need to steal. She just needed to ask. Anything she took was with my permission." He gripped her throat.

"Let go of me, you bastard," she muttered, gasping for air.

As the scene unfolded, bodyguards moved within two feet of the arguing couple, drawing weapons and preparing to take action. Conner stepped up and laid his hand on Thurman's shoulder. "Orson, your children are in the car. They can see you."

Thurman released his wife. "Get out of my life," he yelled at her. "If you attempt to enter the gate leading to MY house, you'll be shot on the spot. I knew I was being betrayed by someone close to me. Now I understand why the informer wouldn't give me the name. Of all people, I never thought it was you." His eyes bore into hers. "Get out of my sight."

"You murdered our son. Have you no shame?" Then she turned away from her husband and, to my surprise, headed to me. "Sally, can I talk to you?" she whispered.

Relieved I didn't have to chase her down the hill to get my ring, I said, "Of course." I walked by her side up the incline, further away from the parked cars.

Behind us, I heard Conner say, "Have Mark take Orson and his children home." I glanced over my shoulder and saw Thurman and two men trudging down the hill. Conner still had four bodyguards close by.

"This is far enough," she said, focusing on my face. "He won't leave you alone, will he?"

"Who?"

"Crussett. Conner. Your boyfriend."

"Tessa, I was dating your son when he died," I said, trying to figure out what she wanted. "I've never dated Mr. Crussett."

"Are you going to lie to me too, just like Orson?" she asked, her lips jutted out in a pout.

"Is this what you want to talk to me about? My relationship with Mr. Crussett?"

"No." She raised the chain around her neck revealing my ring. "This."

"How did you get my cousin's ring?" I said, not wanting to admit it was mine. The stabbed victim at the warehouse would've identified it by now.

"Your cousin's?" She cocked an eyebrow and shook her head. "How I got it isn't important. What is…is the magical power this ring holds," she said as a bald man with a thick neck, dressed in a suit, came down the hill and stopped ten feet behind Tessa.

From the way his eyes were fixed on me, I wasn't sure if he was there to protect Tessa or me. Footfalls pounded against the ground behind me. I expected Conner would be within earshot any minute. "Power? What are you talking about?"

"I've had it analyzed. No one has a clue why it can't be worn. It jolted one so hard when he tried to put it on that he ended up with two broken fingers. Since the experts in the field couldn't give me any answers, I took it to my psychic. She claims it's been bewitched by a spell. That's the only reasonable explanation."

Being bewitched is a reasonable explanation? "Huh?" I asked, thinking Tessa had watched too many movies and they were affecting her gray cells.

She continued, "A bullet struck a woman's forearm at a warehouse. She wore this ring." Her eyes dropped to my bare arms. "You don't have even a faint scar. I've seen pictures of Conner's girlfriend, the one that looks just like you and supposedly died in a warehouse fire." Tessa glared at me. "Somehow, you rose from the dead. I'm convinced this strange ring has healing powers and you're the vessel for them." She dangled it back and forth between her fingers. "I want to be able to wear it. You can make that happen."

I recalled Mason saying something about me being a witch at the abandoned cement factory. Could Tessa be T? Not wanting anyone to know I possessed unusual abilities, even though they weren't founded on her false premise, I had to sway Tessa in believing there wasn't anything unusual about me or my ring.

"You've got it wrong. I'm Sally Jablon, and the first time I saw Mr. Crussett was at Sammy's when I was there with your son. Do you know the place?" I suspected Tessa was the woman who had called me the night before.

A hint of a smile crossed her lips. "Yes. I've been there a couple of times." Stroking my ring, she peered behind me, probably checking on Conner and his men. "Sally, I'm not going to spar with you over this issue. Either you fix this ring so I can wear it, or you're going to be the next one that needs a coffin," she said in a soft voice so only I could hear her.

My eyes moved to the guy standing a short distance behind her, and I assumed he had been stationed there to carry out the threat if I didn't comply. Suddenly, a throbbing pain started at the base of my skull and inched up. My fingers and arms tingled and jerked. I clutched my hands to try and stop the spasms running up my arms. My vision became cloudy. I felt the earth move underneath me, and my legs wobbled. My throat swelled, restricting my breathing. I opened my mouth and gasped for air. A gurgling sensation rose in my throat and I screamed, "My ring." I blinked, hoping to clear the fog consuming my mind. Without warning, my arm flew up, smacking into Tessa's chest, and my finger wrapped around my ring.

"No," Conner yelled, leaping into me.

A gunshot rang out.

With my ring secured in my fist, I tumbled to the ground. Conner landed on top of me. Gunfire and loud voices erupted around us. Warm liquid oozed down the front of my dress. My eyes sprang wide open. I could only see shadows and silhouettes moving around. A whooshing sound swam through my head, preventing me from grasping what anyone was saying. Using all the energy I could muster, I slipped my ring on my finger. The noise occupying my head ceased. My vision returned, and I found myself staring at one of Conner's bodyguards, a man I recognized. Then panic hit, sending adrenaline pumping through my veins, as I saw the blood splattered on my dress and Conner lying motionless next to me being attended to by his bodyguard.

"I've stopped the bleeding, Mr. Crussett, but try not to move," the guard said. "An ambulance is on the way."

"Is she okay?" Conner mumbled, lightly squeezing my arm.

I closed my eyes, grateful he wasn't dead.

The guard looked at me. "She wasn't hit."

A siren blurred off in the distance. The sound kept getting louder.

Conner's bodyguard rose to his feet, went and talked to two other men. I spotted a man on the ground ten feet away with blood pooling around him. From the awkward position of his body, I figured he was dead. Attempting to recall what had happened, I vaguely remembered I couldn't control my fingers as they gripped my ring. After that, everything was a blur. Who fired the first shot and why?

I turned on my side and cringed when I saw the tourniquet, fashioned out of a torn shirt, on Conner's arm. I caught a whiff of his masculine smell, a smell I could never forget, and softly stroked his cheek. "Are you badly hurt?"

"No. I'll mend." His eyes met mine and a faint smile crossed his face. "I'd take a bullet for you any day of the week."

"Someone tried to shoot me?" I said, pretending to be shocked by that revelation, though I assumed Tessa had carried out her threat when I touched my ring. But doing it in a public place with Conner and his men close by, seemed like an unreasonable move, putting her own life on the line. On top of that, if she thought there was any chance she could garnish the power she believed my ring held, she would have destroyed that opportunity. Maybe her plan was to shoot me, not kill me. Or maybe it was to shoot Conner to get him out of the way.

"Sweetheart, you can't swipe something from someone when that person has guards positioned nearby."

"But it was my ring."

Red-and-white lights flashed in the direction of the pavement. The siren whined, and then stopped.

"We know that. Tessa knows that. But the ring was in her possession. Given your proven skills, I would have expected you to stealthily sneak into her house and snatch it when she wasn't looking. Not yank the chain off her neck."

"Over here," a guard yelled, standing five feet from us and swinging his hand in front of him, motioning toward Conner.

When the paramedics arrived, they were told I also needed to be taken care of. I quickly stood up and convinced them I was perfectly fine. I scanned the area, looking for Tessa. She was gone.

Within ten minutes, Conner was strapped to a gurney. "I want Sally to ride in the ambulance with me," he said to the paramedic.

"Conner, I want to go home and clean up. Then I'll come to the hospital." I turned to the paramedic. "Which hospital?"

Before the paramedic could answer, Conner asked the closest bodyguard, "Is Mark back?"

"Yes. He just pulled in a few minutes ago."

"Sally, I want you to go with Mark. He'll take you to your place. Will you do that for me?"

Seeing his pale face, his blood soaked suit, and his bandaged arm, I said, "Yes."

Walking down the incline next to the gurney, I looked at the remaining parked cars, searching for Reese's. The black Volvo was nowhere in sight, and neither was Reese. I watched the paramedics load Conner into the ambulance and drive away.

One of Conner's men opened the back door of the Escalade. Climbing in, I caught a glimpse of a tall man getting into a Mercedes. Kendall.

41

DAMAGING EVIDENCE

I strolled into the hospital with a bodyguard by my side. He led me up the elevator to the sixth floor, down a hall, and around a corner to a small hallway with only one door leading to a hospital room. A guard stood by the door frame.

Inside the room, Thurman and his son occupied two chairs, but the bed was empty. "Where's Conner?"

"In surgery," Thurman said, standing up and gesturing for me to take his seat.

Before I could tell him I'd get another chair, a bodyguard strolled in carrying two. He placed them on the other side of the bed. Then Thurman proceeded to tell me the bullet had lodged in Conner's arm. The doctors were removing it and repairing the damage.

"Any idea how long the surgery will take?"

He shrugged his shoulders. "Maybe a couple of hours."

I eased down in a chair as I wondered why Dwayne had accompanied his father to the hospital. I could understand Thurman being here since Conner's injury occurred at Mitt's funeral, but to drag a 16-year-old with him seemed a little strange. "How long have you known Conner?" I asked so we wouldn't be sitting in silence while we waited for Conner to return from surgery.

"First met him when he was Dwayne's age," Thurman said, patting his son's leg.

A guard entered the room and whispered something to Thurman. Then Thurman rose to his feet. "Problems," he said. "Miss Jablon, if Conner returns to his room and he's conscious, will you let him know I'll be back as soon as I can?"

I nodded. "Certainly."

Thurman turned toward his son, "Dwayne, Mr. Crussett might not be able to talk to you for hours. Why don't you come with me, and you can see him tomorrow?"

"No, Dad. I'll stay."

He laid his hand on Dwayne's shoulder. "Mr. Crussett is well protected. He's got it covered. You sensing he's in danger won't be new news."

"I knew something was going to happen to Mitt and no one listened to me. I need to talk to Mr. Crussett."

"Okay, but if you get tired of waiting, I don't want you leaving here alone. Call. I'll have someone come and get you. Understood?" Thurman said in a firm tone.

"Got it."

When Dwayne and I were alone in the room, I asked, "Do you have the ability to sense when someone is in trouble?"

"Sometimes," he said with his eyes fixed on the floor. He fidgeted with his hands and adjusted himself in the seat.

"Have you had that ability long?"

"Yeah," he mumbled, tapping his bottom lip with his index finger.

His body language told me he was hiding something. If he truly had the ability to sense when someone was in trouble, I doubted he'd be able to survive in that household. Organized crime families are seldom not in danger. Otherwise, they'd never need bodyguards constantly hanging around. Then I remembered never noticing any bodyguards when I went out with Conner before I discovered he was a member of a crime family. Now, I knew they were always close by and just hidden from my view.

I moved to the door and eased it shut. I sat beside Dwayne in the chair Thurman had occupied earlier. "Dwayne, any idea why you're sensing Mr. Crussett is in trouble?"

"Well…"

"I'm very good at keeping secrets if that's what you're worried about. I won't tell a soul without your permission."

"Well…," he muttered as his drawn eyes gazed at me. His face was etched with worry.

I felt he wanted to unburden something that had been weighing heavily on his mind, but he had trust issues. "Did you overhear someone talking about Mr. Crussett?"

He nodded. "Yeah."

"Your father or one of his employees?"

"Not about this."

"Your mother."

He nodded and his eyes became moist. A tear leaked out of the corner.

He swiped it away with his fingers. "She wants my dad dead."

I thought he had heard too much of his parents' argument and rubbed the boy's shaking hand. "Dwayne, I'm sure your mom doesn't want to hurt your dad. She was upset at the cemetery. People often say things they don't mean when they're angry."

"No. It wasn't today." He squeezed his eyes shut, bent his head, and cradled his forehead in his hand.

I hadn't expected to hear that. Since someone could open the door any minute, I needed to move this conversation along at a fast pace. "Listen Dwayne, I might be able help. Why don't you tell me what you know?"

"How can you help?"

"Let's me just say, I have some useful skills in dealing with trouble."

He sat up straight and his eyes popped wide open. "You...Were you the one that stabbed a guy at Buckley's warehouse?" he asked, and I assumed he had picked up that bit of information from eavesdropping on a conversation.

I wanted him to know I was a competent fighter, but, at the same time, I didn't want him to relay my exploits to his father. "Can you keep a secret?"

"Sure. I won't tell anyone it was you."

I smiled to myself, relieved I didn't need to verbally confirm it. Changing the subject and trying to figure out his relationship with Conner, I asked, "Are you and Mr. Crussett buddies?"

He shook his head. "No. When he comes to see my dad, I'm always shooed upstairs."

Why would Dwayne be concerned about a man he hardly knew? "Are you hoping if you tell Mr. Crussett whatever you heard before he finds it out on his own, that you might be able to get him to leave your mother alone? Is that what this is about?"

He shook his head again. "No. If she kills Mr. Crussett, my father will be next."

Wondering why he believed that, I asked, "Dwayne, have you told your father what you heard?"

"Can't," he said, running his hands through his hair.

"Why?"

"Monique. I promised I wouldn't tell him about her, and I always keep my promises. A lot of business goes on with just a handshake. If your word can't be trusted, no one will ever want to do business with you."

I suspected the handshake thing was something his father had drilled into him. From my exposure to an organized crime family, I knew first hand that was how they conducted business. Though they kept records, nothing was in writing between the parties. I also knew how customers were dealt with if they didn't pay up. "Monique? Monique Torren?"

"Yeah, you know her?"

"No, but I've heard the name." The kid was holding back. If I was going to help him, I needed more information. "So you're planning to warn Mr. Crussett he's in danger. He'll ask you why, and you'll tell him you overheard your mother talking about him. Right?"

He bobbed his head.

"Mr. Crussett will want to know what you heard. What will you tell him?"

"Mom and Monique had just come down to breakfast. They thought I was still at my friend's house. I slept overnight, but got dropped off early. I was in the pantry getting a box of cereal. Monique said something about a van with blood stains. Next I heard 'Kill Crussett and Orson.' That's when I ducked down in a corner so they couldn't see me if they went in the pantry. Monique always says bad things about my dad. I think she hates him."

Monique had been missing for a while, but Dwayne didn't seem to know about that. Was she really missing?

Dwayne went on, "She said something about working with Uncle Buckley. Then she wanted him to shoot Mr. Crussett. After that, someone would kill Dad."

"Uncle Buckley. Is that Mason Buckley?" I asked for verification.

"Yeah. He isn't really an uncle. He's my dad's best friend." Dwayne shook his head. "Him doing business with Monique and Mom, something's wrong."

"Is it possible they were talking about one of Buckley's sons—Mase or Reese?"

"Hmm." Dwayne squinted and scratched his forehead. "Just heard Monique say Buckley. Guess it could be." He lowered his head and clasped his hands together. "Do you think Mr. Crussett will help me?"

"What do you want him to do?"

He raised his head. "Get rid of Monique," he said, clenching his teeth.

Did he want a permanent solution or only to get her out of his parents' lives? Would a 16-year-old request a hit?

"I know if she was gone," Dwayne said, "Mom wouldn't be so weird. Whatever Monique wants Mom to do, she does it. She's like a little puppet. Mom used to be nice to Dad. Not anymore. They argue all the time now. She never asks me about school or anything. She blew up at Candace just because Candace dumped the rest of her cereal in the sink and didn't run the garbage disposal. Mom never acted like that. It seems like she's getting worse. Whenever the house phone rings she yells at me if I answer it. No one can answer it but her."

"When was the last time you saw Monique?"

"She only stays at our house when Dad's gone. Must be a couple of weeks."

"You heard them talking two weeks ago?"

"Yeah. Something like that."

"Then why didn't you try to contact Mr. Crussett earlier?"

"I wanted to figure out what was going on with Uncle Buckley first. I just don't know if he's still Dad's friend or not. And the guys that guard our house have seen Monique there. I hoped one of them would say something to Dad. And then I didn't hear about anyone getting hurt except for the guy at Buckley's warehouse. I thought maybe Monique had changed her mind, but then, Mr. Crussett…" The ringing of my cell phone briefly interrupted him, "got shot."

I fished my black phone out of my purse. Gazing at the name, I said, "I need to take this. I'll be right back." I pushed the door open, quickly moved around the corner, and down the hallway out of the earshot of Conner's men. "Hello, Father. I've got my ring."

"I've heard," he said, his voice heavy with concern.

"Is something wrong?"

"Yes. I had hoped to leave you out of this, but we need to move fast and there isn't another Tegen close by."

"Move fast?"

"Wendy Adams had four revenge killings. The last victim she preserved and stuffed into a rolled up sofa bed. The body was discovered before we could recover it. A poisoned victim we could handle. Leaving him wrapped in a web causes problems. The medical examiner has already identified the substance and has called in a spider expert for confirmation."

"And who is the expert?" I asked, suspecting it might be Father.

"That's how I learned about the examiner's findings. They've booked me on a six o'clock fight tomorrow morning. I don't plan to get on that plane, unless the body hasn't disappeared by then."

"Who's the victim?"

"I'll explain everything later. Right now, I need you to help get the body out of the medical examiner's lab."

"Okay," I said hesitantly, doubting I could lift the body by myself. "Oh, you said help. Who's going with me?"

"Kendall."

I cringed hearing his name.

"He has all the details and a plan. He's been following you around all day trying to talk to you, but you haven't been alone. He'll meet you on the hospital roof. With Conner's men keeping track of you, can you manage to get up there unseen?"

"Yes," I said, picturing the window in Conner's hospital room.

"He's waiting for you there."

After we said our good-byes, I walked at a brisk pace back toward the room and thought about sending Dwayne on an errand.

Before I reached the door, it opened and Dwayne came out. He stopped by my side. "Need a Coke. You want one?"

"No. I'm good." I went into Conner's room, closed the door, removed my shoes, and stuck them in my purse. After opening the window and forcing out the screen, I slid out, crawled above a row of windows, and scurried up to the roof.

When I planted my feet on the solid surface, Kendall, wearing hospital scrubs, strode around the mammoth air condition condenser. My stomach churned and spine stiffened. "What's the plan?" I asked over the lump forming in my throat.

"You distract the guard at the lab and I'll take care of the body."

"But first how am I going to get out of the hospital without anyone spotting me?"

"I've taken care of that."

"We can't climb down. There are too many people and Conner has a few guards stationed outside."

"This way." He tilted his head toward the roof's hospital entrance.

I obediently followed him into the building's stairwell and down two flights. He opened the door to the eighth floor. There, he led me to a supply room with a sheet-covered gurney inside. I assumed it was waiting to be used in my hospital escape.

His dark, sinister eyes glared at me. "Get into this," he demanded, holding up a body bag.

Had Father not asked me to help, I would've protested. Instead, I took the offered bag, lowered it to my feet, and wiggled into it with my purse draped over my shoulder. Holding the rim of it above my head, I said, "I can't zip it from this angle."

While I gripped the top of the bag, his oversized, rough hand moved over my fingers, and I dropped my hold.

He lowered the edge. "Put this on." He handed me a rolled up rubber thing.

I stretched it out and saw it was a mask of an elderly woman, complete with gray hair. I tugged it over my head and lined up the openings over my eyes and mouth. It fit snuggly against my skin. "Done."

He stared at my mask covered face, and then picked me up and laid me on the gurney. "Close your eyes and keep them shut," he ordered.

I jerked when something cold and slimy touched my eyelids. "What's that?"

"It hides the seam." He zipped up the bag, enclosing me inside.

The door squeaked open and the wheels creaked as he pushed me along. I heard voices, the shuffling of feet, and the ping of the elevator. While we descended, I suspected some of Conner's men were busy searching for me, and wondered if we could get out of building without being stopped.

"Open the bag," a husky voiced man said, halting my speculation.

"There's nothing in this bag except for a dead old lady," Kendall said in an even tone.

The gurney swung sideways, striking a hard surface. "A woman is missing," the husky-voiced man said. "No one is leaving the hospital with anything large enough to conceal her. "Now open that damn bag or you'll be joining the woman inside."

The metal zipper rattled. The plastic bag crackled. Bright light penetrated through the rubber mask. I held my breath.

"That sure isn't her," the husky-voiced man said. "Zip it up."

I sensed darkness descending over me again. The wheels rolled along a smooth, hard surface. A few minutes later, the gurney bounced and swayed. A loud clang reverberated. Then, the gurney was pushed up an incline.

A car door clicked shut. Without Kendall saying a word, the engine roared to life, the vehicle jerked, and it moved. As traffic sounds erupted around me and my face itched from the rubber mask, I felt irritated I hadn't been freed from the body bag. The itching was driving me crazy. I ran my fingers over my eyelids, touched the firm jelly-like substance Kendall had applied, and eased a fingernail under it. Gripping the stuff between my thumb and forefinger, I carefully peeled it away from one eye at a time. Confident I had removed all the goop I slowly opened my eyes and saw the inside of the body bag. Then I pulled the mask off and twitched my jaw back and forth.

I inhaled and exhaled deeply, found the end of the zipper, and forced my finger through a small opening. As I was about to unzip it a thought sprang to mind. Did Kendall have a reason for leaving me concealed inside the bag? Was this how he planned to get into the medical examiners lab? Then I sighed, recalling Kendall telling me my job was to distract the guard. *Can't do that in a body bag.*

A short while later, the vehicle stopped and the hum of the engine ceased. Car doors squeaked open. The bed of the vehicle wobbled. The bag zipper slid open and Kendall's head loomed above me.

"We're here," he said, yanking down the body bag. His dark, penetrating eyes studied my face, sending an eerie sensation up my spine. Father had mentioned he had hoped to leave me out of this mission of retrieving the body, but there wasn't another Tegen close by to help. I was sure Father knew the affect the Tegen enforcer had on everyone near him. Kendall handed me a long blonde curly wig. "Put this on."

I quickly obliged. The bangs on the wig hung down below my eyebrows, making it difficult to look sideways. If I peered up my vision would be obstructed by the dangling strands.

"You'll go through the side entrance, turn right, and down a flight of stairs at the end of the hall. There is a small office right outside the lab. At this time in the evening, there should only be one person on duty. He could either be in the lab or in the office. Your task is to keep him in the office until an alarm goes off. Don't touch anything."

"About how long will that be?" I asked, freeing myself from the body bag.

"Less than fifteen minutes." Kendall climbed out the vehicle.

Reaching the back door, I jumped down from the hearse onto asphalt, and saw we were parked in an alley behind a police cruiser next to a three-story brick building—a place I recently visited when two police officers questioned me about Mitt. "We're going into a police station?" I asked, staring at the structure.

"Yes."

"I've been in that building before. Someone might recognize me."

"Just follow the path I dictated and you shouldn't have any problem. When you leave, head to that car," Kendall said, pointing to the police cruiser in front of us, "and lie on the backseat floor.

I nodded as questions buzzed through my head, but I didn't want to linger in the alley, thinking someone might spot us. I pivoted away from Kendall, eyed the side entrance, and noticed a card-reading box attached to the frame. I swung around to ask Kendall about it. He was gone.

Hoping the door was unlocked, I hurried to it. I pulled the bottom of my blouse out of my slacks, and covered my palm as I clutched the doorknob. Just as I feared, the doorknob wouldn't turn. "Great," I mumbled and studied the card reader. I doubted I could break into the police station without drawing unwanted attention. Then the door partially opened. I braced myself, expecting a police officer to come strolling out. I came here to help remove a poisoned victim. Leaving another one behind definitely wasn't part of the plan. Yet, I needed to get inside. Did I have another option?

The door began to slowly close without anyone stepping out. Before it slammed shut, I stuck my foot between it and the doorframe. Wondering if Kendall had pushed the door open, I peeked into an empty hallway and entered. I turned right and hurried to the brightly-lit stairwell. Tucking in my blouse, I rushed down to the office. No one was in the sparsely furnished room. At the far side were double-doors with round windows in them. I went and peeked through one of the windows and saw a thirty-something, thin man with horn-rimmed glasses perched on his narrow nose, wearing a white lab coat. He was busy straightening up a row of medical instruments. I knocked on the door.

He raised his head, looked at me, and marched toward the doors. He pushed them open. "Can I help you?" he asked with a creased brow.

"Yes. My uncle's body was here a few days ago. My aunt wants me to meet her at the funeral home, and I can't reach her on her cell phone. Can you give me the name of the funeral home?"

He stepped into the office, and I noticed 'Erick' embroidered over the lab coat pocket.

"You're not supposed to be down here. No civilians unless they're accompanied by an officer."

I touched his arm and moved closer to him. "Please, Erick, can't you help me?" I asked, gazing into his magnified brownish-green eyes.

"Well, I guess it can't hurt." He walked to the file cabinets. "What's your Uncle's name?"

"Brad Barstow," I said, giving him a made-up name.

"That doesn't sound familiar," he said, thumbing through the cabinet drawer. He pulled out a file and glanced inside it. "Only one Barstow. A woman. She was here two years ago." He put back the file. "Are you sure his body was taken here?"

I sank down into a chair, bowed my head, and rubbed my forehead. "Isn't this where car accident victims go?"

"Only bodies of individuals who died under unusual or suspicious circumstances are brought here. Well…they're not all brought here. Baton Rouge has other medical examiners' labs. Was there something unusual about the car crash?"

"It was real bad. Three people died. One of the policemen who came to the accident gave me his card. He works here, so isn't this where the bodies would have gone?"

He shook his head.

Tears ran down my cheeks and I cupped my head in my hands. "Where could Uncle Barstow be?"

"What's the name of the officer?"

"Officer Sloan," I stuttered, feigning emotional distress.

"Hmm. Have you got his card with you?"

I shook my head. "No."

Erick flipped through a notepad on the desk. "There isn't an officer here by that name. Could it be Stowne?"

"Maybe. I feel so confused."

"Let me—" he began.

A high piercing alarm buzzed and smoke billowed out around the double-doors. Erick charged to the doors and squinted at the windows to see what was happening. I jumped to my feet, charged up the stairs, and edged by several officers in the hallway. Each carried a fire extinguisher and it appeared they were heading toward the medical examiner's lab. To my horror, Detective Karl Gilbert, one of the officers who had questioned me about Mitt, was among the group. But it seemed like all of his attention along with his colleagues was consumed by the smoke drifting up the stairwell. I turned my face away from the officers, flattened myself against the wall, and continued to the door. I rushed out. As I sprinted to the police car, I noticed the hearse was gone. The cruiser's backdoor stood wide open and the engine hummed. Without looking around for Kendall, I leapt into the backseat, pulled the door shut behind me, and dropped to the floor. A few seconds later, the cruiser pulled away from the police station.

After we had driven a while, the sound of traffic grew louder and light streamed through the car windows. I looked over my shoulder and saw street lights, lit up billboards, and multi-colors reflected from the buildings. "Where are we?"

"Not far from the hospital."

Wanting some answers before I climbed out of the car, I said, "I thought we went there to retrieve a body, not to burn the place down."

"The lab will sustain some smoke damage from the body being incinerated. Nothing else burned."

"Incinerated? How did you manage to get the temperature that high?"

"I'll drop you off a block from the hospital," Kendall said, ignoring my question.

As a Tegen enforcer, Kendall's chosen profession meant inflicting the ultimate punishment to convicted Tegens. I envisioned flames shooting through guilty members as a wave of terror ran through my body. Incineration left only ashes with no evidence the charred remains once embodied a Tegen. My stomach tightened into a knot as the image of Wendy engulfed in flames sprang into my head.

The car eased over to the curb. I had more questions for Kendall, but I'd rather leave them unanswered than spend another minute with the Tegen enforcer who occupied the driver's seat. I pulled off the wig, dropped it on the backseat, and exited the vehicle without us exchanging any more words.

42

DEADLY OCCURRENCES

As I walked to the hospital, I saw a black Volvo turning into the parking lot and flinched. Could it be Reese? Thinking it over, I stepped into the shadows between two parked trucks and called Father.

"Problems?" he asked

"No. It's all done. You don't need to board a plane in the morning."

"Did it go smoothly?"

"Yes, except I saw one of the detectives involved in Mitt's case when I was leaving the station. I wore a wig and doubt he caught a good glimpse of my face. But in case he did, I'll have an alibi lined up."

"Anyone else see you?"

"Erick, the guy I kept distracted while Kendall took care of the body. Who was Wendy's fourth victim, the person who went up in flames?"

"Your building superintendent, Mr. Hawkins."

"The Super? Why did she do that?"

"Based on her account of the event, he came to your apartment when you weren't there to discuss a confrontation she had with a tenant the prior evening."

"She slammed Esther's hand in the door. Esther told me the Super came to her rescue."

"Yes. That's it. He mentioned he wanted her out of the building. She refused to leave, and told him you'd never allow her to be kicked out of the building. He said, 'We'll see about that,' and stormed down the hall. Wendy followed him back to his apartment. She doesn't have an ounce of remorse for her action. She felt the killing was justified."

"The third victim. Who was that?"

"An investigator. A man hired by Hank Davidson's parents. Kendall discovered his remains in the basement of your apartment building."

"Hank's been missing for over a year. The investigator just caught up to Wendy. What took him so long?"

"Mrs. Davidson had been devoting every waking hour searching for their son. The family recently received a large donation to help broaden their efforts. They hired an investigator. He was on the job less than a week when he paid Wendy a visit."

"He could have threatened her or something. Maybe she had no recourse," I said, and then wondered why I had this need to defend her.

"Wendy said she followed him to the back door of the apartment building, and then he got aggressive. It doesn't matter if that poisoning was self defense or not. One revenge killing is not allowed. She carried out at least two. Even if the killings of both Mr. Hawkins and Mr. Steinberg, the investigator, were justified, the verdict would be the same."

I had the urge to ask if Wendy had been punished. Yet, after everything that had transpired within the last twelve hours, I didn't feel prepared to handle any more bad news.

"Sara, it's time you came home. We can minimize, but we can't completely stop the ripple effect of Wendy's actions. Too many people believe she was your cousin. She stayed with you. Mr. Steinberg's organization has launched an investigation searching for his whereabouts. You're already involved in the investigation regarding Mr. Thurman. Mr. Hawkins died under suspicious circumstances in your apartment building. You need to leave Baton Rouge before the police and investigators start digging into your background."

"But our computer expert has that covered."

"I don't want to take any unnecessary chances. I want you out of there."

"My project. It's not finished."

"Sara, this isn't negotiable," he said in a firm tone, and I knew there was no point in arguing with him about it. "You can have two days. Friday morning, you're going to follow the outlined procedure we discussed in Bismarck and come home. The documents will be delivered to you Thursday morning."

We said our good-byes. Concerned about how badly my project had gone so far and irritated Brett had sent Wendy to me, I trudged through the hospital parking lot.

If I hoped to accomplish anything, I had to find a way to keep Conner out of harm's way without his knowledge. He had been shot trying to protect me. I couldn't let that happen again or spend my time worrying about him. My pulse quickened and a tingly sensation pulsated through every inch of my body just thinking about him. Oh, how I longed to be snuggled in his arms and feel his lips on mine. I shook my head. How can I love and be repulsed by the same man? He gives orders to kill people or destroys their lives without any remorse. What is wrong with me?

Nearing the hospital entrance, I almost stumbled into the back bumper of a black Volvo. I ducked down, peered around the vehicle, and scanned the people wandering in front of the hospital and in the abutting section of the parking lot. Four men, dressed in suits, paced back and forth and checked the area around them. Another two wearing jeans and sport coats along with a casually dressed woman who had a large bag slung over her shoulder were chatting to each other. Something about the stiff way they were standing and one guy's hand under his coat, told me they hadn't come to the hospital to visit a loved one. One of the men turned toward the parking lot. Focusing on his face, I recalled seeing him at Monique's. He had helped Leon search the backyard, looking for an intruder. I doubted the threesome were Conner's employees, but I couldn't rule out that possibility. My gaze swept over the parked cars, searching for Reese. Not spotting him anywhere, I thought he might be inside, or the Volvo next to me, wasn't his.

Assuming at least four of the guys by the doorway were part of Conner's crew, I straightened up and headed in that direction. I sensed seven pairs of eyes on me as I entered the hospital. Two of the suit-clad men followed me in. One spoke into a headset attached to his ear.

They both went up in the elevator with me and stayed close behind while I walked at a brisk pace to Conner's room. A man standing by the door opened it as I approached. Stepping inside, I saw Conner sitting up in bed with a pillow behind his back, a sheet covering him, and his arm bandaged from his shoulder to below his elbow.

"Where have you been?" he snapped.

Seeing his pale face and the worried look in his brown eyes, I ignored his tone. "I'm glad to see you, too." My eyes drifted around the room. "Has Dwayne left?"

"Over an hour ago."

Resisting the urge to embrace him, I eased down in the chair next to the bed. "Did he get a chance to talk to you?"

He adjusted himself in bed, stretched out his undamaged arm, and moved his hand over mine. "Before we discuss Dwayne," he said in calm tone, "will you please tell me where you have been?" He squeezed my hand.

"I had some personal business I needed to take care of. Nothing to do with Buckleys, Thurmans, or anything we've discussed. Will you do something for me?"

"What?"

"If anyone asks, I was here all the time. Okay?"

"Personal business? And you need an alibi?" he asked, suspicion apparent in his voice.

I raised an eyebrow and briefly pressed my lips together. "Is that a problem?"

He studied my face. "No. Not at all. May I ask, who might be inquiring?"

"No," I replied, giving him a coy smile. "Can we talk about Dwayne now?"

His hand caressed my cheek. "What do you want to know?"

"He wanted to ask your assistance regarding a situation," I said, trying not to spill very much in case Dwayne had hesitated.

"Did he tell you about it?"

I nodded.

He went on, "Part of the situation has already been handled. The other part is strictly family business, and they'll have to work it out. And I'm not planning to become anyone's victim."

"Can you give me just a little bit more clarification?" I asked, holding up my hand with my thumb and forefinger slightly apart.

A faint smile crossed his lips. "I thought I made myself completely clear."

"Oh, come on. How about if we start with Monique? Is she out of their lives?"

"Dwayne will never have to worry about her again."

His quick response reinforced my belief that she was dead. He had told me earlier he wasn't involved in her disappearance. Now I suspected he lied and would never confirm he had given the order. I moved on to another question, "Did he mention to you that Monique slept over at his house sometimes?"

"Yes, but I already knew Monique and Tessa were lovers."

"And Thurman didn't mind that?"

He shrugged his shoulders. "Monique isn't the first woman who has stayed in Tessa's bedroom."

"She doesn't share a bedroom with her husband?"

He shook his head.

"Thurman knows about his wife?"

"Has for years. They had an agreement."

Here I thought she was jealous over Thurman's mistress. Boy was I wrong. "Then why did she kill his mistress?"

"Don't know the facts. I'd just be speculating."

"Okay. Speculate."

"Tessa's involvement with Monique started shortly before Thurman's mistress disappeared. At the cemetery, Tessa claimed Victoria was stealing from them. I suspect the thief was Tessa. She used Victoria as a cover-up. Mitt, who carried out the execution, probably had no idea his mom was the culprit. This is shear speculation, I have no proof. But around that same

274

time, Monique received three hundred grand in cash."

"Cash? Is that why you couldn't trace the money?"

"Yep."

"Mase's cell phone. Is Tessa the T contact?"

"That would be my guess."

"Any idea what they're working on?"

"Not yet." He caressed my arm and flashed me a mischievous smile. "This is so interesting. Sara cringed when business was discussed, and Sally, who resembles Sara in every way, thrives on it. So tell me Sally, are you here to wreak havoc on my business?"

I wondered how long he had suspected I was his enemy, but I wasn't surprised he had figured it out. "Is that what you think?"

He nodded. "Yes. But sweetheart, if the Crussett family never did an ounce of business in Baton Rouge again, it would hardly faze us." He touched my cheek and his eyes glowed. "You're just going to have to work a little harder."

"Let's get back to Dwayne's situation. Does Tessa know Monique's fate?"

"Yes. She ordered the kill."

"Huh?" I said in disbelief. "So it wasn't you?"

"I already told you it wasn't. Don't you trust me?"

I wanted to shout "No," instead I said, "Then how do you know Tessa was involved?"

"Leon, one of the guys you killed at the shack, spread the word."

"Leon? There was a time he stood guard by my apartment door. Exactly who did he work for?"

"I've already told you people can be bought. In the end, he was on T's payroll."

Trying to figure out how that worked, I asked, "If Tessa is T, she hired him?"

"Not directly. Mitt used to do the recruiting. After his death it went to Mase, then Don."

"What about Reese?"

"Don't know how that decision was made, nor what they're hoping to accomplish. Maybe we'll never know."

"Why?" I asked, wondering if Don, Reese, and T had already been slated to join Mase.

"Tessa's action regarding Victoria has rattled Thurman."

"He's going to murder his wife?" I asked, thinking about Dwayne and Candace.

A knock on the door startled me. Aware danger lurked in the hospital, my eyes darted to the door. It swung open and a middle-aged, tall, muscular man, wearing a lab coat, strolled in. "How are you feeling, Mr. Crussett?" he asked, moving closer to the bed.

"The pain killers are working."

The man reached into his pocket and pulled out a syringe. Recalling an experience I had the prior year, wearing a white uniform did not always mean the person belonged in the hospital. I leapt to my feet, looped around the bed and inched my way between the stranger and Conner. "Conner, have you seen him before?"

"No," he said, his voice dragging. "Can I see your credentials?"

"This is ridiculous. I'm Dr. Mitchell," he said, pointing to his name tag.

"That doesn't prove you're Dr. Mitchell," Conner said, and then looked at me. "Get Max. He's in the hall."

While my eyes remained fixed on the doctor, I backed to the door and pushed it open. "Max, come in here." As I waited for Max to enter, the stranger's eyes scanned me from head to foot. No one stepped into the room.

"Hey, Max," Conner yelled from the bed. Still, no one entered.

I raised my foot and pushed the door open wider. I stuck my head out and peered into the hallway. An immobile man sat slumped against the wall with his head bent down and a food tray splattered on the floor next to him.

I heard noise behind me and spun around as the stranger gripped Conner's good arm and raised the syringe in the air, prepared to plunge it into Conner's chest. "No," I screamed, lunging toward the assailant. I slammed him into the nightstand. The medical supplies on it tumbled to the floor with a loud clang. The assailant smacked my head with the back of his hand. Ejecting my needles, I grabbed that hand, twisted it and flipped him, sending him sprawling across the room and the syringe flying under the bed. Conner flung his legs over the side of the bed. It appeared he planned to join in the fight. "Stay put," I responded in a firm tone.

The phony doctor jumped to his feet and charged toward me. I dodged out of his way, but he still managed to smack his fist into my upper body, knocking the wind out of me. He gritted his teeth, raised his fist, and pulled it back. As he propelled it forward toward my jaw, I blocked the blow and pounded my fist into his face. Blood spewed from his nose. I swung to the side, lifted my leg, and kicked him in his chest with all the force I could muster. He stumbled backwards. I struck a blow to his jaw before he gained his footing. The assailant swayed and wobbled, then landed on the floor in a heap.

Expecting we might have more bad company soon, I locked the door and forced the back of a chair under the doorknob.

"Where did you learn to fight like that?" Conner asked with a perplexed expression on his face.

Sliding the window wide open, I said with a smile, "Natural ability."

Conner grinned. "Sure."

I began dragging the assailant across the floor.

"Want my help?"

"No. I want you to stay in bed."

"My men can take care of the guy."

"I doubt the man lying unconscious in the hallway is going to be helpful."

"Only one guy?"

"Yes."

"Any blood?"

"We can talk after I take care of this fellow," I said, moving toward the light switch. "I'm going to turn off the light." I flipped them off, went back to the window and tried to raise the body as moonlight streamed into the room.

"You planning to toss him out."

"That's the plan."

"Sara, ah, Sally, I can have him removed without drawing any attention."

I knew he was capable of that, but the stranger I held onto had been poisoned. He needed another cause of death. Dropping six floors to the ground would take care of that problem. "I want to handle this."

Using all my strength, I pushed his head and upper torso out of the window. I took a deep breath, lifted up his thighs, and shoved the body out. Hoping I didn't have any spectators, I quickly closed the window and drew the drapes. After turning back on the lights, I sank into a chair. "That guy must have weighed over two-hundred pounds."

"Definitely," Conner said, climbing out of bed.

"Conner, please stay in bed."

"I wasn't shot in a leg," he said, swaying and rocking on his feet. "I am perfectly capable of walking."

Suspecting whatever anesthesia he had been given hadn't completely worn off, I hurried to his side. "No, you're not." I put my arm around his waist to help him. "You're going back to bed."

"Sally, I can do this," he said, stumbling toward the closet.

"No, you can't. You're going back to bed."

Reluctantly, he accepted my assistance. When he was stretched out on the bed again, he said, "Can you get my cell phone out of my pant pocket in the closet? Is the guy lying in the hallway bald?"

"Yes," I said, opening the closet door.

After I handed him the phone, he punched in a number. "Trouble here. Max is lying in the hallway, either unconscious or dead. Nick's gone," Conner said in a harsh, angry voice, "... Yes... take care of him."

From his tone, I suspected Nick, whoever he was, would soon be among the missing. Never to be seen again.

As Conner continued his call, I heard feet pounding on the hallway tile floor. Glancing at the clock on the wall and seeing the hands at 11:05 p.m., I suspected the feet didn't belong to the hospital staff. Conner was busy on the phone, and his reinforcements would be here soon. If not, the guy who just went out the window might be having company.

"...we'll do that," Conner said, and clicked off. "They're on their way. We're to stay put."

Pounding on the door and rattling of the hinges echoed through the room. "I'm not sure if the folks in the hall want to wait that long. Have you got a gun?"

"No. I seldom pack," he said.

I knew that was true from living with him for three years. Guns were not part of his normal wardrobe.

I bent down, raised my pant leg, and pulled a knife out of the sheath attached to my calf. "I guess this will have to do."

"You come prepared."

"Business necessity," I said as the door split from a sharp blade penetrating through it. "Aren't they concerned about the other patients, hospital staff?"

"With the commotion they're making—very unprofessional," Conner said, shaking his head. "It won't be long before we hear sirens."

The door burst in half and wood slivers exploded across the room. One man charged in with his gun drawn, and another man lingered by the doorway, watching. My moves were swift and concise. I scraped the man's face with one hand and plowed the blade into his stomach with the other. Blood saturated his clothing. As he staggered, his pistol discharged. The bullet struck the wall, sending pieces of plaster over the bed. I gasped when I saw the hole in the wall was less than a foot from Conner's head.

Loud voices and crashing sounds, like carts being tipped over, drifted into the room as a barrel of a gun suddenly poked me between my shoulder blades. "Miss Jablon," a man with a harsh, cold voice said, "you're lucky you're still breathing. We were told to capture you alive, but not your boyfriend."

Conner tumbled from the bed, out of the man's line of sight. The assailant clutched my arm, swung the pistol around my shoulder, and, in the process, made a deadly mistake of brushing against the needles protruding from my fingers. Ignoring the scratch marks, he pulled me toward the other side of the bed, the place where Conner had hidden from the stranger's view.

A burst of gunfire rang out from behind me. The bullets lodged in the assailant's back. Blood spurted from the wound, spraying onto my blouse and slacks as the would-be killer sank to the floor.

The throbbing sounds of sirens came from the parking lot. The flicker of strobe lights illuminated the drapes casting faint colors of blue and red across the walls.

"Got here as soon as we could, boss," a muscular man with a thick neck said, helping Conner off the floor and into the bed.

Lifting his head, Conner looked at me as a warm smile played on his lips. "You okay?"

I bobbed my head up and down.

"You have no idea how relieved I felt when that guy said he wasn't here to kill you."

"But you?" I retrieved my knife from the stabbed victim's stomach and used his slacks to clean the blood from the blade.

"I never would have dropped to the floor if you were in danger."

Sitting down in the chair next to Conner, I slipped the knife back into the sheath.

Another man clad in a suit, peeked into the room. "Boss, company is on their way up the elevator."

"You know the drill," Conner said.

Two women and one man, all dressed in hospital uniforms, rushed into the room. A crowd gathered by the doorway. The man who helped Conner into bed, maneuvered around the debris and bodies to the door. Out of the corner of my eye, I watched as he cautiously exchanged his pistol for one held by another guard. Then he moved to the foot of Conner's bed, blocking the gawkers in the hallway from seeing him.

At the same time, the medical people knelt down and checked the men bleeding on the floor. "This one's still alive," a woman said, referring to the stabbed victim. "Let's get him into surgery."

I wanted to tell them not to bother, but having him die during surgery would mask that he had been poisoned. The commotion in the hall became louder and more hospital workers entered the room pushing a gurney and talking among themselves.

Conner leaned closer to me, took my hand, and whispered. "Do you want my men to get rid of your weapon before the police arrive?"

"No," I whispered back. "I doubt they'll search me."

"True. Who would think you could handle a 250-pound guy?"

"Exactly," I said with a smile, then my eyes moved to his bandage. "How's your arm?"

"Numb. The wound required an extensive amount of repair. Otherwise, I'd be out of here." He cocked his brow. "And we would have missed all this fun."

After the gurney carrying the poisoned victim was wheeled out, two men wearing sport coats and three uniformed policemen stepped inside. Detective Gilbert, the police officer I spotted earlier at the police station, was among the group.

He eyed my blood-stained outfit while his team secured the crime scene and removed the spectators lining the hallway. "Miss Jablon," Gilbert said with a nod of his head. His attention turned to Conner. "Mr. Crussett, can you tell me what happened here?" He pulled out a notepad and gestured to the other suit-clad man to join him.

Conner filled them in on some of the facts, but added a few of his own. "A doctor was checking my vitals when the stabbed victim came in and pulled a weapon from his jacket. The doctor attempted to shield me, but the gunman knocked him into the nightstand, pounded his fist into the doctor's head, rendering him unconscious. Then the assailant threw the doctor out the window."

With trembling lips, I nodded in agreement. "It was terrible. That poor doctor ended up giving his life protecting a patient."

"Who stabbed him?" the Detective asked.

"The gunshot victim," Conner said, waving his hand toward the body on the floor.

"Robb," Gilbert said to the man leaning down by the body and searching his pockets. "Does he have a knife?"

"No knife, except this," he said, holding up a Swiss army knife. "The blade's clean."

"See if the medical staff removed it, and took it with them."

Robb stood and left the room.

"Who shot that guy?" Gilbert said, motioning toward the body on the floor.

"The shot was fired from the hallway. I didn't see the shooter's face," Conner said, then turned to me. "Did you, Sally?"

I shook my head.

"Miss Jablon, how did you end up with blood on your clothing?"

"Hearing the first shot and seeing the guy stagger, I ran toward the bathroom door as a second shot ran out. I was too close to the guy. Blood splattered everywhere. I dropped to the floor, thinking the guy in the hall was going to shoot me next." My eyes lowered to my clothing. "I didn't know this much hit me." I looked at Conner. "I can't stay like this. I need to go home and change."

"We'll deal with that after the detective is finished with his questions."

I pinched my blouse with my index finger and thumb and pulled it away from the spots where the blood soaked garment stuck to my skin.

"Driving over here, I was told you had bodyguards," Gilbert said, his eyes darted to the guard still standing at the foot of Conner's bed. "Where were they when this went down?"

"Outside, except for one—"

I interrupted, "I went to get Conner's guard when the man was fighting with the doctor. Conner's guy was lying on the hallway floor with his head on a plate full of food. Is he still out there? Is he okay?"

"There was an unconscious man in the hallway. He's being taken care of. I don't have the prognosis yet."

I inhaled deeply. "Thank goodness he's not dead. I thought he was."

"Mr. Crussett, why were guards outside? Were you expecting trouble?"

"As I'm sure you know, last year my brother died in a suspicious fire," he said.

Every muscle in my body tightened, knowing I was responsible for his brother's death.

Conner squeezed my hand and went on, "After that, I've stayed on high alert along with my family, and we'll continue that until the police can either rule out foul play in my brother's death, or the culprit is put behind bars."

"That doesn't explain why they were outside and not in the building close to you."

"Officer, everyone needs a break sometime. Would you stay cooped up in the hospital when you were given the opportunity to get some fresh air?"

Without answering, Detective Gilbert skimmed over his notes. "Can you tell me how the gunman was dressed?"

Conner released my hand and rubbed his chin. "Casual. Slacks and a short-sleeved shirt."

Thinking about the clothing worn by one of the threesome I noticed outside the hospital entrance, I added, "The shirt was striped, red and white. The stripes were wide. The pants were a light brown." I swung my head toward the door and pressed my lips together. "His hair... his hair was a medium brown."

"And you didn't see even part of his face?" the detective asked with a tinge of suspicion in his voice.

I shook my head. "No. I just caught a glimpse of the back of his head when he started down the hall after he shot the guy."

A nurse entered the room, pushing a wheelchair. "Mr. Crussett, we've prepared another room for you on the fifth floor."

"Can you give us just a few more minutes?" Gilbert asked the nurse.

"Certainly," she said, backing into the hallway, but remained right outside the door.

"Mr. Crussett, do you know why you were targeted?"

Conner shrugged. "No. Maybe an unhappy investor. You know, my family owns several investment companies. Unfortunately, people lose money sometimes. The police have been looking into that angle regarding my brother's death."

Robb rushed back into the room. "No knife," he said. "It wasn't in the victim. The nurses and doctor didn't see it."

"Mr. Crussett, may we search your bed?"

"Can it wait until I no longer occupy it?"

"How long will you be staying in the hospital?" Gilbert asked.

"Until sometime tomorrow afternoon," he said, glancing at the clock. It said 12:39 a.m. "I mean until sometime this afternoon."

Gilbert jotted down the information and asked, "We'd like to examine your bodyguards' pistols."

"No problem," Conner said, "but I can assure you their weapons weren't fired."

"We just want to rule out that possibility." He looked over his shoulder. "Robb, take care of that."

As Robb stepped toward the guard at the foot of the bed, the guard pulled back his suit jacket, raised his weapon with his thumb and index finger out of his holster, and handed it to the police officer.

Robb examined and smelled the pistol, "Not this one," he said to Detective Gilbert.

"Make sure he's not carrying one on his calf," Gilbert said.

Before Robb could bend down, the guard raised his pant legs, revealing his socks and holster-free calves.

Gilbert nodded. "Check the others," he said to Robb

After Robb scurried out into the hallway, Gilbert turned his full attention on me. "Miss Jablon, were you at the police station earlier this evening?" he asked, eyeing me suspiciously.

I had expected him to ask me about it when he first arrived, possibly recognizing me under the long blonde wig that only covered part of my face. Not now. Maybe Conner mentioning a fire triggered a possible connection. "No. I've been here since four o'clock. Do you want me come there?"

"No. We had an incident earlier and in the confusion I saw a woman resembling you in the back hallway, a place unescorted visitors are not allowed."

"I was either in surgery or recovery until around seven," Conner said. "Sally was here waiting when I was brought to this room. A guard was here all the time. He can vouch for her presence. What was the incident?"

"An unexplained fire in the medical examiner's lab."

"Much damage?" Conner inquired

"A corpse burned. Nothing else." Detective Gilbert briefly studied my face, and then wrote something down in his notepad. He pivoted toward the doorway. "You can move Mr. Crussett now," he said to the nurse.

When Conner was settled into another room, I said, "Why didn't Detective Gilbert ask you about your injury? You were shot in the afternoon, and then a gunman appeared in the hospital. Surely, he should have thought there was a connection."

"Hospital records don't show I'm a gunshot victim."

"Huh?"

"I had an accident at the cemetery, being struck by a crane digging a hole." He flashed a smile. "No gunshot wound."

"But there were bodies. How can you explain that?"

He cocked his head and squinted. "There were bodies?"

"You know darn well there were bodies."

Without showing any emotion, he shrugged his shoulders. "Maybe one of my men can recall seeing bodies. Do you want me to ask?"

I rolled my eyes, figuring everything had been covered up, though I suspected there were some witnesses that didn't work for Conner or the Thurmans. How did he get them to remain silent? "Were there any other casualties after you were carted away?"

"No innocent people suffered from the occurrence at the cemetery. A few cell phones and cameras did. Is that what you want to know?"

I inhaled deeply and let out a calming breath. "Yes."

"Who did you cremate at the police station?"

"No one. Remember, I was here all evening." I glanced at my watch and rose to my feet. "It's after two. I'm beat. I'm going home."

"Phil will drive you."

Heading down the hall, I saw a suit-clad man standing by the elevator and heard heavy footsteps behind me. The elevator doors slid open. The two men followed me inside, and they remained close to me until I unlocked my apartment door.

43

THE CARNAGE

My eyelids fluttered when my cell phone rang. Feeling groggy, I grabbed the noisemaker from the nightstand and stared at the screen while waiting for the ID to come into focus. Brett.

"Hello," I mumbled into the black phone.

"Sara?"

"Muh huh."

"Are you still in bed?" he asked sounding baffled.

"Mm Hmm."

"It's almost noon. What did you do last night?" he said in a cool tone.

Blinking, I cleared the fog from my head and sat straight up. "Brett, I've had a lot of late nights working on my project. Nothing you need to be concerned about," I said with an edge in my voice.

"Sara, sorry. It's just…it's just that I've heard Conner's in town. Is that true?"

Besides Father, the only other Tegen who knew he was here was Kendall. Suspecting the later had squealed to him, I replied, "Yes, but it wasn't by design. He just happened to show up. I didn't search him out if that's what you're implying."

"No. Are you seeing him?"

"Not in that way. Brett, the last man I slept with was you. In Jackson," I snapped, though stretching the truth.

"How much longer are you planning to be there?" he asked in a warmer tone, though I sensed anger behind each word.

"I'm leaving on Friday." Attempting to draw his attention away from Conner, I said, "Do you think they'll hand down my punishment as soon as

I arrive?"

"No. The Council isn't scheduled to reconvene until a week from today."

The Council didn't always stick to a schedule if pressing matters took precedence. "Wouldn't my sentencing for harboring Wendy be considered an emergency meeting?"

"I doubt it, and besides they'll wait until after Wendy's sentence has been carried out."

"She's not—"

"No. Kendall is the enforcer on the case, and he had to resolve several loose ends first. He'll be back in Bismarck sometime over the weekend. I suspect it will be handled the day he returns."

The image of Wendy's mother flashed into my mind. Tears streaming down her cheeks and her face etched with grief. I swallowed hard as I held my own tears at bay.

"Sara?"

"I'm still here. Are you still unreachable?"

"Yes. I should be through with this exploration on Saturday. Even if the job isn't done by then, I'm flying to Bismarck. I want to spend time with you before your sentencing and help you through it. But if you need me now I'll drop everything."

"No. I'm okay."

"I need to go. The van's about ready to pull out. Sara, I love you, and don't ever forget that."

"I miss you," I said, truthfully. Then the image of Conner bounced into my head and guilt surged through my body. I hadn't physically cheated on Brett, but I couldn't control the thoughts that kept creeping into my mind. "See you when you get to Bismarck." I clicked off and stared at the black screen as conflicting emotions bombarded me. I desired and craved both men, but I knew Brett could be part of my future. Conner could never be more than the present. I couldn't go with him to Houston without being targeted by his family. He'd probably die trying to protect me, and I couldn't tell him I didn't need his protection. If I told him the truth about me, which would be breaking another Tegen rule, eventually he'd try to exploit my abilities and I'd be busy undermining his business from within. A business I was still determined to destroy. How could we possibly exist together?

As much as I wanted to climb back under the covers and sleep a couple more hours, I couldn't spare the time. In less than forty-eight hours, I'd be boarding a plane. My thoughts drifted back to Conner, and based on the conversation Dwayne had heard between Tessa and Monique, I was sure Tessa was behind last night's attack in the hospital. Why did she want Conner dead? If she wanted her husband dead, Conner wasn't standing in her way. He wasn't in town to protect Orson. Until yesterday, Tessa lived with Orson. She must have had numerous opportunities. Killing him in their home would be tricky with their children and his guards nearby, but when he was out and about she probably often knew his location. Wanting Conner dead first made no sense to me. Yet, I had a nagging feeling she wouldn't relent until either he was dead or she was. Conner had guards, but they hadn't managed to keep him safe last night. Had I not been there, he wouldn't have survived. In the short time I had left here, I couldn't ruin Thurman's business, but I might be able to put a halt to Tessa's plan.

I slipped on my sweats, fed my spiders, and brewed a pot of coffee, then retrieved my computer. I clicked to the surveillance program, and held my breath, fearing the tracking device might have been discovered. My lips curved up when I saw the blue bleep on the screen clear across town, nowhere near Mase's apartment or his parents' house. Yet, I had no idea where Reese lived. Could it be at his place? I tapped on the blip, and my eyes opened wider when I recognized the street, Fulmer Lane, on the screen—Monique's. Since Orson had kicked Tessa out of *HIS* house, was she staying there? At the house of a former lover she had executed?

Planning an outing to Monique's house, I turned off my laptop, stuck it in my backpack, and changed into black clothing. I expected I'd be followed to my destination, but that wasn't going to sway me to stay away. I didn't have the time to arrange an elaborate scheme to prevent me from being tailed.

Since I didn't want Conner calling me during my outing, I picked up the green cell phone and called him. After we greeted each other, he said, "The way things are going around here, I probably won't be released until early evening."

"Problems?"

"No. Just a small blood clot in my arm that's being dealt with and the police are swarming around asking more questions. Nothing I can't handle. What time are you coming here?"

"Well...," I said, hesitantly.

"You are planning to come here, aren't you?"

"Well, I need to run a few errands first."

"Errands? What kind of errands?" he asked in a suspicious tone.

"To buy a few things. I don't have a large wardrobe, and the dress I wore to the funeral and the outfit I wore to the hospital are ruined."

"Could I send someone to shop for you?"

"No. I like shopping."

Commotion and muffled loud voices came through the telephone lines, giving me the impression some people had entered Conner's room.

"Just a minute," he said, and I wasn't sure if he was talking to me or someone in the room. "Sally, ahh, it might be better if we catch up later. I'll call when I'm released."

"You no longer want me to come there," I asked, confused why he had suddenly changed his mind.

"Yes."

"Are the police in your room?"

"A relative," Conner said. "Talk to you later." He disconnected.

As I turned off the green cell phone and dropped it in my backpack, I understood why Conner didn't want me showing up at the hospital. I knew all of his relatives. I didn't doubt he would do whatever it took to protect me from anyone associated with Thurmans, but his family would be a whole different kind of trouble.

I drank a glass of *venotrolia*, flung my backpack over my shoulder, and nibbled on a wheat cracker as I left my apartment. Two bodyguards paced the hallway. When they saw me, one began speaking into his headset. They followed me to my car. Not surprising, an Escalade with its motor running was parked beside my vehicle.

Driving out of the parking lot, the Escalade was right behind me. A block later it was joined by another Cadillac. From past experience, I doubted I could lose the tail, but if I tried and didn't succeed, at least the surveillance vehicles would become well hidden. And since I didn't want the Escalades in plain sight, either parked behind or in front of me on Monique's street, I took a sharp right, then left and continued meandering through alleyways, neighborhoods, parking garages, and up and down numerous highways. When I could no longer see them, I pulled over to the edge of the road and checked the Dodge for tracking devices. After I removed three, I jumped back in the vehicle and continued roaming through city streets for another ten minutes. Not spotting any Escalades or any other cars following my erratic path, I headed to Monique's.

I parked in my usual spot, a few hundred feet from Monique's driveway. Glancing through the windshield, I wished it weren't so bright outside. Not a cloud in the sky. Though I wore dark clothing, I'd be easy to see if I had to move out of the heavy foliage. Determined to at least disguise my face, I unzipped my backpack to pull out my ski mask, and then remembered I no longer had it, Reese did.

Feeling annoyed that I hadn't replaced it, I slid out of the Dodge, fastened on my backpack, and made my way to the woods in front of the steel-and-glass house. As I stealthily moved closer to the house, I saw a black Porsche parked by the garage. Assuming it belonged to Monique, I wondered who had been driving it since it wasn't there the last time I checked out her house. Could it be Tessa? After all, she had probably given her the money to purchase it.

The gleam of the sun striking metal and glass shined through the heavy foliage while I ducked behind an overgrown cluster of bushes. Peering through some of the branches, four other cars came into view—a dark green Mercedes, Mase's Mustang, a black Volvo, and Don's red Corvette with the white stripe on the side.

Scanning the area in front of the house, I observed a crew-cut, blond-haired man pacing near the door. His arm muscles stretched out the short sleeves on his polo shirt, and he wore a holster, the handle of a pistol protruding. Occasionally, he stopped and glanced over the area between the road and the house.

I crept around the edge of the bushes, remaining out of the guard's view, to see the front windows from another angle, one not obscured by the sheen of the sun on the glass panels. My mouth fell open and I gasped when I spotted a blowtorch at the corner of the structure. Why would they have a blowtorch? None of our spiders had ever been set loose around Monique's. Mitt had been taken here after he had been poisoned. The police and everyone believed he had died from the gunshot wound to his head. Not a word had been spoken about the possibility of another cause of death.

Another casually attired man emerged from the side of the house, and like the man in front of the building, wore a holster strapped over his chest, but he also had the butt of a rifle sticking up in the air behind his shoulder.

My eyes fixed on the blowtorch again. Had the guy who left the cement plant before the fighting ensued learned about Wendy's spiders? Was that the reason he took off in a hurry? No one inside Monique's house knew Wendy was no longer a threat.

Not wanting to test that theory and find someone chasing me with a blowtorch, I retreated farther back into the foliage and scurried up a tree with thick branches well covered with leaves. I settled down on a limb about twenty feet above the ground. There, I quietly removed my backpack, and nestled it in the groove of three attached branches, making sure it couldn't easily tumble. I unzipped it, looked through the compartment, and pulled out my directional mike. After attaching the earpiece, I pointed the device toward the house, and flipped it on. Loud static blurred through it. I jerked. A twig snapped. Leaves floated to the ground.

Turning down the volume, my eyes darted toward the guards, searching for signs they heard the noise in the foliage. Neither guard glanced in my direction as they chatted. Relief flooded through me. I turned up the volume. The static had dissipated.

Reese's voice came through the earpiece, "…explain it."

"I have," Tessa said.

"No, you haven't. I still can't figure out how you sold Mase on this whole scheme."

"But we're so close."

"Shooting up a hospital room? You call that close?"

"We'll have that covered when he's back in his hotel room," another female said. A voice I didn't recognize. Does Tessa have a new lover already?

"What about-," Reese began, and then a soft crackling sound came through the device.

I shook the mike. The unwelcome noise stopped along with the voices. Not a peep could be heard. I flipped the switch off and on.

Don's voice flashed through the receiver, "She's on board?"

"As soon as Crussett's dead," said the woman with the unrecognizable voice.

"That family's pretty close," Don said. "No one will suspect?"

"I've spent the last week in Houston. It's all taken care of. Conner's girlfriend killed his brother. She doesn't believe he didn't play a role in it. Revenge."

"This whole thing smells wrong to me," Reese said. "Mase is still missing. I doubt he'll ever be found. Someone in that family will get a whiff of this. You can't wipe out Orson and Conner at the same time without bringing trouble. Old man Crussett will have us all dead and buried before we know what hit us."

"Reese, besides our new partner, the rest of that family will believe Orson was behind the hit. We've gone over this before. You need a little trust."

"Don't have it. I'm outta here."

Furniture scraping on the tile floor, crunching of paper, and shuffling of feet vibrated through the directional mike.

"Come on, Reese. We've come so far."

"Come so far? Yeah. Mitt's dead along with at least six other guys plus the ones who were at the cement plant, the ones missing with Mase. Bodies stacking up everywhere. Dad's business will probably be ruined. I just don't see this ending well. Mase fell for your plan lock, stock, and barrel. I don't."

The front door flew open. Reese stormed out. A woman with long blonde hair stepped out after him. "Reese, come back. At least think about it. It'll work out," the woman yelled, standing by the door.

Ignoring her pleas, Reese climbed into Mase's Mustang, started the engine, and inched it out of its tight parking spot between a Mercedes and a black Volvo. As soon as he cleared the vehicles, he gunned the engine and sped out of the driveway, running over the edge of the grass next to it.

I stared at the woman on the porch, blinked, and rubbed my forehead. Monique? How? Conner thought Tessa had killed her. Had someone ordered a hit on her so they staged the whole thing? A smoke screen?

Monique moved back into the house, slamming the door behind her. "He'll be back. He's just upset about his brother. Nothing to worry about."

"You don't think he'll go to Crussett?" Don asked.

"No," Monique said. "The van's still at his dad's place. Buckley isn't going to move it with Crussett in town. Reese knows if he mentions a word to Crussett, he'll be putting his dad's life on the line. The way Crussett operates, I doubt he'll stop with the dad."

"Yeah," Don mumbled. "I heard after his girlfriend was murdered, over twenty guys were executed."

I cringed. Twenty guys. Then I shook my head. That many might have perished in the fire, but I doubted Conner would go on a killing rampage. His nephew, Caden, shot me. Then Caden went into a coma from poisonous venom running through his veins. Poisonous venom I had injected into his body. He never opened his eyes again. There wasn't anyone left alive to blame.

"The guy can be vindictive," Tessa said. "Come tomorrow that won't be a problem."

A faint sound behind me drew my attention away from the steel-and-glass house to the street. I removed the earpiece and listened intently. Wheels softly crunched the pavement's graveled shoulder and car doors creaked open. Pressing my lips together, I suspected Conner's men had tracked me down, though I couldn't understand why they would've parked so close. As I continued focusing on the area behind me, I heard muffled voices and footsteps barely making any noise as they moved lightly in my direction.

Slowly and quietly, I turned off the directional mike, slipped it into my backpack, and zipped it up. Then I gripped the bag in my hand and climbed ten feet higher into the tree. From my new vantage point, I had a better view of the house and I could see branches swaying and glimpses of men moving toward the house. I attempted to get a headcount, but the heavy foliage occasionally obscured my view, not allowing me to see all of them at the same time. Though I couldn't manage to get a total count, I knew there were at least ten men working their way to the house. As they moved closer, I saw they were all dressed in black and heavily armed, and then figured I wasn't their mission.

Watching them inching through the bushes and trees, I pondered who might have sent them and came up with three possibilities—Orson wanting revenge for Victoria's death, Conner to get even for the attack at the hospital, or Buckley finding out Monique, the woman who had put himself and his family in danger, was still alive. I also realized I had only captured snippets of the plan, not the big picture. What would they gain if they managed to kill both Conner and Orson? Maybe the group had stepped on the wrong toes before I even arrived in Baton Rouge. The men prowling around below me might not be employees of anyone I knew, although, I doubted that. But one thing was for sure: the people inside that steel-and-glass house were in imminent danger, and I wasn't going to budge from this tree to help them.

I observed four men with pistols stretched out in their hands creeping around the rear of the garage and moving toward the backyard. Another six or seven spread through the foliage ten feet from the driveway and dropped to the ground. The two men patrolling the steel-and-glass house were still chatting and oblivious to the advancing ambush.

The cracking sound of a branch being broken alerted them. The patrolling men leapt around, grabbing the handles of their pistols at the same time. They were too late. Their weapons never left their holsters before a burst of gunfire struck them and shattered the house's glass panels.

A man charged out of the house firing an automatic rifle as bullets sprayed over the bushes from the barrel of a rifle sticking between the broken glass and a steel beam on the second floor.

Somewhere below me, a machine gun went into action, plowing bullets into the running man. He landed in a puddle of his own blood.

Screams echoed from within the structure while another burst of gunfire crackled, sending the smell of acrid smoke through the air. A fusillade of bullets thudded against the house's steel frame as the assault continued on the occupants.

Just when I thought the shooting had ended, a single shot rang out from inside the house. A second later, another one followed. Then silence descended over the scene. No more screams. No more gunshots.

"All clear," a man yelled, stepping out of the bullet-ridden house with a rifle slung over his shoulder.

The men on the ground rose from their prone positions and holstered their weapons. I noticed them slipping on gloves.

"Five minutes," one man shouted as he rushed toward the house tailed by the other men in the front yard.

Within a few minutes, a man hurried out of the house and charged to the Porsche. He held up what appeared to be a set of keys and climbed into the vehicle. The engine roared to life. The vehicle pulled out the driveway as another man leapt into the Mercedes. The Mercedes flipped a tight u-ey, hitting a small bush in the process, and barreled away from the house.

Then a man stepped out of the house with a wrapped bundle over his shoulder that I suspected had a body secured inside and trudged up the driveway. Shortly after that, another man walked out of the building also carrying a bundle.

"Time's up," a man shouted.

I watched a handful of dark-clad men charge out of the house and up the driveway. Off in the distance, sirens blared. Assuming this was their destination, I wanted to get out of the tree. But since I didn't know if the assailants were a friendly lot or employed by a Crussett enemy, I stayed put for another minute, giving them time to get away.

As I scooted down the trunk, the siren's throbbing sound became louder, confirming they were headed to Monique's. Avoiding trees and bushes, I sprinted through the foliage and ran to the Dodge. I threw the backpack on the backseat, slid behind the steering wheel, started the car, and drove away from the damaged steel-and-glass house, a place I'd never visit again. When I reached the main highway, two police cruisers zoomed past me. Glancing out my rear view mirror, I saw them turn onto Fulmer Lane and hoped whoever had called the police hadn't paid any attention to my car parked nearby.

44

WARNINGS DELIVERED

I mentally replayed the discussion I overheard before the slaughter team arrived and wondered if Conner was still in danger. No one inside Monique's house could have survived the attack, but Monique had said Conner would be handled in the hotel. Would the hired assassin learn his or her employer was dead, possibly killed by the target?

Worried about Conner, I turned onto a residential street and pulled over to the curb, out of view from any emergency vehicles that might be headed to Monique's. Leaning over the back of the seat, I grabbed my backpack, retrieved the green cell phone, turned it on, and called him.

"Where are you?" he hissed.

Irritated, I snapped back, "Mr. Crussett I am not, I repeat NOT, your employee. I will go wherever I please without asking your permission."

"Well…ah—"

"Stop," I said, interrupting him. "Are you in your hotel?"

"Yes. Are you coming here?" he asked, the harshness in his tone gone.

"No. Listen. Someone there is going to attempt to kill you. I don't know any other details. So be careful." Having said what I wanted to tell him, I disconnected and turned off the cell phone as anger boiled up inside me. Here, I had attempted to be pleasant to him, not overly, but civilized. How could he talk that way to me if he's hoping to have a relationship with Sally, or renewing one with Sara?

A tear trickled down my cheek. Wiping it away, I closed my eyes as conflicting emotions welled up in me. Why did I feel so confused when it came to Conner? All the good times we had shared flooded into my mind, drowning out the corruption that surrounded him. The glare of bright headlights shining through the rear view window brought me back to the present. I shielded my eyes and realized the sun had set.

The vehicle stopped behind me. Was it just a coincidence it happened to park near me or had the occupants recognized my car? Staring at the rear view mirror, I focused on it. A black Cadillac Escalade. The passenger door opened. Without waiting for the person to climb out, I turned the key in the ignition, pushed the accelerator, and flipped a u-ey. A few seconds after I hit the main highway, the Escalade was less than a car length from my bumper. Driving back to the apartment, I never went over the speed limit or made any attempt to lose my tail.

I pulled into the apartment building's parking lot followed by an Escalade. A police cruiser and a white van with the police department emblem on the back double doors were parked by the entrance. I didn't see anyone outside.

Stepping into the building, I saw the super's door stood wide open. I peeked inside. The couch was tipped over, drawers stood open, magazines and papers were spread on the floor. A team, some wearing white lab coats and the others police uniforms, was going over every square inch of the place.

An officer, carrying several full plastic bags, moved toward the door. I pivoted around and headed to the elevator. Before it stopped on the first floor, a suit-clad man stood by my side.

As I anticipated, he followed me to my apartment. I opened the door, and the wonderful aroma of lilacs wafted out. In the center of the table sat a huge bouquet of lilacs and red roses. I leaned over it and inhaled the luscious smell. Conner. How could I hate the man?

The landline phone rang, startling me. I expected Conner was on the other end. Doubting I could avoid him completely before I left town, I answered it. To my surprise, Mrs. Adams was the caller.

"Since we talked last, have you heard from Wendy at all?"

"No," I said as my heart ached for Wendy's mother.

"She's not at her friend's place in Florida. I've called all of her friends I know. No one has seen her. She still hasn't turned on her cell phone. Wendy's taken off like this before, but she always calls after a few days. Not this time. Another investigator wants to talk to her about Hank. He wanted to know where she went when she left our house. I'm sorry, dear, but I ended up giving him your address. I hope you don't mind."

"No. That's fine. I want to do whatever I can to help," I said, hoping I'd be gone before he showed up at my door.

"Before she left did she mention anything about Hank to you?"

Without hesitation, I replied, "No."

"Hank's mother thinks he might have disappeared on purpose because he was in trouble. Once, when he was a sophomore, he had some kind of gambling problem. His folks had to mortgage their house to take care of it. She knows he'd never ask for help again." Mrs. Adams paused, and the sound of deep, shaky breathing came through the line.

"Mrs. Adams is something wrong?"

"Well…do you think…maybe…he called Wendy…and…and she's with him?"

"I guess that's a possibility," I said, thinking the poor woman was clinging to the possibility nothing bad had happened to her daughter.

"If the investigator finds Hank, then we'll know for sure. I sure hope she doesn't stay hidden like Hank. Will you let me know what the investigator says to you?"

"Sure. I'll call after he talks to me." I bit my lower lip and my stomach churned. I hated lying to Wendy's mother. Yet, there wasn't an alternative.

As we hung up, I noticed the light on the answering machine blinking. Five messages, two from Detective Gilbert, one from Conner, one from the apartment management company, and one from Reese. All wanted return calls. I played them to catch the time of Reese's message. Its 6:32 p.m. time stamp, meant several hours after the carnage at Monique's and since he left shortly before the assassins showed up, I wondered if his call had been by design. Curiosity made me dial his number.

We greeted each other, and then he got right to the point of his call. "Tessa is pretty upset you took Wendy's ring from her. She wants it back and I'm afraid it could get ugly. With Mitt's killer still on the loose and Mase missing, I just hate seeing all this trouble. I talked it over with my folks, and we're wondering if you'd consider selling it?"

What a surprise. Of all the possible reasons running through my mind why Reese would call me, the ring wasn't one of them. Obviously, he knew nothing about the slaughter, so I could cross the Buckleys off my list. That left Thurman and Conner.

"Sally?"

"Oh. It's Wendy's ring. I'd have to ask her, and right now I have no idea where she is."

"She left town without it, so it can't be that important to her. Name a price."

"Reese, can you give me a couple of days? I'll call around and see if I can track her down."

"Great. I think I can stall Tessa a few days."

"Thanks. Wendy's always short on money. Who knows, she might go for it," I said, stringing him along, wanting him to believe I had no personal attachment to the precious jewel.

I clicked off, thinking he would probably learn about Tessa's fate sometime tomorrow. Then my ring would cease to be important to him. If by some chance it still was, I'd be back home, untraceable, and a long distance from Baton Rouge before he came looking for it.

I glanced at the clock and decided I'd return Gilbert's calls and the one from the property management company in the morning. Wondering if Conner's call could also wait, I grabbed a Coke from the fridge. While I sipped on it, I pulled my green cell phone out of my backpack and clicked it on. The message icon lit up with a small 6 in the corner. All the messages were from Conner. Anger in his voice began in the second one and grew with each succeeding message. Listening to the sixth one, he sounded almost out of control, ordering me to call him. That cinched my decision, no call to Conner.

I gazed at his peace offering, the fragrant lilacs, as I mulled over if there was anything left I could accomplish in Baton Rouge before I boarded the plane. Part of the conversation I had overheard at Monique's bounced into my head. Someone in Conner's family wants him dead. A female. My first and only guess was Melanie, Conner's sister-in-law, the wife of the brother I killed. Since Monique and Tessa had met their demise, I figured the threat against Conner died with them. Yet, maybe revealing a family member had been on their team might cause turmoil in the close knit Crussett family. I had been physically tortured by that family because they suspected I knew who killed Conner's brother. How would they handle a relative scheming to kill a member of the bloodline, the one running the family business?

While I was enjoying thinking about the family scuffle, a knock echoed through the apartment. I opened the door. There stood Conner with his bandaged arm in a sling and in that hand he held a bottle of wine. In his other hand he carried a large bag of take-out Chinese food.

"Thought you might be hungry," he said with glowing eyes and a sensual smile, a smile I thought about often.

I still felt irritated about his cell phone messages. Had I not been pressed for time, I would have sent him away so he could think about keeping his temper under control, at least around me. Not wanting him to think for one minute that his behavior had been forgiven, I decided to stall the inevitable. "Mr. Crussett, you're wrong. I'm not hungry."

"So we're back to formal addresses, Miss Jablon?" he asked, handing the bag of food to the guard next to him.

Without being invited in, the guard walked by me.

"Hey," I said as he sat the bag on the table. "No one said you could come in here."

Ignoring me, the guard went back out into the hallway.

"I brought all your favorites," Conner said.

"How do you know my favorite Chinese dishes?"

"An educated guess," he said with a mischievous smile. "I had planned to share some interesting information I just heard, but if you're not…"

Determined to cause some chaos in his organization, I couldn't do it with him standing in the hall. "No, I'm interested. But before I invite you in, I'd like the guards at the door to leave when you leave," I said since I didn't want them near when the package from Father arrived. "There are police swarming the building, and your men might draw unwanted attention to my apartment."

"Yes, I know. Let me check on a few things first. If things seem in order, I'll have them removed. Will that work?"

Not pleased with his answer, but thinking it was better than an outright no, I gave him a curt nod. "Come on in."

Stepping into my apartment, he brushed my arm with his and briefly touched my hand. A tingly sensation pulsated through my body as my desire for him surfaced. I inhaled deeply reminding myself what I felt for Conner was wrong. He was a murderer and destroyed lives.

While he lifted cartons out of the bag, I set the table. He attempted to open the bottle of wine with one hand before I took it from him and finished the job. "I'll pour," I said, filling the wine glasses.

I hadn't realized how hungry I was until I ate the first bite. When my plate was empty and my stomach full, I asked, "What interesting information did you just learn?"

Conner laid down his chop sticks and took a sip of his wine. "Rumor has it that Tessa Thurman ordered a hit."

"On Orson?"

"No. It occurred at Monique Torren's house." He studied my face. "Do you already know about it?"

"Why would I know about it?"

"When my men finally tracked you down, you were a couple of miles away from her house."

"Now that you mention it, I had been tailing Reese and he went there. When he left so did I. I lost him and pulled off the highway to locate him."

He filled our glasses. "And how were you going to do that?"

"Through a tracking system," I said, since it no longer mattered. Reese and his remaining family weren't key players in the drug business. From everything I had learned, they stored drugs for Thurman, but they weren't distributors. The exception had been Mase. "You're not the only one who uses that system."

"But Reese wasn't driving his car."

"How do you know that?" I asked, suspecting the group who invaded Monique's place was probably Conner's guys.

"We were tracking Reese's Volvo. It never left his folks' place."

"My tracking device is on Mase's Mustang, the vehicle Reese has been driving off and on since his brother disappeared."

"Interesting." His tone suggested he didn't know that, which I doubted.

Every time I've tried to figure out how many men Conner had in Baton

Rouge, it seemed more show up. They were everywhere. If he was concerned about Reese, at least one guy would be keeping close tabs on him. Maybe that's it—he's not concerned about Reese at all. "Who did Tessa order a hit on? And why at Monique's?"

"The house is owned by a corporation with only two stockholders. Tessa is one of them. The place has no close neighbors. A convenient location."

"Who was the target?" I asked, feigning ignorance.

"You didn't see it go down?"

Conner held a good poker face, emotionless. He was an expert at lying to me. He had done it so many times when I lived with him, and I always believed him. Now, I studied his face for any sign that he knew the truth. There it was, a slight flicker in his brown eyes. Skeptical? No, that wasn't it. He knew I was there. None of the men roaming through the foliage could have seen me, but someone must have spotted my Dodge. Thinking about the pictures of my escapades he had shown me in his car, I wondered if I had been tailed to Monique's. That didn't make sense. His anger radiated through his cell phone messages. He didn't know where I was. I had been parked at the side of the road for a long time before the Escalade showed up. I must be reading his eyes wrong. Then what did it mean? Was he behind the hit and he was checking how much I knew?

"Sally, did you see it go down?" he asked again.

"No. I didn't hear any gunfire before I left. Oh, maybe the person wasn't shot. Is that it?"

"My source claims there was an attack on the place. Tessa wanted everyone inside dead."

"Claims? So you don't know if there was an attack?"

"It's a verily reliable source. That road has been blocked by the police. Crime scene tape surrounds the place. Something definitely went down. The number of victims hasn't been confirmed yet. There could be survivors."

"When will you know?" I asked, certain no one could have survived that barrage. And if they had, they would have been wiped out after the assailants entered the house. Not one gunshot rang out then, but two bodies had been removed. I suspected one belonged to Tessa. She couldn't be blamed as the culprit behind the plan if her body was found among the victims.

He downed the rest of the wine in his glass. "Sometime today when you were keeping an eye on Reese, did you by any chance happen to overhear anything said?"

"As a matter of fact, I did, but you're not going to like it."

"And why is that?" He topped off my wine glass and filled his.

"It involves your family."

He cocked his head and narrowed his eyes. "My family? What did they do? Or are they in trouble?"

"You're in danger from a family member."

"Who?"

"A woman. They just referred to the person as a she."

"Who's they?" he asked, adjusting his arm in the sling.

"Tessa, Monique and Dan."

"Monique?"

"Yep. She's alive," I said, though I knew that was no longer true. "Tessa never killed her."

"What did they say about the woman?"

"Let me recall." I leaned an elbow on the armrest and tapped a finger on my lower lip. "Whatever the overall scheme of the group, they said the woman would be on board after you had been killed. Someone said something about revenge. The woman believes you played a role in your brother's death. Anyway, something like that."

Conner's eyes dropped to the table. He tented his hands and rubbed the pads of his fingers together. "Did they all buy it?"

"You don't think it's true?"

"A possibility."

"Monique said she had been in Houston last week checking to make sure the woman was still on board. She told the others the woman would be once you were dead. I guess she wouldn't be part of the group unless that happened. Oh, Reese was against it. He didn't want any part of it. He said something about your dad would kill all of them."

"That's true."

"That's when Reese stormed out. Monique went after him, but he wouldn't talk to her."

"Reese isn't like his brother. He never carries a gun. Not even hidden someplace in his car."

That explains why Reese wasn't among the guys at the old cement factory. "Any idea how he got roped into the whole thing?"

He shook his head. "No, but I suspect his brother dragged him into it before he knew any facts."

"He offered to buy my ring."

"Huh?" Conner squinted. "When?"

I held up my hand and admired my precious gem. "He called and left a message. I called him back when I got home. He said Tessa wanted it and she'd stop at nothing to get it. He mentioned Mitt and his brother, and he didn't want any more trouble. I told him the ring was Wendy's. To appease him, I said I'd try to track her down. The way he sounded, he'd pay top dollar for it."

"Top dollar? Reese isn't wealthy. He never mentioned a price?"

"No. There is no way I would sell my ring at any price, so that was a moot point. However, he did say he had talked it over with his parents, so I figured they'd be footing the bill."

"That makes sense."

"How?"

"Some people have the impression you are my girlfriend. If someone went after you, they'd have me to deal with. On top of that, old man Buckley is storing a stolen van, the one on the pictures you so graciously sent me."

"I didn't send you any pictures."

"You're still sticking to that story?"

"Are you planning to do anything about the van?"

A slight smile flickered on his face. "There you go again, asking a question before you answered mine. But I'll answer it. The Buckleys are safe. They didn't intercept the van, kill the driver, or steal the merchandise. The van can stay in that shed indefinitely."

Conner probably liked having it there. It gave him an edge. As long as it was there, they'd never mess with him for fear he'd send men snooping around their warehouse. From the conversation I overheard at the Buckleys, they thought if the van was discovered they'd all end up in the ground.

He stretched his hand across the table and laid it on top of mine. "Sally, I have to leave here on Saturday. Will you go out with me tomorrow night?"

"Are you going to come back here?"

"It all depends on you." He flashed me a smile. "Will you still be here scheming how to destroy my business?"

"I haven't made any travel plans."

Conner's cell phone buzzed. His jaw became rigid and his eyes narrowed as he pulled it out of his pocket. He glanced at the screen. "This can wait until I know if we have a date."

"Let me think about it." I wanted to say yes, but my reasonable side kept hollering no. Somehow I had to appease my internal struggle, and I knew feeling Conner's body next to mine would only lead to more heartache.

"While you're thinking about, I need to deal with a relative." Conner rose to his feet.

Standing up, I asked, "Who?"

"Carter."

I sucked in air, not because I feared Carter, but I didn't want to be placed in a situation where I might have to kill another one of Conner's relatives. I had poisoned Cameron, Conner's brother, and Cameron's son, Colin. Carter was also one of Cameron's sons. A college kid who I suspected was now learning the ropes of the family business. I liked him. Unfortunately, he had been born in the Crussett family and destined for a life of crime, just like Conner. "He's here checking up on you?"

"No. He came wanting my assistance on a matter. He was surprised I had been shot."

"You didn't tell your family?"

"No. I didn't want them to know very much about the business in Baton Rouge." He came closer to me and traced a finger along my cheek bone. "Sally, I want you in my life," he said, his eyes gazing into mine. "I'd like nothing more than to have you live with me again, but I doubt I could keep you safe from my family. I thought I could keep Sara safe, but I failed her." Pain etched his face. "I've run it through my mind often trying to figure out what I could have done differently to protect her." Using his good arm, he pulled me tight against his body. "You'll be safe going out with me. No matter what you've done. I'll never harm you. Do you believe me?"

"Yes," I said as tears stung my eyes. I nuzzled into his shirt, wiping my eyes on it and hoping he wouldn't notice.

Someone knocked softly on the door.

"That's my signal. I wish I could stay longer." He gently placed his hand under my chin and raised my head. "I'll always love you." He bent down and kissed me, a long passionate kiss. I should have pulled away from him. Instead, I returned his kiss just as passionately.

His face glowed and he smiled ear to ear. "I'll call you in the morning," he said, opening the door.

45

LIES

At ten the next morning, a courier delivered the packet from Father. Before I closed the door, I glanced up and down the hall. No sign of Conner's men. I doubted they would have been removed if he didn't know Tessa was dead. I also doubted Thurman would confess to Conner that he had killed his own wife, the mother of his children. Since Conner knew Tessa's fate, that only left one possibility—Conner was responsible for the slaughter that occurred at Monique's.

From what he said last night, I actually believed he hadn't been involved. Maybe it was just wishful thinking that he wouldn't lie to me. But then again, I had also lied to him and suspected I hadn't fooled him for a minute. Regardless of how angry he sounded in the phone messages, he probably knew my exact location all the time since my car was parked on her road. His men wouldn't have missed seeing it.

Not wanting to dwell on my stupidity any longer, I opened the package and spread out the contents: four airline tickets, four passports, four driver's licenses, four credit cards, and money. I'd be leaving Baton Rouge at 7:55 a.m. under the name Kristine Hart. "Hmm. Strange," I murmured. Not a name with the initials S.J. Tegens chanced their names often, but always tried to maintain the same initials. Maybe Father thought Conner would put two and two together since Sara Jones and Sally Jablon were the same person. No one wanted to take the chance of him following me. Glancing through the other airline tickets, they all had different passenger names—Cindy Ross, Maxine Levitt, and Francine Thomas. I was being routed through Florida, Boston, and New York. I'd have to exit the secure area and go through the security screening again after check-in at each stop.

That meant I'd be destroying the documentation applicable to each name when I no longer needed it. It also meant I'd have to travel with three outfits plus wigs, hats, and sunglasses so I could change and disguise my appearance at each location. My last plane was scheduled to touch down in Bismarck at 11:47 p.m.

I had planned to only take carryon luggage with me. Now I wasn't sure if that would work. My travel itinerary would give me sixteen hours to imagine the punishment waiting for me in Bismarck, and I anticipated I would put every minute to use worrying about it. Though I had no idea what the punishment would be, it had to be bad. Neither Brett nor Father would even tell me how others were punished for harboring a sought-after Tegen. And Brett was flying in town to help me through it, which was definitely not a good sign. With an accelerated stress level, could I manage to go without *venotrolia* for sixteen hours?

Just worrying about it made my mouth dry and my throat burn. I rose, hurried to the bedroom fridge, and grabbed a bottle of *venotrolia*. Two swigs and the bottle was empty. That confirmed what I feared, I couldn't go sixteen hours without the delicious substance.

I sat back down at the table and noticed the edge of a note sticking out of the top passport. Reading it brought a smile to my face. Father had made arrangements for someone to meet me at each stop. That person would provide me with a change of clothing and beverage. He wanted me to travel light. No checked luggage.

Feeling relieved, I gathered up all the documents, put them back into the padded mailer and stuck it in my backpack, my only carryon luggage. I headed into the bedroom and began emptying out my drawers. I hadn't finished clearing out the dresser when the doorbell buzzed.

Closing the bedroom door behind me, I stepped to the apartment door, opened it, and found myself face-to-face with Detective Gilbert. A uniformed policeman stood by his side.

"Miss Jablon, we'd like to ask you some questions about your superintendent. May we come in or would you prefer to answer them at the station," he said, eyeing me suspiciously.

"By all means, come in," I said, opening the door wider. "Please have a seat."

Detective Gilbert sat on the couch. The uniformed officer remained standing.

"How well did you know the superintendent?" Gilbert asked.

"Is the Super in trouble or something?" I asked, since Sally Jablon shouldn't know the man was dead.

"No. He's dead."

I gasped. "Dead? How?"

"It appears he died from a poisonous spider or insect bite in this building. Due to the unusual condition his body had been found in, his death was classified as suspicious. While his body was in the medical examiner's lab an intruder entered and burned the corpse."

"Burned it? Why?"

"That's what we are trying to determine."

I shivered. "What about the poisonous spider or insect? Do I need to move?"

"An exterminator has already fumigated the basement, the superintendent's apartment, and the apartments surrounding it. Now, he's working on the second floor. He anticipates having the building completed by Sunday."

"Do I need to do anything before he shows up?"

"It's all being coordinated by the building property management company. Haven't they contacted you yet?"

"Well…they left a message on my answering machine to give them a call, but I assumed it was about raising the rent, not poisonous bugs. I guess I better return the call. Has anyone else died?"

"No other similar incidents have occurred in your building since Mr. Hawkins' body was discovered on Monday."

"Anyone before him?" I asked, sounding anxious.

"No. Let's get back to Mr. Hawkins. How well did you know him?" he asked, and then his eyes slowly swept over my apartment.

"Not well at all," I said while he stared at the closed bedroom door. "He came here once to fix the kitchen faucet. That's it. We never even talked when we ran into each other in the hallway."

His attention returned to me. "Did you see him talking to any of the other tenants in the building?"

I shook my head. "No," I said and changed the subject. "Have you found who killed Mitt yet?"

"We have a strong lead we're working on."

"I sure hope whoever did it gets locked up soon." Tears pooled in my eyes and I swallowed hard. "I'll never forget him. Such a wonderful man." I dabbed my eyes with the back of my fingers. "His murderer needs to be punished."

"I can assure you that the guilty party will be brought to justice, Miss Jablon." His eyes drifted to the closed bedroom door again. "On another matter, when was the last time you saw Tessa Thurman?"

"Tessa? Has something happened to her, too?"

"No. We'd like to ask her a few questions and haven't been able to locate her."

"I haven't seen or heard from her since Mitt's funeral."

"How well do you know her?"

"Not well at all. I met her when Mitt took me to a barbeque at his parents' house, and I saw her at the funeral. That's it."

His brow furrowed. "I understand you drove with her and her children from the funeral home to the cemetery."

"Yes, I did. She was so kind to invite me to join her family that day, but she knew how much Mitt had meant to me. She's a lovely woman."

He rose to his feet and gave me his card. "Give me a call if she contacts you."

"I will." I walked him to the apartment door.

"Thank you for your time," he said and briefly looked at the bedroom door. Then he left with the uniformed policeman.

Did he think I was hiding Tessa in my bedroom? I moved to the window, hoping the Escalade had left. No luck. It was prominently parked across the street. Irritated, I went into the bedroom and began emptying another drawer. The landline phone rang. I picked up the receiver and listened to a prerecorded message from the building management company. It said they were doing their annual bug and spider extermination in the building. My floor was scheduled for Saturday. Cringing at the thought of all that pesticide, I hung up before the message ended, relieved I'd be gone along with my spiders before then.

My green cell phone buzzed. Seeing Conner's name appear on the monitor, I answered, "How's your arm?"

"Much better."

"Is your relative still in town?" I asked, thinking that would deter Conner from trying to see me. As much as I would have liked to spend time with him, I couldn't allow my emotions to take control of me. He had lied to me and who knows how many people he had sent to their graves since he arrived in Baton Rouge. I had to keep him out of my life. In order for that to happen, I needed a solid plan to escape my apartment without being followed.

"Yes. He's flying out this afternoon. How about this evening? Are we on?" he asked with apprehension in his voice.

A lump formed in my throat. "Yes," I lied. "There's a spider problem in the building."

"Poisonous?"

"Yes. The superintendent died from a poisonous spider."

"Wendy?"

"No. She didn't know him, but maybe one of her spiders got away from her. That's all I can figure. There are exterminators working in the building. It's not safe for you to come in here. I'll meet you out front. What time?"

"Seven."

"I'll see you then."

"Remember, I love you," he said, his voice soft and sad, leaving me to believe he doubted I'd be there.

Disconnecting, I thought, *Am I that transparent?* Maybe I imagined his tone because of the guilt creeping through me. Soon I'd be out of his life again, and he'd be out of mine. I couldn't waiver. I had to stay the course regardless of how much my heart ached for him.

The landline phone rang.

"Who now?" I said out loud as I picked up the receiver.

"Hello."

"Miss Jablon?"

"Yes."

"I'm Samuel Spencer, and investigator for Clawson Investigation Corporation. We're trying to locate your friend, Wendy Adams."

"Yes, her mom called me. She mentioned you were looking for Wendy. When Wendy left here, she said she was going to visit a friend in Florida. I've only known Wendy for less than a year. I don't know the name of the friend she intended to visit."

"Her mother gave us a list of Wendy's friends that were in her phone book. We've contacted all of them. No one has seen Wendy. I'd like to talk to you about her. I could be in Baton Rouge tomorrow if there's a time that would be convenient for you."

"My schedule is pretty full. How about Saturday?"

"I can arrange that. What time?"

"Early afternoon. But I don't see how I can be very helpful. I only know a few of her friends."

"Even a little bit of information might lead us in the right direction. I'll call when I get in town and we can tighten up the time. See you on Saturday." He disconnected.

I leaned back in my chair, thinking how right Father had been. I did need to leave Baton Rouge. Mitt's ongoing investigation, Mr. Hawkins' and the investigator's deaths caused by Wendy, and now the shooting at Monique's house had been added to the pile.

When I didn't show up for my date, Conner would come looking for me or, maybe with the building's spider problem, he'd send someone. Staying in my apartment for the night wasn't an option. I decided I would check into a hotel near the airport.

I got a pen and a notepad and jotted down everything I had to take care of before I left the apartment building. Agnes was on top of the list. I wrote her a letter telling her I had to leave town. All of her things along with her repaired walker were in her bedroom. The rent was paid until the end of the month so she could take her time in collecting them along with anything she wanted in the apartment. I asked her to call goodwill and give them the remaining items. Then I went on to thank her for doing such a good job in pretending to be my grandmother. At the bottom of the letter I wrote: "P.S. Please burn this letter and the envelope."

I addressed the envelope to her at her sister's house, slipped the letter in it along with twice the amount of money I owed her. Sealing it up, a tinge of sadness swept through me, I wouldn't be able to say goodbye to her in person or even on the phone. No one could know I was leaving. Agnes had played her role to perfection. I felt like I was losing a grandmother. Grandparents had always been nonexistent in my life.

Next on my list was cleaning up my computer's hard drive. I didn't want to travel with anything on it about drug businesses. I was probably being paranoid, but I didn't want to take a chance with the heightened security at airports. Especially, since I'd be going through four security screenings. I emailed all the folders on it to a secure email account set up by our Tegen computer whiz.

I only had three bottles of *venotrolia* left in the small fridge, and planned to take two with me. The third one I opened and drank while I tossed replaceable items from my backpack. Then I continued cleaning out drawers and my closet, putting everything into large plastic bags except for a nightgown and two outfits—one to wear tomorrow and one to put on after I showered. I took the plastic bags to my car and placed them into the truck.

After I showered and dressed, I moved my spiders into the ovoid container and put it along with some toiletries into my backpack. The cage and my dirty clothes went into a garbage bag. Then I went through the apartment wiping down everything I had touched. Satisfied I was finished with the apartment, I hung my backpack on my shoulder, picked up the garbage bag, and headed outside. I dropped the garbage in the metal bin near the apartment back door.

As I climbed into my car and noticed a tall figure stepping out from behind the garbage bin, I shuddered. Kendall.

46

DEPARTURE

I briefly closed my eyes as chills swept through me. Opening them, a thought flashed into my head. He's here to make sure I get on the plane. That's all. Since I had no intention of skipping my flight, I had nothing to fear from Kendall.

I drove toward the mall with the Escalade a few cars behind me, easily visible through my rear view mirror. Probably another type car was also tailing me. I kept glancing around to see if I could determine the other car, but each time I thought I'd identified the suspect car, it vanished from sight.

A couple of blocks from the mall, I stopped at a goodwill collection box near a gas station with an automatic car wash. I unloaded the bags from the trunk and placed them in the container, and then I drove to a gas pump and filled the car. The Escalade was parked by the curb. The driver hadn't made the slightest attempt to hide from my line of sight.

I headed to the car wash. As soon as the soapsuds covered the Dodge, I slipped on a pair of latex gloves and went to work wiping down the interior of the vehicle.

I pulled into the mall parking lot and parked in an empty slot wedged between two large vehicles—one a truck with oversized tires and springs that lifted it almost three feet from the asphalt; the other a tall delivery van. I took the green cell phone out of my backpack, vigorously rubbed it with a tissue, and laid it on the floor of the vehicle. I stepped out of the vehicle, closed the door, and took off my gloves. I planned to send the car keys along with a note where the car could be found to the rental company when I reached the hotel.

Moving around the truck, I looked for the Escalade and found it on the next row in a spot where the passengers couldn't have observed me in my car. I walked to the mall entrance. A man dressed in a suit opened the door for me and followed me inside. I wandered in and out of the shops buying a few miscellaneous items while he continued to keep track of me. I ate a late lunch at the food court a few tables away from my bodyguard. I was tempted to ask him if he wanted to join me, but I resisted the urge.

I headed to a familiar department store and purchased a skirt, sweater, and a pair of sandals, making sure he couldn't see what I was buying. Then I went down another corridor and noticed a mailbox by the side entrance. I dropped Agnes's letter in it with the bodyguard hot on my heels. I assumed he thought I was planning to leave the mall through that exit. I turned, almost bumped right into him, and moved further into the mall. I stopped at a small boutique that carried intimate apparel, a store I had patronized several times and knew the layout.

Like I had hoped, the guard didn't follow me in. He stayed by the entrance. I picked up a few things to try on. The sales clerk took them from me, ushered me into a dressing room, and hung them on a hook.

"Let me know if you want a different size," she said with a smile.

I bit my lower lip. "I've got a problem."

She raised an eyebrow. "Do you need help trying these items on?"

"No. That's not it. My ex-boyfriend's been following me from work and all through the mall. He's standing right by the entrance. He's violent. Last month he sent me to the hospital." My eyes became moist. "I just can't go through that again."

"Let me call the police."

"It won't help," I said as tears drizzled down my cheeks. "I have a restraining order. It doesn't do any good. I just moved and I don't want him to know where I live. Besides that entrance," I nodded toward the place the guard stood, "is there any other way out of here?"

"Well...well," she hesitated, "there is a back door through the storage room."

"Can I go out that way?"

"It's only for employees."

"Please," I begged, wiping my eyes with a tissue.

"Well, I guess it won't hurt." She glanced at the clothing hanging on the hook. "Do you want to try any of these items on first?"

"No." I touched the lacy nightgown. "They're lovely, but I'm afraid if I'm in here too long, he'll come in looking for me."

"Give me a second," the clerk said and went out of the dressing room area. "Debbie, can you watch the counter? I'm helping a customer try on some clothing."

"Sure," I heard a woman respond.

The sales clerk returned, led me to a door at the far end of the dressing rooms, and through their storage area to a solid metal door. Unlocking it, she said, "Good luck. I'll try and stall him if he comes in the store to look for you."

"Thank you," I said, squeezing her arm. "You have no idea how much I appreciate this."

She gave me a warm, sympathetic smile as I stepped out the door.

I walked at a brisk pace to the department store's exterior entrance, the familiar store where I had made a purchase twenty minutes earlier. There, I hurried to the women's restroom on the second floor. I went into the handicap stall, removed the price tag and changed into the outfit I purchased, a knee-length, pink-and-black patterned skirt, a pink cotton short-sleeved sweater, and brown leather sandals. I pulled a short brown wig out of another shopping bag, placed it on my head, and tugged my hair under its rim. I rolled up the outfit I had been wearing and discarded it in the restroom's garbage container. I hid my eyes behind oversized sunglasses and placed my backpack in a shopping bag. Carrying the bag, I headed toward the mall exit near a bus stop without ever looking over my shoulder. Hordes of people came and went from the mall all the time and I remained vigilant not to make any gestures or movements that could draw unwanted attention.

Over a dozen people were at the bus stop. I edged my way into the crowd. Five minutes later, a bus cut to the curb. I didn't care what route it was taking. It was going away from the mall and that was all that mattered. After I climbed in and settled into a seat, I pulled out my black cell phone and called several hotels until I found one located a mile from the airport that offered shuttle service to the airport. I made a reservation under the first name I'd be using on my flights, Kristine Hart, and secured it with a credit card issued to her.

Putting the phone back into my backpack, my eyes roamed over the contents. "No. No," I yelled, realizing a terrible mistake I had made.

The eyes of all the passengers in the bus darted toward me. Feeling self-conscious, I held up my hand. "Sorry. It's nothing."

I pressed my eyelids shut, bit my lower lip, and rubbed my forehead. How could I have forgotten them? All my planning went up in smoke. The two bottles of *venotrolia* weren't in my backpack. I couldn't leave them behind in my apartment. I had to go back for them. I checked my watch: 4:43 p.m. That gave me over two hours to retrieve them and leave before Conner showed up. I contemplated taking a taxi to my apartment and decided against it since it could raise suspicion. If any of Conner's men had returned, they'd know I was up to something.

Reluctantly, I piled out of the bus with five other passengers at the next stop. I went to the other side of the street and waited ten minutes before a bus arrived. I eased down into a seat behind the driver and gazed out the window as it drove along, stopping every few blocks to drop off and pick up passengers. The bus made an unexpected right turn. I leaned around the partition separating the driver from the passengers and asked, "Is this bus going to the mall?"

"No. If you want to go there you'll have to catch the 209."

"Where?"

He made his next stop and said, "Take bus 220 on the other side of the street. Get off after it turns to connect to 209."

"Thanks." I exited the bus, headed across the street, and glanced at my watch: 5:03 p.m. I still had plenty of time to get the *venotrolia,* but I felt edgy and kept stepping out from the curb, looking for the bus.

After I was situated on bus 209, I ran my newly devised plan through my head to make sure I didn't screw up again. The Dodge would be left in the apartment building parking lot. I'd stick the *venotrolia* in my backpack, depart through the bedroom window, make my way behind buildings for several blocks, and then call a taxi. I figured from getting into my car at the mall to calling a taxi shouldn't take me more than an hour.

It was 5:35 p.m. when I scooted into my car, removed the wig, and drove toward the apartment building. Suddenly, the traffic came to a complete halt. A siren erupted somewhere behind me. My lane of traffic and the one to my right were packed with stopped cars. A police cruiser travelled on the other side of road, going against the flow of traffic and dodging cars along the way.

As the minutes ticked by, I tapped my fingers on the steering wheel and chewed nervously on my lower lip. Finally, at 6:09 the traffic began moving again. Twenty-six minutes later, I parked behind my apartment building, quickly wiped off the steering wheel and door handle, and climbed out.

A police car sat empty near the backdoor with its engine running, and I hoped if something else had happened or been discovered in the building, it didn't have anything to do with Wendy as I rushed to the elevator. The doors opened and out stepped Detective Gilbert and a uniformed officer.

"Miss Jablon, we've been trying to reach you. We'd like to discuss Mitt Thurman's case and the disappearance of Tessa Thurman with you."

"Tessa's missing?"

"Yes. Can you come to the station tomorrow?"

"I'm getting my hair done in the morning. I could come any time in the afternoon."

"Around two?"

I nodded. "See you then." I got on the elevator.

When I reached my apartment it was 6:47 p.m. Short on time, my adrenaline spiked and my heart pounded in my chest. I put the *venotrolia* in the backpack and secured it to my back. Before I climbed out the window, I decided to check if the Escalade was back since I hadn't noticed it following me to the apartment. Conner's men could've been inside the mall searching for me when I drove off.

Peering out the window, I didn't see an Escalade parked across the street. Thinking it might be on my side of the street, I leaned forward and gazed down. There, pacing in front of the building was Conner. He looked so handsome in his navy blue pinstriped suit with his arm in a sling. A soft breeze blew through his hair. I touched my cheek, recalling the spot where the tears he had shed landed the day he thought I had died. I swallowed hard as a battle raged in my head. The same battle I had been fighting since I had seen him at Sammy's: part of me trying to squash what I felt for him, and part of me longing to be in his arms. My desire for him was wrong, but sometimes it consumed all my thoughts.

He looked up, toward my window. I ducked to the side. Then I stared out the window again. He was still pacing and I sensed he was nervous, probably fearing I'd stand him up or call and say I couldn't make it.

I had no idea what type of punishment awaited me in Bismarck, but I did know the man pacing the sidewalk loved me. He'd taken a bullet for me. My heart took control of my body, suffocating all my coherent thoughts. Instead of climbing out the window, I went out the door and headed toward the man I could never forget.

ABOUT THE AUTHOR

Inge-Lise Goss, USA Today Best Selling and Multi-Award Winning author, was born in Denmark, raised in Utah, and now lives in the foothills of Red Rock Canyon with her husband and their dog, Ted. She spends most of her time in her den writing stories. There, with her muse by her side, her imagination has no boundaries, and her dreams come alive. When she's not pounding away on the keyboard, she can be found reading, rowing, or trying to perfect her golf game, which she fears is a lost cause

Visit www.Inge-LiseGoss.com to learn more.

www.ingramcontent.com/pod-product-compliance
Lightning Source LLC
Chambersburg PA
CBHW071241170626
46809CB00001B/39